Praise for the Amanda Dc

A high-adrenaline plunge into the dar
of homegrown terrorism.
— *Publishers Weekly* (starred review)

A great evocation of the lakes, the beauty and the power ... Amanda Doucette
is somebody I'd like for a friend.
— Maureen Jennings, author of Murdoch Mysteries

Masterly ... it's the wilderness that provides the story's passion.
— *Toronto Star*

Leaves one wishing to know more about Amanda Doucette. She is a plucky,
adventurous, smart, caring person with an exciting, globetrotting career and
the potential for many great stories.
— *Ottawa Citizen*

Fradkin populates her series with real people whose lives encompass more
than solving the odd crime. Keep 'em coming.
— Booklist

A simply riveting read from first page to last by a master of the genre.
— Midwest Book Review

Readers of Tana French and Deborah Crombie may want to investigate.
— *Library Journal*

Fradkin's forte is the emotional cost of crime.
— *Ottawa Citizen*

If you want to get a real feel (and fear) of the woods, this is the book for you.
— *Globe and Mail*

A terrific read.
— *Winnipeg Free Press*

Praise for the Inspector Green Mysteries

For those who like a solid classic mystery with added character,
Inspector Green is perfect.
— *Globe and Mail*

In a modern crime fiction universe in which protagonists are expected to have
weaknesses as well as strengths ... Barbara Fradkin's Inspector Michael Green
has always been among the most, well, human.
— *London Free Press*

Interesting characters, plenty of local colour, a clever plot that keeps
the reader guessing.
— Canadian Book Review Annual

A perfect blend of mystery and suspense.
— Charlotte Austin Review

Fradkin weaves a complex problem into a novel that works on two levels:
as a mystery and as a spotlight on a serious Canadian social problem.
— *Hamilton Spectator*

Fans of character-driven police procedurals will be satisfied.
— *Publishers Weekly*

A fast-paced crime thriller [featuring] a breathtaking plot with
so many twists and turns.
— Bibliophileverse

Fradkin brings the legacy of the Holocaust centre stage, casting the unfolding
historical revelations as integral pieces of the crime puzzle. The interplay
between past and present makes the events and the people they
affected come alive on the page.
— *Quill & Quire*

Once Upon a Time is so much more than a mystery; it is a story about people
pushed to the edge, about families, about desperation, about love. Rarely does
one find such depth in a novel of any type.
— *Storyteller Magazine*

Fradkin's writing captures it all. Great narrative, dialogue, and suspense.
— Reviewing the Evidence

WRECK BAY

Amanda Doucette Mysteries

WRECK BAY

An Amanda Doucette Mystery

Barbara **Fradkin**

DUNDURN
PRESS

Publisher and acquiring editor: Kwame Scott Fraser | Editor: Allister Thompson
Cover designer: Karen Alexiou
Cover image: shutterstock.com/Harry Beugelink

Library and Archives Canada Cataloguing in Publication

Title: Wreck Bay / Barbara Fradkin.
Names: Fradkin, Barbara, 1947- author.
Description: Series statement: An Amanda Doucette mystery ; 5
Identifiers: Canadiana (print) 20220284547 | Canadiana (ebook) 20220284555 | ISBN 9781459743878 (softcover) | ISBN 9781459743885 (PDF) | ISBN 9781459743892 (EPUB)
Classification: LCC PS8561.R233 W74 2023 | DDC C813/.6—dc23

We acknowledge the support of the Canada Council for the Arts and the Ontario Arts Council for our publishing program. We also acknowledge the financial support of the Government of Ontario, through the Ontario Book Publishing Tax Credit and Ontario Creates, and the Government of Canada.

Care has been taken to trace the ownership of copyright material used in this book. The author and the publisher welcome any information enabling them to rectify any references or credits in subsequent editions.

The publisher is not responsible for websites or their content unless they are owned by the publisher.

Printed and bound in Canada.

Dundurn Press
1382 Queen Street East
Toronto, Ontario, Canada M4L 1C9
dundurn.com, @dundurnpress 𝕐 f ⊚

To readers everywhere

Times Colonist, *September 19, 1971*
Wreck Bay Fire Claims One Life

A fire in a temporary dwelling on Long Beach turned deadly yester-day when the body of a young mother was discovered in the smoking ruins of her beach home. Patricia Decker, 19, lived in the Long Beach community with her six-month-old son and the baby's father, neither of whom was home at the time of the fire. Police are currently searching for a neighbour who has not been seen since and who may have infor-mation relevant to the case.

The cause of the fire is unknown, but the commune dwellings are notoriously unsafe, and fires from candles and open firepits are com-mon. This hazard has been a concern to local officials for years, and with the creation of the national park, efforts are underway to move residents to safer housing inland.

CHAPTER ONE

"I think that's a crazy idea."

Amanda pulled back in annoyance. In true cop fashion, Chris had maintained a poker face throughout her entire explanation, without betraying any reaction until she'd asked him what he thought.

"What do you mean, 'crazy'?" she demanded.

"I mean you know nothing about the West Coast."

"Since when has that stopped me from doing anything?"

He smiled and leaned over to draw her closer, but she withdrew to the other end of the couch, where she snuggled Kaylee instead. The dog stretched sleepily and thumped her tail. "I'm serious, Chris. I've been giving my next tour a lot of thought, and this is a great idea." Watching him slowly shake his head, her anger flared. "You've got to stop going all protective cop on me. I've been in more dangerous situations than this and dealt with far more dangerous men."

"It's not just the men," he said. "It's the isolation in unfamiliar territory. You don't know the ocean, the tides, the sudden storms. Not to mention the cougars and bears and wolves."

"I'm not going to be alone," she shot back. "I'll have at least one local tour guide, probably two, and a counsellor from the addictions centre."

He winced. To his credit, he tried to hide it, but in the shadows of dusk, his tightened lips were enough.

"It *is* the men," she said. "I could take any other group on an expedition out to the Pacific Rim and you'd be fine with it, but because it's men with an addiction history, you're all freaked out."

With a sigh, he unfolded his tall, lanky frame from the sofa and went to fetch the bottle of wine that sat on the table amid the remains of their dinner. He paused to glance out the picture window of their bungalow at the glossy black of Deer Lake. Pinpoints of golden light from other homes flickered against the water, and in the quiet, a distant motorboat droned.

She held up her wineglass for a top up, reluctantly acknowledging that he couldn't stop himself from worrying. Being a police officer meant he had to respond to people in peril, whether from criminals, accidents, or their own stupidity. He saw dangers where others did not.

She softened. "I don't want you to worry, honey. I've had several preliminary conversations with the executive director of the addictions umbrella organization in Victoria, and she's all for the idea. She told me she's already talked to a counsellor who's keen. A man who grew up on Vancouver Island. The ocean, the islands, and the forests were his playground as a kid, and he's eager to go. And we're not talking about active addicts here, or dealers —"

"But —"

"These are guys who've gone through the programs and are staying clean. Yeah, some of them have done time for petty theft or other minor things, but now they're burned out, past their prime, and just trying to rebuild the lives they messed up. I told the ED that I wanted guys who'd burned their bridges with their families and need some way to reconnect. To find some hope."

"And they're going to find this paddling around the islands and hiking through rainforests?"

She gritted her teeth at the hint of condescension. "No, they're going to find it by working together and sharing challenges. I don't need your permission to do this, you know. But I'd like it if you cared — at least a bit — about what I'm trying to do."

He sipped his wine and twirled his glass. "It's noble. Just a bit …"

"Quixotic?"

He grinned. "I know the guys you're talking about. We see them all the time, pick them up, put them in the drunk tank, release them in the morning to do it all over again. They're not bad people. They just don't know what else to do."

"But these guys *do* want to do something else! It's a requirement for the trip. That, and the fact they have an estranged adult son. Taking them out into the wilderness and forcing them to do things together, I hope it will help them both."

"This woman from the addictions centre …"

"Bonnie Pamiuq."

"She's going to vet them carefully? No violent criminal history, no mental health issues?"

She nodded. "No serious mental health issues. No one's going to be squeaky clean, otherwise they wouldn't be in this situation."

"What does Matthew think? Have you discussed it with him yet?"

She sensed him wavering and slid back over toward him. She felt the soft caress of his sweater against her cheek and breathed in the musty scent of wool. How she loved this man! They had survived the entire pandemic in isolation together in this remote corner of the country, and she had found a peace she'd never expected. Never before had she gone months without being on the move, always on to the next project. To the next crisis demanding her help.

Only as the days grew longer and the first buds of spring began to emerge had she felt the first faint stirrings of discontent. Not with Chris, but with herself. She'd spent her life on the front lines, helping those in need in struggling corners of the world, and she felt restless to find that purpose again.

She twined her fingers through his as she considered how to answer him. Matthew Goderich was her oldest, dearest friend. They'd met when she was an aid worker in Cambodia and he a war correspondent covering a regional conflict. When she'd barely escaped from Nigeria after a brutal attack, he had covered every inch of her harrowing journey across unfamiliar, inhospitable land. When she'd fled back to Canada to recover, unable to face another overseas post, and had instead taken up a charitable crusade closer to home, Matthew had returned home to Canada to run it with her. He was her right-hand man and a master of logistics, finances, and technology. He believed in her cause. More, he believed in her. He knew her deepest fears and demons, as well as her propensity for finding trouble, and he was going to hate this idea as much as Chris did.

"I wanted to tell you first," she replied finally. "I told him only that the next trip would be this summer on Vancouver Island. I'll probably tell him when we're standing outside the office of the treatment centre." She chewed her lip and steeled herself to deliver the next news. "I've booked myself and Kaylee on a flight to Victoria in three weeks."

He recoiled. "Kaylee! Do you have to take her? Poor girl, in the hold for hours!"

"She's a service dog. She'll be on the plane with me. And I've booked myself on business class."

Kaylee had raised her head at the mention of her name and was looking at them with concern. When Amanda called her over to join the snuggle, Chris leaned across to scratch her ears. "This place will be so empty with you both gone."

"I know. But I need her. I'm much better, but I'm not a hundred percent." *Probably never will be*, she added to herself. But that was something she didn't dare tell him. He might never let her out of his sight.

Amanda had lost count of the number of airplanes she'd flown in, the number of times she'd gazed out the window with curiosity as the plane banked over some faraway land and settled in for a landing. Over flat ochre deserts, craggy treeless mountains, tiny chequered farms, and ramshackle sheet-metal shantytowns.

Very little took her breath away, but as the Air Canada Airbus skimmed over the ocean past scattered green islands and descended toward Victoria International Airport, she found herself holding her breath. Despite travelling all over the world, she had never visited Canada's far west coast, so she had chosen a window seat for her maiden voyage.

It had been cloudy and raining for much of the flight across the British Columbian interior, robbing her of the chance to see the jagged, snow-cloaked peaks of the Rockies, but the clouds tore apart and the sun broke through just as they left the mainland to fly over the Strait of Georgia to Vancouver Island. The sun twinkled on the waves and on the miniature boats that ploughed a V as they wove through the islands. She felt a rush of joy. It was going to be a beautiful trip. The landscape was perfect for the renewal of hope. No wonder this green, sunny island had been a spiritual mecca for wandering souls for centuries. If it was possible anywhere, this was the setting where the lost fathers and sons in her group would find each other.

Inside the airport, the magic vanished. The building bustled with travellers scurrying through its wide, brightly lit halls, dragging their suitcases and juggling passports, phones, and sometimes small children. On top of the clamour, the constant bursts of PA announcements jangled her nerves. Kaylee clung to her side, wide-eyed. Amanda had brought only a carry-on and Kaylee's crate so that she could skip the baggage carousel and escape into the midday sun as quickly as possible.

Outside, she ignored the taxis and scanned the line of waiting cars. Matthew had told her to look for an orange Kia Soul. "Trust me, it stands out in a crowd," he'd said.

And sure enough, she'd only just spotted the little orange box when she saw the dumpy middle-aged man beside it, waving his arms. He was wearing his trademark battered fedora, a cherished legacy from his overseas tenure that also served to hide his bald head, and a brown leather jacket of comparable vintage. A big smile bubbled up inside her. How she had missed him these past two years!

After a long hug and a few minutes of roughhousing with Kaylee, he busied himself loading the suitcase and crate into the hatch, avoiding her gaze. Was he thinner? More haggard? Or did they all look older after two gruelling years of the pandemic?

Finally, seated in the car, he grinned at her. "You look great. Chris been treating you well?"

She nodded, wary of discussing Chris with Matthew, who'd never quite believed that the straitlaced Mountie was wild enough and impassioned enough to keep up with her. "But you're not looking your best."

He flushed. "Thanks a lot."

"Are you hungover, or is there more?"

"Hungover?" He snorted. "O, ye of little faith."

She said nothing. Waited. He started the car and eased away from the curb. For a few minutes, he concentrated on navigating out of the airport. "I'm having some health issues."

Anxiety spiked through her. "Matthew!"

"Don't freak out on me. It's nothing."

"What's nothing? What, Matthew?"

"I think I'm just rundown. The pandemic was a damn hard time. I'm a man of action, and I like to be on the move. To have everything come to a crashing halt, to be stuck in my two-bit apartment by myself for two years — man, that was hard, Amanda!"

As she absorbed this with dismay, guilt settled in. She should have called him more often, talked about projects they could do by virtual meetings or phone. She had been in rural Newfoundland, where the fears and restrictions of the pandemic had barely touched them, whereas he had been in dense, teeming Toronto, the early epicentre of Canada's pandemic crisis.

"So, anything else besides rundown?"

"I'm out of shape." He shrugged. "Too much lying around, and I probably drank too much. I know I didn't eat properly — you know me and cooking — and it caught up with me. I'm not in my thirties anymore, like you and Chris."

She wasn't letting him off the hook so fast. "What does out of shape mean?"

"Just tired. No big deal."

She reached over to touch his arm. "What does the doctor say?"

"We're working on it. I see the doctor again in a couple of weeks."

"Then maybe you shouldn't …"

"Shouldn't what?" He flushed. "No, no, this won't interfere with anything."

"But you need to put your health first."

"And do what? Sit around for another few months doing fuck all while you're out here doing another adventure tour? No, this is just what I need. A cause. A new challenge."

She eyed him thoughtfully. It was true, his colour was better now that they were talking, and he looked energized. But she knew there could be a lot more wrong with him than he was willing to divulge. He would run himself into the ground for her Fun for Families charity. For her. Just as he had run himself close to death chasing down her dangerous story in Africa.

"Okay," she said, "but promise me —"

"Yes, Mom, I'll keep you posted. Now let's get this show on the road. Where are we going?"

Half an hour later, they were parked in a suburban shopping mall lot facing a glass wall of generic storefronts featuring everything from yoga to jewellery. The first to spot their destination, Amanda pointed. "It's on the second floor."

The addictions centre offices weren't flashy. There were no window banners or logos, merely a modest sign on the door next to the jewellery shop: *Island Recovery, Second Floor.* Matthew cast her a doubtful glance.

"It's an umbrella organization," she said. "It provides most of its services through other social services agencies. But it's quality, not glitz, that counts."

She opened the door, and Kaylee strained on the leash as they climbed the dark, narrow staircase to a glass door with a stencilled logo depicting a family beneath the arch of a rainbow. Kaylee dragged them excitedly through the door into a clean, bright reception area with couches, potted plants, and a receptionist's desk. Although the hours on the door suggested it was open, there was no one at the desk, and a closer look at the furniture revealed its wear and age.

Almost immediately, one of the doors along the corridor flew open and a woman emerged. Like Amanda, she looked in her mid-thirties but with greater attention to style. Her hair was a soft teal, and discreet tattoos of geometric patterns encircled her wrists and throat. She had chosen a deliberately hip but professional look — jeans and tailored red jacket — and Amanda suspected her suede ankle boots had not come from the bargain bin. But then the woman probably had to spend a lot of her time cajoling public officials and private donors to part with their money. Mastery of PR would be essential.

But the woman who greeted them exhibited neither polish nor artifice as she rushed across the foyer like an excited schoolgirl, hand outstretched and a huge smile on her face.

"Bonnie Pamiuq," she exclaimed, shaking Amanda's hand until her teeth rattled. "Omigod, what an honour to meet you! I've followed your charity since the beginning, and to think you've chosen the Island and our very own Island Recovery for your next trip, I'm just … speechless!"

Amanda could almost see Matthew rolling his eyes, but she felt an instant affinity for the woman. Kaylee, too, seemed to approve, wiggling happily when Bonnie knelt to scratch her ears. Anyone Kaylee approved of won extra points. Once Bonnie stood up, Amanda introduced Matthew.

"Matthew handles all the financial and logistical details. He'll be the first to tell you I'm no good at either, so if this works out, you'll see a lot more of him. I'm not looking for a big, splashy event. I want it to be meaningful for the men who participate. If it works, it might serve as a pilot project for other groups. I wish I could help way, way more of them, but unfortunately I'm only one person and I won't sacrifice quality for quantity."

"That's what I love about your work," Bonnie replied. "You understand change has to be personal. Come into my office. I've got a coffee maker in there, and there's someone I want you to meet."

She led them down the hall to an open door. Like the foyer, the room was flooded with natural light and crammed with plants. Bookcases overflowed with files, binders, and books on addiction, and the desk half buried in the corner was surrounded by mismatched chairs. A man was settled in one of the chairs, studying a computer propped on his lap, but when Bonnie burst into the room, he jumped to his feet, catlike and agile.

Amanda barely suppressed a gasp. He was built like a weightlifter, almost all muscle and sinew. He had a shaved head but a full beard of greyish red steel wool and startling blue eyes set deep into his leathery face. Tattoos ran up and down almost every inch of exposed skin, including a small one of a peace symbol on his left temple.

Bonnie laughed. "Yes, he makes quite a first impression. Amanda, meet Michael McTaggart. Tag to his friends. He's the counsellor who will go with you on the trip."

Good God, has the man done time? was Amanda's first thought. At her side, she sensed Matthew stiffen, as if he'd had the same thought. Perhaps sensing their alarm, Kaylee remained by the door, watchfully still. But Tag merely smiled and extended his hand.

"It's an honour." His voice sounded aged by years of cheap booze and cheaper cigarettes, but to her surprise, his hand was soft and warm. "And here's Kaylee." He knelt and patted his knee to call her. She came warily, and he held out his hand for her to sniff. Amanda was pleased he hadn't pushed it. For all his bulk, maybe he had a gentle side.

"In your emails, you mentioned the Tofino area," Bonnie said. "Have you finalized what you'd like to do on the trip?"

She shook her head. "That's what the next couple of weeks are for. I've done quite a lot of reading, so I know about potential activities. Kayaking, hiking, biking, exploring First Nations traditions. But now I want to visit the area to meet with local tour guides before I decide the exact itinerary. I know Tofino gets a million tourists a year, and I don't want us to be in the thick of that."

Bonnie pulled a face. "Tag and I discussed that. We think you should plan for June or September to avoid the crush, and he suggested he go with you on the scouting expedition. He has lots of outdoor experience around here, but he's eager to see the Pacific Rim."

"Oh, good," Amanda said, but doubt must have crept into her voice, for Tag cocked his head.

"Is there a problem?"

Amanda was about to be polite but stopped herself. There *was* a problem. She didn't know this guy from Adam, and she always liked to do things solo. She didn't want to be tripping over him every time she set off anywhere. After a moment of tense silence, during which she tried to formulate a tactful reply, Tag finally nodded. "I've done time, yes, if that's what you're wondering. Two years for assault and robbery. And I'm a recovering addict."

"But that's all behind him," Bonnie interjected. "He upgraded his education in prison and has gone on to qualify as an addictions counsellor. Now he's continuing his —"

"Book learning doesn't matter, Bonnie, if Amanda is uncomfortable." Tag's tone was gentle, but there was a firmness to the man. A clarity of intent. *What the hell?* Amanda thought. *Is he going to go all alpha on me?*

"It'll be fine," she said. "I like to do things my way, and on my own terms. Just so you know."

"I'm sure Tag can work with that," Bonnie said cheerfully. "When are you planning to leave?"

"As soon as I can organize the gear and rent a car," Amanda said. "Thursday?"

Matthew had been sitting quietly, but now he looked both alarmed and dismayed. "Amanda, we have stuff to discuss. Costs, budget."

She smiled. "That's what phones are for, Matthew. I have some ideas on paper, but I want to check them out on the ground to see if they're practical. It should only take a week or two."

Bonnie was making some notes on her laptop and nodded enthusiastically. "And Matthew, while they're gone, you and I will go through the list of potential clients. Tag has thrown in some names, and I know others. We can narrow it down and start getting the paperwork rolling." She grinned. "Consents and waivers and other bureaucratic evils."

CHAPTER TWO

In pictures, the western edge of Vancouver Island looked like a jagged tangle of tree-covered islands, rocky shores, and sparkling inlets. Dark, hunched mountains brooded in the background. As she drove down the sole highway connecting the Pacific Rim area to the more settled east coast, Amanda was struck by some of the resemblances to western Newfoundland. The trees were taller and denser than Newfoundland, scoured as it was by the brutal North Atlantic, but the round, towering mountains and deeply cut fiords were the same.

Amanda had to devote much of her attention to navigating the highway through the twisting, mountainous terrain, and she was grateful Tag was content to watch the countryside in silence. He'd offered to drive, but she'd wanted to send a clear message that she was in charge. Tag looked like a man used to acting on his own wishes. She was anxious to make it to Tofino early enough to explore a little, so although they both stared in wonder at the magnificent old-growth forest of Cathedral Grove and the spectacular cliffside drop to Kennedy Lake, she didn't stop.

Tofino and its sister town of Ucluelet had sprung up at opposite ends of a peninsula that jutted into Clayoquot Sound. At one time, the main industries had been logging and fishing, but now a national park had taken over much of the peninsula, famed for its endless, soft sand beaches, and the main industry was tourism. Traffic on the highway was heavy with RVs, campervans, and pickups festooned with surfboards, kayaks, and canoes. As they approached the coast, Amanda kept a wary eye open for the crass development and tawdry commercialism that buzzed around most tourist meccas.

But so far, beyond the roadside surf shops, the scenery was peaceful. After a brief stop at the park visitor centre to pick up literature and ask about group permit requirements, they headed down the long highway through the park toward Tofino. Amanda noted with excitement that a beautiful new bicycle path ran through the forest alongside the road.

"That would be a great activity for our beach days," she said.

He squinted through the trees, distracted. "Sure. Or we could give them some choice for those days. There's surfing, paddle boarding, cycling, swimming ..." He chuckled. "Or maybe just lying in the sun."

She turned her attention back to the park. Discreet signs announced the beaches, but nothing could be seen through the tall evergreens until they came to the turnoff to Incinerator Rock, where for the first time she caught a glimpse of the pale sands and rolling surf of fabled Long Beach. Tag strained to peer through the window, and his blue eyes drank in the sight.

"We'll be back," she said before he could ask. "Let's stretch our legs and get something to eat."

As they passed out of the park, signs to resorts and private mansions dotted the ocean side of the road, hinting at luxury perched on the edge of the sea, but nothing was visible through the veil of lush green trees. Gradually the town began to emerge from the green. Hotels, kayaking centres, surf shops, and restaurants, and before she knew it, they were driving through the centre of a classic beach town with boutiques, funky little houses painted bright colours, hand-scrawled menus on restaurant walls, and everywhere motifs of the sea — fish, seashells, boats, anchors, and vistas of beach — intermingled with First Nations art.

This was Tofino, a jewel cradled by the blue-green waters and lush islands of Clayoquot Sound. Beneath the shadow of silent, brooding mountains, the town was alive. Parked cars lined every side street, and she noticed with dismay that lines of customers snaked out of the restaurants.

A mix of emotions gripped her. Nature had created perfection, and humankind was swarming all over it. "We'll have to get the group out of here," she said. "This is not the escape I had in mind."

"Beyond this town is wilderness. The islands are barely touched by tourists. Just First Nations communities. There should be plenty of escape." He was peering at street signs, and now he pointed. "Look for a parking spot. There's something I want to check out. Then we can grab some takeout."

They finally found a parking spot opposite the town's museum on the harbourfront and clambered stiffly out of the car. The mid-afternoon sun shone brightly in the cloudless blue sky, and a warm breeze redolent with salt, fish, and gas fumes rippled in off the inlet. Kaylee leaped out of the car and headed eagerly to the nearest patch of green. As she waited, Amanda took a deep breath and took in the scene. Boats of all sizes and types bobbed in the wooden slips, and a float plane was just revving up its propeller. Shorebirds of all sorts wheeled overhead, screaming and fighting over scraps.

A perfect day to explore. She glanced at her watch. Hunger was beginning to gnaw at her stomach, but they had only an hour to settle in at their B&B before their meeting with the first kayak tour company. Tag had drawn up a short list and promised they'd find the perfect fit for their needs.

"All these guys have been doing this forever and know every inch of the coast," he'd said. "And they'll each put their own creative spin on your ideas."

She'd had some doubts about Tag during that first meeting. Matthew had even more, and she hadn't even mentioned the ex-con line on his resumé to Chris. But as she trudged beside him along Main Street, she had to admit he was proving useful. He had given the activities a lot of thought and done some preliminary research into what companies could provide.

"It's busier than I expected," she said, dodging a surfboard as she raced to keep up with his long stride. Even her sturdy hiking boots didn't help her reach five foot three, and her backpack felt heavier than her. Kaylee tried to sniff things on the fly, her tongue lolling with excitement.

Where are the takeout places anyway? No sooner had she asked herself the question than Tag veered off the sidewalk at a modest little house advertising e-bikes. A woman emerged through the front door, and her eyes flicked nervously over Tag before she pasted an expectant smile on her face. In his soft, polite voice, Tag asked about the e-bikes.

As the woman unlocked an adjacent shed, Amanda hung back. "Wouldn't ordinary bicycles be better?"

"I want to check these out," Tag said as he pulled one out. "Maybe you can bike for miles at a stretch, but our old-timers can't. It's sixteen K along Long Beach alone. I think these might be good for our group, at least for the dads, who are mostly over sixty and not in the best shape."

The e-bike looked ordinary, except for a small electric motor mounted on the frame. She had to admit it was a good idea. After spotting Kaylee, the owner disappeared back inside and came out with a small bike trailer. "These are custom designed for pets. It would be perfect for your dog. And we have luggage trailers as well."

Tag stepped astride the bike. "Try it. Have you ever ridden an e-bike before?"

Amanda felt a flash of annoyance. "I drive a motorcycle, and I've driven scooters all over the developing world. If I can navigate Bangkok, I can manage that nice flat path we passed."

He laughed. "Ouch. What do you think? We could leave the car for today, rent these, and use them to get around town. No parking issues."

"It's an idea," she said, almost against her will. She asked the woman a few questions about cost and availability and soon found herself dishing out money.

Tag had booked two rooms in the Silver Surf B&B perched on a point on the far edge of town. "The owners are long-time residents. They should know everything about everybody."

The short ride there was exhilarating. The fresh air, infused with both ocean salt and evergreen forest, was glorious, and the electric motor made the small hills effortless. She spilled into the Silver Surf B&B, red-cheeked, shiny-eyed, and energized by the prospect of her tour. As she sat on her private terrace to eat her fish wrap, she breathed in the mountain air and revelled in the view. Below, the ocean lapped gently against the rocks, and in the distance the rounded tops of the island mountain range peeked through the trees.

When she stepped back inside, her eyes were drawn to the painting hanging over the bed. Bold sweeps of forest green and cerulean blue captured the jagged silhouettes of fir trees and mountains, gilded in the sunlight. She checked the artist's name, *Anonymous*, scratched in small, spiky strokes in the corner. She had heard that the Pacific Rim was a haven for artists of all sorts, and there were more galleries per square foot in Tofino than anywhere in the world. Perhaps she'd find this artist's work for sale in one of them.

Tag had set up a gruelling schedule of meetings with kayak companies that afternoon, and by the time she'd unpacked, washed up, and taken Kaylee for a brief break, they had just enough time to cycle back downtown for their first appointment. The official company office was a modest room in the back of an art and espresso bar on Campbell Street, but they found the owners, Charlie and Nash, down at their dockside shed, cleaning a tandem kayak. Every inch of shed space was taken up with racks of paddles, life jackets, skirts, and other accessories. Outside, brightly coloured kayaks were stacked on racks by the slip.

The two owners abandoned their cleaning to greet them with broad smiles and extended hands. Beyond the smiles, they couldn't have looked more different. Charlie, who took the lead, looked as if he'd just stepped off a surfing beach in California. Deeply tanned, blue-eyed, and blond, his lean, muscular body belied his age until Amanda noticed the web of crow's feet around his eyes. He did his best to be friendly and welcoming, but she sensed a wariness in his expression whenever he looked at Tag. Was she imagining it?

By comparison, Nash showed no such tension. He was slender, almost delicate, with dark eyes, high cheekbones, and a glossy black ponytail that fell long and straight down his back. He was content to let Charlie take the lead.

"If you go with our company," Charlie said, "Nash here will be your tour leader, and he'll take along two or three staffers, depending on your numbers. Let me show you some of our ideas."

He laid a battered map on the counter and began to orient them. For nearly an hour, they discussed routes and camping options, pointed out the activities and sights each offered, and outlined the skill requirements of each option. Amanda's excitement grew as each trip sounded better than the last. Should they take three days to dawdle around the protected archipelago of the Broken Islands south of Ucluelet or take a longer trip through Clayoquot Sound around a wilder island controlled by the Ahousaht First Nation?

Tag wanted to stick to the busier, more protected islands closer to Ucluelet, whereas Amanda was drawn to the less travelled wilderness that would present more challenge and encourage more bonding and co-operation.

"Most of the guys don't have the skill to handle the tides, wind, and swells," Tag said. "Too much could go wrong. The guys need to have fun. They don't need to be terrified."

She eyed him thoughtfully. Despite his physique, she judged he was at least fifty. He'd been in their shoes. She loved the adrenalin rush of being on the edge, but perhaps he was right. Maybe after years of living on the edge, they just wanted to feel safe.

At the end of an hour, Amanda thanked them and headed off with a stack of documents about the trips. After two more visits to tour companies and more stacks of documents, her head was spinning, partly from the deluge of information but also from hunger. She headed for the Java Bean, the art and espresso bar on Campbell Street.

"Food. And we can discuss."

The smells of exquisite coffee and baking greeted them as they approached the door. The shop was packed with chatter, and the line to order food snaked toward the door. Tag scowled glumly at the lineup.

"Order me an Americano and a bean salad. I'll get a table outside with Kaylee."

Left to her own thoughts, Amanda shrugged off his surly mood and glanced at the paintings on the walls. Some listed prices or the artist's contact information. The artwork was eclectic and striking, but all had the vivid colours and free spirit of the West Coast. One artist caught her eye. They had painted wilderness scenes of rock and ocean and trees, but using bold, unexpected colours that contrasted light and dark. Deep red mountains, jagged yellow pines that exploded into stars, shadowy black water. An artist not tied to reality, pouring their emotions onto the page.

After she'd picked up their order, she carried her tray over to the largest painting for a closer look. It had no title or price, and the artist was listed as *Anonymous*, like the painting in her room at the Silver Surf B&B.

"I really love that artist's work," she said as she sat down opposite Tag on the patio. "I wonder who it is."

Tag glanced through the patio glass and frowned at the paintings. "Weird, if you ask me. Never seen a yellow fir tree before."

She laughed. "It's yellow in his imagination." She considered the black ocean, with its hint of dark shapes below. "Not exactly a happy work, but it's got a lot to say."

"Never really did get art," Tag replied, digging into his bean salad. "But there's plenty of it in this town. Every second person who came here figured they were a Picasso."

"Maybe the place inspires art. Its beauty cries out to be captured."

"More likely the LSD. Or the mushrooms. I'd say that's what that guy is on. And he probably wants two thousand bucks for his yellow tree."

Later that evening, Amanda was sitting on the terrace of the B&B with her laptop on the tiny bistro table. Beyond the point, she could see the golden glow of twilight setting fire to the ocean. Shafts of coral and pink shot up into the clouds. It was magical, and she decided then and there to capture the memory.

"I found the perfect painting to commemorate my Pacific Rim tour," she told Chris when his broad, crinkly grin filled the screen. He looked dishevelled and worn out, but it was the middle of the night in Newfoundland, and he had just returned from the scene of an accident between a moose and minivan in Gros Morne. No matter how many warnings were posted, some tourists never learned.

"Can you show it to me?" he asked.

"I don't have it yet. I have to find the person who painted it. I saw it in a café in Tofino today, but I didn't have time to ask about it. We had meetings with kayak companies all afternoon."

"And how did that go?"

"Great. The companies are all really good and mostly do the same trips, so it will come down to who can handle the group size, provide enough tandem kayaks, and work within our dates."

"Why tandem kayaks? They're more unwieldy."

"I know, but they're more stable and provide the perfect solution to differences in skill and endurance. Some of our fathers may be over seventy. And as a bonus, it will strengthen the father-son bond." She hesitated. "It was Tag's idea, actually, but it's brilliant."

Chris waited a beat and dropped his voice. "How is Tag working out?"

She looked out over the shimmer of sunset, searching for careful words. "I think he'll be fine. He's a good match for the type of men in the group and sees problems I don't. He's no nonsense, down-to-earth, a man of few words."

Chris grunted his skepticism. "What's on the agenda for tomorrow?"

"We're going to start looking into nature hikes. There are dozens of trails, some along the coast and some inland into the old-growth forests. Tag has to go back to work in Victoria in a few days, so I'll stay on to check out some of the hikes."

"You'll be careful? There are cougars and wolves —"

She rolled her eyes, and he held up his hands in surrender. "Sorry, babe."

"I'll get a guide for the big trips. There's an overnight one in a First Nations tribal park that I'm really excited about. It's guided by the local Ahousaht, and we may be able to work with them on restoring the nature trail along the coast, which was closed for the pandemic and is overgrown. I think that would be another good experience for our men. The First Nations have a lot to teach us about reconnecting with nature and supporting each other. They've had to do so much rediscovery and healing themselves."

He cocked his head and smiled gently. "I wish I was there. I miss you."

"I wish you were here too. You'd love it. It's so different from the East Coast. Maybe after my tour ...?"

"Maybe." He didn't give a commitment, but she heard the longing in his voice. Summer was a very busy tourist season in Gros Morne National Park, and the Deer Lake RCMP detachment was usually kept running flat out. This year especially, a deluge of tourists was expected now that pandemic restrictions had lifted and travel had resumed.

She savoured the thought as she shut her laptop and went inside to review her plans for tomorrow. Maybe they could include another visit to the Java Bean to find out who Anonymous was.

The breakfast room in the B&B was a warm expanse of natural wood and floor-to-ceiling windows that welcomed the dappled sun into the room. As Amanda made a beeline for the empty table by the window, she spotted Tag standing in front of a painting in the far corner. He was motionless, and he didn't move even when she approached. For a man who claimed he didn't "get" art, he was certainly studying it carefully.

The paintings hanging on the cedar-panelled walls were an eclectic mix of landscapes, streetscapes, abstracts, and people. This one was a portrait of a young woman sitting on a massive driftwood log in front of a makeshift beach shack. Her sun-bleached hair fell long and straight to her waist, entwined with pink flowers and beads. She was half-turned, looking out to sea.

The painting wasn't perfect; the perspective and lighting were off and the strokes rough, but the woman radiated life. At first, Amanda couldn't read the expression on her face — sad, awe-inspired, regretful — but finally settled on wistful. As if longing for something far out to sea.

"That's mesmerizing, isn't it?" she murmured.

Tag jumped and swung on her, tensed for a fight. She took a quick step backward. An instant later, his fists relaxed and he dropped his gaze.

"Sorry," he muttered, "I didn't hear you."

She hesitated but decided not to pursue it. Instead, she leaned forward to peer at the painting, which was signed *AK*. "This looks like the hippie sixties. I wonder what AK stands for."

Tag spun on his heel. "Like I said, they're a dime a dozen. Let's eat. We've got a big day."

As they took their seats, she eyed him warily. His expression was businesslike and his tone brusque. Was this partnership going to work? And how effective could he be as a counsellor with this much tension coiled up inside? Only once the breakfast arrived — a delectable spread of locally smoked salmon, capers, red onions, and apple slices on an open-faced bagel — did he sit back and relax. He grinned at the man who brought the food, the owner himself, whom Amanda recognized from the day before. Bald as a billiard ball with a face so creviced by years of sun and ocean wind, it was impossible to guess his age. The name on the Silver Surf B&B was H&H Keenan, but he had introduced himself simply as Keener.

Keener gave Tag a cool look. "Welcome back, Tag. You back for another —?"

"We're here to plan a group tour," Tag interjected briskly. "Only staying a few days."

Amanda studied him curiously. Why hadn't he mentioned he'd been here before? But given his mood, she decided the question could wait. Instead, she gestured out the window. "This is a beautiful spot. How long have you been here, Keener?"

"Here at the Silver Surf B&B? Or in Tofino."

"Both."

"Longer than you've been on the planet," he replied with a wink. "I slid across Canada in free fall and landed on Long Beach in 1968. Just visiting, I figured. Sowing my wild oats. I spent a couple of years in the hippie commune at Wreck Bay until the park drove us out, then banged around a few years on logging crews, and finally got into the accommodation business in 1978."

Tag had just bitten into his bagel, but now he snorted. "Accommodation business! You said you found this piece of vacant forest and pitched a few tents for the hippies."

"Yeah, but it grew. I built the original B&B in '85 and expanded it in 2006. This one will see Helen and me into our sunset years."

Another couple had arrived and taken a seat at the next table. Keener nodded toward them. "Coffee to start?"

Amanda watched him head back toward the kitchen and saw him glance briefly at the painting of the woman. *AK*, she thought. *Could that be Keenan?* When he returned with the coffee pot, she gestured to the painting. "That beautiful portrait. Did you paint it?"

Emotion flitted across his face. Surprise? Sorrow? "No, I don't have that talent." He swept his hand around the walls. "I just support other people's talent."

"Do you know anything about the artist, AK?"

He busied himself pouring coffee. "That was done years ago. He's long dead now. Listen, I better get back to the kitchen, or Helen will have my hide."

Amanda was still trying to analyze his abrupt change of mood when she felt Tag's gaze on her. "Like I said, a dime a dozen. Back in those days, the hippies used to trade paintings or jewellery or whatever they could make for food or drugs or a place to stay. Everybody thought they were Picasso."

"Still, it meant enough to him that he kept it through all those years of tents and renos."

"Tourists like that shit. It's part of Tofino's romantic past, before it all got fancied up for the millennial surfing crowd."

CHAPTER THREE

Amanda and Tag spent the morning gathering material at the Pacific Rim visitor's centre and hiking the short ocean trails around Ucluelet. Kaylee was thrilled to chase sticks across the flat sand and over the rocky outcrops. As the sun rose overhead, they stopped on a bluff overlooking the spectacular expanse of Long Beach. The pale sand glistened in the low tide, and jumbles of huge driftwood logs lay helter-skelter above the high-tide mark like a giant game of pick-up sticks. Although the beach was gorgeous, Amanda was dismayed by the crowds. Teenagers played Frisbee, and out in the ocean, surfers battled the huge, rolling waves. Lovers strolled hand in hand along the water's edge, and children splashed and screamed in the shallows.

A day or two of playing at the beach might be fun for the group, but it was not a place to seek peace and intimacy, to build bonds away from the madding crowd.

Tag was watching a group of beginner surfers struggling to stand upright as the boards hurtled toward shore. A smile twitched on his lips as one of them pitched into the waves with a shriek. "I used to do that. Not sure I could do it now."

"I tried it once in Thailand years ago, and it was really fun. It might be something for our group to try. Push their comfort zone and make them all learn together."

He was wearing wraparound sunglasses and a ball cap pulled low over his shaved head, making his expression almost inscrutable. "It takes considerable upper body strength even to get up. Remember, most of the fathers are nearly twice your age."

"Fair enough, but I'm keeping the idea in my back pocket. How can anyone come to Tofino and not try surfing?"

He grunted. "Let's carry on. All this ocean air is making me hungry."

"Okay, let's go back to that café in Tofino, grab some lunch, and look over these hiking brochures. I want to ask the owner about that artist, Anonymous."

"What's with you and these artists? First AK and now this guy."

"I love art, and I like to buy original paintings directly from the artists to remember the places I've been to. The house I share with my partner in Newfoundland is full of art from all around the world. Each tells me a story."

He shrugged as if the idea were entirely foreign to him and turned to lead the way back toward the car. Back at the Java Bean, with Kaylee tied up on the patio, Amanda found herself standing in line with a perfect view of Anonymous's yellow tree across the room. It was even more evocative from a distance.

Behind the counter was an older woman who seemed to be overseeing the food preparation. She had a broad, friendly face, a chipped front tooth, and a bird's nest of wiry grey hair that she had struggled to tame into a braid. The owner, perhaps, Amanda thought. When she reached the counter, she caught the woman's eye.

"Are all these paintings for sale?"

"Most. The prices are below."

"What about that one by Anonymous?"

The woman gave a dreamy, broken-toothed smile. "Isn't it marvellous? But no, that particular one's not for sale."

Amanda's heart sank. "Why not?"

"Artist's choice. Too personal."

"I love it. It's so raw."

"Raw. That's a good word for it."

"Who's Anonymous?"

"He's shy. He only sells through his dealer."

"And who's that?"

"Me."

"Oh!" Amanda laughed. "Well, how can I find out about his other work?"

The woman glanced at the line of customers growing restive behind Amanda. Her gaze came to rest on Tag, who was outside with Kaylee, and she stared. Squinted. For a moment, it seemed as if she'd lost her train of thought, but then she said, "Come see me at closing time. We'll talk."

When Amanda arrived at 9:00 p.m., the café was in shadow, with a single splash of light on a table in the corner. The woman was sitting alone at the table with a baguette and a spread of cheeses and fruit in front of her and an open bottle of Laughing Stock Syrah from the Okanagan Valley at her elbow. She had taken off her shoes and propped her wrinkled bare feet on the chair opposite. She gestured Amanda to a third chair and, without even asking, poured her a glass of wine.

"Laughing Stock," she said, waving the bottle. "Mostly I just like the name, but it's a damn good wine. I know who you are. I'm a tremendous admirer of your work, and we were all very excited when we heard you'd chosen the Pacific Rim for your next Fun for Families adventure."

Amanda sipped the wine, which was as smooth as silk. "We?"

"Just a bunch of old broads who cut our activist teeth on the Clayoquot Sound anti-logging protests in the nineties and who get together to plot mischief and keep the guys in power on their toes." She wiped her hand on a brightly coloured napkin and held it out. "Nancy Rowley."

Her strong, brisk handshake made Amanda smile. She liked this woman already. "Pleased to meet you, Nancy, and I remember my mother talking about those protests when I was growing up. Chained to trees, staring down the bulldozers. Those were wild times. My mother has carried a placard or two of her own over the years."

"More than one or two!" Nancy exclaimed. "She's one of the originals! In fact, I knew about her long before I learned about you. No wonder you turned out as you did. How lucky you were to have such a powerful inspiration growing up."

Amanda chose her words carefully. She had heard this refrain often from people on the outside looking in. People who saw Susan as the brilliant scientist, never-say-never crusader, and fearless feminist. People who didn't know Susan the mother who balked at kissing a scraped knee or hugging her children when they had a nightmare. A mother so high up on her own pedestal that everyone else in the family felt small.

Finally, she settled on a safe answer, the answer she had come by grudgingly over time. "Yes, she certainly taught me how to fight for what I believe in. This cheese is wonderful, by the way. Perfect with the wine."

"Local sheep cheese." Nancy cut her another slice. "I don't lay on a spread like this for everyone, you know. But we want to support your efforts here on the Island the best we can. The Old Broads are at your disposal."

Amanda laughed. "Thank you, that would be super. Maybe you can prepare picnic lunches for some of our excursions. I'm hoping to find some activities that are more off the beaten track so our group can connect without tripping over tourists at every turn."

"Yeah, we're victims of our own success here in Tofino. We get a million visitors a year in this area, and it's getting harder and harder to avoid the crowds at the popular spots. But if you go north a bit, only a couple of islands up, you'll be in wilderness. There are guides who can set that up for you, and I can connect you to them. The Wild Side Heritage Trail run by the Ahousaht on Flores Island takes you through some of their culture and heritage, which is fascinating. And yeah, I'd be honoured to collaborate with them on food."

They sipped wine, nibbled cheese, and spent the next while discussing what islands were accessible, where the landing spots and trailheads in the backcountry parks were, and what special touches the First Nations guides might offer. Amanda felt her excitement rising as she jotted down notes. Finally, she thanked Nancy and sat back with her wineglass, which Nancy had filled yet again.

Nancy grinned. "Now you want to know about my mystery painter."

"I do." Amanda gestured to the painting of the exploding yellow tree. "That painting is so striking. Are there others like it?"

Nancy pointed to some smaller landscapes around the room. Brooding mountains in purple and black; towering ocean waves; tall, sunlit spruce. Amanda selected another slice of cheese, picked up her wineglass, and walked over to examine them. "They're very competent and would look beautiful in any living room, but they're not ... alive like that one."

Nancy chuckled. "Yes, well, they're normal. They're what he paints when he wants to be normal."

Amanda turned, puzzled. "Is that a choice for him? You mean he takes hallucinogens to get this effect?"

Nancy twirled her wineglass and pursed her lips as if debating how to answer. "His name is Luke. I'm very protective of him. Many of us old-timers are. He … struggles to cope. That …" she gestured to the yellow tree, "that is more his natural state. He works hard to keep a lid on it. These other paintings, he does those to sell to make a living. They're popular, and they help to keep him afloat. Plus, his needs are simple. He lives mainly off-grid and doesn't have many expenses."

Amanda walked over to study the tree. "Does he ever do any other paintings like this one that he does sell?"

Nancy hesitated and shook her head. "Rarely. Most people aren't interested, and I think that wounds him. He's private."

"*I'm* interested. Can I meet him and talk to him about it? Is he here in Tofino?"

"He's a bit of a recluse. Has been for decades. He lives on the northern part of Flores Island. That's one of the more remote islands in Clayoquot Sound that I was talking about, where the Wild Side Trail is."

"Would he come into town to meet me?"

"Nope. Not unless he needs supplies. And it's not easy to contact him."

"Can I get to his place by water taxi?"

"I'm not sure I …" Nancy rocked back in her chair and gazed at the star-sprinkled sky.

"I'm sorry," Amanda said. "I shouldn't put you on the spot. Maybe he'll come into town sometime when I'm back here with the group."

"He's very special, that's all." Nancy shook her head as if to dispel her doubts. "I guess I'm protective, but I shouldn't be. Not with you. You of all people will understand him. I'll set up a taxi for you, and I'll send some rice, sugar, and coffee up for him. He'll be happy to get those, and it'll break the ice."

Amanda felt a rush of excitement at the thought of the adventure. "That would be great, and at the same time, Tag and I can check out possible remote hikes on the island."

"Who's Tag?"

"My co-leader, Michael McTaggart." Amanda remembered her odd reaction to him earlier. "You saw him this afternoon. Big guy with a red beard?"

Nancy's nostrils flared. "Where's he from?"

"Victoria. Why?"

"It's just ... never mind. But I wouldn't take Tag."

"Why not?"

Nancy ran her tongue over her broken tooth as if weighing her words. "He's imposing. Luke might get scared."

Pim looked as if he had spent his entire life at the wheel of his boat, pounding through the waves in the ocean sun. His face was a maze of wrinkles. Layered in a combination of plaid shirt and faded windbreaker, with a tuque pulled low over his ears and a pair of fisherman's boots on his huge feet, he stood in the little cab in the centre of the boat, hunched against the chilly spring wind and squinting through the spray at the ocean ahead.

The boat was an old, open-hulled ocean skiff made of steel painted many colours over the years. Even with twin outboards, it hardly looked big enough to handle the big water, but Nancy swore Pim knew the whims of the ocean currents and the coastal rocks better than anyone else on the west island. He chose his customers carefully and preferred to spend his days out on the fishing grounds rather than ferrying tourists around.

He seemed comfortable with his own company and barely spoke to Amanda as they drove up the inner coast of Flores Island. Amanda evaluated the route curiously. Because the passage was narrow, it was protected from huge ocean swells, and much of the land was wild, with towering stands of evergreens descending straight to the rocky shore. In the narrow coves, seaweed and driftwood were tossed up on the rocky beaches, but there was little place to land a convoy of kayaks or set up camp.

Along the way, they passed a salmon fishery that she studied with interest. Later, Pim slowed to weave through a narrow passage in the shadow of a looming mountain, and seals sunning themselves on a rocky shoal lifted their heads to watch them lazily. As the boat rounded the top of the island, the wind picked up, churning the waves. Kaylee flattened her ears, and Amanda pulled her tuque more firmly down on her head. Soon, Pim steered toward a small, protected cove tucked between two rocky headlands and barely visible through the trees. As they drew nearer, she saw a battered steel boat moored to a rough-hewn wooden dock. The tide was retreating, leaving gentle bubbles on the pebble beach, and a line of jumbled driftwood and kelp farther up the beach marked the high-water point. Pim guided his boat to a perfect docking behind the other and tossed the bowline up onto the dock.

Kaylee leaped out with relief and began to race around the shore in search of treasure. Amanda clambered out, stiff from the constant pounding of the boat, and secured the line. Looking around, she smiled as she breathed in the clear, fresh air. Seaweed, salt, fish, and spruce mingled with the lingering diesel from the boat. An old canoe lay farther up the beach, tucked under a sturdy spruce and covered by a tarp. Beyond it, a camouflaged path ducked into the trees and headed inland. Almost undetectable if you didn't know where to look.

She stood still a minute, tuning her senses. The silence and isolation felt absolute, and at first she could hear nothing but the soft bumps of the boats against the dock. But as she listened, sounds began to separate out. The rhythmic swish of the waves, the drone of a seaplane, the call of shorebirds. Overhead, an eagle flashed white in the sunlight. In the distance, an animal grunted. A sea lion? Wolf? Cougar? In spite of herself, a shiver ran through her. She dug her bear spray out of her pack, hooked it to her waist strap, and took a deep breath, excitement overcoming trepidation. *I can do this!*

She glanced at Pim, who was tying up the boat. "What a beautiful place, Pim. Thank you. You don't have to stay, but can you come back for me in four hours?"

He shook his head. "Too dangerous. We stick together. It's a long hike up to his place. There are wolves on this island, and bears and cougars, so put the dog on a leash too."

She didn't argue. She was grateful for the company. She wasn't sure why Nancy hadn't wanted Tag along. Yes, the man was imposing, but was Luke really that easily spooked, or was there another reason? Amanda had been forced to give Tag a half-baked excuse about covering more territory quickly if they split up for the day. Tag hadn't objected, saying he had some things he wanted to check out on his own. She'd left him heading south toward the beaches on his e-bike.

Pim started up the path with an easy, long-legged stride that left Amanda scrambling to keep up. They were immediately swallowed up by a dense forest of moss-draped hemlock, spruce, and massive red cedars with trunks thicker than the span of her arms.

"Amazing trees," she said.

"Some of them are a thousand years old; one of the few old-growth forests left in British Columbia."

"Was there any logging in here?"

He nodded. "For a while. Lots of my people got jobs in logging, me too. But it destroys the forest, the soil, the streams, and the salmon grounds. Our whole way of life. So, we're going back to our traditional ways. Respect for the land."

The path was narrow, choked on both sides by lush ferns and bushes with bright pink flowers.

Pim touched one tenderly. "Salmonberries. Delicious in August," he said before turning to continue the climb. The fresh scent of cedar mingled with the damp, musty loam of the rainforest. The path meandered up and down around rocky outcrops and fallen trees, over rotting roots, and through mossy bogs, slowly climbing as they hiked inland, clapping their hands at blind turns to alert the bears to their presence.

There were no markings on the trail, but Pim kept up a steady pace as she clambered and slipped and scrambled in his wake. Once, she was sure they were completely lost, until they came across a crude boardwalk spanning a rushing stream. In the canopy high overhead, crows, ravens, and jays shrieked and flapped as they followed their progress. She was drenched in sweat and breathing heavily by the time they reached a small outcrop of windswept rock and paused to look out to sea. From this vantage, the ocean was a swirl of blue, green, and silver, and farther out, a long green tongue of land jutted south into the sea. Another island?

She looked at her watch. They'd been walking for nearly an hour. Surely, they should have arrived by now, but all around them the tall, dense forest loomed untouched. With no trail markings, did Pim really know where he was going? There was no internet or mobile coverage, only trees and a narrow path that drew him forward through the bush.

"Are we close?" she panted as she gulped water and offered some to Kaylee.

He glanced at her with a half smile. "His camp is just through the trees. Maybe a hundred metres."

Pim was a big man. Intimidating, like Tag. "Okay, you wait here. I can manage from here." She sensed his hesitation. "He might be scared by two people."

"He knows I'm here."

"How does he know?"

"This is his forest. But you're safe." Pim gestured to Kaylee. "Okay, follow the dog."

The path was a faint thread weaving into the bush. Unnerved by the vast trees and the dark silence, she took a deep breath and clutched her bear spray and Kaylee's leash, determined not to be afraid. In her heyday, she'd been in scarier jungles than this, but fear felt like her constant shadow these days.

With a nod, she plunged into the woods, letting Kaylee lead with her nose to the ground. Soon, up ahead, she glimpsed the diagonal line of a roof cutting through the trees, and gradually a cluster of cabins emerged. The largest was built of elaborately etched logs that glistened like honey in the sun. It had a peaked roof, a door, and two windows facing west toward her. In front of it was a clearing with a stone firepit, a chicken coop, and two sheds, and to the south of the cabin was a cleared garden with a fence and roof of chicken wire. Two chickens strutted around the yard, and a goat looked up in surprise. Everything looked hand-hewn, and both the door and the chicken coop were painted with brightly coloured nature scenes. The chicken coop had the playful saying *Come in and Lay Awhile* painted across it, and on the transom over the cabin door were the words *Heaven's Door*.

Of all the odd features of the cabin, however, none was odder than the round wooden tower that rose above the peak of the roof. It reminded her of the widow's walks on the old fishermen's houses on the East Coast, where women would watch for their men returning from the sea. The tower soared about fifteen feet above the roof, with spiral steps carved out of the massive core and a perch at the top. From that vantage, could Luke see the ocean and his private cove? Had he seen them arrive? If so, he hadn't come out.

She walked around the property, greeting the goat and the chickens, which were squawking at Kaylee, and studying the plants in his garden. They were just sprouting, but she recognized carrots, potatoes, lettuce, and various kinds of squash just beginning to flower. Other leafy greens were unfamiliar. Herbs, drugs, or home medicine? Wooden rain barrels caught the runoff from the roof and funnelled it into furrows in the garden, and another rain barrel fed a large clawfoot tub that sat in the yard.

For safety, she kept Kaylee on the leash, but the dog pulled excitedly as she snuffled in corners. Amanda called out a greeting. Nothing. She knocked softly on the cabin door, but there was no answer. Intrigue gave way to disappointment. Surely, he would have heard the animals, so unless he was fast asleep inside, he was not home. The main cabin door was secured with a wooden latch that held firm when she tried it. Across the clearing was a smaller cabin, which she'd assumed was a storage shed until she saw the words painted over the door: *There but for fortune.*

She felt a twinge of apprehension. The door itself was slightly open, and in spite of herself, she was drawn to it. She eased the door open farther and peered through the crack. The room inside was bathed in light from windows on three sides. She barely registered the easel, the wooden stool, and the shotgun hanging by the door, because the whole was overwhelming. Walls, ceiling, and floor were covered in paintings that blended one into another. Vivid reds, oranges, and yellows, softer greens and purples, angry shouts of black. Some paintings were wild explosions of colour that swept over the wall, others were intricate close-ups of a leaf, a moth, or a human hand.

She moved into the room to look more closely. The hand was dirty, its nails torn and bleeding. The red explosion on the wall looked like a human heart, gaping open and spraying blood onto a naked body purple in death.

Higher up, a human head, eyes squeezed shut and mouth open in a silent howl. And pressed to the temple, the muzzle of a gun.

Horror raced through her. She stumbled backward, and for a moment, terrifying memories flooded through her, of guns and screams and flames. She clutched Kaylee's leash and turned to flee from the room, but as she reached the door, she spotted a man hiding behind it, peering around it at her. His eyes were wide, reflecting the fear she felt.

"Luke?" she managed.

He edged farther into view. "What? Who?" His voice was rusty, and he seemed to grope for long-forgotten words. Kaylee barked ferociously, and Amanda backed up, sucking air into her lungs as she tried to calm down. She had been prepared for unkempt hair and beard, ragged clothes, and filth, but not for this. His pure white hair fell in a neat braid down his back, and a matching beard in a braid hung down in front.

He was beginning to shrivel with age, but he was still a tall, powerful man. He was wrapped toga-style in a red-and-white blanket bearing a Haida design, which was an odd contrast to his blue eyes and pale, freckled skin. And beneath it, both his hands and bare feet were speckled with paint and mottled with purple and white scars. His face was a web of crevices, with more scarring on one side that twisted the corner of his mouth. A single teardrop was tattooed below his left eye. He looked like a new-age Moses coming down from the Mount.

Beside him, within easy reach, was the shotgun.

Through her own panic, she recognized the man was afraid. As afraid as her. She held up her hand. "I'm sorry," she managed. "I don't mean to ... the door was open."

His eyes filled with reproach. "This is mine. My place."

"I know. I didn't mean to upset you." She groped for some way to reassure him. "Nancy told me where to find you. I am interested in your paintings. Not the touristy stuff at her shop, but ... your real art."

He stood in the middle of the room and looked around. Bewilderment chased the fear from his face. "What do you want with it?"

He kept his gaze averted, and instinctively she sensed that face-to-face contact was uncomfortable for him. She gestured to the paintings stacked against the wall. "If you are willing to share any, I would like to buy one."

"This ... this ..." He swept his paint-stained hand around him. "This is not for sale."

"I know. Because this is your own private hell."

He stiffened and shot a glance at her. She felt as if she were teetering on a tightrope, with nowhere to go but forward. "I recognize it. I have my own. My name is Amanda, and I too live with nightmares like this in my head. Not exactly the same, because I don't know where yours come from, but the feelings are the same. Terror and guilt and pain that are almost unbearable. The feelings are hammering to get out. This is how you get them out."

He still didn't speak, but he was quivering, and his eyes were glassy. "Let's go outside," she said, walking toward the door. "I'm sorry, I shouldn't have come in here. It's too private to share."

He backed out of her way, his head down. Once they were outside in the sunlight, she breathed a sigh of relief and moved away to give him some space. Kaylee had been pressed to her side protectively, but now she wagged her tail and crept toward him. At his feet, she rubbed against his knee. He reached down and stroked her silky fur with an awkward hand.

As Amanda watched, a calm settled over her. "Your paintings are unflinching. If you do want to sell any of them ..."

"Where do your nightmares come from?"

She was startled, and doubts crowded her mind. He was so fragile that he didn't need her horrors added to his own. But he had raised his head and met her gaze for the first time. His eyes, deep-set and webbed by age, were a pale blue. He seemed to be looking for a connection. But did she want to revisit that time, after working so hard to move past it? His painting of the face and gun had shaken her, and old memories were roiling.

"From Africa," she said carefully. "I am — was — an aid worker working with Save the Children. Except one night, I couldn't. The village was attacked ..." She clenched her jaw and looked at Kaylee, longing to call her back but sensing that Luke might need her more. "Set on fire. The children were kidnapped, and the villagers —"

He stopped patting Kaylee and, feeling his imperceptible distress, the dog nuzzled his hand gently.

"The villagers died?" A bare whisper.

"You don't need to hear this," Amanda said. "I'm sorry. I'll go. I'll speak to Nancy about buying one of your paintings in the shop." She picked up Kaylee's leash and headed toward the path.

"You'll come again?"

She turned to him in surprise. He stood in the middle of his clearing, a man safe only in his self-chosen exile, but inviting her in. It was no time to be coy.

"Yes."

CHAPTER FOUR

Nancy was smiling ear to ear. "I was hoping you were the right person!"

They were sitting on a pub patio overlooking the inlet. Pushing aside her half-eaten fish and chips, Amanda reached instead for her beer. It was her first taste of Tuff Session Ale, a kick-ass pale ale from the local Tofino Brewing Company, but it wouldn't be her last.

For a few minutes, they watched the gulls squabbling over scraps on the wharf while Amanda figured out a response. She still felt unsettled by her encounter with Luke and by the memories it had stirred up.

"I'm not a therapist, Nancy," she said finally. "Beneath the surface, I'm as fragile as he is."

"Not by a long shot," Nancy said, scooping a juicy chunk of fish out of her chowder. "You've chosen to stay engaged in the world, to turn your experience and your emotions to something good. Luke almost never talks to anyone, and the longer he's up there alone, the more disconnected he becomes."

"I'm not sure that's all bad. He's created quite a pleasant little world for himself. Maybe that's all he wants or can handle."

"But he's still stuck in the seventies," Nancy said. "He's not getting any better."

Amanda pictured the white hair and the deeply wrinkled face, the hands speckled with liver spots as well as paint. "How long has he been up there?"

"In that cabin, about thirty years. Before that, he was on Meares Island for a while until the area got too crowded with visitors for his liking. So, he moved up to that remote part of Flores Island, which is mostly Ahousaht First Nations territory with a provincial park on the western half. When he first moved up there, he kept an eye on the park for the park rangers, reporting trouble or poor conditions. It's a wilderness park with no facilities, but it's getting more popular now that the Wild Side Trail is there. Everyone wants wilderness, it seems. He doesn't like all the people. Sometimes I worry that ..." She broke off, shaking her head, and took a sip of wine. "I don't want him to go completely off the rails and do something that will get him locked up."

Amanda's eyes narrowed. "Has he been locked up before?"

"No! At least, not in jail. But some of us old-timers, and the Ahousaht, keep an eye out for him, to buffer him from too much contact."

Amanda thought about the paintings in his studio. About his reclusive life and his fumbling communication. "Did anyone ever find out what's wrong with him?"

"I was only a teenager back in the sixties, but I did know him. We were both part of the hippie commune at Wreck Bay until the Feds made the whole beach a park and demolished the commune. He spent the better part of the time stoned. LSD, hash, mushrooms — you name it. The local doc figured it fried his brain. That happened to some of those kids."

Amanda shook her head. Clouds had begun to mass overhead, and a chilly breeze tugged at her jacket, but she barely noticed. "I think it's more. There's a reason he took all those drugs. He's suffered a lot of pain."

Nancy played with her napkin. "What did he tell you?"

"Nothing. But something happened to him, and I'm not sure, after all this time, that he'd be able to get over it. Or that he should even try."

"But he wants to see you again."

"So he says."

"Then that's a big step! Don't you see? You can't turn your back on him now."

"But I'm only here for a short time," Amanda said. "And I'll repeat what I said at the beginning. I'm not a therapist."

"Don't be. Just be a friend. You'd be the first he's had in a long time."

"Matthew, I'm staying a couple of extra nights up here," Amanda said. She was sitting on her bed with her laptop propped on her knees. Since the pandemic began, almost all their long-distance communication had been by Zoom, which wasn't perfect, but she really enjoyed being able to see him. Although not the scowl that flitted across his face.

"Why? What's going on?" he asked.

"Nothing. It's just a big place with lots to investigate." Vague and evasive, but true. She had no intention of telling him she was going up into the wilderness to talk to a hermit who had avoided civilization for half a century and who might be more than a little bit crazy. She'd given Nancy's suggestion careful consideration over the past couple of days while she continued her trip planning. In fact, she'd tried to dismiss it, but in idle moments her thoughts kept drifting back to the strange old man hidden away from the world with his fear and his sadness.

"Did Tag put you up to this?" Matthew asked.

Amanda was surprised. "Tag? No, he's going back by plane to-morrow as planned. He has commitments in Victoria." She hesi-tated. She really had little idea what Tag had been up to the past couple of days. He'd been off doing his own thing, with vague ex-planations like following up on details. She assumed he was pulling some things together. Not worth complaining to Matthew about. "He's been fine. He has good connections, and we've got a lot done. I just want to follow up on some loose ends."

"Do you want me to come join you?"

There was both wistfulness and worry in his tone. She knew he'd never stop trying to protect her, to keep her from getting her-self into trouble. He and Chris had both appointed themselves her guardians. No matter that she neither needed nor wanted that.

"No, no. Tag should have a lot of information already, so you and he can move forward on some of the logistics."

Matthew made a face. "That'll be a barrel of laughs. Does Chris know you're staying up there?"

"It's not the end of the earth, Matthew! They even have decent organic coffee and five-star resorts. Honestly!"

"That doesn't answer my question."

Irritation flared, but she tamped it down, reminding herself this was what most people did when they cared about each other. The boundaries between friendship and family had blurred between them long ago. Matthew fretted while her own mother was oblivi-ous, and her brother, engrossed in making millions in China, didn't even know where she was.

"I'll call him in the morning. It's the middle of the night in Newfoundland. Now, have you and Bonnie finalized the list of who's coming yet?"

He sighed and sat back. "Working on it. There are so many men in need. So many who want to reconnect with their families. We're having trouble paring down the numbers."

"I know. Our programs are always like that. They're like pilot programs to see what works and what's really needed. I always hope a local agency will pick up the idea and run with it." She grinned. "Maybe you can use your charm on Bonnie. You'll enjoy that."

He chuckled, but she could almost see the faint redness creeping up his neck. Matthew had been chasing conflicts around the world for decades and more recently had been traipsing across Canada for her charity, staying in one short-term rental unit after another with no chance to lay down roots or build any lasting relationships. She felt partly responsible for his loneliness, especially now that she had found someone else to share her life with. He could do a lot worse than Bonnie. Not that he would ever let Amanda play matchmaker, but she'd noticed he came alive whenever he mentioned her name.

They talked business for a few more minutes before signing off. "Say hi to Chris for me," he said, his way of reminding her not to leave the man in the dark. In truth, she wasn't sure what she was going to tell Chris. She had finally told him about Tag and was pleased that he hadn't leaped on the next plane to come to her rescue, but she suspected a half-crazy hermit in the middle of the wilderness might be a step too far. It was almost a step too far for her.

The next morning, she gave Chris the same vague explanation she'd given Matthew, and then after breakfast she set off to drive Tag to the airport, which was halfway between Tofino and Ucluelet.

"I'll be back in Victoria soon," she said as they headed out of town. "Probably in a day or two. I just have one remote hike I want to check out. The one on Flores Island run by the Ahousaht."

"I would have liked to do that one."

She glanced at him, wondering why he hadn't mentioned that before. "There was only so much time."

On the roadside up ahead, a small sign with a single word caught their eye. *Cemetery.*

Tag chuckled at the narrow lane almost hidden in the brush. "Talk about hiding your dead," he said. "There's not a single building around. I wonder how old it is."

"The town's European settlement only dates back to the mid-1800s." As they passed by, Amanda peered down the road, and a thought struck her. "Maybe there's an AK buried there."

Tag glanced at her. "Do you want to check? It might be interesting to see some history, and we've got time."

She did a U-turn and took the narrow, nondescript road into the forest. They bumped along the road for a short distance until they were stopped by a barrier. Up ahead, she could see a gate and wooden fencing surrounding a simple pioneer cemetery. Tacked to the fencing were the familiar signs: *Bear in area* and *Cougar in area*. She kept Kaylee on a tight leash as she climbed out of the car.

The place was deserted. No cars, not even a parking lot, no gatehouse or other structures. Just a couple of fenced enclosures containing one large stone memorial and a scattering of gravestones. All around, the forest pressed in.

"Don't people die around here?" Tag muttered as he set off down the road to the entrance. She followed, curious to see who would be buried here. Inside, the gravestones were an eclectic lot, some worn and barely legible while others were quite new. A few had flowers and other signs of care.

Tag went his own way, wandering among the stones and reading inscriptions, while she began a methodical search for the initials AK. The names told many tales. Father and son dead on the same day, husband and wife thirty years apart. A daughter two months old.

"Maybe many people are buried elsewhere," she called as she reached the last row of stones without having any luck. "Probably with family wherever they came from."

Tag had stopped in front of a small stone plaque inlaid into the grass and was studying it thoughtfully. She came to join him. "*My Nootka Rose, September 19, 1971*," she read. "That's touching. I wonder if it's a child."

"Somebody who was loved. They didn't have much money, whoever they were." He glanced around at the towering trees. "But around here, who needs fancy?" He glanced at his watch and spun on his heel. "But now we'd better book it."

After dropping Tag off, she visited a bakery and an arts supply shop, stowed all her purchases in her knapsack, and went in search of Pim. She found him joking with some fishermen down at the dock. He wrinkled up his face in alarm when she asked him to take her and Kaylee back to Luke's cove.

"You're going again?"

"He asked me to come."

He shook his head in disbelief as they settled into the boat. One of his friends unhitched the dock line. "You stay with her this time, Pim," he said.

"It's a good idea," Pim said as he pushed away from the dock, but Amanda was reluctant.

"Luke invited me, and I think it's a big step for him. I don't want to upset him."

Pim started the engine in a cloud of fumes and accelerated across the channel toward Meares Island. The noise of the engine made conversation difficult, but she could tell by the grim set of his jaw that the discussion was not over. Kaylee took up her favourite perch in the bow, her tongue lolling and her red fur rippling in the wind, seeing nothing but adventure.

A boat crowded with young people and surfboards roared past them, laughing and shouting over the noise of their engine. Amanda watched them grow smaller until they disappeared around a rocky point.

Pim scowled. "Fools. Too many shoals there to go so fast."

He threaded his old skiff expertly through the passages and islands past the village of Maaqtusiis and up the inner coast of Flores Island, pointing out birds, seals, and majestic trees. Seaplanes overhead and periodic flotillas of kayaks were the only disruption to the wilderness peace. Halfway up the island, however, they spotted the boat of rowdy surfers pulled up in a small cove bracketed by rocky outcrops. They had piled out onto the pebble beach and were unloading hampers and bags. Amanda counted four men, all young, lithe, and deeply tanned by the ocean sun. Someone had turned on music, blaring techno across the water. Pim's lips tightened.

Just as they were passing, a smaller, blue-and-white striped boat carrying a surfboard roared up the strait. At the last minute, it veered into the cove and pulled up beside the first boat. A man leaped out amid shouts of greeting. Sunlight glinted off his wet, windblown blond hair as he tied his boat to a log and dived into the shallow water, surfacing two seconds later amid shrieks. Soon they were all splashing each other.

Pim muttered something about cracking their heads open on the rocks as he opened the throttle on his boat. As they neared Luke's cove, Amanda scanned the mountainside and spotted his tower peeking over the treetops. If he wanted to, he could see everything coming and going, she thought with an unexpected shiver.

Close to shore, Pim shut off the engine and let the boat drift gently up to the dock. She gathered up her knapsack and Kaylee's leash, preparing to secure the boat, but Pim didn't move. "Luke is not always the same. One day he's okay, the next day he's hiding behind a tree, seeing things. Too much acid. Or too many bad memories." He gestured to the path. "He may not even remember who you are."

She nodded. "I'll be careful. I won't stay if he's upset."

"He's old, but don't be fooled. He's very strong."

Amanda clipped on her bear spray. "I have Kaylee."

Kaylee wagged her tail at the mention of her name. Pim grunted. "She's not a guard dog."

Amanda chuckled. "No, she's a Toller, sunniest dog on the planet. But she will defend me if she has to."

Pim crossed his arms and thrust out his chin. "It's better if I stay with you this time."

"How about you wait at the lookout again? I have my hunting whistle. If you hear it, come running."

He heaved a sigh, tied the boat, and led the way up the path, stoic and silent. For his size, he was remarkably fast and sure-footed. When they reached the lookout point where she had left him the last time, she stopped to catch her breath. "I know you're worried, Pim. But he invited me, and I don't want him to think I don't trust him."

"You shouldn't."

"I don't think he wants to hurt anyone."

He leaned against a tree and eyed her thoughtfully. "The first sign of trouble, the first sign that his mind has gone somewhere else, you get out of there." He paused and squinted up the path ahead as if debating whether to say more. "Luke is not a bad man, but he has ghosts. I know about such things. In our village, our Elders still have nightmares about Christie Residential School. Some of them see things too and change their moods in an instant. So I know."

Amanda felt a rush of overwhelming sadness. So much suffering in the world, so many wounded souls. "It must be awful for them."

He nodded brusquely. "You hang on to that whistle. I'll be right here."

CHAPTER FIVE

Amanda headed up the rest of the way, holding on to Kaylee's leash and keeping a sharp eye out for trouble. Ahead was the final outcrop. *Not far now*, she thought, pausing to listen. There was nothing but the call of birds and the swish of wind through the trees. As she bent her head to clamber up the rocks, a shadow fell across her path. She recoiled instinctively and looked up to see Luke standing at the top, watching her. Kaylee barked and wagged her tail, but he didn't move. Amanda tried to read his expression. Was he happy to see her? Angry at the intrusion? Did he even remember her?

She forced a calm she didn't feel. "Hello, Luke, it's Amanda."

He didn't smile but gave a faint nod and turned to continue up the path. Was that an invitation? After a brief hesitation, she followed. For the tenth time, she wondered why she was doing this. There were many other paintings she could choose from. What compelled her to see this strange, troubled recluse again? What drew her to him? A sense of pity? A desire to help? Or a feeling of kinship. What made her presume he wanted her help, let alone her pity?

Chris had once told her she was a sucker for suffering. "Isn't that a good thing?" she'd retorted. "Isn't it better than callous indifference?" He'd hugged her close and murmured in her ear, "I don't want you to change. I just want you to find a balance. Not everyone wants their lives fixed."

Luke had spent almost her entire lifespan in this self-chosen isolation. He was not at peace — that much was clear from his paintings — but perhaps it was the closest he could get.

When they reached his compound, a brisk wind was blowing off the ocean, bringing with it the distant crash of waves. Amanda was glad she'd packed a jacket. Luke was dressed in ordinary clothes today: a pair of baggy khakis worn threadbare at the knees and frayed at the cuffs. His multicoloured, beaded suede jacket had been mended many times. He had lit a fire in the stone pit, and a pot of water was simmering over it. Spread on the stone beside it was a hunk of cheese and some bannock.

"Did you …?" she began in surprise.

His gaze slid toward her briefly. "I saw your boat. I'm glad you came."

"You invited me."

He blinked nervously. "Most people are afraid of me."

"People are afraid of what they don't understand."

He sat cross-legged by the fire and poured hot water into a cup before sprinkling in some dried leaves. "Do you think you understand?"

"A little, maybe. I know …" She searched for safe words. "You have an artist's soul, full of feelings."

He held out the cup to her without reply. Without meeting her gaze.

"Aren't you having any?"

"I only have one cup."

The profound loneliness of the statement echoed between them. "I wish I'd known. I would have brought you one from Nancy's place." She hesitated. "If you don't mind, we can share this cup."

He shrank back. A step too far, she realized. To change the subject, she reached into her backpack. "I brought you some paints, though," she said, spilling the tubes of paint on the ground. "The gallery helped me choose them."

He picked one up and examined it carefully. "I usually make my own paints."

"Then these will be different. They're acrylic, and the gallery told me they're colours that are difficult for you to make. Something for you to experiment with."

He picked up another tube, opened it, and peered at the hint of pink inside. A smile flitted across his face as he set it aside. "The colour of a smile. For my soul. My feelings."

She relaxed. He was staying with her. "How long have you been an artist?"

"As a child, I drew sketches of little things I saw. But paintings like this? Since I came to Tofino."

"When did you come?"

He hesitated as if searching the distant past. "Time blurs because for so long it didn't — doesn't — matter. But I remember the beginning: 1969. I was twenty."

"Why here? Why Tofino?"

"Friends told me about a commune. They said it was safe, you could live for free on the beach, everybody was looking for peace. For safety." He shook his head ruefully.

As part of her research into the area, she had read about the hippie commune that had sprung up on the beach and adjacent cliffside near Tofino. The B&B owner had mentioned he was part of it himself. Communes were magnets for dropouts, flower children, and dreamers seeking a utopian world order built on sharing, spiritual renewal, and enlightenment through mind-expanding drugs. Some were fleeing trauma, but most were just seeking an escape from the pressures and expectations of what they perceived as the materialistic, spiritually bankrupt rat race defined by their parents.

She did not think that was Luke's story, but did she dare ask him? Was it any of her business? Instead, she gestured to the compound around her. "But the commune wasn't enough?"

He scowled. "They tore the camp down. Set fire to our home."

A brief flash of memory made her shiver. "I'm sorry. Who?"

"The government. We were a menace, they said. We stank, there was filth and garbage all over the place. Drugs. They wanted a park for nice, clean families to visit."

"Oh," she said noncommittally. She could see why a beach full of drugs and garbage might not be popular. She took a sip of tea as she weighed her words. "That must have been hard. What did you do?"

"The fire." He shifted. His gaze darted around the clearing as if looking for an answer. "It was a bad time for me. I don't want to talk about it."

She thought about his facial scar, the flames painted across the ceiling of his studio, and the terror stamped on his memory. His words came much more easily to him than on her first visit, and she was anxious not to drive him back into silence. "It's okay, you don't have to. I know about fires. That fear stays with you."

His breath seemed to quicken, and he wound a piece of grass tightly around his finger. She was looking for a way to distract him when he abruptly stood up. "Let me show you some paintings."

This time he led her not to the shed where his tormented paintings were, but to the main cabin with its message carved over the door: *Heaven's Door.* Kaylee rushed inside, ever eager to explore, and began to nose around the corners. Once Amanda's eyes adjusted to the dimmer light, she took in the sparse, soothing surroundings. It was one big room, bathed in pale light from windows on all sides. She barely noticed the mattress, chair, wood stove, and primitive kitchen that made up the furnishings, because the far wall of the room was dominated by a massive tree trunk that formed the base of the tower on the roof. The trunk was intricately carved into shelving and nooks that held his paints, brushes, jars, and palettes, all meticulously cleaned.

Almost every inch of the remaining wall space was covered by paintings, and more were stacked against the walls. Unlike the paintings in the shed, these were mostly soothing: misty purple mountains, waves racing green and blue up the shore, jagged multi-coloured rocks, boats, cabins, village scenes. They were fanciful colours and somewhat abstract, but they reflected loneliness, awe, and occasional joy, not terror.

Amanda smiled. "This is your safe place."

He was standing in the open doorway, watching her as she walked around the room. "Do you have one?"

She was going to say no. Since that terrifying night in Nigeria, she had never been able to find a lasting peace. A peace she could rely on without the sudden threat of flashback or triggers. But then she realized that was no longer true. "I do. My home in Newfoundland. Sitting on the patio, looking out over Deer Lake."

"Alone?"

Once again, she hesitated. That was a delicate question. Her safest place was lying in Chris's arms, but it was clear Luke lived alone, and she didn't want to break the tenuous connection they had found. "Sometimes," she finally said. "There can be great peace in solitude."

A helicopter thundered low overhead, and he glanced anxiously back up at the sky. As it swept over the trees, he flinched and retreated to sit in the corner, wrapping his arms around himself. Watching his frozen mask of fear and his rigid body, she recognized the signs of a flashback. The clatter of a helicopter had transported him back in time. She didn't move in case she triggered panic, and she kept her voice calm.

"That's just tourists, getting an aerial tour of Clayoquot Sound."

He swallowed. Nodded.

"But it brings back something else, doesn't it?"

He didn't answer, but she began to put together the pieces. The helicopter, the yellow trees, the blood-spattered heart: 1969. "Were you in Vietnam?"

He stiffened and shot her an alarmed look. The roar of the helicopter was fading, and with it, his panic. "Who says that?"

"No one. It's just your age and the fact you came here in 1969. I know thousands of war resisters came from the US to Canada back then, and many ended up here."

He said nothing, but he quivered.

"I know it was a terrible time, Luke. And I've seen this destruction over and over. Victims of war, child soldiers, even civilians like me, who can't forget what we saw. What we did. So many things trigger memories."

Taking a chance, she went to sit on the ground closer to him. "Let me make us some fresh tea, and we'll take it outside into the sunshine."

"Sometimes ... sometimes I can't tell what's real," he said. "I see things. People come to visit me from my past, and I don't know if they're real. I smell things. Burning. Trash burning. People burning."

"That's a smell you never forget," she said. Her heart began to race. Did she dare go further? Up on a mountaintop, all alone with this fragile stranger? She had often talked about her memories in her therapy sessions over the years, and yet they felt more vivid here in this lonely cabin than they ever had in the psychologist's office. "Fires still scare me too. Even barbecues, the smell of steak ..."

He unwrapped his arms in surprise and nodded. "I can't eat meat. I can't kill a living thing. I can't watch its life fade away. Not now." He lifted his head to look overhead. "I flew in those helicopters. I saw the fires and the black smoke that boiled up. The smell stays in your nose, on your clothes, your hair, your skin. I could never get clean." He looked at his scarred hands. "Even now, sometimes."

"Did anyone help you? I mean, afterward?"

He shrank back. "How? How do you erase that? What we did? What I did? Whole jungles napalmed, just so we could kill the Viet Cong hiding in them. Beautiful forests gone. Villages vaporized. Children, pigs, chickens, cows … running." He shut his eyes as if to block out the memory. "The VC, they hid in tunnels. And in the villages. Everywhere! I was in the jungle, and I couldn't find my unit. There was a woman. A villager. I was crouching behind a tree, holding on to my M16 for dear life. I was so scared she'd see me. But then her son, just a little boy, saw me and came running. He had a gun, and I …" He sucked in his breath. Whimpered. "Trust no one!"

Amanda knew the terror of not knowing whom to trust. Of being on the run in a desperate bid for safety. Hiding in ditches and deserted homes, avoiding panicked villagers and deadly Islamic terrorists alike.

Luke had been in a war far from home, far from a world that made any sense to him, thrown into a kaleidoscope of shifting meaning, cascading from safety to threat, good to evil, in shapes he no longer recognized.

As had she. During her time in Northern Nigeria, the community had been happy and peaceful. It had been desperately poor and extremely conservative, with hospitals and proper schools far away. There was never enough water, and the meagre crops were always on the brink of shrivelling up. A travelling medical clinic visited once a month but was barely able to treat even minor ailments. The government, with its pomp and corruption, seemed uninterested and far away, but with the help of various NGOs, the community was becoming a hub for both education and health care. Charities were working together to build a proper school with walls, desks, and a roof.

Teachers and health workers were being trained, and basic texts and manuals for reading and math had been delivered. The faces of those eager young workers like Aisha were etched in her mind. The pride and hope they felt, their excitement at watching the students learn, especially the girls who were catching a glimpse of a new future. Perhaps that's what had caught the attention of the extremists.

Sometimes she had flashbacks of the guards, little more than boys, clutching their AK-47s and turning to flee in their Jeeps, leaving nothing but dust and the staccato drumming of gunfire. The predators descended in one brutal swoop, clad in black against the night, Islamic flags billowing, machetes dripping with blood, the stench of gunpowder and smoke carried on the wind. Screams, flames, fleeing shapes backlit by orange. The young teacher, the nurse ... cut down in midflight. Someone yanked her to her feet and dragged her into the night, past the village, past the perimeter road, away from the bullets chewing up the ground around her. Still the ferocious grip on her arm propelled her forward. Until with a sudden jerk, the grip loosened. Aisha's eyes wide and white in her black face as she melted to the ground. Her co-worker. Her friend. "Run, run," she'd said, the last words she uttered as those big, beautiful eyes grew dim.

Amanda ran. *Trust no one!* Luke had said. She shut her eyes now as she remembered that desperate flight to freedom, never knowing at each encounter whether she'd be met with food or a bullet. Not knowing, until a month later in the safety of Lagos, the fate of that village and those children. Eighty-nine dead. Two hundred and ten kidnapped.

Luke was watching her now as she pulled herself slowly back to the present. She breathed deeply to calm her heart rate. *Ride it out*, she'd been taught. She'd come a long way back in five years, and she knew she would find her footing again.

"People think I'm crazy, you know," Luke said.

She focused on him. "Do you think so?"

"Sometimes." He unfolded himself from the bed and walked over to look at one of his paintings, a tranquil beach at low tide, with sandpipers pecking through the seaweed and a hint of whimsical shacks huddled against the dunes in the distance. There were no people in the scene.

"This is an old painting," he said. "From the way it used to be."

"On Long Beach?"

He nodded. "Wreck Bay," he said and pointed to a brightly painted lean-to propped up by huge driftwood logs at the edge of the scene. What looked like seashells and wind chimes were strung across the front. "That was my place. They tore all this down. We were a tiny corner of the beach. Long Beach is ten miles long, and we just wanted one corner. But they tore it down."

She scanned the other paintings. "Your villages are empty. You have no people in these paintings. Only in your studio."

His eyes flitted to a painting turned against the wall in the corner before he looked away hastily. She approached and turned it over. It was indeed a person. A young woman half-turned away, gazing down the beach. Her long, sun-bleached hair cascaded down her back and over her naked breast.

Amanda peered more closely. A small pink flower was tucked behind her ear. "Who's this?"

He turned toward the door abruptly. "Pick a painting if you want, and then you should go," he said and walked out.

Outside in the bright afternoon sun, they stood in awkward silence. Amanda wanted to apologize for turning the painting around, but she was concerned any more mention of the woman would upset him further. In the distance far below, she heard the drone of motorboats. Scraps of laughter drifted on the breeze. Luke's mood blackened further.

Amanda trod carefully. "Do you have a painting you'd like me to have?"

"Not her," he said before disappearing back inside. After a few minutes, he emerged, empty-handed. "It's hard to part with any of them. They are my life, my memories. But I know what I would like to paint for you. Come again in a few days and I will have it."

Her heart sank. She was already several days behind her scheduled departure. "I have to go back to Victoria in the morning."

He risked a glance, and she saw the dismay in his gaze. "I will be here when you come back. Will you come back?"

She turned to gather up Kaylee's leash. "Yes, I will," she said as she headed toward the path. Before the forest swallowed her up, she heard once again the shrieks of laughter over the sound of the boats down below.

It felt like a violation of this sanctuary and of the peace Luke was trying to find. As she walked down to meet Pim, she wondered what Luke would paint for her and whether he would put a person in it. As a sign of progress and reconnection.

Her thoughts returned to the painting of the young woman on the beach. Had she seen that woman before?

CHAPTER SIX

The morning sun spilled through the venetian blind into Bonnie's office, casting ribbons of light over the slumping stacks of files on her desk. Her teal hair glowed eerily, and Matthew suppressed a laugh as he entered the room. She had ditched the pricey hip look in favour of striped, wide-legged pants paired with a simple white T. He suspected she'd look good in a potato sack.

As he did with all attractive women, he'd already taken note that although she wore chunky artisan rings on almost all her fingers, her ring finger was bare. As a result, he'd chosen his own clothes with uncharacteristic care. Instead of the battered fedora that bore every scar from his years on the front lines, he'd covered his bald spot with a black beanie and was wearing his newest pair of blue jeans and a long, loose black shirt that deftly concealed his paunch.

She grinned up at him from behind a hank of hair. "I was just looking over your estimates. It's going to be steep, even if we rent a bus to get them there."

He nodded. "I'll work the donation angle the best I can, but prices are high out there, especially in high season. I was pushing Amanda for the Great Bear Rainforest, but she thought Tofino would offer more diverse activities. And she is right. Lots of people interested, and donations are good."

"Yes, they've been good for us too. Clever woman."

The hint of doubt in her voice gave him pause, and he eyed her keenly. "Amanda doesn't do this for the money, you know. Not the money for her tours or for the charities we choose. The charities were an afterthought when we discovered that ordinary people were looking for small ways to make a difference. For Amanda, it has always been about building bridges and healing. About giving people hope."

"I wouldn't have accepted if I thought otherwise, Matthew. I'm really looking forward to the itinerary she comes up with. Tag says her focus is on activities that make fathers and sons work together. He is on his way in from the airport right now to give us an update."

Matthew felt a twinge of disappointment. He'd been looking forward to this meeting all week. It was a ray of light and joy in his dismal round of medical appointments and tests. His cocktail of drugs was wreaking havoc with his digestion. He'd had to give up his taste for Thai and Indian food, curtail his intake of red wine and fine Scotch, and most recently rich cheeses. He'd been in Victoria more than two weeks and had only eaten the famous fish and chips from Red Fish Blue Fish down on the waterfront once. He'd spent half the night in pain and regretting it.

Now he couldn't even enjoy the thrill of a harmless flirtation without the brooding presence of the tattooed, bearded hulk.

Bonnie cocked her head. "That's okay, isn't it?"

A knock at the door cut off his answer, and a moment later the Hulk himself appeared, breathless and energized. Matthew noticed he was more freckled and sunburnt, especially on his shiny, shaved head. Sea, sand, and sun obviously agreed with him.

They shook hands, and Bonnie wasted no time. "Tag, since Amanda's been delayed, I hope you can provide us with some specifics so we can move forward. We're working with a very tight deadline if you still want to do this in June."

Tag filled them in on the camping and kayaking tours already lined up. "All that's left is finalizing some hikes."

"Is that what's she doing now?"

"She wanted to check out a multiday hike, but she should be back by tomorrow." Tag paused. "Unless she's hooked herself up with some handsome, half-naked artist."

Matthew's lips tightened. "That's not her style." Hearing his prim tone, he tried for a casual shrug. "I know she was interested in a particular painting and was going to track the artist down."

"That shouldn't take long," Tag said, stretching out his long legs and forcing Matthew to tuck his feet to the side. "You can cover all of Tofino in an hour."

Matthew bristled. "The artist isn't in Tofino. He's living on a mountaintop somewhere."

Tag's grin vanished. "Where? Who?"

"On some island north of there. She said it was a hermit named Luke. You heard of him?"

Tag's eyes narrowed, as if he was thinking, but Matthew sensed he was figuring out how to react. Finally, he forced his body to relax as he shook his head. "They're a dime a dozen, those guys, and the more mysterious, the better. I can hardly wait to see what crap he pawns off on her."

By the time she and Pim arrived back down at Luke's cove, Amanda was sweaty and hot. The sun blazed high in the blue sky, tempting her with a swim, but a brisk wind was blowing in from the west. A worried frown flashed across Pim's face, but he said nothing as he started the engine. After navigating out of the cove, he headed west instead of east back toward the inner passage. Amanda knew that ahead lay the open ocean.

"Scenic route?" Amanda asked.

Pim's face was impassive as he studied the horizon. Far out over the ocean, a band of cloud gathered. "There's a storm blowing in, but not for a few hours. Sometimes the ocean is too rough once we get past the peninsula, but this afternoon should be fine. This is a good time to see the outer side of the island and the Wild Side Trail that you're interested in. It's rugged and more off the main tourist route. There are big cliffs and waterfalls along here. And if we're lucky, gray whales in Cow Bay."

As they rounded the top of the island, the wind and ocean swell picked up. Waves hurtled against the black rocks, shooting spray high into the air. Pim swivelled to point at the land opposite, where a deep fissure cut into the shoreline.

"Hot Springs Cove is just ahead over there," he shouted.

Just then, the boat was slammed with the full force of the ocean. Chilly headwinds tore through her T-shirt, and she scrambled to pull on her waterproof jacket. Kaylee retreated to cower in the bottom of the boat, and Amanda clung to the gunwales as she strained to look at the rugged shoreline. The famous Hot Springs had been on her list as the final activity, but she could see nothing but rocks, trees, and rolling swell.

"Is it worth going to?"

Keeping his gaze fixed on the ocean ahead, he shouted above the roar of the boat. "Too many people. You should come to the hot springs near my village, Maaqtusiis."

The boat pitched and slammed against the waves as he threaded through the swells and skirted deftly away from the jagged rocks on the shore. Amanda's heart was in her mouth. The wind whipped away words, so for a while neither of them spoke. Pim kept his eyes glued to the wave pattern ahead, with occasional glances at the shore, where the surf crashed onto the scoured black rocks. One miscalculation and they could easily be dashed to bits.

Up ahead, steep, barren cliffs plunged into the sea, and then the shoreline cut into a deep fiord with a spectacular waterfall at the end. Pim edged into the narrow chasm to give her a glimpse.

"It's all provincial park up this side," he said. "Those kids we saw on the other side? I want to see if they came down this shore or over to Hot Springs. I want to see what they're up to."

They chugged down the ragged coast, skirting shoals while Amanda kept a sharp eye out for rocks below the surface. Finally, the jumbled, tree-lined shore gave way to a curving sweep of pale sand. She saw a couple of surfers paddling in the waves and the outline of two boats pulled up on the beach, one of them a small blue-and-white striped powerboat. Someone had lit a fire with the driftwood on shore, and as Amanda and Pim drew nearer, she saw the group sitting on logs, laughing and passing a bottle around.

Pim's lips tightened. "Drinking and driving a boat don't go together. The park and the Ahousaht have rules, but it's a big park, easy to hide in, and people like this don't take care of it. Luke used to help when he was younger. The park ranger paid him to keep watch. Stop trouble."

"Really!" Amanda tried to picture the diffident recluse with the long, white hair confronting troublemakers.

Pim nodded. "He did have good times. He'd come to visit us in the village, share stories, and join our Smudging Ceremonies and Sweat Lodges. We tried to help him understand his visions, be more in harmony with himself." Pim gestured with his hands as he tried to explain. "But people like this, they just laugh at him. One time a bunch of yahoos from Ontario chased him off this beach, throwing rocks and calling him crazy." Pim shook his head in disgust. "He never came back."

A swell of anger tightened her throat. Luke's hold on reality was so tenuous and vulnerable to threat that at that moment he might have been right back in Vietnam.

"Poor man," she said, moving closer so they could talk without shouting. "Are there very many yahoos who come to this area?"

"A few. Some come to party. They get drunk, loud, and do stupid things for thrills. But most visitors understand the Pacific Rim is a very special place. They want the adventure and the experience of wilderness, and they try to respect it even if they don't always know how. But this group ..." He gestured to the cluster of young men on the beach. They seemed to have split up, three of them remaining around the campfire while the other two were paddling in the surf and diving off the rocks. Amanda heard scraps of angry shouting between the two groups.

"Here's what I mean about doing stupid things," Pim said. "Those kids aren't experienced surfers. They don't know how to read the waves and tide, or the rocks hidden underneath. It's not safe to surf or dive here. The tide is coming in, and the ocean currents are very tricky. Riptides can suck you out to sea, and underwater shoals can crack your head open in an instant."

He aimed the boat to shore and killed the engine to allow the boat to grind up on the sand. The campfire group watched in silence, but the two surfers approached. Behind goggles, their expressions were hard to read, but Amanda recognized the man with the sun-bleached hair who had arrived later in his own boat.

Kaylee leaped off the bow, relieved to be on dry land, and snatched up a piece of driftwood before racing up the beach to greet the pair. The darker, stockier man broke into a grin and bent to toss the stick, sending Kaylee off like a shot.

Blondie was scowling. "Is there a problem?" It was a challenge, not a question.

Pim folded his arms. "Just a warning. It's not safe to surf or dive here. Besides the rocks and the undertow, there's some weather coming in."

"Who are you? The cops?"

"I'm with the Ahousaht Council. We oversee this land."

"But this is a public park, not your reservation. Or your business."

The shorter surfer had wandered up. He held up his hands. "Hey, look, dude, we don't mean any trouble. We just thought it was a beautiful beach, a nice spot to grab a bite and take a swim."

The sun was still high, but the wind off the open ocean was strong and biting. Although not as frigid as the North Atlantic, Amanda knew the water would be bracing. Pim's expression didn't change. "It is. I'm just warning you —"

"You made your point," Blondie snapped. "Now why don't you and your girlfriend and your mutt go on your way."

Amanda's temper flared. "Look, you moron, he doesn't want you to get killed, okay! We stopped as a courtesy. He knows these waters; you evidently don't!"

Blondie pushed his goggles back on his head, revealing pouchy blue eyes shot through with red. Up close, she could see he was pushing fifty but trying to cling to his fading youth. Wrinkles crisscrossed deep into his tan, and his grey roots were showing. Alcohol wafted around him, and he wavered slightly, way past being safe either to surf or pilot a boat. He stepped forward, and his friend reached for his arm.

"Richie, let's drop it. Go grab some lunch."

Richie shook him off. "Piss off, Dov. I only get one fucking week, and it's a free country. No nosy Indian who thinks he owns the whole fucking island is going to order me around."

Amanda opened her mouth to fire another shot, but Pim shook his head faintly. Without a word, he turned and headed back to the boat. Amanda called Kaylee, and the dog plodded toward her, her head down, obviously reluctant to leave the game and get back on the high seas. Once he'd shoved off and started the engine, Pim turned to look at her. His face was unreadable, but his dark eyes burned.

"I'm sorry, Amanda. That guy was looking for someone to fight with, and it wasn't going to be me."

Wind and rain lashed the B&B most of the night, and Amanda slept fitfully, worried that poor weather would scuttle her plan for the next day. When she woke in the early morning, the rain had tapered to a drizzle and the wind had died, but thick fog obscured the mountains and curled in and out of the trees beyond her window. According to her phone's weather forecast, however, that was supposed to burn off in a couple of hours, leaving a glorious, sunny day. *Let's hope the forecasters got it right!*

She let Kaylee out and stood for a few minutes, breathing in the damp, clean air and watching the raindrops shimmer on the trees. Through the fog, the ocean surf sounded muffled and far away. She tossed the ball for Kaylee a couple of times and fed her before heading down to breakfast, anxious to get an early start on her ambitious day. She was planning to hike the Wild Side Trail at the south end of Flores Island. The ten kilometres of coastal trail through the park reserve was not strenuous, much of it running along beautiful white sand beaches, so five kilometres a day might not be too taxing for the older fathers in her group. From what she'd seen from Pim's boat the day before, the views should be breathtaking. Apart from the idiots they'd met farther north, the beaches were almost empty, and they would have their pick of soft, flat places to pitch their tents.

Pim was going to drop her off at the trailhead in Maaqtusiis and pick her up at the end of the trail in Cow Bay, but he was adamant that she not hike alone. He had arranged for his nephew, a forestry student at the University of Victoria, who was acting as a guide during the summer, to go with her. "He's very smart, and he can teach you all about our history and the plants and animals along the way."

Amanda had not objected. Anyone who hiked wilderness trails alone in areas with no cellphone coverage was a fool. She had done most of her packing for the hike the night before: food, high-energy snacks, plenty of water and a water filtering pump, an emergency aid kit, layers and changes of clothing, an emergency blanket, personal locator beacon, compass, and matches. She hoped to do the trip in one day but had packed for overnight. Pim would supply a detailed map of the trail but said his nephew knew every rock and tree.

As she sipped her first cup of coffee and waited for her waffles and maple syrup, she glanced around the room. None of the other guests were up yet, so she enjoyed the solitude. Fog still shrouded the distant mountains, but pale yellow light was beginning to wash the sky overhead. For a while, she watched a pair of little birds arguing over a feeder outside the window before her attention was drawn back inside. The painting of the woman caught her eye. Cup in hand, she strolled over for a closer look. The young woman was half-turned, her honey-blond hair entwined with pink flowers and tumbling down her back to her waist.

Amanda's breath quickened. It *was* the same woman she'd seen in Luke's cabin! The same beautiful hair, pink flowers, and wistful look. This artist was AK. She realized she didn't know Luke's last name, or indeed whether Luke was the name he'd always gone by.

Keener emerged from the kitchen with a plate of waffles piled high with strawberries, whipped cream, and maple syrup, but he stopped short at the sight of her. His eyes darted to the painting. She returned to her seat and waited until he'd put her plate down and topped up her coffee.

"Wow! This looks delicious, Keener!" She laughed. "Sorry, do you have a real name? A first name?"

"Everyone calls me Keener."

She waited, but he didn't elaborate. "Okay. Keener it is. I'd like to know more about that painting."

"Why?"

"Because there's a painter up on Flores Island who has a portrait of the same woman."

Keener blinked. "You can hardly see her face."

"The same hair, same carriage."

"Believe me, the long blond hair, flower child look was ubiquitous back then. If you didn't have long, straight hair, you ironed it."

Amanda ignored the deflection. "Who is she?"

"Just a girl who was here during the hippie days. It was a long time ago, and I was a kid."

"Is she still around?"

He seemed to hesitate. "Most of those who came for the counter-culture went back to their real lives."

It wasn't really an answer, but she let it go. "Did you know her?"

"We all knew each other. We were literally one happy family."

"Then who was AK?"

He was beginning to edge away. Since there were no other customers in the breakfast room, she sensed something about the painting bothered him. "*K* ... Keenan? A relative? Is that why you've hung on to the painting?"

"It's a nice painting, and it reminds me of those days. They were very special days."

"I'm sorry. I didn't mean to pry. You said he died, so if the story is too personal —"

Keenan grew red. "It's not too personal. It's just ... he died a couple months after he painted that, and I was there. That's why I keep it."

She dropped her gaze, ashamed. "I'm sorry. Sorry I reminded you."

"You didn't remind me. Not one day goes by that I don't remember. Now, I don't mean to be rude, but it's my day off and I promised Helen I'd prep for tomorrow before I left."

She hesitated, debating whether to pry further. His face was still flushed, but the tension was easing from his body. "I ... I do have one more question, if you've got time. I'm trying to find out about the artist up on Flores. His name is Luke. He says he was here in that hippie commune in the late sixties. Did you know him?"

"Like I said, I was young."

"Can you remember anything?"

He shrugged. "I knew about him, but I steered clear. Luke was 'out there,'" he made air quotes, "even for those days."

"What do you mean?"

"You never knew what he would do. He ended up carted away to the funny farm."

"Hamish Allister Keenan!" came a shriek from the kitchen. They both started and turned to the kitchen door, where a very large woman with a halo of white hair and a flour-dusted apron stood with her hands on her hips.

Keener reddened and ducked his head. "Busted."

"Hamish," Amanda said with a grin. "That has potential."

CHAPTER SEVEN

When she met Pim at the boat, the sun was already melting the fog, and by the time they docked at the village of Maaqtusiis on Flores Island, the sky overhead was a cloudless azure. Amanda heaved a sigh of relief. She really wanted to fit in this hike, but Matthew would kill her if she stayed away much longer.

Unlike Pim, his nephew Gilligan was a short, skinny young man with narrow shoulders, an acne-scarred face, and lank, greasy hair. But his wide, infectious smile lit up his face. Four village dogs swarmed them immediately, checking out Kaylee, but both Pim and Gilligan chased them away.

"They're friendly, but they'll come on the whole trip with us if we let them, and you don't want that," Gilligan chuckled. Despite his size, he grabbed Amanda's backpack and slung it over his shoulder, along with his own. *Do I look old and feeble?* Amanda wondered as she protested.

He shook his head. "I've walked this trail a thousand times. I don't need to admire its beauty, but I don't want you to miss a single moment. And there are lots of wolves around, so please keep your dog on a short leash or she'll be dinner."

After that dire warning, he set off at a brisk, cheerful pace along the moss-covered boardwalk that wove into the rainforest. Amanda trailed about thirty feet behind him to get an unimpeded view. The rez dogs, she noticed, were also trailing along at a respectful distance, but she had her hands full coping with the trail. Initially the going was rough as they ploughed through thick undergrowth, balanced on precarious boardwalks over bogs, and navigated muddy streams. She was grateful for Gilligan, because sometimes the path was indiscernible through the bush.

"Yeah, there were no tourists through here during the pandemic," Gilligan explained when she inquired. "It needs work. We're getting to it."

Along the way, he paused to explain sites central to Ahousaht history and culture — sacred prayer pools, important battles, and legendary people. After sweating and slogging through the forest for some time, Amanda stopped to give herself and Kaylee some water. There was no ocean in sight, although she could hear the distant call of shorebirds above the murmur of the surf. She began to worry that the trek would be too challenging for the fathers in the group. Yet they were only just getting started!

As if by magic, the canopy lightened up ahead, the dense brush thinned, and within minutes the trail opened onto a wide beach swept with dunes. The ocean was still angry from last night's storm, and foamy breakers raced up the fine sand. Green islands dotted the horizon offshore, and the purple mountains of Meares Island loomed in the distance. Kaylee tugged on the leash, eager to be free. When Amanda pulled a ball from her fanny pack, however, Gilligan shook his head.

"A running dog would be perfect prey."

Kaylee danced around in excitement as Amanda apologized and put the ball away. Instead, she took off her hiking boots, plunged her hot, sore feet into the cold water, and strolled along the water's edge, enjoying the cold rush of sea. Kaylee soon forgot her disappointment as she poked her nose at the shells and ropes of kelp and watched the sandpipers scurrying along the shore ahead of them.

At the end of the beach was a craggy, rocky headland that looked daunting. Gilligan instead turned inland to follow a sign to a barely visible trail that led through soggy bush to a wooden bridge over a rushing stream before heading back to the next beach. Each beach seemed wilder and more beautiful than the last; sweeping coves of white sand nestled between headlands of ragged, black, barnacle-encrusted rock. Churning mist shot up from the breakers as they crashed onto the rocks. Spruce trees clung to the crevices, silhouetted against the azure sky, and countless birds wheeled overhead in search of sea creatures left in the tidal pools. Here and there, a seal basked in the sun on a rock.

They ate lunch sitting on a huge driftwood log on a long, curved stretch of beach, deserted except for excited seagulls wheeling overhead. Amanda snapped photos, enthralled. She turned to look at the backdrop of rounded, green mountains farther north, where Luke lived. Peaceful. Uninvaded.

Mostly.

A seaplane droned low overhead, and a flotilla of kayaks paddled by. When she and Gilligan reached the first spectacular beach of Cow Bay, she was frustrated to discover the group had pulled their bright red and yellow kayaks up on the sand and were playing Frisbee barefoot in the breakers. Another group was farther up the sand, cooking hot dogs on a beach fire. The shrieks of laughter seemed an intrusion. Out on the bay, whale-watching tour boats rocked in the swell, their engines growling. Kaylee tugged on her leash, eager to chase the Frisbee, but after a polite greeting, Gilligan and Amanda moved on through quickly.

"We're not yet in high season, so this will get worse," Gilligan said. "But it's the economy of the area, and it brings in money to the Ahousaht. If we manage it wisely, we can show people the beauty without destroying it."

To Amanda's relief, the next beach was deserted, and they stopped for an afternoon snack on a driftwood log. Gilligan told her the farthest beach was about half an hour away, beautiful for camping.

"Do you think my group can make it that far?" she asked.

"Up to you. There are some challenging parts near the end. If your group plans an overnight camp halfway, you should do it easily. Depending on the weather, of course. Up ahead we're in the wide-open Pacific, so it can get rough really fast."

She pointed to the next rocky headland. "Is it safe to traverse that instead of going inland, just for a change?"

He nodded. "The tide is coming in, so it may be tricky, but we can try. Just stay away from the water's edge, because a rogue wave can easily sweep you away."

They set off over the rocks with Gilligan picking the safe way forward. He clambered cautiously, testing his footing and avoiding slippery seaweed. Amanda paused to peer in the tidal pools, fascinated by the crabs, anemones, urchins, and starfish clinging to the rocks in the warming water.

As they topped a crest of the rocks, the next beach lay ahead of them in the distance, serene, empty except for the jumbles of driftwood above the high-water mark and the ropes of shiny seaweed dotting the sand. Breakers rolled in, gathered, and hurled themselves up the sand. Amanda paused to snap some photos.

"Uh-oh."

She glanced up at Gilligan, who was standing at the edge of a drop up ahead, his binoculars in hand.

"What?"

He gestured. "There's a boat cracked up on the rocks."

"Anyone in it?"

He shook his head. Gripping Kaylee's leash, she picked her way forward to stand beside him. Peering down, she spotted the boat nestled in a dip in the rocks near the edge of the beach. Gilligan lifted his binoculars to scan the beach. "No one around. But that's too small a boat to navigate this outer side of the island unless you really know what you're doing." His brow furrowed in worry. "And we haven't met anyone on the trail walking out."

She trained her own binoculars on the boat. After focusing, she moved her binoculars slowly over the markings on the side. There was no surfboard in the boat, probably lost in the crash, but the blue and white stripes along the sides were familiar. She sucked in her breath.

It was Richie's boat.

"I know that boat. There were some surfers farther up the coast yesterday, and this boat belonged to one of them. A guy named Richie."

"I don't recognize it," Gilligan said. "Did this dude tell you where they planned to go next?"

She shook her head. "He blew us off. Pim was pissed. But there were other people and another boat."

"Same size?"

"Bigger. But pretty loaded up, so it would be hard to transport another person, especially in the rough seas yesterday afternoon."

"We'll go down and look for him on the beach, and double back along the inland trail. He may be injured."

Gilligan picked up the pace, leaping agilely from rock to rock and leaving Amanda to make her own way. By the time she caught up with him, he had examined the boat, which had a huge gash punched in its side, and was down on the beach, scanning the tree line with his binoculars.

"The propeller was sheared off," he said. "If that happened out on the sea, he would've had no control and would've foundered on the rocks. I don't see any sign of him, but let's check the bush inland. If this happened last night, he would have tried to get shelter from the storm." He pulled out his marine radio. "Meanwhile, I'm going to call this in. We need a search and rescue team ASAP."

While he spoke to the Coast Guard, she walked slowly along the beach, picking her way through the debris and logs washed up on the shore. Plastic bottles, bits of netting, rope, and decayed fish. She saw no trace of footprints. She had almost reached the next headland when Gilligan joined her.

"A SAR boat is on its way, and Uncle Pim can bring some guys from the village by boat."

Kaylee whined, and Amanda glanced down at her. She was facing the next rocky headland with her ears forward and her nose sifting the air.

"What is it?" Gilligan said, sniffing the air himself. "Does she smell something?"

"Yes, but it could be a rotten fish or deer, or even a seal. But —" Kaylee's hackles had risen slightly, and Amanda felt a twinge of alarm. "This is not normal excitement. We should check this out."

"SAR will be along soon."

"But if it is him, he could be hurt and may be in danger when the tide comes in. I have an emergency first-aid kit, and I know how to use it. We should at least treat him."

Without waiting for an answer, Amanda started over the rocks, letting Kaylee lead the way. The dog tugged gently on the leash, and Amanda had to keep a firm hold while she picked her way from rock to rock. Kaylee whined and began to quiver. Something was spooking her. Amanda's heart pounded as she neared a crest in the rocks. At the top, she stopped to look. Down below in the distance was an object lying on the rocks, twisted as if flung like a rag doll by the merciless sea.

"Fuck," she muttered, pulling out her binoculars. She scanned the rocks until the object came into view, focused them, and took stock of the shape. A man, wearing a neon-yellow jacket and hiking boots. His damp hair was plastered to his head, barely recognizable as blond.

At that moment, in the distance, came the roar of a large boat.

The sun hung low over the ocean, sending a shaft of white glare dancing across the waves. Amanda was sitting on a driftwood log up at the top of the beach where they'd been instructed to wait, but Gilligan paced restlessly nearby. Amanda hugged her knees and tried to quell the sick feeling in her stomach. She hadn't liked Richie — he was a racist, loudmouth jerk — but he didn't deserve to die. Not in the horrible way he had, alone, frightened, and trying to crawl to safety. As she hugged her knees, she noticed the sand was churned up at her feet, with the indistinct outline of footprints washed out by the rain. Curious, she glanced behind her and picked out a faint trail of trampled grass leading into the bush. Likely the inland trail around the headland. Otherwise, the beach below the high-tide mark was pristine. Where were his buddies, and why had he been left alone to die?

She turned back to the investigation unfolding on the beach, wondering whether she should mention the churned-up sand. The SAR Zodiac sat on the shore while the team stood by to see if they were needed. They had called 911 dispatch to report the death, and soon two Mounties from the Tofino detachment had roared up in their own Zodiac. After briefly checking the body, they had called their commander, who arrived in a larger police boat with a young female officer. The detachment commander, a grizzle-haired sergeant with a florid face and no neck, hesitated before hefting his gut and clambering up the slippery rocks to check on the body. Two of the officers pulled a roll of crime scene tape from the Zodiac and began to spool it around the rocks.

The police have a process to follow, she told herself. *They will talk to us soon enough.*

The sun dropped lower, gilding the ocean tips. Amanda drank the last of her water and closed her eyes to centre herself. When footsteps crunched up the sand, she opened them again to find the sergeant standing over her. Kaylee wagged her tail, but he ignored her. In a soft, subtle French-Canadian accent, he introduced himself as Sergeant Saint-Laurent and recorded her contact information before asking her to recount the events of the afternoon. He listened deadpan as she described their hike.

"We saw the boat first, and were worried."

Saint-Laurent's eyes scanned the beach, narrowing. "Where's the boat?"

She gestured over the previous ridge. "It had been tossed up on the rocks. There's a big hole torn out of the hull."

Gilligan had moved to stand beside her. "Not a big enough boat for these seas, anyway."

Saint-Laurent signalled to his female sidekick. "Check out that ridge for a boat, put some tape around it, and get the licence number." As the woman moved to go, Saint-Laurent snapped his fingers. "And Janine, take some photos. A detective from General Investigations will be coming from Courtenay, probably won't get here until tomorrow morning, so let's get the preliminaries done." He squinted at the sinking sun, shaking his head in disapproval. "I hope the coroner gets here soon."

Once the constable had scampered off toward the ridge, Saint-Laurent turned back to Amanda, his florid face sober. Amanda gestured to the faint trail. "I notice the sand is disturbed here. Could that be relevant?"

Saint-Laurent cocked his head to study the scene, then humoured her with a smile. "Not likely. That trail goes around the headland, and people like to hike in there. And that log you're sitting on is a popular picnic spot."

"Still, it looks …"

"All in good time, Ms. Doucette. Did you hear anything or see anything this afternoon before you found the body?"

She shook her head. "It was surprisingly peaceful. Just two groups of kayakers on the first Cow Bay beach."

"Did you know the deceased?"

"No, but Pim and I met him yesterday. His name is Richie, and he was with a group of tourists who were paddle surfing and playing on a beach farther up." She paused. "The others had come in a bigger boat, but he had his own boat. Pim tried to tell them it was dangerous to surf or swim, but he was belligerent. Drunk." She gazed down the beach at the solitary shape sprawled on the rock, broken and twisted. Mixed emotions swirled through her. "He was pretty nasty to us, Pim especially."

Saint-Laurent made some notes. "I'll need to talk to Pim."

"He's on his way," Gilligan said. "I called him. He's going to take us back to town."

Saint-Laurent turned to look out to sea. At that moment, a small speck of a boat appeared and disappeared in the swell. Five minutes later, Pim manoeuvred his boat up near shore, secured it with anchors, and walked up the beach toward them. After taking some preliminary details, Saint-Laurent led them down to the police Zodiac and pulled out a creased, battered map of the island. He grinned at the junior constable as he unfolded it.

"Old-school. Never crashes on you, never corrodes or loses a signal. Show me the beach where you saw them."

As the officers crowded around, Pim bent over the map, which Amanda could see was detailed enough to show every cove and beach. He tapped his finger just below the midpoint of the island. "This beach here. We'd cleared the peninsula and were in open ocean. Dangerous for a small boat even on a calm day. And if he was out in the storm last night or the fog this morning ..."

The junior constable peered at the map. "That's not far from Loony Luke's place. He can see much of this coast from up on that tower of his."

Amanda was about to object, but Saint-Laurent nodded, as if Loony Luke were a perfectly normal name. "Someone is going to have to talk to him to see if he saw anything. Maybe the kids visited him."

The constable's eyes lit up. "Yeah, like that time a couple of years ago! Remember how he threatened —"

Saint-Laurent grabbed his arm. "That's good, Brandon, you can interview him. Take someone with you. But not tonight. Morning's good enough."

The low drone of an approaching plane rose above the sound of the waves, and Saint-Laurent glanced up as a single-engine De Havilland Beaver circled above the beach. A smile spread cross Saint-Laurent's face.

"The Red Baron is here. Never misses a chance to take that plane out to crazy places. I think the whole reason Moretti took the coroner's job is so he'd have an excuse to fly. The more remote the body, the better." His smile broadened. "And I bet he's brought along the lovely Meridia Santos. He rarely misses a chance to do that either, strictly for her medical expertise, of course. But even he can't land in that surf. Radio him to dock at Hot Springs, and we'll pick him up there."

Amanda was beginning to feel weak from fatigue and hunger by the time the police Zodiac reappeared with the coroner. As it ground up on shore, Saint-Laurent and the other officers walked over to meet the coroner, who was already standing on the gunwale. He jumped off into the shallow water and turned to offer the woman a hand. Amanda was amused to see she ignored the offer and leaped down with the grace of a cat, black bag in hand. She was already halfway across the beach toward the rocks by the time the coroner and the police caught up with her. Even from a distance, Amanda could hear the coroner's loud, excited voice bragging about the record speed of his flight.

Once they were out of earshot, Amanda turned to Pim with dismay. "I've got a bad feeling. What do you think Luke will do when the police show up to talk to him tomorrow? Especially Mr. Sensitive there."

Pim shrugged. He was watching the group pick their way over the rocks toward the body. The coroner leaped from rock to rock, lithe and reckless, while the doctor moved with careful precision. From Pim's scowl as he watched the coroner, Amanda suspected a history between them.

"Hard to say," Pim replied eventually. "Luke has his good days. They might get lucky."

"I'm not so sure I like those odds, Pim, especially with a guy who calls him Loony Luke. Luke might freak out, and if he freaks out, it could end very badly."

Pim shifted his gaze from the coroner, who was now bending over the body. "The cops know him. They'll be careful." He exchanged a glance with Gilligan. "Probably."

"They better not send Paulsen," Gilligan said.

"Who's Paulsen?"

Pim grunted. "Tofino detachment's enforcer. Big on muscle, not so big on sensitivity. He's old-school. Every detachment needs a Paulsen to keep the drunks and smartasses in line, but for a situation like this ..." Pim shook his head. "I doubt the sarge would send Paulsen."

"Except maybe as backup, if he thinks muscle is needed," Gilligan said. "The sarge can be a hardass too."

Amanda had been watching the exchange, feeling increasingly uneasy. "Luke's an old man," she said. "He's not going to need that kind of muscle."

"He's strong as a bear," Pim said. "Don't kid yourself."

"And besides ..." Gilligan began before Pim shook his head.

"Besides what?"

"Nothing," Pim said. "Just when he's having one of his spells, when he goes somewhere else in his head, who knows."

Amanda looked from one to the other, sensing a pact of secrecy. "What was that incident that young cop, Mr. Sensitive, started to mention? When Luke threatened someone?"

For a long moment, Pim gazed at the cluster of people on the rocks, seemingly absorbed by the action. Finally, without looking at her, he said, "A group of kids landed their kayaks on his beach, and they were horsing around, collecting starfish and clams, smoking weed, playing music. Harmless stuff. Luke came down and chased them off with his shotgun. They complained to the cops that a crazy man tried to kill them. Not true. Luke hates killing and would never hurt anyone. He just shot the gun into the air. Luke's a crack shot. If he wanted to kill them, they'd be dead. Anyway, the cops charged him. It could've been serious, but we — I mean the village — told them he was harmless, just frightened. We said we'd take care of it, keep an eye on him. So, they just took away his shotgun and left him alone."

As a fleeting memory stirred, Amanda felt a quiver of alarm. "But he has a shotgun. I saw it in his shed."

The small group was making their way back down the headland to the beach. Pim's nostrils flared as he drew in a sharp breath. "Yeah, well, he shares this island with cougars, wolves, and bears. We weren't going to leave the man all alone up there with no protection." He started to edge away toward the group conferring on the beach. "Let's go see what the plan is. But ..." he leaned in toward her, "don't say anything about the shotgun for now, okay?"

CHAPTER EIGHT

Saint-Laurent and the coroner were sharing a laugh, but as Amanda, Pim, and Gilligan approached, they quickly grew serious. Saint-Laurent took charge. "You three are free to go. We have your statements and your contact details. For the moment, this is in the hands of the coroner's office. Mr. Moretti has arranged for the body to be transferred to Victoria for autopsy."

All routine so far, Amanda thought, but Pim was less reassured. "As a representative of the Ahousaht Council," he said stiffly, "I'm responsible for ensuring the community's safety. Is there —"

"There's no risk to the public, Pim," Saint-Laurent interrupted. "Dr. Santos here has pronounced death — a formality — and Wes Moretti and I have set the wheels in motion for the death investigation. Right now, it looks like an accidental death, but we'll wait to see what the post turns up."

"What was the approximate time of death?" Amanda asked.

A frown of annoyance flitted across Saint-Laurent's face at the intrusion. Before he could cut her off, she held out her hand to Wes Moretti. "I'm Amanda Doucette, Mr. Moretti. I'm the one who discovered him, along with Gilligan here. Pim and I also talked to him yesterday afternoon, very much alive, although drunk."

Wes raised an eyebrow and gave a slow smile as he looked her up and down. "Yeah, he looked like a man who likes his drink. What time was that?"

Amanda ignored the leer. "Three thirty. So, he had to have died in the past twenty-four hours." She glanced at the doctor, who was jotting down notes. "When do you think he died?"

Meridia Santos glanced up impatiently. "It's not my field of expertise, and it's a challenge to estimate time of death when the body has been in frigid seawater. We don't know how long he was in the water either. But we've taken all the appropriate temperature readings, and we'll leave that to the pathologist."

She folded up her notebook as if to leave, but Wes didn't move. "There's always the tide schedule. He was above the high-tide mark, and he looked like he sustained a crack to the head. Probably when he was thrown up on the rocks, but he may've already been dead. My money's on the last twelve hours. Not hundred percent, but likely —"

Meridia was already heading toward the Zodiac. "Wes, I have to get back to the hospital."

"Yep," Saint-Laurent said. "And we've got to get on with the identification, find his pals, and notify his next of kin before some joker posts it on social media. I'm going to close off this entire end of the trail. An Ident officer and a detective will be here in the morning, and anything we find out, we'll pass it on to Wes."

It was past 10:00 p.m. by the time Amanda dragged herself back to the Silver Surf B&B. Kaylee was starving, but despite the long day, Amanda could barely summon the appetite to eat. Her stomach was in knots. Another body. Sometimes she felt cursed, stalked by tragedy and death no matter where she went. She longed to talk to

Chris, to see his crinkly smile and hear his calm, practical voice. But it was three o'clock in the morning in Newfoundland.

There was a light on in the kitchen, and she slipped in, hoping to get a sandwich or a croissant to tide her over. The buttery, yeasty smell of fresh baking enveloped her, and she found Helen bent over the kitchen counter, spooning filling into tiny tarts. Danishes sat cooling on the table, golden brown and oozing fresh fruit.

Helen smiled as she looked up, blinking sweat from her eyes. "Want one? They're for breakfast, but honestly? This is the best time to eat them."

Amanda selected an apricot Danish and perched on a stool by the table. Keener's wife reminded her of an oversized cherub, round and dimpled, with rosy cheeks and innocent blue eyes, but Amanda suspected that behind that guileless smile, she was the real boss of the operation.

"Long day?" Helen asked, holding out a cold beer. "Or would you rather have tea?"

Amanda shook her head and thanked her for the beer. She hadn't the energy for a discussion of the day's events, a conversation that might take more than half an hour. "Hamish not helping you?" she asked instead.

Helen laughed. "Oh, don't let him hear you call him that. No, this was his day off. He'll be on a six a.m. tomorrow. At least, he better be, no matter what state he's in when he rolls in tonight."

Amanda felt the last of her energy slipping away. "I'll keep my breakfast simple then," she said, waving as she headed for the door.

"There will be fresh fish," Helen called as a parting shot. "That is, if he has any luck today."

Back in her room, she propped herself up in bed with her laptop to make notes on the day, but within minutes, she was asleep. Kaylee woke her at six thirty in the morning, whining to go out. Afterward, Amanda stumbled around the room, foggy-brained and grimy, feeding Kaylee and fixing herself a cup of coffee before returning to bed with her laptop.

"Hey you," Chris said. His big, crinkly grin filled the screen briefly before fading. "You look like a cat dragged through the hedge backwards."

Emotion flooded through her, closing her throat. She managed a choked laugh. "My best look. I ... I couldn't wait to see your smiling face."

"What's wrong, Amanda?"

"Oh, it was a great day yesterday. Amazing beaches, beautiful blue sky, wild ocean, peace ... Up until the moment we came upon a dead body."

"What?"

She gave him the barest details, forcing herself to sound dispassionate and in control, to stop him from worrying about her. She hated people worrying about her, as if they didn't think she was strong enough to manage her own life.

"The cops will do their investigation, and the coroner has ordered a post-mortem, but it looks like a boating accident. The man's boat wasn't big enough to handle the seas and besides that, he was probably drunk. At least he was when I saw him the day before."

"Where was that?"

She hesitated. Was that an innocent question, or was there a hint of suspicion in his tone? "Pim and I saw him and a group of friends on another beach on the same island." She paused to brace herself. "We'd gone up there to meet with Luke again. Remember Luke, the reclusive artist I told you about? Coming back, we ran into the group surfing. It was just a random meeting, nothing peculiar, but then the next day ..." Her voice caught. She clenched her jaw to steady it.

He reached his hand up to the screen as if to touch her. "Honey," he said gently, "this is not your fault. You didn't do anything. The sea can be cruel."

The dam threatened to break. How well he knew her! How well he understood the crazy thoughts she had. Too much death, too many dead bodies strewn across her life. She should learn to trust him. To lean on him.

"There's more." She chewed her lip. "The beach where we saw the group wasn't far from where Luke lives, so the cops are going to pay him a visit today. They *say* it's to find out if he witnessed anything or knew the man."

"As they should."

"I know. But I don't think they'll handle it right. He's … he's fragile, and if they challenge him or come across as accusing him of anything, he may freak out. He may get hurt."

"I'm sure they'll treat him like they would anyone else. Like an ordinary witness."

"But you know what can happen when an unstable witness panics. Some people — just the sight of a cop, with the uniform, the gun, all the equipment, can set them off. And Luke already has a reputation as crazy."

"Then the local police will have worked out a strategy ahead of time." He smiled. "We're not all yahoos, you know."

She wanted to believe him, to back away and let others do their jobs, but she knew something the police didn't: Luke had a gun. If they knew that, chances were they'd be even more confrontational, escalating the situation and putting Luke at even greater risk. But if they didn't know it, they themselves might be at risk. Pim insisted Luke would never hurt anyone, but if he was back in Vietnam, terrified for his life, anything was possible. As she herself knew well.

She wanted to tell Chris about the gun and get his advice, but she knew he'd relay the information to his Tofino counterparts. He would have no choice. And in the police response, a fragile old man who was just trying to stay safe might get shot.

She could think of only one way to defuse the situation. She knew Chris would hate it, but she had to tell him something. If she kept him totally in the dark, he'd be furious, and rightly so. Trust was a two-way street. Yet how could she tell him only half a truth?

"Earth to Amanda." Chris had cocked his head, and his smile had turned quizzical. Then it slowly disappeared. "Amanda, you will stay out of it, won't you? Promise me?"

"I can't promise you that."

"Let the police do their job! If you get in the middle of this ..." He broke off, leaving the implication unsaid. She had gotten in the middle of things before and had sometimes barely escaped with her life.

"I won't put myself in danger, honey. I promise you that. But I do understand how he might react, and more important, he trusts me. I hope I can help."

Matthew was sitting at a patio table overlooking Fisherman's Wharf, sipping a delicious espresso and gazing out over Victoria's inner harbour. As usual, it was buzzing with boats of all sizes, from water taxis to large luxury yachts. This was his favourite way to start the morning: bright, warm, and washed by a gentle ocean breeze that brought a tang of fish and salt to the air.

He was supposed to be working up a revised budget, but he was actually playing on the internet, checking world news sites and scrolling through Twitter. Reading about world dramas was familiar and oddly comforting, like sitting down with an old friend. It was all his mind was up for now. The news from the doctor wasn't good. The cancer had spread. Not just one smudge on a chest X-ray, but two. "The radiation helped to slow the spread," the doctor had said brightly, "because it's not in your lymph nodes yet, but we'll need a second round of chemo before we can operate."

He hated the chemo. It took days out of his life each week. What was the point of this half-life, he'd retorted with a snarl that was probably unfair. It wasn't the doctor's fault that he'd smoked for over thirty years, not the doctor's fault that he'd breathed the air of some of the most polluted cities in the world for almost as long.

Too late, he'd returned to the safety and sanity of Canada, where he'd given up cigarettes and most of his high-adrenalin lifestyle, but the seeds of the cancer had already been sown. Now, another round of chemo. During the pandemic, while Amanda had been sequestered in Newfoundland, he'd been able to hide the whole drama from her, but eventually he'd have to tell her the full story. He was only functioning at half throttle, and she was far too attuned to suffering not to notice.

Buried under the pile of the discarded *Times Colonist* newspapers, his cellphone rang. His spirits lifted as he groped for it, hoping it was Amanda. *Chris Tymko*, the call display announced. Although their relationship was civil, Matthew had never been able to move beyond the twinge of jealousy and the belief that deep down, he wasn't right for Amanda. Chris never called him. Something must be wrong.

"Chris!" he answered cheerfully. *Short and simple. Let the man lead.*

"I'm glad I caught you. Have you talked to Amanda recently?"

"A couple of days ago. Why?"

"She's done it again. Got herself right smack in the middle of trouble, intent on going even deeper."

Matthew listened with growing dismay as Chris told him about the discovery of a body on the island during a hike. He felt a stab of sorrow. It didn't sound as if she'd gone looking for trouble this time, but once again, it had found her. This was an extra layer of trauma she didn't need.

"But the real problem isn't the dead man," Chris said. "It's the artist who lives on the island. Did she tell you about Luke?"

"Some. I know she wants one of his paintings, and I know he's a recluse. Lives off the grid."

"Yes, and several bricks short of a load. Amanda is worried about how he'll react when the cops go to interview him. I told her to trust they know what they're doing, but you know Amanda."

Yes, and I also know country cops, Matthew thought. *Not always the most up to date on deescalation techniques.* "What's she planning to do?"

"She promised me she wouldn't put herself in danger but I'm pretty sure she's going to insert herself in the middle of that confrontation."

As Matthew sorted through possibilities, he watched a small seaplane circle overhead, aiming for the aerodrome in the distance and gauging the clutter of boats in the way. Precision to the square inch. "You could call your colleagues in Tofino and give them a heads-up."

"I could. And maybe I will. But Amanda would be furious. You know how she is about …" He trailed off.

"About us meddling? Yeah."

"So, I'm hoping for a more indirect approach."

Oh, you want me to meddle. "What do you want me to do, Chris? I'm way down here in Victoria."

"That's where I want you. I'm way the hell the other end of the country. Start by trying to persuade her not to get involved."

"That's not going to work, so what's Plan B?"

"I want you to find out what you can about this guy Luke. I don't even know his last name, so I can't look him up on police records. I want to know who he is, and most important, does he have a history of violence? Then I'll know if I should warn the local RCMP."

Barbara Fradkin

Matthew's thoughts were already racing ahead. This was an assignment he could really sink his teeth into. Way better than budget revisions. This was what he'd done all his life. He started thinking of his contacts. He had almost no contacts on Vancouver Island, which wasn't exactly a hot spot of conflict on the world stage. But he did know Bonnie, who would be pretty plugged into the legal and mental health networks in the area.

And for what it was worth, he knew Tag.

CHAPTER NINE

Amanda had packed for the day trip quickly, eager to get an early start to Flores Island once again. She knew the police would be back there as soon as it was light, because in a death investigation, time was always of the essence. Evidence decayed and witnesses forgot. The Ident team would be at the site of Richie's body, and the detective would be planning interviews with hikers, kayakers, and locals who might have witnessed anything relevant about either the accident or the beach party earlier. And someone, perhaps even the detective, would be going up the mountain to interview Luke. Almost certainly accompanied by some brawn.

She was alone in the breakfast room and had barely sat down when Keener slumped out of the kitchen, bleary-eyed and unshaven. While he poured her coffee with a slightly unsteady hand, she scrutinized him. Was it just a lack of sleep after his night off, or was he hungover? The faint smell of weed wafted around him.

She refrained from comment and kept her voice cheerful. "Any fresh fish today?"

He looked bewildered. "Fish?"

"Helen said you went fishing yesterday."

"Oh. No, no luck." He shrugged. "Too rough. What'll it be?"

Not trusting him to manage anything beyond frying an egg, she chose eggs and toast. When he returned with her plate, he looked marginally revived, so she smiled as she thanked him. "Did you hear about the man who drowned off Flores Island yesterday?"

He flinched as he nodded. "It's all over town. That kind of news always is."

"What are the rumours?"

"Drunk? Stupid?" His eyes narrowed. "I hear you found him."

"I did. It was a shock. Does anyone know who he is?"

"Not that I heard. A tourist, probably. A cop came by earlier, asked Helen if we knew him or if he was staying here. They're asking all over. Not just about him but about his buddies."

"I guess they'll identify him sooner or later. They have a first name — Richie."

"Helen told the cop they should probably check out the campgrounds at Chesterman Beach. Lots of surfers stay there."

Amanda nodded, resisting the urge to probe further. *I'm not getting involved*, she chided herself. "The police can probably track down his boat too. The rental company will have records."

"Not many boat rental companies out here, at least official ones. The ocean is too dangerous to risk inexperienced yahoos going out there and cracking up. Case in point."

"But unofficial ones?"

Keener shrugged, probably reluctant to give up any of his friends. "Where are you off to today?"

"Back up to Flores Island. You remember that artist I asked you about? He's doing a painting for me, and I want to check how it's coming along."

Keener busied himself pouring her a second coffee, gripping the pot hard to steady his hand. Just then a couple entered the dining room, and he straightened, put on his professional face, and mumbled a final, curious comment.

"Watch yourself."

———

It was a glorious day. After its earlier rage, the ocean slumbered peacefully in the sun and the breeze was so gentle it barely stirred the trees. As Amanda walked down toward the docks, however, her heart began to race. Sweat slicked her palms, and she gripped Kaylee's leash tightly. Was she up for this? Did she really want to revisit the images of yesterday? The sprawled, twisted body, the mangled head ...

You won't be going anywhere near the site of the death, she told herself firmly. *Pim will take us up the quieter inside channel.*

When she'd raised the idea with him the night before, Pim had not been eager to take her anywhere. He'd assured her that he and the other villagers would check on Luke to make sure he was prepared for the police visit. As she neared the docks now, she spotted him by his boat, talking to the young female officer from yesterday. Janine Somebody. Neither of them had seen her, so Amanda slipped behind a nearby boat shed and strained to hear. The waves and the growl of motorboats snatched away much of the conversation, but she heard the phrases "crack shot," "wilderness survivor," and "into custody for assessment."

The officer looked more worried than angry as she turned to go. "Leave it to us, please, Pim," were her final words. Amanda waited another minute to see what Pim might do, but he turned to check his motor. When she approached, he eyed her levelly.

"I don't think you should go. Don't get in the middle of this."

She suppressed her own qualms. "Pim, I value your judgment and knowledge, and I want you to come with me. But I understand if you'd rather not. I'll figure out something."

He eyed her suspiciously. "Do you even know how to handle a boat?"

"I've driven every kind of ramshackle contraption in the Far East, most of them barely afloat. These are luxury yachts."

Grudgingly, he grinned and reached out to help her into the boat. Kaylee shrank back, no longer a fan of bouncing waves on the open ocean. Effortlessly, Pim lifted her aboard, where she stood sulking as Amanda strapped her into her life jacket. Amanda suspected she was thinking that no self-respecting Toller needed a life jacket. *Suck it up, princess. This is the frigid ocean.*

The trip up the inside channel past Meares Island and along the inside shore of Flores was uneventful. She spotted the police boat at the entrance to Ahousaht Harbour, but there was no sign of the drama no doubt unfolding on the other side of the island. They passed a group of kayakers and exchanged greetings, but otherwise the channel was empty.

As was the little landing cove for Luke's cabin. Luke's boat was gone. Pim paused to study the ground. A jumble of footprints, including their own, was visible on the pebble beach, but it was impossible to discern any pattern. Had the cops come and gone? Or had Luke fled at the first hint of them?

"Well, that's that," Pim said. "Let's go."

Amanda had an uneasy feeling. "We should check to see if he's there. Make sure he's all right." Seeing the skepticism on his face, she pressed on. "One man is dead, Pim! We don't know what's happened to Luke."

"Maybe he doesn't want us to know."

She turned toward the path. "Please, Pim. We're here."

He sighed. "We should leave this to the police," he muttered, even as he tied up his boat and turned to follow.

They said little as they made the trek through lush bogs and dense stands of towering trees, clambered over fallen logs and scrambled up steep slopes, finally nearing the summit before stopping to catch their breath and take a drink. They stood in the small clearing overlooking the forest and distant ocean. Amanda knew they'd be visible from Luke's tower if he were keeping watch. She suspected he'd designed the path with the clearing so he could see danger approaching.

She started to speak, but Pim held up a hand to silence her. For a few moments he stood motionless, listening, before shaking his head.

"He is being very quiet," he said. "I smell no fire."

"Does he always light a fire?"

Pim's face was pinched with worry, but now he grinned. "He likes his coffee."

"Should we make noise? Let him know we're coming?"

"He knows. He has four solar-powered trail cams in the woods. One at the cove, one by his cabin, one down the trail, and one ..." He nodded to a tall fir at the edge of the clearing. "Right there."

"Trail cams! Luke?" she exclaimed incredulously.

Pim's grin widened. "Yep, motion-activated. Nancy set him up with them this spring when he started getting upset about the tourists coming. He'd never seen technology like that, and he was like a little kid when he first got them. He watched every animal that went by at night."

Amanda thought back to the second time she'd visited. Luke had met her at the top of the escarpment, as if he'd known she was coming. She glanced at Kaylee, looking for signs of excitement. The dog's head was raised, and her ears were forward. Her tail wagged slowly, but Amanda sensed uncertainty. Puzzlement. Was there something else in the woods?

Pim had already started forward. To avoid unpleasant surprises, Amanda kept a tight grip on Kaylee's leash as she fell in behind. Soon they crested the hill and stood at the edge of the compound. Other than the hens wandering around their enclosure, the place was empty. Even the goat was gone. Amanda felt a prickle of alarm.

Pim called out. No answer except a flurry of clucks from the hens.

A peek through the window of the main cabin revealed that it was empty too. Everything looked normal, from the folded blankets to the clothing hanging over the stove, but Luke was nowhere to be seen. They headed for the House of Horrors, as she'd come to think of his studio. The door was unlocked, and she opened it gingerly, still haunted by the images inside. Beside the door, the wall was empty.

"The shotgun is gone," she whispered.

Pim nodded, his face grim. "He would take it if he was going into the interior."

"I thought you said he never killed anything."

"Everyone kills, if they have to."

Amanda shivered, remembering the moment in Newfoundland when she had stared down the barrel of a rifle and felt the trigger beneath her finger. How close she had come. She shut her eyes. *That's over. Come back to the present.*

Inside, the room was bathed in midday sunlight. The walls still screamed of his torment, but it was the painting in the centre of the room, still on the easel, that caught her attention. It had not been there before.

It was a painting of a field on fire, the wind whipping tongues of orange and red through the grass. A woman filled the foreground, her arms outstretched, her long honey-blond hair streaming out behind her as she ran. In the distance, running toward her with her own arms outstretched, was a little girl with the same long, honey-coloured hair and an expression Amanda couldn't decipher. Not quite terror, not quite rapture. Was it hope?

A lump rose in Amanda's throat.

Footsteps sounded behind her. "He's gone," Pim said.

Amanda nodded. "This is what he painted for me."

Back outside, Amanda stood in the middle of the compound, try-ing to recover her composure. "Do you think the cops have already been here and arrested him?"

He looked doubtful. "They wouldn't have risked the trip in the dark last night, and they'd have had to leave pretty early to get here ahead of us. They would leave more prints on the shore. I didn't see anything. No one was on that beach after high tide, which was at five thirty this morning."

"Should we go look for him?"

Pim shook his head. "If he's hiding, we won't find him. Luke knows this island better than anyone. If he doesn't want to be found, no one will find him."

She thought about the resources police search teams had at their disposal: K9 units, heat-sensing helicopters, night-vision goggles, and more. They would grid the island and search it section by sec-tion. The noise of the helicopters alone might trigger his panic.

Pim was studying her as if debating how much to tell her. "Luke knows a few things about hiding," he said finally. "He spent two weeks in the jungle in Vietnam, trying to get back to his unit. Nothing but his M16 for company, he said. Sometimes, when he's scared, he's right back in the jungle, hugging his rifle."

She took a deep breath. "And now he has his shotgun."

They both stood in silence, reflecting on what that meant. That if the cops did find him, the end might not be pretty.

"Do you know where he is, Pim?"

"Nope. He draws a line. There's a lot of Luke that's off limits. But there's a big, empty wilderness out there, not just on this is-land, but across Millar Channel on the mainland. The cops would have to bring the entire RCMP force to search it all. Why would they spend that much effort? They'll concentrate on the accident scene and try to piece together what happened. They'll look at the storm, the currents, and the tide to come up with the best theory."

She frowned. "Do they always do that? I mean, isn't it obvious what happened? He got caught in the storm, he was inexperienced, and the boat was too small. The boat either capsized or cracked up on the rocks. Either way, he didn't stand a chance."

Pim wandered over to let the hens out to roam. He watched in silence as they strutted about, happy to be free. Kaylee eyed them curiously but made no move to chase them. The stick at her feet was far more interesting.

"There's a few things they have to figure out," Pim said finally. "Why was the guy's boat on one headland and his body on another? The body was just above the high-water mark. That means it was washed ashore around high tide, either around five o'clock yesterday afternoon, about when you and Gilligan found him, or four thirty the morning before."

Amanda thought back to that afternoon. "I wonder why his friends didn't report him missing."

"Maybe they weren't real friends, or they left before him."

"Even so, they must have known he might have trouble in that boat," she said. "You'd think they'd check on him."

"Maybe they did. Maybe the cops have a whole lot of answers by now."

She was replaying the scenario in her head, trying to imagine whether Richie drowned out at sea or whether he'd been trying to swim to shore and been battered on the rocks. A head wound would have produced a lot of blood, but there was none on the rocks, suggesting he'd died before washing ashore. If so, what had he cracked his head on?

Something about the scenario puzzled her. "You said he was just above high tide?"

"Looked that way from the water marks. The cops will be checking that this morning."

"How could a body get *above* the high-tide mark?"

"Sometimes there's a rogue wave. And during the storm, the waves surge higher."

"That means he likely went into the water before or during the storm."

Pim looked unconvinced. "He could've been in the water a long time before he was washed up."

"What time did you say high tide was yesterday?"

"About five o'clock. The tables will say exactly. I'm sure the cops will figure all that out."

"And the previous high tide? The one that happened during the storm?"

"About four thirty in the morning? Still pitch black. Sunrise isn't for another hour."

"No one with any sense would be out on the water then."

"Like I said, he could have gone in the water earlier."

She scoured her memory of that afternoon when she and Pim had seen him. There had been no one on the beach except the surfers, and farther down in Cow Bay, some kayakers. But there had been a couple of boats out in the bay, mostly whale-watching tours. And with all those witnesses in the whale boats, surely someone would have seen his boat foundering on the rocks and reported it. Or had he stayed on shore alone, trying to wait out the storm, and ventured out in the early hours, too drunk or stoned to judge the danger?

There were a lot of questions for the cops to answer. But the question that haunted her most was what did Luke's disappearance have to do with it?

CHAPTER TEN

Once again, Matthew dressed with care, cultivating a casual but sophisticated air: sandals, black jeans, and a T-shirt with a Haida motif. He'd bought a new fedora from a wharf-side stall, and he practised different angles in the mirror until he settled on his old standby, pushed back over the bald crown of his head.

When Bonnie had accepted his lunch invitation with delight, he was hopeful that signalled more than a business meeting. He knew it was still a long shot, but his medical troubles had brought a sense of urgency he'd never felt before. *Carpe diem.* He felt vaguely foolish. In the old days, when he was younger, slimmer, and his title of overseas correspondent lent him a certain cachet, he'd had no trouble attracting women. The hint of danger in his job was like an aphrodisiac that drew women to him. He'd been at the top of his game, and his cocky confidence was contagious.

But now, what was he? A middle-aged has-been working behind the scenes as a glorified tour operator, with an uncertain future and little to show for his exciting past but a couple of unwelcome lesions on his lungs.

Bonnie was on her way up, poised, attractive, and confident in her future.

His stomach twinged, adding a layer of worry. Was this a new symptom? A new cluster of the little bastards colonizing his gut?

Wanting to set a casual tone, he had suggested Barb's famous floating fish and chips restaurant on Fisherman's Wharf. But what could he safely eat?

Shut up, Goderich. Time to go and just be the man you used to be.

She was waiting for him at a picnic table, wearing a large-brimmed red hat and purple-rimmed sunglasses that hid much of her face, but not her broad smile at the sight of him. Feigning nonchalance, he picked up two beers from the nearby brewery, hoping she wouldn't notice his hands shaking. All through lunch, conversation lurched from one trivial topic to another as he struggled to find a path forward. But words died in his throat. Who was he kidding? Why was he even here?

By the time she pushed her empty plate aside, she gave him the perfect escape.

"Any word from Amanda on when she's coming back?" she asked, reminding him what Chris had asked him to do.

"Actually, she's had a small delay. Did you hear about the boating accident on Flores Island? A man was killed."

Alarm froze her smile. "Amanda was involved?"

"She found the body. So there has been police follow-up, and she's worried about that artist who lives there. The one I mentioned the other day?"

"Why?"

"He's ..." Matthew groped for words. "Well, that's Amanda for you. Do you know him? He goes by the name of Luke."

She shook her head. "There are quite a few artists and hippies living off the land up there."

"This guy is apparently very fragile mentally. He's older, and I guess he's been through some stuff, has some PTSD. Amanda didn't elaborate. But you know the mental health services on the Island. Do you know who I could talk to? I'm worried about what Amanda's getting herself into."

"PTSD? Is he a residential school Survivor?"

"No. I don't think he's Indigenous."

Bonnie tugged her lower lip for a moment. She was all business now, all hint of flirtation gone and with it what was left of his resolve. "If it's PTSD you're looking at, you want to talk to Dr. Saul Vetner. Retired now after a heart attack, but he was our go-to guy for advice on PTSD. A powerhouse. He taught at the Island medical program at UVic, ran a private practice, and consulted to just about every hospital on the Island. Lucky for you, he lives right here in Victoria." She pulled out her phone and flipped through it until she found his contact. "Tell him I sent you. I don't think he'll mind; he hates being retired."

Judging by how eagerly Saul Vetner agreed to talk to him, Matthew suspected Bonnie was right. He was afraid he'd have to book an appointment sometime next month, but the man suggested drinks later that afternoon. Matthew had a brief twinge of worry that his gut couldn't manage another drink on the same day but he angrily brushed aside the fear. Surely he hadn't fallen that low!

Matthew suggested a wine bar on Cook Street, not far from his apartment, and when he arrived, Saul Vetner was already there. He looked like a tall beanstalk bent over by a strong wind. He was a mass of wrinkles and ropey muscles, his handshake crushing and his golden-brown eyes intense.

"I appreciate your making the time to see me," Matthew began, but Saul waved the preamble aside.

"I've been checking you out. Impressive resumé. And your request intrigued me. I'm not as plugged in as I used to be, but I still like to keep my hand in. So, tell me about this artist of yours."

"I've never met him, you understand. I only know what my friend Amanda Doucette has told me."

"Yes, I checked her out too. I'd heard of her, of course, and as a life-long student of PTSD, I've been fascinated by the path she's chosen."

The waiter brought them both menus, and Saul waved his away while ordering an Okanagan Syrah. He winked. "Good for the heart, they say. You should have the same."

Do I look that ill? Matthew wondered, but he acquiesced. Saul also ordered a cheese platter.

"Not good for the heart, but who wants to live forever? Sorry, continue. Amanda and the artist."

"He's a recluse living alone in the wilderness, off-grid. Amanda first contacted him because she wanted to buy one of his paintings. But she's had a few meetings with him, and now something has happened."

Saul leaned forward, his gaze alert and piercing. "What?"

Matthew described the boating accident on the artist's island and the police investigation. "It seems routine. There's nothing to suggest it was anything but an accident, but the police will have to interview the guy, and Amanda is worried about his reaction. He's fragile, apparently, and might panic. Overreact."

The wine arrived, and they both took the time to savour their first sip. Saul rolled the wine around on his tongue with a satisfied smile before setting the glass down. "Has she witnessed any violence, any outbursts?"

"She's telling us very little. She doesn't like us being overprotective. And it's in her nature to see the suffering in people. Their humanity, not their danger."

"But you're worried about the danger."

Matthew nodded.

"How old is this man?"

"Elderly, I gather. He's from the hippie commune era down in Tofino."

Saul's eyebrows shot up. "Really! Then residual damage from drugs may also be at play. LSD, STP, methamphetamine, and other hallucinogens did a number on quite a few brains."

"Yes, I've seen a lot of that over the years," Matthew said ruefully. "But I think PTSD is the bigger concern. That's why Amanda cares about him. It's what binds them together. Amanda spent more than a year in therapy recovering from her own trauma, and she still wrestles with its lingering effects. She says she understands his fear and pain, but I worry that bond blinds her to other things. He's been outside normal society for almost fifty years. He's only taken care of himself. She says she trusts her, but honestly, a man who's been cut off for that long, does he even know what trust is?"

"He has no other relationships? He's an artist. If he sells paintings, he must have some interactions with people."

"I guess. But she can't even find out his last name. Everyone just knows him as Luke."

Saul paused, a morsel of cheese halfway to his mouth. He grew very still. "Luke?"

Matthew's eyes locked on Saul's. "You've heard of him, haven't you?"

"I can't discuss anyone specific."

"Was he a patient?"

"I'm sorry, I can't discuss it."

"Tell me at least that. Did you ever treat him?"

"No, I never treated him."

"But you know who he is, what he's been through."

Saul slipped the cheese into his mouth and shook his head as he chewed.

"Look," Matthew said impatiently. "If you never treated him, there's no patient confidentiality issue here. And Amanda is the most wonderful, caring person in the whole world. She thinks she can help this guy. I need to know if he could kill her."

Saul swallowed the cheese, picked up his wineglass, and stared into it as if the answer lay in its depths. Finally, he set it down untouched. "Luke's the reason I went into psychiatry. I was part of that hippie commune in 1970. I … I was a draft resister. In 1969, I graduated from university, and my deferment was about to expire. So I packed up, left California, and hitched my way up to Vancouver Island. The word was out about the communes up here, and being a surfer, naturally I headed to Tofino. It was a wild time. There were a lot of us, most of us evading the draft, but a few were deserters. They'd served one tour in Vietnam, and they were never going back. There were underground networks on the US military bases giving advice on how to escape the barracks, how to get into Canada, where to go, how to get fake papers. It's estimated half a million soldiers deserted during that war, although only a fraction came to Canada."

Matthew was too young to remember the turmoil of the Vietnam War, but he had seen similar scenarios play out in other parts of the world. Desperate people fleeing for safety, entering the dark world of false papers and bribes in their bid for a tolerable life. Although the stress of fleeing the United States was less extreme, it would still be a heart-wrenching choice.

Saul gave a sad smile, as if caught up in the memory. "Overall, the deserters were a very different breed of man. Resisters like me, who'd never seen war, who'd been sheltered by college, came up here and joined the fun. But the deserters — those who'd been drafted straight out of small-town high schools, who'd gone overseas and lived through the horror of war — some of them were very damaged. They were haunted."

"Luke was one of those?"

Saul nodded. "Something was eating him up. He took every drug on offer, spent his days in a stupor or high as a kite. I didn't understand it at the time, but his self-medicating was to escape the memories and the flashbacks. And I got to thinking … we, the United States of America, have ruined this poor man's life and how many other young lives with this vicious, senseless war? Maybe once he'd been a hopeful, idealistic kid who thought he was serving his country and even liberating the Vietnamese, completely ignorant of the political forces of which he was a pawn."

Saul had grown red as he talked, and now he broke off to reach for his wine. "Sorry, talking about this still burns my ass, as you can tell. So yes, I can see where your Amanda gets her passion. She's seen first-hand the destruction those in power cause to the poor pawns at the bottom of the heap."

Matthew had forgotten both the cheese and his wine. "Just because it's unfair or understandable, it doesn't make him any less dangerous. Prisons are full of guys who have been unspeakably abused. Did you ever know Luke to be violent?"

"It was a long time ago."

"I know it was. But I'm asking."

Saul sighed. "There was an incident. A fire in the commune. It was never clear whether it was an accident or he set it on purpose. But a close friend of his, a woman, died. He ran away, and when he was found, he was having a frank psychotic break. He was committed to a psychiatric facility, where he stayed for a long, long time. And I went to medical school."

Matthew was in his element. He loved ferreting around for old bits of news and piecing together the story from the disparate fragments he uncovered. The internet, the archives, and the musty shelves of libraries all held pieces.

Saul had not remembered the name of the dead woman or the exact date of the fire, although he knew it was in the summer of 1971. Too long ago to have left much of a trace online and probably too obscure to have made it into any newspaper big enough to have a searchable digital archive. He might be reduced to spending hours scrolling through reels of mind-numbing microfilm or trying to track down another aging hippie who'd been on Long Beach at that time.

But the internet was the place to start, at least to narrow down his microfilm search. To his delight, he quickly discovered that Vancouver Island's major newspaper, the *Times Colonist*, had recently created a searchable archive of issues back to 1858. As he browsed through it with various keywords, he slowly pieced together a picture on the turbulent history of Long Beach and the Wreck Bay commune. Violent confrontations between local people and rowdy Long Beach campers increased during the 1960s and reached a crisis in 1970, when the federal government intervened to convert the whole coastline into a national park. The Wreck Bay commune had taken over the southern corner of the beach to establish its close-knit community and had tried to separate itself from the rowdy beach crowd, but it had nonetheless been folded into the park boundaries. Over the next year, the squatters were evicted, and all the tent cities and ramshackle homes were demolished — some of them intricate architectural marvels and others little more than canvas tossed over driftwood.

Years of communal living, complete with its own social support network, barter economy, and close friendships, were destroyed in the summer of 1971. According to the town officials, the beach had become an eyesore and a health hazard, with stoned or high residents walking around naked, dirty, and spreading disease, copulating and defecating wherever they wanted. They ruined the natural beauty of the place for everyone else. The idea that it was an attempt at the utopian ideal of freedom and community was lost on the rest of the populace.

Some of the squatters dismantled their homes and moved inland to more appropriate campgrounds, but others resisted, stubbornly ignoring the eviction notices. Their dwellings were either demolished or burned down. This was the first mention of house fires that Matthew had come across, but he doubted park officials would have burned down a home with someone inside.

However, during the heyday of the beach culture, accidental fires were not uncommon. Beach bonfires on Long Beach gathered huge stoned and inebriated crowds who raced cars up and down the beach and set fire to anything that could create a spectacle. Many of the commune structures were made of salvage siding, canvas, and sisal, propped up by driftwood and heated with whatever fuel they could find. Incense was burned and candles were set in the sand inside, easy to kick over.

One of these seemed a more likely scenario for the fire. As he waded through the digital archives of 1971, he found most of the Tofino news related to the creation of the Pacific Rim National Park — championed, he noticed with a smile, by Prime Minister Pierre Elliot Trudeau — as well as the fights between residents and squatters and the dismal state of Highway 4, which was the only road connecting the west coast communities to the rest of the Island. There were scattered reports of fires, most related to beach parties.

Then the headline seemed to leap out of nowhere. *Beach Fire Claims One Life.* Finally! He clicked on the article.

> A fire in a temporary dwelling on Long Beach
> turned deadly yesterday when the body of a young
> mother was discovered in the smoking ruins of
> her beach home. Patricia Decker, 19, lived in the

Long Beach community with her six-month-old
son and the baby's father, neither of whom was
home at the time of the fire. Police are currently
searching for a neighbour who has not been seen
since and who may have information relevant to
the case.

The cause of the fire is unknown, but the
commune dwellings are notoriously unsafe, and
fires from candles and open firepits are common.
This hazard has been a concern to local officials
for years, and with the creation of the national
park, efforts are underway to move residents to
safer housing inland.

From there, the article switched its focus to similar fires, to the
appalling sanitary conditions on the beach, and to the government's
cleanup efforts. Matthew scanned editions for the following two
months but found no further mention of the incident. If Luke had
been found, the news had not merited mention in the *Times Colonist*.

But at least he had a date, September 19, 1971, and the name of
the victim. That was enough to focus the search at the Royal BC
Museum, which housed the archives of the small, local newspapers.

Stabbing pains were shooting up his back. He tried to convince
himself that it was from sitting hunched over his computer for too
long, but in the old days he could have spent the entire day flipping
from one screen to another, piecing together a story. Surely, he was
just out of shape. He brushed aside the niggle of fear that the little
bastards were making inroads into his spine.

He stood up to stretch and fought a brief wave of dizziness.
*Fuck! Don't do this to me! I'm not old, just nudging fifty-five. Still
plenty of life to live. A walk might clear my head and limber up my
back.*

But he knew he was kidding himself. He had packed a lot into the day already, and even if the archives were still open, he had reached his limit. So he phoned for pizza delivery and called it a day.

The next morning, he felt revived enough to tackle the walk from his condo sublet to the Royal BC Museum along the two-kilometre path through the meandering gardens of Beacon Hill Park. Tall trees provided shade, and the ponds and fountains offered a cooling view, but by the time he arrived at the museum, he was puffing and bathed in sweat. But he had made it! If he walked downtown every day, he'd soon get his stamina back.

The archives were attached to the magnificent, modern Royal BC Museum that sat on the most famous crossroads in Victoria, opposite the harbour, the BC Legislature, and the grand fortress of the Empress Hotel. He smiled at the museum's tall, imposing totem poles as he walked down the steps to the elaborately carved wooden doors. The archives housed microfilm copies of two local west island newspapers that had flourished during the sixties and seventies: the *Westcoaster* and the Tofino-Ucluelet *Westerly News*. The *Westcoaster* had suffered the fate of community newspapers everywhere, replaced by bloggers and social media gurus, but the *Westerly News* still existed. After registering, he made a beeline for the bank of microfilm filing cabinets and was soon sitting at a microfilm viewer with a stack of reels at his elbow. He picked up the 1971 reel of the *Westerly News* and steeled himself.

He hated searching microfilm. Fast-forwarding through the moving pages always provoked nausea and a headache. He shut his eyes as the pages whirred by, stopping briefly to check dates. When he reached August, he backed up a little, curious to see whether there were any articles involving Luke or Patricia before the fateful day. Were they active in protests against the park? Had there been any run-ins with neighbours or with the locals?

Nothing, until he hit September 20, when the screen filled with a flurry of articles and grainy photographs of the flimsy buildings on fire, of residents running back and forth from the ocean with buckets, and of the charred skeleton of what had once been a plywood, driftwood, and canvas home, now reduced to some wisps of smoke, blackened logs, and a single pole still standing.

Matthew could see that the homes in the community were packed one next to the other, often sharing walls, support posts, and community courtyards. Blackened laundry, kettles, and pots were strung across the courtyard, and a firepit sat in the middle, perilously close to the walls. Given a brisk ocean wind, it could all go up in a flash.

No wonder the authorities had wanted it shut down and cleaned out!

The September 20 article focused on the efforts to put out the blaze and rescue Patsy, as she was called. Luke only merited a brief mention as missing and unaccounted for, but as a neighbour and regular visitor at Patsy's home, there was some concern for his safety.

The September 27 edition was flooded with articles. Follow-up about the arrival of fire specialists to investigate the blaze, the removal of Patsy's body to Victoria for autopsy, and the intensifying search for Luke, who'd been seen fleeing from the home shortly after the fire started. More grainy photos, of Patsy with her baby in her arms, backlit by the ocean and smiling into the camera, her long hair whipping in the wind. Another of a scruffy, long-haired group gathered around a beach fire. Patsy was identified as third from the left, next to her an unnamed man with his arm around her, and at the far end, a starvation-thin young man who was now missing and under suspicion. All elbows, knees, and wild hair, and identified as Luke Lafferty.

Bingo.

CHAPTER ELEVEN

Back at his favourite waterfront restaurant, Matthew ordered a prawn salad and threw various combinations of Luke Lafferty, Tofino, Long Beach, and artist into Google searches in an attempt to drill down into Luke's past. But 1971 was too deep to drill. He unearthed colour pieces from as early as 1995 about the talented but reclusive artist known simply as "Luke." Rarely a last name, although he'd been variously called Lafferty and Loveless. He had avoided social engagements and gallery appearances and had priced his paintings at barely ten dollars until a local Tofino gallery owner took him under her wing.

There was no information on his capture after the fire or on his committal to a psychiatric institute. No mention of a criminal past. Matthew noted the gallery owner's name and then puttered around on official sites without much luck. Finally, with his coffee grown cold at his elbow, he glanced at his watch. A quick calculation told him it was nearly seven o'clock in Newfoundland. He phoned Chris and caught him just as he was leaving work.

"I've got a name — Luke Lafferty or possibly Loveless — and some background info," he said, "but there's not much other trace. He's a reclusive artist who avoids the limelight. He has no obvious footprint, like he doesn't trust big government and is trying to stay under the radar. No driver's licence, social insurance number, or credit rating. Maybe you'll have more luck through official channels than my backdoor routes. But I did find out he was an American Vietnam war deserter who probably got into Canada illegally, maybe under an assumed name, and he lived in a drug haze on a commune in Tofino and later spent some time in a psychiatric institution."

"When was this?" Chris barged in tautly.

"Fall of 1971 and onward. There was an incident at the commune …" Matthew summarized the fire, Luke's disappearance, and his mental breakdown. Chris listened until Matthew mentioned the dead woman.

"Jesus," he muttered.

"This is where you come in. I don't know if he was ever charged or if the investigation ever determined the cause of the fire or her death, but it should be in RCMP or BC Coroner's records."

"Yeah, buried in some remote archive somewhere," Chris grumbled. "But I'm on it. Was there any local speculation that the fire was deliberate? Or that the woman was targeted?"

Matthew hesitated. Chris was a cop, and a cop's mind, understandably, always went to the dark side. "Not that my source reported. But Luke did know the woman."

"'Know' like in a relationship?"

"Possibly. There was a child."

Chris muttered another oath under his breath.

"But there was also a husband, or at least a partner, so —" Matthew broke off as an idea struck him. He knew the dead woman's name, and although marriage records for 1971 were not yet available to the public, he had his ways. Why had he not thought of that before?

But Chris was one step ahead. "Classic love triangle. A recipe for murder. What was the woman's name?"

"Patricia Decker. She went by Patsy. But I can check that avenue, if you check into the criminal angle."

"No, I'm on it. What else am I going to do with my long, lonely off-duty hours?"

Matthew had already decided that regardless of what Chris found, he would pursue this idea himself. Patsy Decker had been a fresh-faced, happy woman in the bloom of youth and health. She'd had long honey-blond hair, not unlike Amanda's. A prickle of unease ran up his spine.

Their little bungalow echoed as Chris walked through the front door. No Kaylee to greet him, no sounds of Amanda puttering in the kitchen. Evening sun flooded in through the floor-to-ceiling windows in the living room, but for once, the vista of Deer Lake sparkling in the sun did not cheer him up. After nearly two years of pandemic togetherness, Amanda had become as much a part of him as breathing. She'd been gone less than two weeks, with many more looming ahead, yet already his heart ached with the loneliness of her absence.

He knew he couldn't ask her to give up her work. Not only would that be selfish and unfair, but her passion for her charity was one of the things he loved about her. But they could not go on like this much longer. The unpredictable RCMP postings were bad enough, but with them both constantly on the move, how could they build a future and a family together?

He grabbed a beer from the fridge, headed out onto the patio, and sank into a chaise longue. Propping his laptop on his knees, he booted it up to access the RCMP database and promptly hit his first snag. The Canadian Police Information Centre was the go-to database of all charges, convictions, and custodial sentences, but it was only established in 1972. Unless Luke Lafferty's case had dragged out in the courts for over a year, or he had later run-ins with the law, there might be no record on CPIC. And sure enough, a check revealed that although there were a few men with the same name, there was no trace of a Luke or Lucas Lafferty or Loveless in the right age bracket, which meant that any charges and convictions would have occurred prior to 1972. It also meant that even if he'd gone to jail, the sentence had been short.

Frustrated, he sipped his beer and considered his next course of action. He could access the coroner's report into Patricia Decker's death, but it would take days, if not weeks, to fight through the red tape. He could try to get the report of the fire commissioner's investigation, but that would also take time. The case was fifty years old. He wasn't even sure how the jurisdictions and legalities operated in 1971 British Columbia.

He needed an inside source — a local colleague on Vancouver Island or at least in British Columbia who could open doors for him. As the sun sank, he browsed staffing assignments, but the long shadows of night were creeping across the lake before he found a familiar name. Sergeant Travis Nihls, his old boss during his very first posting at Fort Simpson in the Northwest Territories. Nihls had been a hardass back then, all rulebook, buzz cut, and ramrod spine, but years in the North had gradually made that spine more flexible and his mind less reliant on procedural manuals and more on what actually worked in the rugged, sprawling hinterland they serviced. To Chris's delight, he discovered that Nihls, after a brief try at being a big-city cop near Vancouver, was coasting toward retirement in a similar rural detachment on north Vancouver Island, an unspoiled wilderness of trees, bears, rivers, and spectacular salmon fishing.

He sent Nihls a brief email asking the best way to access old BC Coroner's and fire investigation reports, left his phone number, and went inside to scrounge up some dinner. He'd only just taken some chili out of the microwave when his phone rang.

"You talking about the Tofino boating fatality?"

Travis's voice had taken on a rougher edge, but Chris recognized it immediately. "How did you know?"

"Small world out here," Travis replied. "That's the biggest excitement the guys have had all year. Major Crimes and Ident called in, all available personnel called in to assist in the search for the missing hermit. And we got birds in the sky, K9, ERT, the works."

Chris felt a twinge of alarm. "Why? Is the death suspicious?"

"Preliminary word is possibly. There are some contradictions in the post findings. DOA had no water in his lungs."

"That doesn't mean —"

"I know, but there are no signs consistent with asphyxia at all."

"Maybe he went into cardiac arrest when he hit the water. If the water's as cold as the North Atlantic, the shock can kill you instantly."

"It looks like it might be a blow to the head that killed him. And I'm guessing you're calling because your girlfriend is right in the thick of it."

Chris was briefly at a loss for words. It was a small world indeed if his old boss knew about Amanda. As if reading his mind, Travis chuckled. "She's been in the news a few times, so she's hard to miss, and you've had a mention or two yourself."

Chris sighed. It wasn't the first time Amanda had been embroiled in a crime, and she was a celebrity in his own Deer Lake detachment, but he hadn't realized her notoriety, and by extension his, had reached RCMP detachments across the whole country. Chris was not a fan of notoriety. As a shy Prairie farm boy, he was more comfortable with vast open skies and endless fields than with the bright swirl of the limelight. He argued that it interfered with the effectiveness of doing his job, but in reality, it embarrassed him.

Forcing a chuckle, he shifted the focus. "I'm worried about what Amanda has gotten herself into. She's met this hermit whose name is Luke Lafferty or maybe Loveless, and in case she gets in deeper, I want to know what we're dealing with. He was implicated in a fire in a Tofino commune back in 1971 that killed a woman, but I don't know how to get at those records from way out here."

Travis waited no longer. "What do you need?"

"Coroner's report on the woman's death. Patricia Decker. I'm guessing she was born in the early fifties. And the fire commissioner's report on the fire. And any report on the RCMP investigation."

Travis grunted. "You want the moon too? That'll take a while longer."

"The moon? Nah." Chris laughed. "Just lend me a spaceship."

"Give me a day. I gotta consult my busy calendar. This hermit — was he ever charged in that fire?"

"Not sure. My source says he ended up in a mental hospital."

"Ah. An NCR, or whatever it was called back in the dark ages. Insanity plea, I think."

"I couldn't even find a charge."

"Okay, well, like I said, give me until tomorrow; 1971 in Tofino? There'd probably be some old-timers from that detachment still alive and kicking somewhere."

They chatted some more about general news, and Chris was smiling as he hung up. Travis had certainly mellowed now that retirement was imminent and the brass had no power over his future. But Chris chafed at the idea of waiting until tomorrow for answers. Surely there were other leads he could follow up. Patricia Decker, for example, and the other man in the love triangle. When a woman was killed, violent jealousy was often a factor. And violent men rarely changed their spots.

While he ate his chili, he puttered around on the internet, researching various word combinations but learning nothing. He tried a Zoom call with Amanda, which she didn't answer, watched the news, and tried another Zoom call that also went unanswered.

His last thought before he drifted into a restless sleep was of Amanda. Where was she and, damn it, why wasn't she answering?

Amanda had told both Nancy and Pim to let her know if there was any word on Luke. Reluctant to leave the Pacific Rim area while his fate was unknown, Amanda had occupied herself with a guided kayaking trip in the Broken Islands archipelago south of Tofino, testing the route and working the kinks out of the schedule. Although the sun was out, the weather was blustery, and she needed all her strength and focus to fight the wind and waves as they crossed from island to island. The tour guide, Nash, zipped effortlessly ahead, spinning his kayak on a dime and neatly dodging the waves that hurtled at them.

This is supposed to be the easy paddle, she thought as she punched her paddle forward. *If this is easy, "difficult" must be impossible.* As a lake kayaker, she struggled to adapt to the constant swell and chop and the sudden blasts of open ocean. How would the older men in her group cope? She had envisaged a three-day paddle, with overnight camping on a couple of the sheltered islands. The sons, most in their thirties and forties, were probably strong and fit enough, but their fathers, battered by years of addiction and hard living, would struggle.

Since Kaylee had barely tolerated the open ocean rides in Pim's water taxi, Amanda had left her in the care of Keener at the Silver Surf. It was almost six o'clock by the time she dragged her weary body back there, and Keener met her outside with a very excited whirlwind of a dog. He still looked worn out, but he mustered a smile.

"She's quite something," he said, shaking his head. "Energy to burn and too smart for me."

Amanda knelt down to sweep Kaylee into her arms for a hug. "Oh dear, I hope she wasn't a nuisance."

"No, she's a sweetheart. She brought a smile to the faces of all the guests."

Amanda followed him and Kaylee through the breakfast room toward her own room, and once again her attention was caught by the painting of the woman with the honey-blond hair. She stopped for a closer look. The style was quite different from the one in Luke's cabin — the brush strokes were clumsier and the colours less nuanced, giving it an amateurish look — but Amanda was almost positive they were of the same woman.

"I saw a painting almost identical to this in Luke's cabin," she said. "Who is she?"

Keener had already turned away, his face darkening. "Like I said, just a hippie from the commune. Girls like that were everywhere."

"Yet you kept it."

Keener shrugged. "It suits my theme. Sun-bleached blond on the beach."

"Could the artist be Luke, the hermit on Flores Island? One of his earlier works?"

Keener's agitation flared. "It's a nobody, long dead. Forget it."

He veered abruptly into the kitchen, cutting off further discussion, but his agitation puzzled her. She'd clearly touched a nerve. The young woman, or the artist? After changing and feeding Kaylee, she headed out to the Java Bean in hopes of finding Nancy. The minute she opened the door, the mingled scents of fresh baking, garlic, and lemon greeted her, and she realized she was starving. Nancy was behind the counter, sweaty and red-faced as she juggled a line of trays.

Amanda leaned toward her to place her order. "I'll be out on the patio. When you have a minute, I have a question about Luke."

Nancy herself brought out her order of fish tacos and plunked herself down in the chair opposite. With a sigh, she wiped her forehead and blew hair out of her eyes.

"I'm getting too old for this shit."

"Sorry, I know this is your busiest hour. This can wait."

"I've been on my feet for six hours. This is my excuse to sit down." She signalled to a young woman clearing tables nearby. "Jesse, be a doll and bring us a bottle of that Sauv Blanc, will you?" She swung around to watch the girl's progress until she disappeared inside, then shook her head. "The town has been nuts! People flooding into town all day long. Reporters, cops, other search officials, rubberneckers, all trooping through here to grab a bite before heading off to Flores Island."

"Any news on that? Have they identified the victim?"

"Some rich guy from California, I heard. Staying at the Wild Point Inn. They come up here thinking they know everything about surfing, but the weather, the tide, the shore, and the wave patterns are all totally different. They say he didn't even have the right-sized boat!"

Amanda hesitated before casually lobbing her next question. "What about Luke? Have the cops questioned him yet?"

Nancy's face grew serious, and worry puckered her brow. "I don't think so. There's an island-wide BOLO out on him and his boat, and the longer he's missing, the more suspicious it looks. They're throwing everything they can at the search. Helicopters, dogs, ERT ground search, even drones, although trying to see anything from the air in that forest is a waste of time."

"I'm worried for him."

Nancy eyed her sharply, as if to gauge her sympathies. Finally, she nodded. "Me too. And the longer it takes to find him, the angrier the cops will be. They'll have him tried and convicted before they even bring him in."

Amanda felt her way forward cautiously. She suspected Nancy knew much more than she was revealing. "He gets flashbacks from Vietnam. The helicopters and uniformed officers bristling with guns, him being on the run — all that might totally freak him out. He might panic or dissociate and do something …" She shook her head sharply. "I don't know what he'd do if he was cornered."

The young waitress arrived with the wine and two glasses. "Anything else, Nan?"

"No thanks, Jess."

Jesse flashed her a wide grin and headed back inside. Nancy smiled fondly. "That's my granddaughter, Jesse. We've got a chronic labour shortage out here, and she helps me out with the odd shift in the summer while school is out." She leaned forward to pour two generous servings of wine and took a long, grateful sip. Then she licked her lips and said, "Getting back to Luke, they may not find him."

Amanda thought about his missing boat. "You think he's gone farther north?"

A shrug. "Possibly. But Luke rarely goes far. He hasn't been into town in four years. I meet him in Maaqtusiis. Flores is … his sanctuary. He knows every tree, rock, and hiding place on it."

"But dogs …"

"He would foil dogs."

"But sooner or later he'd have to come out. To get supplies at least."

Nancy gazed out at the slowly descending darkness and said nothing for a long time. "He has his ways."

Amanda thought of Pim and the Ahousaht community who had welcomed him in, shielded him, and tried to heal him. Did Pim know where he was, and would the police pressure the community into betraying him?

Nancy broke into her thoughts. "Poor crazy bastard," she murmured.

"He painted a picture of me, you know."

Nancy arched her eyebrows.

"We were talking about our experiences in war. I told him things I never told anyone. About the missing girls and the jihadists burning down the village, about fleeing for my life, about my flashbacks and nightmares. He painted me a picture about that."

Nancy's eyes widened. "He's never, ever opened up to people before. Not even me."

"I saw the paintings in his studio. Some of them are really raw. I think the fact I recognized the feelings is what opened the door." She hesitated. Studied the wine in her glass. "He has a painting of a young woman, looking away, staring off into the ocean. It's beautiful. Sad but hopeful at the same time, like she's searching for someone. There's a similar painting at Keener's B&B. It's not as skilled or powerful, but maybe he was just learning. But it's signed *AK*, and Keener says AK is dead."

A velvet twilight was beginning to settle in, and the patio twinkled with garlands of tiny lights. Kaylee had given up all hope of table scraps and had stretched out under the table to snooze. Nancy sipped her wine. "That was painted a long time ago."

"So, it was Luke after all?"

"No." Nancy hesitated, and then set her glass down as if making up her mind. "I mean AK's been dead a long time."

"Did Luke know him?"

Once again, Nancy stalled. "This is ancient history, Amanda. But yes, we all knew each other."

From her reluctance, Amanda guessed there was a whole lot more to the story. Her curiosity was piqued, but it was private history and really none of her business unless Luke was making a connection between herself and this young woman. Given his fragile hold on reality, the thought was unsettling.

"Is this woman still in the area? She'd be around seventy by now."

Nancy shook her head. "Nope. Also dead. Like I said, ancient history."

But not to Luke. And not to Keener either, Amanda suspected.

CHAPTER TWELVE

Chris was out on a call, following up on a missing hiker report on Gros Morne Mountain, when Travis phoned back the next day. It took all Chris's willpower to let the call go to voice mail. By the time the hiker was found, and he had a free moment back at the station, it was nearly six o'clock.

"I'm still working on the official reports from the coroner and fire commissioner," Travis said, "but I did touch base with one of the local Mounties on the case back then. He claims to remember your Luke Lafferty well, and he's still got enough marbles that his recollection may be accurate. He said once the fire got started, everything went up in flames like a matchbox. The plywood walls, the wall hangings and beaded curtains they hung between the rooms — it all just took off. Lafferty was spotted fleeing the scene with a bundle of clothes in his arms, stark naked and screaming. Mind you, stark naked was pretty much the norm in that crowd back then. He was picked up three days later wandering around Ucluelet, wearing his clothes at least but talking to himself and hallucinating. Which wasn't all that unusual with that crowd either. But three days in lock-up didn't bring him back to earth, so he was sent to Nanaimo for a psych eval and then shipped off to Riverview Psychiatric Hospital on the mainland. I'm still tracking his progress from there. My colleague thinks he was shipped back to a hospital on the Island when Riverview downsized in the late seventies, and eventually dumped back on the street like the rest of the mentally ill. Supposedly treated in community clinics, but we all know what that meant. Anyway, he resurfaced on Meares Island — that's just north of Tofino — in the mid-eighties and had a homestead there until it got too busy with tourists and logging surveyors roaming around. He's been up on Flores Island for almost thirty years now, mostly minding his own business as long as he's left alone."

"And if he's not?"

"Well, there was one incident of threatening to shoot some noisy tourists, but it was resolved without charge."

"What about the fire? Or Patricia Decker?"

"My contact couldn't remember what the investigation revealed. The official reports would have come out months later, dry as dust. But no charges were laid in the fire or in her death."

"So, Luke Lafferty was in the clear?"

Travis paused. "Well, you know there's an ocean of difference between cleared and not charged. Probably by the time the reports came in, he was locked up in Riverview hundreds of miles away, so the case wasn't pursued."

"Okay, thanks, Travis. When those reports come in, will you let me know?"

"I could. But you got any leave coming? You could come out to beautiful Vancouver Island. They're seconding me down to Tofino to beef up the search effort, and we could meet up for a beer. And you could see first-hand what your girlfriend is up to."

Chris was cruising down the Trans-Canada Highway on his way home from the station when he called Matthew to report his findings. He loved the fact that it was an easy ten-minute drive along the lakeshore, with almost no traffic and pristine, green mountains as a backdrop. He had already consulted his schedule and couldn't see a way clear to take a holiday for at least a month unless he pleaded family emergency, so he let the possibility percolate in the back of his mind without mentioning it while he filled Matthew in on Nihls's findings.

"We don't know all the details about the fire or what Luke has been up to since," he said, "but you can probably learn more at your end than I can from here. And see if you can track down more on Patricia Decker's death. She may still have friends or family in the area."

Matthew sounded fuzzy and tired and for once didn't leap at the chance to dig into a story. "Okay, but it was a long time ago. I'm not sure it's relevant to what he's like now. The guy's over seventy years old."

"But you love that kind of stuff! Have you talked to Amanda recently? I can't reach her, and all this stuff about Luke isn't exactly reassuring."

"I was about to phone her when you called. She's still out in Tofino, embroiled in this whole Luke mystery. I'll pass this on, although it's unlikely to change her mind."

"I know." Chris paused. He sensed the shared worry and weariness in the man's voice. "Keep me posted, will you? I feel awfully far away."

When Matthew hung up, he felt vaguely unsettled. Chris had caught him having an afternoon nap on his couch to replenish his strength, and the man's observation had cut a bit too close to the bone. Was he losing his drive? His passion to get to the bottom of every mystery that presented itself? Had he become so focused on himself and the invisible enemy gnawing away at his body that he'd stopped caring about the world beyond? Even about Amanda?

Angry at his weakness, he shoved himself off the couch, opened his laptop, and typed *Decker Tofino*. There were a couple of references to Patricia's death in the history of the park, but nothing else. Nothing on Canada 411. No other Deckers at all. If Patricia had any siblings or cousins, they did not live on Vancouver Island. When he broadened his search, he located a handful of Deckers scattered throughout Canada, but cold calls yielded nothing. None of them knew anything about a Patricia or Patsy who'd died in Tofino in 1971.

Nowadays, however, many people only had cellphones, which made tracking down potential Deckers much more difficult. Then Matthew remembered there had been an infant son who'd survived because neither he nor his father had been home at the time of the fire. No names, but those should be easy enough to track down.

Vital statistics like birth and marriage records were not available to the general public, making a direct approach difficult, and although they could often be accessed by combing through newspaper archives or church records, it was a frustrating, time-consuming, and often wasted effort. So, he turned to one of his favourite search tools: Ancestry.ca. Some time ago, he had figured out a backdoor access to the records, and once in, he started with a fictitious ancestor named Decker. That proved too broad, creating a spider's web of connections all over the world. But once he added Patricia and Canada, the search narrowed to one cluster in an extended family. One Patricia was born in Moncton, New Brunswick, in 1886 and another in 1910, also in Moncton, who died in 1949 in Sarnia, Ontario. A third, born in 1951 in Sarnia to a brother of the second Patricia, had died in 1971.

Gotcha. This Patricia was listed as having one son, name unknown. The tree ended there, but beside Patricia's name, listed as the father of the child, were the initials AK, followed by a question mark.

AK.

A familiar surge of adrenalin galvanized him as he went back up and across the family tree, searching for a close contemporary relative of Patsy who might remember her. Patsy had no siblings, but her uncle had three children roughly Patsy's age. One had died in 1965, another had apparently emigrated to Australia, but few details were listed about the third: Thomas Mosley Decker, born 1953.

Matthew threw the name into Google, searching for a cellphone number or address. Although there were no direct hits on the name, he did find a T.M. Decker who was a philosophy professor at Waterloo University in Ontario. *Worth a shot*, he thought as he placed a cold call.

He had his cover story ready to go that was as close to the truth as possible. He explained that he was a history student at the University of Victoria, doing research on the old hippie commune of Tofino, and he wondered whether the man was any relation to the young woman who'd died there in 1971.

There was silence on the line for a moment. "How very odd," Thomas said eventually in a thin, high-pitched voice.

"In what way?"

"Well. It's just … this sudden interest in Patsy. Yes, she was my cousin. I'm sorry, who did you say you were?"

Patiently, Matthew repeated his cover story, adding a personal twist this time to add credibility. His mother had been in the commune, and had told him crazy stories about the place, but she died when Matthew was just a kid, leaving Matthew with many questions about her past. "Do you know anything about Patsy's life in Tofino?" he asked.

"Not much. I visited her there once, but we weren't close. She'd rather … chosen a different path."

"Do you know anything about her husband and son? Where they are now? Maybe they can help me."

"Husband?" Thomas gave a dry cackle that might have been scorn. "If you could call it that. I heard he was dead, years ago. Not long after Patsy."

Matthew felt a twinge of alarm. Had Luke done something? "Was he sick?"

"No, overdose. There were a great many bad drugs around. People cultivated and mixed the most outlandish things. Magic mushrooms were big. Your mother probably only told you the half of it."

"Did you meet her husband on your visit? I'm trying to find the husband's name to talk to his relatives too. Were his initials AK?"

"No," Thomas said doubtfully. He chuckled. "I confess I remember very little about the trip. I went out there for a month when I graduated from high school. One of those 'show the boy the world' ideas of my father's. Sarnia was a pretty small, pedestrian place. They got me drunk, stoned, high, and laid until my parents got wind and shipped me back east on the train. Patricia and what's his name — Bernie? Bertie? Something very un-hippie-like. Anyway, they tripped with the best of them."

"What about the baby? Wasn't there a baby?"

"Yes, Patsy was pregnant, and they kept joking about how enlightened the baby was going to be."

Matthew winced at the implication. Back in 1971, perhaps there had been less information on the damaging effects of drugs on the unborn child. "Bernie? Can you remember his last name?"

"No. But I believe he contacted my father after Patsy died, asking if we'd take the baby."

Matthew felt a surge of hope. "And?"

"Dad said no. He was just getting us out of his hair and looking forward to his freedom with his new girlfriend. He was never too keen on the whole fatherhood experience anyway and was only too happy to slam the door behind us when we left."

"What happened to the baby? Did someone else in the family take it?"

"Not ours." There was a pause over the phone. "However, I don't see how all this is relevant to your mother. Why the particular interest in Patsy and the baby?"

Matthew thought fast. "Well, that's the thing. My mother was close to them before then, used to babysit the baby. When she heard about the fire, she always wondered what happened to the baby. I forget its name. Do you remember?"

"Not the slightest idea. Something odd. One of those flower child names."

"Right. A plant?"

"Or a celestial body. Moonbeam or Jupiter." Thomas snorted. "I doubt he's kept it."

"My mother wondered if the father's family took him. In my mother's memory, I'd like to see if …" Matthew let his voice trail off, hoping it was enough.

"Oka-ay." Thomas sounded unconvinced. "Well, my guess is the baby was probably adopted."

Matthew cast about for one more small toehold. "Did you ever meet a man called Luke at the commune? Was he connected to Patsy and this Bernie character?"

There was silence. A deep breath and a muttered *Good Lord*. "Loony Luke. That's what they all called him. For a while they thought he set the fire, but the cause was never determined. It's more likely someone just forgot a candle. Rather a pointless end, isn't it? No grand drama, no great tragic end, just a candle sputtering down." Another silence. "Hmm. I wonder whether my father remembered that when the fellow called last month."

Matthew was instantly alert. "What fellow?"

"I have no idea. Dad took the call and couldn't remember the fellow's name, if he was even told. I try to stop Dad from answering my phone because he gets conned by telemarketers and scammers, or he forgets to pass on important messages. I got rid of the landline to avoid that, but he answered my cellphone while I was out in the garden. There's a pad of paper in the kitchen where he's supposed to write things down, and there was a single word on it. *Patricia.* I asked what that meant, and at first he thought it must have been his sister, but I reminded him she'd been dead for over seventy years. I asked if it could be about cousin Patsy who died in the fire, and he said yes, that was it. The man wanted to know about the fire and about Patsy's husband. Dad has a peculiar memory; he remembers all about Patsy's childhood. She was something of a wild child, too wild for Sarnia. I was half in love with her as a child because she was so free and full of adventure. She was listening to Elvis Presley and rock 'n' rolling at beach parties when she was barely fifteen, and finally busted out altogether at seventeen to hitchhike across the country. Landed up in that commune on Vancouver Island."

Not wanting to disturb the flow of memories, Matthew had said nothing but was jotting rapid notes. Now he interjected, "Why Vancouver Island?"

"Because it was as far away from Sarnia as you could get?" Thomas chuckled. "Actually, Dad thought she was chasing some boy she met on the road. That sounds like Patsy, always hoping the next one would be better."

"Was it this man Bertie?"

"I don't think so. I think she met Bertie in the commune."

"Do you know where he was from?"

"I don't …" Thomas was silent a moment. "But he might have been local. He had family there. Most of the commune came from somewhere else — lots of Americans, and Canadians from out east — and they kept to themselves. But Bertie seemed to know a lot of people."

It was a small tidbit, but one more clue to the mystery husband's identity. To Matthew, it had started off as little more than a curiosity, but now that someone else had been inquiring about the man only a month ago, the mystery took on much greater importance.

"Did your dad, or you, have any clue who this guy was who called?"

"No. And if he gave Dad any explanation, Dad couldn't remember it. But I was afraid he might be after our money. The family's not wealthy, but there is money, mostly in real estate in the GTA, and this man seemed very keen on the family tree. But he used the name Patricia, not Patsy. No one who knew her called her Patricia."

"What about his phone number? Would it be in your call history?"

"The call was, yes. I was curious, and a bit worried about what Dad might have told him. But it was an unknown caller."

ID blocked, Matthew thought. Now his curiosity was really piqued. What would anyone have to hide, or gain, from inquiring about a couple of people who'd been dead more than fifty years? He was just getting ready to thank the man and sign off when Thomas broke into his thoughts.

"Keen. I knew that rang a bell."

"Keen?"

"That was the so-called husband's last name. Something like that."

CHAPTER THIRTEEN

Amanda had no further excuse to stay in Tofino. The search for Luke continued, but despite all the manpower being thrown at it, there had not been a single sighting of him. Pim was being very evasive; if he knew anything about Luke's whereabouts, he was keeping it to himself. So far there had been no official conclusion on Richie's death — lab tests ongoing — although rumours about murder swirled. Suspicion was settling firmly on Luke, but the police had also intensified their search for the rest of the group that Richie had been with.

All this was reported to Amanda by Nancy, who seemed to be at the centre of the village grapevine. On the final evening of Amanda's stay, she brought a bottle of her favourite red, along with a tray of cheeses and fruit, and joined Amanda at her table on the patio.

"I've earned this," she said, putting her bare, wrinkled feet on the chair opposite. "It's still crazy around here. The rubberneckers are getting bored, as are the reporters — nothing new to see — but the cops are still swarming around. That crowd that Richie was with is their new interest."

"What have the cops found out?"

"Four twenty-somethings from Ontario. They were staying at the Chesterman Beach campground near the Wild Point Inn, but they packed up and took off the day after Richie's death. They'd been there a week, all staying together in a campervan with an additional small tent, but only the driver of the campervan had signed the register. Dovid Lantos, twenty-nine. Israeli."

"Israeli?" Amanda said with surprise as she sliced into the slab of local Brie. "He's a long way from home."

Nancy shrugged. "We get all nationalities here. Anyway, he's from Toronto, where I hear they also have all nationalities."

"This is true." Amanda thought back to the men she'd seen that afternoon on the beach. The smaller one had been deeply tanned and had tried to persuade Richie to leave Pim alone. Had Richie mentioned his name? The word *Dov* tugged at her memory. She had thought Richie was insulting him for his peacemaker stance, but perhaps it was his actual name.

"I think I met Dovid," she said. "Seemed like a nice man. He did have a slight accent, but I thought it was Middle Eastern. So, the cops haven't found them yet?"

"The cops are crawling all over Vancouver Island, so they will. The group had the campervan rented for four weeks and still have another two weeks to go. The cops have plastered the Island with alerts, and they're checking campgrounds across the Island, but so far the group hasn't turned themselves in."

Amanda tried to piece together her impressions of that encounter, as well as the one earlier in the day. The five did not appear to be travelling together. The camping foursome had been in one boat and Richie in his own. When Richie showed up in the morning, they had seemed happy enough to welcome him, but she had the impression he hadn't been as welcome in the afternoon. In fact, he seemed angry that they had taken off without him. Had they been actively avoiding him? Not that she would blame them. Richie was the kind of drunk who could quickly ruin the fun for everyone else. Had the dispute escalated after she and Pim left, and had it ended in violence? Or had they simply chased Richie off the beach into the dangerous open sea?

"Do the police think their behaviour is suspicious? Do they think Richie's death was more than an accident?"

Nancy plucked a grape off the tray and popped it into her mouth. "The word I'm hearing is maybe. He had no frothy fluid in his lungs, which I understand is not definitive, but it means he probably didn't drown, and the shape of his head wound, the likely cause of death, doesn't seem consistent with the sharp rocks where he was found."

"But there are rocks everywhere, and there'd be even more sticking out at low tide. He could have hit any of those."

Nancy nodded, still chewing. "The body was probably buffeted around by the surf afterward. The blood on the head wound was washed away, and any chance of matching it to a specific object also washed away. The police are working on possible scenarios, and the microscopic tissue analysis still needs to be done, but so far the evidence doesn't fit with an accident. One of the scenarios I hear the guys talking about is that he was hit on the head with a heavy object and then taken out to sea and thrown overboard to make it look like a boating accident."

Stifling her alarm, Amanda cast about for objections. "But what about the boat? It was found close by and pretty banged up. That makes it consistent with an accident."

Nancy shrugged. "Who knows? The police are working with tidal and weather charts, as well as oceanographers, to see where he likely went into the water. Then they'll be able to narrow down the crime scene to do more specific analysis. They may find the object that killed him, for example, or signs of a scuffle or blood on the shore. Assuming it took place on the shore at all instead of inland, of course. Searching all that dense forest would be impossible."

Amanda felt a chill. The dense forest was Luke's home turf, a fact that was no doubt on the police's mind as well. But if Luke had killed Richie in a fit of anger or panic, would he bother to take the body out to sea to create such an elaborate misdirection? Would he bother to set the boat adrift? Or would he simply bury it in the woods to be reclaimed by scavengers and nature?

As she thought about the police theory, another thought struck her. If Richie's body had been dumped at sea, whoever did it had probably expected it to sink, never to be found. She knew from Chris that a dead body usually sinks for a few days before rising to the surface, and if the water is cold enough, it may not rise at all. The killer hadn't counted on the power of wave and tidal action to keep it moving. Would Luke, who had lived half a century by the sea, have made that mistake?

"You seem to get all the inside gossip," Amanda said as she sliced off a piece of cheese and slipped it to Kaylee, who instantly perked up. "Is there any gossip about why he was killed?"

Nancy laughed. "Next to hairdressers and bartenders, I've got the best gossip channel in town, but give me some time. Cops are in and out of here all day long, venting their frustrations to each other and wanting to be the first to score big news. Right now, they're thinking Richie was maybe a drug dealer, because …" She shrugged. "Rich, middle-aged man with international connections, that's the obvious line of reasoning. Not likely a sex smuggling ring." She laughed again at her own joke and reached for another grape.

It was nearly 11:00 p.m. by the time Amanda stumbled back into the Silver Surf B&B. Light shone through the solitary window in the kitchen. Was Helen hard at work on her morning pastries again, or was Keener getting a head start on a spectacular breakfast con-coction? She would miss this place almost as much as Nancy's Java Bean when she returned to Victoria, but her waistline warranted at least a brief reprieve. After changing into pyjamas, she propped herself up in bed and opened her laptop to check her emails. Most of them were business queries or confirmations that were beyond the powers of her weary, wine-sodden brain, but two emails from Matthew jumped out at her. *Call me* read the subject line of the first, and three hours later, *CALL ME ASAP!!* sent an hour ago.

WTF? she thought as she connected his number. Matthew was not an alarmist. He was protective of her, but after ten years in desperate, violent corners of the world, he found little here in Canada to trigger the panic button.

He answered on the first ring, as if the phone was at his elbow. "Jesus, don't you check your emails?"

She was taken aback by his angry tone. As always, her defiance flared. "When I find time. If the world was blowing up, you could have called."

"Okay," he said more calmly. "I got distracted."

For the first time she heard the weariness in his voice. She soft-ened. "What's up, Matthew?"

"Chris and I have been doing a bit of digging into the situation in Tofino. I mean the death of this guy Richie and ... your artist friend, Luke."

"Chris? Why?"

"Don't get defensive, Amanda. Because we have the resour-ces. Chris has been able to tap into RCMP sources. That comes in handy, you know."

Her curiosity got the better of her annoyance as she listened to him summarize the latest information Chris had gleaned from his old RCMP colleague. The coroner's office had concluded that Richie's death was the result of blunt force trauma to the head and that his body had been moved, possibly several times, after death. He had likely died between 4:00 p.m. the day before and noon on the day Amanda and Gilligan found him. Homicide by person or persons unknown.

"Moved several times?" Amanda said with surprise. "Do they know where he was killed?"

"Forensic analysis of the trace debris on his body and clothes could take weeks, even months. If there is even any left after soaking in the ocean."

"Who do they suspect?"

There was a pause. Amanda tensed, guessing what came next. "The people he was with the day you first saw him," Matthew said, "and ..."

"And Luke."

Another pause. A softer voice. "Yes, Luke. We've found out more details about him too."

Once more, she quelled her objections while he told her about the fire on the commune, the death of a young mother, and Luke's years in a psychiatric institution.

"That doesn't surprise me," she said. "Apart from any other mental illnesses he may have, he suffers from severe PTSD from Vietnam."

"He was implicated in that fire, but it never went anywhere because he was committed, but he sounds very unstable."

"I know he's unstable. That's why I'm worried about him. But he's struggling to live the best life he can, and as long as people don't threaten him —"

"But something else is going on, Amanda. Someone is stirring up the past about those years on the commune, and that's what has me worried for you. The young woman who died in the fire in September 1971 was Patricia Decker. Her husband, partner, whatever he was, died about a month after her. They had an infant son who I can't trace. He was probably adopted out. But last month someone contacted Patricia's cousin asking questions about their deaths and what happened to the child. Someone is digging."

Amanda was bewildered. The mystery caller couldn't possibly be Luke, who wouldn't even know how to operate a modern phone, let alone track someone down. Could it be just a coincidence that a month after someone was asking questions about Patricia's death, a man ended up dead? Or could there possibly be a connection?

The next morning, she drove as fast as she could back into town and down to the dock, hoping to catch Pim before he went out on the water. Pim was too young to have known Patricia or Luke back in 1971, but perhaps the story of the fire had been passed on in his village. Was Richie's death linked to this past, and was that why Luke had disappeared?

Or was Luke also dead?

As she drew near the dock, she saw a knot of people gathered near the boats, pacing and gesticulating. In the chorus of voices, one voice suddenly rose above the rest, shrill and hoarse with a hint of southern drawl.

"This is bull! My money's as good as any of the rest of y'all!"

Pim stood his ground and spoke too softly for Amanda to hear. His gaze flickered when he saw Amanda approach, and he shook his head slightly.

Facing him, leaning in with her hands on her hips and her feet planted firmly apart, was a short, barrel-chested woman dressed in a jean jacket, cargo pants, and steel-toed boots. Silver glinted through her buzz-cut hair, and deep scowl lines scored her craggy face, but Amanda suspected she could hold her own against any of the men in the crowd.

"The island is closed to the public," Pim said patiently, as if for the hundredth time. "There are no water taxis going to Maaqtusiis."

"I don't give a shit about Maaq-whatever the hell it is," the woman snapped. "I can land anywhere along the shore."

"It's all closed."

"Bull! Y'all can't close off the entire ocean. It's a free country." She paused. "Or is this what passes for freedom up here?"

Despite the silver hair and the stocky build, there was something familiar about the woman. The tone of voice. The condescension. She pulled a wallet from her jacket pocket and began to count out bills. "What'll it cost me? Five hundred? Who's willing to say the hell with the stupid rule and take me up to Flores Island?"

Three of the drivers stood with Pim, but the fourth took a hesitant step forward. Pim signalled for him to stop, but the man squared his jaw and reached for the money. Holding Kaylee tightly at heel, Amanda stepped into the fray.

"You can't go," she said firmly. "It's a crime scene."

The woman turned on her. Up close, Amanda could see the ravages of pain in her face. The deep circles under her bloodshot eyes. "Who the fuck are you?"

"I'm Amanda Doucette, and I —"

"Well, Amanda Doucette, don't butt in where you're not needed. I know damn well it's a crime scene. That's why I'm going!"

She started toward the water, forcing Amanda to step in front of her. "Who are you?" Amanda said. Toe to toe, she knew she was no match, but she was counting on the woman's natural decency. She was wrong.

"That's also none of your business," the woman said, sweeping her aside with a powerful arm. Kaylee barked and lunged forward before Amanda could stop her.

"Watch your mutt," the woman snarled, sidestepping the dog's lunge with an agile leap. The driver had already accepted his five hundred dollars and was starting his motor. The woman jumped in, rocking the boat violently but keeping her footing, and within a minute they were revving away from the dock.

Pim was frowning. "What an unpleasant woman."

"I had another term in mind," Amanda said. "Who is she?"

He shrugged, his eyes still on the boat as it disappeared into the sound. "She didn't say. But she was asking about Luke. She wanted to know where he lived and wanted us to take her there. I told her I wouldn't, and anyway, he's gone inland. Take me there, she said, and I said there are no routes."

"She also wanted to know where Luke came from and how long he'd been here," one of the other drivers interjected.

"We said we didn't know, we keep to ourselves," Pim said.

Amanda replayed the scene in her head. Remembered the woman's anger, the hint of pain, her single-minded determination. Why should she be so desperate to find Luke?

"She didn't give any name?"

Pim shook his head. "But she paid that guy in US hundreds, and she's staying at the Wild Point Inn. So, there's some big money there."

CHAPTER FOURTEEN

The Wild Point Inn snatched her breath away. All glowing cedar and soaring glass, it sparkled like a fine-cut diamond set on a rocky point between two golden beaches. Surf and spray roiled around it, and on the beaches nearby, people strolled and surfers dipped and twisted in the waves.

Amanda walked around to the spacious entranceway and opened the magnificent carved cedar doors. Local art graced the walls. *Paradise, if you have the money to partake*, she thought.

The mystery woman obviously had the money but hardly seemed the type to seek out such elegant luxury. She looked more like a beer and RV park type. On her way to the entrance, Amanda had noticed an RCMP Interceptor discreetly parked by the delivery bay. She recalled that Richie had been staying at the inn, so perhaps the police were conducting follow-up interviews. Unlike the police, Amanda knew she couldn't just march up to the front desk and demand information on a random guest. She needed a more oblique approach. As she'd skirted the exterior of the inn, she'd seen an octagonal, glassed-in restaurant overlooking the ocean. A restaurant was the perfect cover for her presence in the hotel, and she might be able to glean more information through casual conversation with the serving staff than through more formal channels.

As she was escorted to her table in the corner, she was grateful she had dropped Kaylee off with Keener at the Silver Surf. This was far too formal and exclusive a restaurant for a bouncy, overly friendly dog. Guests came here to be pampered. They also paid handsomely for the privilege, she thought as she opened the menu and nearly choked.

Waiters glided discreetly around the room bearing works of art on platters. Their discussions and recommendations were made in hushed tones. These waiters could not be drawn into casual gossip about other guests while pouring her coffee. When she gazed out the window, contemplating alternatives, she spotted a small patio café on the edge of the beach below. Perfect. The servers would be more junior, less schooled in the Downton Abbey rules of service, and less under the eagle eye of the maître d'.

Making her excuses to the approaching waiter, she scurried out and made her way down to the Surf's Up Café. Picking a table by the beach, she settled down to study the menu. At least Matthew wouldn't have a stroke, she thought with relief.

A young woman came over with a big smile on her face and a pot in each hand. "Good morning! Coffee or tea?"

Amanda accepted coffee and stretched out with a sigh of bliss. "What a beautiful place to work! You must meet all kinds of people here."

The girl grinned. "Yes, it's pretty amazing. People come here for a special treat. Birthday, wedding, anniversary. I'll give you a moment with the menu."

She turned and began piling dishes from the adjacent table on a tray. Something in the girl's bent profile triggered a memory. She'd seen this girl before. What a stroke of luck! "You're Nancy's granddaughter, aren't you? Jesse?"

The girl shot her a surprised glance before recognition dawned. "Yes, I am. And you're the woman my nan's so excited about. With the charity tour." Her face darkened. "And you're the one who found Richard Vali's body, right?"

More luck. The perfect segue. Amanda grimaced. "I am. Did you know him?"

"Well, no, not really, like, *knew* him, but I served him a couple of times."

"Poor man. Was he nice?"

Jesse hesitated.

"It's okay, I met him. He could be a bit of a jerk."

Jesse smiled with relief. "He wasn't so bad until he had a few drinks. He made a pass at me, hands like ... all over me." She stuck her tongue out. "It was gross."

"I'm sorry."

Jesse shrugged. "I'm used to it, goes with the territory."

So much for Me Too, Amanda thought. A couple strolled up from the beach and chose a table at the other end of the patio. Jesse gestured lamely. "I should ..."

"Sure, but I'm curious to know more about him. So, if you have a moment later, drop by."

"Umm ... sure. Do you want to order something?"

"Oh!" Amanda laughed. "I guess that's a good idea. Scone and a fruit salad."

Amanda settled in to watch a dog racing down the beach after a ball and wished Kaylee were there. She was a retrieving fanatic and would love it. Jesse returned a few minutes later with her order and stood over her awkwardly. "I don't know what else I can tell you. He was only here a few days. Said he didn't know how long he was going to stay."

"Did he talk about anything? Like why he was here?"

"Well, I guess to go surfing. I think that's what he did when he went off every day."

"I just wondered ... do you know Luke?"

"Like ... the artist? I know Nan helps him, but I've never met —" Her face cleared. "But Mr. Vali did ask about him. He called him the old hermit and, like, asked if I knew where he hung out."

"Did you tell him?"

The girl shook her head, her ponytail whipping. "Nan would kill me if I told. I just told him somewhere on Flores Island."

Amanda's heart sank. So much for her hope that Richie's presence on Flores Island had nothing to do with Luke. Jesse was beginning to fidget and sneak anxious glances at the door. Amanda rushed on.

"There was a woman down at the docks this morning who also wanted to find Luke. She was very upset and insistent. Apparently, she's staying here?"

"Oh, yeah. That's Mr. Vali's sister, DeeDee. She came up here to identify the body and I guess to arrange to take him back home. She's been in full-on warrior mode since she got here. Yelling at the police and calling them a bunch of, like, backwoods bozos for letting a dangerous criminal loose on the streets. She said her father is like ... some big army general down in the States, and he knows the president." She rolled her eyes. "Whatever. Freaked our manager right out."

"Do you know where she's from?"

"Some army base down in Texas, I heard."

Amanda remembered the wide stance and the squared shoulders, the cropped hair and shrill voice, like a drill sergeant barking out orders. "Perhaps the woman herself is army?"

The couple across the way were giving them dark looks, and Jesse began backing away. "Maybe. Sorry, I gotta go."

147

Matthew's spirits lifted at the sight of the name on his call display. He hoped Amanda was returning to Victoria to refocus on the trip, but after the initial greetings, she launched right in.

"Matthew, can you work your internet magic and see what you can dig up on a woman named DeeDee Vali, maybe US military based in Texas?""

"Goddamn it, Amanda."

"I'm sorry, I know this is out of the blue, but I'm really worried. This woman is Richard Vali's sister, and she's already on her way to confront Luke."

"Then tell the police."

"I already did that. They say she's wasting her time because he's gone, and they seem happy to have her out of their hair."

"Then leave them to it, Amanda. Come back."

"I will, I will. I'm just packing up and should be back in Victoria by late tonight. But it would ease my mind if I knew how crazy she is. Two crazy people clashing in the wilderness is a scary thought. Just a quick internet search to see if anything obvious pops up?"

"You mean besides the quick search you asked me to do on the painter, AK? I'm planning a trip here, Amanda. In fact, I have a meeting with Bonnie and Tag in less than an hour."

"I know. I'm sorry. But ..."

He heard the familiar anxiety in her voice and softened. "Let the chips fall where they will, Amanda. If he's that unstable, he shouldn't be running around loose anyway. He should be getting help. Let the police handle it."

In the ensuing silence, he pictured her pacing, as she did when she was torn. When she spoke, her voice was low, as if the acquiescence was being dragged out of her. "Okay. If you look her up and find out why she and Richie were interested in Luke, I promise to pass the information on and let the police handle it."

When Matthew hung up, he sat for a moment staring at his computer screens. An old habit from his years as a correspondent, he had four laptops open to different news sources, and they fed him constant chatter about global crises, when he bothered to pay attention to them. Now one of them was open to his search on AK, which had so far turned up almost no leads. The most promising was a short reference in a digitalized local history book of the Tofino area, written in 1995. No full name was given, but AK was believed to have come from Ontario and joined the artists' colony in Tofino around 1966. He painted local landscapes as well as the life and people of the commune, but many of his works had been lost in a fire. He died of a drug overdose widely believed by those who knew him to be suicide.

None of this told Matthew who AK or the blond woman in his painting were, or why the owner of the Silver Surf refused to talk about a painting he had kept all these years.

Wearily, Matthew threw a few words about Vali, US military, and Texas into a Google search, and multiple hits jumped up on his screen. Patiently he combed through them, determining that Vali was a big name in the military. A Jefferson Damon Vali was a decorated Second World War vet who had died last year after a busy career making money. There were two George Valis, one a George Richard Vali and the other an older, much-decorated general, George Damon Vali, who'd served in the Gulf War, Iraq, and Afghanistan, and had gone on to advise presidents on the handling of conflicts in the Middle East, even after his retirement. Matthew studied his photos with interest. The man looked vaguely familiar, but maybe it was just the chest full of medals and the tough, uncompromising stare. Matthew had seen plenty like him in war zones. Exactly the look you'd want to intimidate the Osama bin Ladens and Saddam Husseins of this world.

Other military Valis has less Google presence, including a
Robert, two Mitchells, and a Dwight. The George Richard Vali had
apparently gone by the name Richard and was not a military man
but rather a financial adviser from Southern California. Most of
the hits related to his recent death, but he was also active on social
media, hustling for clients when he wasn't bragging about his yacht,
his beach house, and his celebrity friends. Lots of grinning poses
with a surfboard, half-naked women, and a can of beer.

But no DeeDee. In fact, none of the military Valis highlighted
were women, although there were female Valis in other lines of
work. Matthew studied the name. Could DeeDee be a nickname,
short for Deirdre? Or could they be initials? He tried D.D. Vali and
combed through various possibilities. He was almost ready to give
up in frustration when he had a brainwave. Richard had left his
Facebook profile public, so Matthew tackled the prohibitively long
friends list. He only had a few minutes to spare before his meeting with Bonnie, but luckily the name Dorothy Dawn leaped out
almost immediately. He did a quick search of Dorothy Dawn Vali
and found almost no internet presence beyond a single reference to
a list of NCOs based in Texas.

Bingo.

He left that search open, grabbed his files, and headed off to
his meeting. Bonnie greeted him with that wide, beautiful smile
that always brightened his mood, and instinctively he straightened
his shoulders and sucked in his gut. Tag nodded tightly but barely
looked up from his laptop. He shifted in his chair, and his leg jig-
gled as Matthew summarized the various contracts he'd negotiated
based on Amanda's plan.

"Amanda promised she's on her way back this afternoon,"
Matthew said. "This incident has shaken her and thrown her off
course, but I think it's all wrapped up now. At least it's in police
hands."

"About time," Tag muttered. "Can I give my report now? I've done my end. I've got all the consents and waivers, and I'm just waiting on a few medicals." He shut his laptop and perched forward on his chair as if to leave.

"Any concerns?" Bonnie asked.

"What?"

"In the medicals. Any red flags, health-wise?"

"None we can't handle. Amanda's been careful to keep the activities geezer-friendly." He managed a tight smile, still on the edge of his chair.

Bonnie laughed. "Now my report —"

"Can I go?" Tag interjected. "I mean, I don't need to be here for the business stuff. And I ..." He twitched. "I have to go out of town for a few days."

"Oh?" Bonnie's eyes narrowed. "Is something wrong?"

"No. Something personal came up. I'll be back in plenty of time for the orientation session."

"Okay. Where can we reach you?"

Tag was already on his feet, and Matthew could see him bristle. "I'll have my phone."

Bonnie watched him bolt out the door, her concern mirrored in her eyes.

"He's wound tight. Is he all right?" Matthew asked.

"I think so. I don't know much about his personal life. I think he has a partner, but I've never met him. Tag has always kept himself detached, but that's to be expected. Jail and life on the street make you cautious, and you learn to keep things to yourself. But I guess ... well, he must have a personal life."

Matthew thought about the twitching and the restless energy. "Do you think he could be using again?"

"Oh, no. I don't think so." Her face clouded with doubt. "At least, I hope not. He's come such a long way. But he's ... I think he's got something on his mind. He's been distracted for a few days now, and I haven't always been able to reach him. There was a woman nosing around yesterday asking questions about him. Really pushy. She wanted his address. When I told him about it, he seemed alarmed. And now ..." She pointed to the door. "This."

CHAPTER FIFTEEN

Amanda had just checked out of the Silver Surf B&B and was driving down Campbell Street on her way out of town when she spotted Pim striding across the street, waving at her. He was backlit by the early afternoon sun, so she couldn't make out his expression, but his step was hurried. Pim almost never hurried.

Concerned, she pulled over and rolled down the window. Kaylee wagged her tail and danced excitedly in greeting, but for once, Pim ignored her. His dark, coarse features were tense with worry as he approached. She thought of the angry woman who had headed up to Flores Island earlier.

"What's happened? Is it about that woman? Richie's sister?"

Pim betrayed no surprise at her identity. He glanced nervously around and leaned through the window. "Luke sent a message."

Her pulse leaped. "Is he all right?"

"He wants to see you."

"Me? Why?"

"He didn't say why. He just asked me to bring you to him."

"Where is he?"

"I'll bring you to him. My boat's gassed up and ready to go."

She was dressed for Victoria, hardly for a trek through the wilderness. "Wait!" she cried, but he was already striding down toward his boat. Hastily, she pulled into a parking spot and jammed a few warm items of clothing from her suitcase into her daypack before grabbing Kaylee's leash and locking the car. She could change clothes in the boat or on shore once they arrived. Her mind was swirling with questions, and her heart pounded, part apprehension and part excitement.

Pim opened the throttle and said nothing as they threaded past Meares Island and raced up the inside channel of Flores. The sky was blue and the breeze seemed soft, but the boat rocked and pounded on the ocean swell. She dug her hiking boots, sweater, and weatherproof jacket out of the daypack and tried to change while clinging to the gunwales. Kaylee perched at the bow, her ears flattened and her tongue lolling with excitement.

Instead of continuing toward Luke's beach, Pim pulled into the small, protected cove halfway up the inner shore where Richie and his friends had first stopped to play. When she shot him a questioning look, he shrugged.

"It's close to where he's staying."

They floated the boat up into a crevice and anchored it at both ends before Pim led the way across the stony beach toward what looked like impenetrable forest. Up close, however, he lifted an overhanging branch to reveal a narrow, partially overgrown path that plunged into the thick, tangled green. He signalled to her.

"This is very rough. Stay close and watch the dog. She'll warn us if there's trouble. Dogs can hear and smell many times better than humans."

Amanda kept a tight lead and a close eye on Kaylee, tensing every time the dog's nose twitched or her ears swivelled. For about half an hour, they tromped single file along the path, clambering up hills and down gullies, floundering across streams, and detouring around fallen trees, slipping, panting, sweating despite the cool, damp forest air. Kaylee was pulling on her leash, tracking the ground with her nose and flicking her ears to pick up tiny sounds, but she acted more excited than afraid.

Sometimes the path forked or intersected other narrow paths leading in different directions, but Pim never hesitated in his choices.

"Where do these other paths go?" Amanda asked.

"Somewhere else," he responded cryptically.

Suddenly, Kaylee's head shot up, and she lifted her nose to sift the air. A low whine bubbled in her throat as she stared up the path ahead. Pim raised his hand and stopped. Together they stood and listened. Above the blood pounding in her ears, Amanda heard nothing but the creaking of boughs and the swish of wind through the trees. High overhead, the heckling of birds. The forest loam was dank and rich with the smell of rot.

Pim turned slowly in place and scanned the woods, raising his head to search the trees.

"What do you think it is?" Amanda whispered.

He shrugged. "Maybe Luke. We're not far now."

She searched the lush, brooding trees for a sign. "His special hiding place is here?"

He didn't answer but began to creep forward. "I don't want to spook him," he whispered.

"But he knows we're coming, right? He asked us to come."

"But he will be afraid. Everyone is looking for him."

Amanda stifled her own breathing and peered around his broad shoulders as they moved slowly along the path. Up ahead, a massive rocky outcrop rose out of the forest, overhung with ferns and moss that cascaded down its cliffside. Pim walked directly up to it and stopped.

"Luke?" he called softly.

Amanda's heart pounded in her ears. Nothing.

"Luke? It's Pim and Amanda."

Still nothing.

Amanda glanced at Kaylee, who was snuffling around the base of the rock with interest. Her tail was wagging. Suddenly she ducked through the ferns and disappeared under the rock, pulling at her leash.

"Where's she going?"

"There's a cave."

"Omigod!" Amanda yanked the dog back quickly. "A bear's cave?"

"No, Luke's cave." He knelt on hands and knees to crawl through the opening out of sight. Amanda gritted her teeth and followed, sinking her fingers into the damp soil and trying not to think what critters she might encounter in the dark. She followed Pim blindly, guided by his grunts as he squeezed through the narrow gap.

Up ahead, he stopped, stood up, and flicked on a flashlight, illuminating a damp, smoke-blackened cavity about ten feet by six. The floor was cushioned with fir boughs, and a makeshift sleeping pallet had been fashioned out of woven branches and soft grasses. A bucket, a ladle, and a small pile of ash in the centre were the only other signs of human habitation.

Pim stood in the middle, his head grazing the ceiling and his forehead creased with frustration. "He's gone."

"Maybe he's just out getting water or food."

Pim shook his head. "His quilt is gone, and his supplies. He's abandoned this camp."

"Does he stay here often?"

"When he feels unsafe. People know about his cabin. If he senses intruders, he comes here."

"But the police have searched all over, including with dogs and heat-sensing aircraft."

"That doesn't go through this rock. And that's why he made so many paths from the beach, to confuse followers." He gestured to the far wall of the cave. "If he's cornered, there's a back exit. He chipped it out himself. It leads to the other side of the cliff. He would escape that way."

"Do you think he ran from us?"

The flashlight carved harsh shadows of worry in Pim's face. "Maybe from someone else."

"The police?"

He said nothing.

"Richie's sister?"

He looked doubtful. "How would she know about this place? Very few of us are trusted to know, and the driver who took her in his boat is not one of them."

She shivered as she pictured Luke crouched in this tiny space, listening for footsteps or for hints of danger in the sudden calls of the animals. Had he felt safe, or trapped? She thought back to his experience in Vietnam.

"I wonder if this place gives him flashbacks of hiding from the Viet Cong."

"He told me once the Viet Cong built tunnels in the jungle where they would hide from the American soldiers. They would disappear and pop up behind them to trap them. That's what gave him the idea of this cave."

She pictured Luke painstakingly chipping away at the stone to create this haven from the enemy. She took a deep, cautious breath of the acrid air to quell her sorrow. "Does he have other tunnels in these mountains?"

"Probably. He has been here many years."

"What do we do now?"

He shrugged. "We go back to the boat, and we wait for the next message."

"I can't wait, Pim. I have to go back to Victoria."

"It won't be long. He will be watching us. He may even be at the boat when we reach shore."

Matthew sat at his favourite patio table with a cup of afternoon tea at his elbow, scrolling through his list of old contacts from his overseas days. The sun had vanished behind billowing grey clouds and the wind off the harbour was biting, but he was determined to enjoy the beautiful setting. Victoria was one of the prettiest cities he'd ever been in, and there had been many. Yachts of all sizes bobbed in the harbour, creating a forest of flagpoles and masts that clanged in the wind like an orchestra warming up. Flowers spilled out of planters everywhere.

The meeting with Bonnie and Tag had unnerved him. Specifically, Tag's strange behaviour and Bonnie's news about the woman inquiring after him had unnerved him. Was this Richard Vali's sister, the same woman looking for Luke? If so, what did she want with Tag? To make matters worse, Amanda had texted to say she was delayed in Tofino. She hadn't given a reason, but he suspected it was Luke. Or this sister. Or both.

He had a contact in communications in the American military from his days covering Afghanistan and Iraq. Owen Rhys was a grizzled old warrior who'd had numerous assignments around the world, and by the time Matthew met him in Afghanistan, he no longer took himself, or life, too seriously. Laughter, friendship, and booze were the best antidotes to the long hours of boredom and occasional bouts of terror. He had no family, no real home, and being on tour was all he knew.

The man had enjoyed hanging out with the Canadians and had struck up quite a friendship with Matthew. Now, Matthew studied his name on his phone. It was a long shot. He hadn't been in touch for nearly ten years and had no idea whether the contact information was still valid. Maybe the guy was in the farthest reaches of Sri Lanka now.

But it was worth a try. He sent off a query to the latest personal email in his files, asking for a video chat or phone call, and then sat back to enjoy his chocolate brownie. He had barely licked the last crumb off his fingers when his phone sprang to life with a WhatsApp video call. He stared at the face in shock. Gone was the ruddy, round-faced Welshman with the twinkling blue eyes. He looked like a lifer on a hunger strike. A corpse had more colour. His jowls and neck hung in loose folds, and his eyes almost disappeared into his skull.

Matthew was momentarily speechless. But the voice, with its hint of Welsh singsong, brought him back. "God, you old bastard! I know I look like shit, but you could try saying hello."

Matthew forced a laugh. "Good to see you, Rhys. How are you?"

"Not quite dead yet. Getting there."

"Jesus. Is it bad?"

"Yeah, it's bad, but I'm still fighting. You know me. But you're a nice blast from the past. I assume you want something from me?"

"I did. But it's not important. Not if you're —"

"Oh, for fuck's sake. I can use a good assignment. I've been stuck stateside for five years now, first pushing pointless pieces of paper around and now spending my well-earned retirement in VA hospitals. So have at me!"

It was the same old spirit, the same voice, and as long as he didn't look at the man, Matthew felt the years falling away. As briefly as he could, he summarized his work with Amanda, her current project, and her discovery of a murdered American named Richard Vali.

"Vali is a Californian in finance," Matthew said, "but it turns out he's from a high-profile US Army family. His sister, DeeDee, also army, has turned up in the area, possibly on the hunt for her brother's killer. There's some secret here that seems to connect Vali to Amanda's artist friend in Tofino." He shook his head impatiently. "I know this sounds convoluted."

A raspy chuckle. "Uh, yeah, but I'm not going anywhere."

"Bottom line, I want to know what we're dealing with. There's already been one murder possibly connected to this secret."

"And you want me to find out exactly what?"

"I want background on the Vali family. Anything that will tell us what their agenda is, what their connection to Tofino is, and something about their character. You can email me any info you get. No rush. I mean, yeah, I'm worried, but ..."

"I can do better than that. I know quite a bit about the Valis. They have a long, storied history in the military, even dating back to the Civil War, and I actually did a piece on them just before I retired."

"I don't need the Civil War." Matthew laughed. "But you can send the piece to me."

"I can give you the unsanitized version right now. Forget the Civil War. I'll start with Granddaddy Jefferson Vali, a Second World War vet who also served in Korea and rose through the ranks. Colonel or something, with enough medals to sink a battleship. When he retired, he went into arms procurement and made a pile of money. Died last year in his late nineties. Old-school steel, that chap. His son Damon — that's Richard and DeeDee's father — is cast from the same mould. All the right career moves, general at the age of fifty-six, served in Middle East conflicts for years. Gulf War, Iraq, Libya, Afghanistan. I met him in Afghanistan. You probably did too. A hardass."

Matthew wracked his brains, and slowly an image emerged from the fog of his memory. Attending a press briefing, the man at the front, built like a linebacker with a barking, take-no-prisoners voice. The man in the photo on the internet. *What a small world*, he thought.

"General Damon Vali went on to serve with the Joint Chiefs of Staff. Like I said, a dynasty. Which his only son chose not to join. Turned his back on all that rah-rah patriotism, apparently. The family must have loved that."

"But his daughter joined."

"Yeah, but only as an NCO. She never cashed in on her name."

Matthew mulled over the information. There was nothing there to link the family to Tofino. "Any skeletons in their closet?"

Rhys laughed, a rattle that started deep in his chest and ended in a cough. For a long moment, he bent over out of sight, and when he reappeared, he was red from exertion. "I'm sure there are skeletons. Well buried to protect the American-hero myth. The clan are hard-right evangelicals, but there are lots of cracks in the veneer. Womanizing, several broken marriages, and word is the sister is lesbian or trans or something. Oh!" Rhys's eyes lit up. "And General Damon started his career in Vietnam, and as we know, that was a shitshow."

Vietnam. Matthew scribbled the word down and underlined it twice. Luke had been in Vietnam too. Could that be the link? Could the secret be something horrific that happened half a century ago on the other side of the globe? A secret that was uncovered when someone began poking around in the past?

"What do you know about his time in Vietnam?"

"Nothing, mate. I was in diapers."

"Can you dig around and find out? See if there were any scandals or questionable conduct?"

"Yeah, I can do that. But in my experience, the best clue is 'follow the money.' And in this family, there's plenty of that. But not back in the Vietnam days."

"But maybe that's where it all started."

After he'd hung up, with Rhys promising to dig deeper, Matthew pondered what he had said. Money or secrets. Or was it both? What secret would be big enough to last half a century?

CHAPTER SIXTEEN

As Amanda trudged back along the path behind Pim, she marvelled at his unerring sense of direction. The forest seemed to swallow them up. Massive trees arched overhead, their limbs draped with tendrils of moss straight out of a horror film. Fallen trunks and rocky outcrops loomed unexpectedly around bends, and the narrow, twisting trails in front of them blurred together. And yet he always chose the right one without hesitation. He said nothing, but she'd learned to appreciate his silence. He was listening to the forest, and pointless chatter would have distracted him from the dangers.

Subtly, a new sound emerged from those of the forest, overlaying the birdcalls and the rustling wind. Kaylee's ears began to twitch, and she strained against her leash, panting. Amanda drew her back and tried to soothe her, but soon even she could distinguish the rhythmic hiss of the ocean and the cries of the shorebirds. Relief surged through her. She was about to speak when Pim stopped and held up a hand, listening. Soon she heard it too, almost drowned out by the ocean but growing louder. A motorboat.

"It's coming closer," Pim whispered. "From the north."

"Luke?"

"Not his motor." He moved at catlike speed down the path, and Amanda slipped and stumbled on the moss and roots as she tried to keep up. The motor was very loud now, slowing as the boat drew near. Up ahead, a shimmer of water winked through the trees. Pim ducked off the path into the dense underbrush and put a finger to his lips. Kaylee went rigid, her gaze fixed up ahead.

"Don't let her bark."

Amanda saw a flash of movement as the boat aimed for the shore. Two figures stood up, and muffled voices rose over the growl of the motor.

"There's a boat!" a gruff female voice shouted. "Is that his?"

The driver's answer was inaudible. Pim crept through the bushes for a closer look. When the engine shut off, the woman's voice was suddenly loud and clear, complaining about wasting the whole goddamn day. The ever-charming DeeDee. The boat rasped ashore on the stones, and DeeDee stood up in the bow to stare at the impenetrable forest.

"Where the hell do we go from here?"

The driver gestured to the woods.

"Y'all better not be jerking me around!"

"There's a path."

She squinted and shook her head in disbelief. Leaping out, she hefted her pack and began to stride up the beach.

The driver didn't move. "We have to secure the boat."

She looked at it lodged in the stones. "It's not going anywhere."

"Yes, it is, next high tide. I lose my boat, it's five grand. On top of the extra grand for this." He gestured to the woods.

She cursed. "Y'all better be right this time," she muttered as she yanked up the boat as easily as if it was a toy. After he'd tied it to a tree, she walked over to peer at Pim's boat. "You know whose this is?"

The driver scanned the beach and the border of brush, his eyes locking briefly on their location. "Nope."

"He's lying," Pim whispered.

"Let's get the lead out. It'll be dark soon," DeeDee snapped, heading for the trees. "Where the hell is this path you promised?"

The driver lifted the branch and led the way forward. "Stick close to me. There are bears."

DeeDee stopped short to stare at him. "Bears? What the *fuck*! You got a gun in that pack?"

He headed up the path, muttering, "We don't shoot bears here."

"Great. Just offer yourselves up for dinner?" When he didn't answer, she scurried to catch up. "Does this guy Luke have a gun?"

"Luke doesn't believe in killing."

"Of course he doesn't. Lucky for you, I brought one."

Amanda felt a chill. A terrified, unstable old man on the run and an enraged, grieving woman hell-bent on finding him. Each with a gun. She glanced at Pim, whose expression was equally grim. "I guess he does know about the cave."

As the pair passed by Pim and Amanda's hiding place, Pim crouched down behind a thick bush and motioned Amanda to follow suit. A growl bubbled up in Kaylee's throat. Amanda clamped her hand around the dog's muzzle and tried not to breathe.

Soon the driver picked up the pace, his long legs covering the ground as he leaped nimbly over rocks and deadfall, widening the distance between them.

"Hey! Slow down, buddy! I'm not used to this jungle."

The driver did not look back. Instead, at the first fork in the path, he veered left and was swallowed up in the massive trees. DeeDee had been running to catch up and was barely visible on the path ahead when she started shouting.

"You little shit! What are you doing?"

Pim parted the bushes and made his way back to the path to peer in the direction they had disappeared. "He's leaving her."

"What, here? To fend for herself?"

"He knows I'm here. He's leaving her to me."

DeeDee's shouting had become a distant roar as she went deeper into the bush. "So, what do we do?" Amanda said. "With all these fake paths, she'll be lost in no time."

Pim sighed. "We follow her. I want to know what she's up to."

Instead of retracing her steps back to the boat, which would have been the wiser choice, DeeDee chose to carry on up the path. Eventually she stopped swearing and concentrated on the ground in front of her. Amanda and Pim kept a safe distance behind, out of sight, treading as softly and cautiously as they could.

At the next fork in the road, she crouched to examine the trail before choosing the one to the right.

"She's good," Pim whispered. "She has some tracking skills."

"She's in the army," Amanda replied, keeping her head down.

DeeDee carried on up the path, alternating between studying the ground and looking up to scan her surroundings. Her expression was alert but unafraid. Each time, Pim and Amanda had to dive into the underbrush to avoid being spotted. Amanda worried particularly about Pim, whose brown leather cowboy hat added an extra two inches to his already substantial frame.

DeeDee chose each fork and crossing with ease, drawing nearer and nearer to the cave. Amanda prayed that Luke had not returned. Once, as they were rounding a boulder, she stepped on a twig, which snapped with a loud crack. Fifty metres up the trail, DeeDee whirled. Amanda dived behind the boulder, dragging Kaylee with her. She and Pim held their breath, not even daring to peek, until DeeDee resumed walking. Now, however, she had reached into her pack and pulled out her gun, a powerful, long-barrelled pistol of some sort, Amanda guessed from its size. Its black barrel glistened dully in the dappled sun.

She crouched back behind the boulder. "Pim, this is too dangerous."

"Then you wait here. Let me handle it."

"No! I'm not risking you either. Let's alert the police."

He looked at her with a faint smile. "These woods are my home. I've been playing and hunting in them since I was four. You, and especially your dog, just make more trouble for me. I can move faster and safer without you. But you stay right here, hidden behind this rock."

"I got you into this mess."

He eyed her levelly. "I make my own choices. Now stay, before I lose her."

Amanda hunkered down behind the boulder, holding Kaylee tight. When the dog began to whine, she clamped her muzzle shut. Then she waited. An eternity. Sifting the sounds of the forest for the first hint of danger. The birds had fallen silent, and sunlight filtered through the swaying tree boughs, creating dancing shadows on the ground. Her heart pounded. Pim was a cautious man, she told herself. He knew how to stalk game; he knew how to spot danger.

A single gunshot cracked the air, sending birds flying from the trees in a whoosh of wings. Kaylee barked. Amanda leaped to her feet, straining to see ahead. She saw nothing but heard a string of curses followed by the faint thudding of boots on the ground. Then, as the birds settled, a faint moan. Fear shot through her. She crept forward, trying to move as quickly as possible while still staying low. She knew she was disturbing the underbrush, potentially giving away her presence, but she had to find out who was hurt.

It was not Pim who had fired that shot.

Where the *hell* was DeeDee? Had that been her footsteps running away? Outrage crowded her fear. What kind of monster leaves a man to die?

Up ahead, the path was almost indiscernible. She hoped she had not missed a turn and lost the path. But Kaylee had her nose to the ground and was zigzagging forward, presumably on a scent. Finally, Kaylee's head shot up, and she focused on a bush up the trail. A bush that was moving. Fuck! Amanda dived off the trail and held her breath. Kaylee was straining at the leash and whining. Over the sound, Amanda heard another moan.

Amanda abandoned all attempt at caution and dashed up the trail toward the bush. Its branches were crushed and its leaves splashed with red. Underneath, sprawled out in a spreading pool of blood, lay Pim.

No fucking signal! Amanda shoved her phone back in her pocket and flung herself down at Pim's side to check his pulse. Relief spread through her. He didn't stir, and his pulse was weak and fast, but he was alive. Blood was pouring from the matted mess of hair on his head. Her emergency training kicked in, allowing her to focus calmly. Head wounds bled profusely, but perhaps this was not as bad as it looked.

She yanked off her backpack and pulled out her emergency kit. She mopped up the blood and poured hydrogen peroxide on the wound. The blood continued to pour as she probed the area with gentle fingers. Was the skull fractured? She felt for jagged edges of bone but didn't dare apply too much pressure. She packed the wound, pressed gently, and sat back to monitor his pulse and wait for nature to work its magic. When the packing was soaked, she added another layer and tried her cellphone again.

His pulse was weakening. She wetted a cotton ball and dribbled some water between his lips, massaged his face and called his name. Still no response. All external distractions receded as she focused on her next steps. She was losing him. She had to get him to the boat. He had a marine radio in his boat gear, and at the worst, she could drive him back to Maaqtusiis for evacuation. If there were still police on the island, they might even catch the goddamn bitch.

She pressed more packing on the wound and wrapped his head in layers of Tensor bandage. That pressure would have to do. She tugged at his shoulders, hoping to drag him down the path. A weak moan escaped him, but she couldn't move him one inch. She guessed she had at least five hundred metres to go.

She foraged around nearby for some way to transport him. Under a nearby bush, she found his leather hat with a bullet hole straight through the crown. Lucky shot or deadly aim? Using the small hatchet in Pim's pack, she chopped off some low-lying branches and used vines and willow to lash together a makeshift gurney that she could drag along the ground. Laying it alongside him, she began to yank, shove, and wiggle him onto it.

His eyes did not open, and the bandage seeped red. She dribbled drops of water on his lips. It was a poor substitute for a transfusion, but it was all she could do. He needed a hospital. She eyed Kaylee questioningly. Could the dog help to pull the sled? Because she only weighed forty pounds, she had never trained for sled work or even skijoring. It was too much of a risk. Instead, Amanda bent to unleash her.

"You stick close to me, princess, while I use your leash."

Kaylee gave a brief, anxious wag of her tail. Amanda looped the leash together with Pim's belt and wrapped them around her shoulders as she'd seen workers do in the Far East. Then she leaned in and tried to pull. It moved a bare six inches and left her gasping. She'd never make it to shore at this rate, and she might kill herself trying. She needed something to slide the sled over.

Cursing the loss of time as Pim's life hung by a thread, she chopped a couple of small, straight limbs off, stripped the branches, and placed them underneath. After some experimentation, she settled on using them as rollers, moving each to the top as it emerged out the bottom. It was pitifully slow, but it worked!

Kaylee led the way, sniffing out the correct trail among the side tracks. As they inched their way back toward shore, Amanda's thoughts circled back to DeeDee. The woman was merciless. She had shot Pim in the head and left him for dead. What was she up to now? Was she watching them, following them, lining them up in her sights for her final deadly shots? Amanda's heart hammered. She pushed the fear from her mind and doubled down on the straps. Grunting and panting down the trail, she knew she was a clear target, but she had no other choice.

Suddenly, Kaylee froze, her hackles rising. Her eyes were locked on the path ahead. Amanda strained to see through the long shadows of late afternoon. Barely able to see a large brown shape. A tree trunk? A boulder? The shape moved. Swayed from side to side as it ambled up the path. A bear! Kaylee barked and started forward. Amanda dived forward to grab her by the collar.

"Kaylee, no!"

Amanda stood stock-still, unable to back up or get out of the way because of the sled. Her bear spray was in her backpack, where it was completely useless. She ordered the trembling dog to lie down and stay while she shrugged off the sled straps and retrieved her pack. The bear had stopped and stood on its hind legs, staring at them. Every muscle in Kaylee's body quivered.

"Kaylee, stay!" Amanda repeated as she unzipped the bag and pulled out the spray. With the spray in one hand, she hoisted the pack on top of her head to look bigger and then waited. Had the bear smelled blood? Were there other animals lurking in the trees, also drawn by the smell?

Her heart was nearly bursting out of her chest. The bear had not moved, but she'd take that as a win for now. She forced her racing thoughts to focus on other strategies. Most of her knowledge about bear deterrence applied to eastern bears. This was also a black bear, perhaps not so different. Making noise might help. She remembered reading about a woman who had turned her cellphone on to play a heavy metal band full blast, and the bear had left. She dropped her voice as deep as she could and began to talk to the bear — gibberish, telling it to move along, telling it she didn't want to hurt it, slowly raising her voice. Kaylee began to bark, and together they made quite a racket. DeeDee be damned.

The bear dropped down on all fours and charged a few steps toward her, sending Kaylee into a frenzy of barking. Amanda raised the spray bottle, but it took all her willpower to hold her ground. The bear stopped, eyed her quizzically, swung its head back and forth, and then slowly turned and walked into the trees.

Amanda stayed frozen for a few minutes before a whimper of relief escaped her lips. She dropped the bear spray from nerveless fingers and sucked in air to slow her pounding heart. Only the memory of the injured Pim forced her to put the pack back on, gather up the straps, and resume her trek. The adrenalin rush had left her weak and shaky. Every muscle in her body screamed, and her heart felt close to exploding.

The forest was growing dark as the evening shadows lengthened. Apprehension at the thought of the approaching night gripped her, and she scanned the dark woods incessantly for signs of the bear. Just when she thought she could not pull the sled another inch, she heard the first faint swish of the ocean surf. She stopped to catch her breath and stretch her aching back. Through the distant waves, she heard an engine cough to life. What the hell? The motor roared, a low growl at first but rising as the boat accelerated into the open water.

"No, no, no! She's taken the goddamn boat!" In her frustration, Amanda screamed into the emptiness of the forest.

"Two boats." The voice, weak and wobbly, came from behind her. She spun around to see Pim's eyes drifting shut, as if the effort of uttering those two words had drained him. But he had spoken!

Tears of relief flooded her eyes, and she redoubled her efforts to drag the sled. Maybe DeeDee had taken the other boat and left Pim's boat, and his radio, alone. Soon they emerged from the forest into the driftwood and boulders of the shoreline. When Amanda scanned the beach, her heart sank. Pim's boat and everything in it was gone. But even worse, so was the other boat.

What the hell? DeeDee's driver? Had he doubled back to shore once he'd abandoned DeeDee and left her to fend for herself in the forest?

She scanned the open water. It was a narrow channel, but because it was more protected than the open ocean on the western side of the island, it was a popular channel for tourists and locals on their way up the coast to the Hot Springs and beyond. She and Pim had seen both motorboats and kayaks on previous trips. Seaplanes and helicopters flew over frequently as well, giving aerial tours or ferrying visitors to more remote areas.

Someone would rescue them. With her outrage and panic back under control, she checked on Pim. He had lapsed back into unconsciousness, and his pulse was still weak and rapid. His breathing was shallow. "Please hang on, Pim," she murmured fervently as she set about making him comfortable, warm, and sheltered from the wind. Afterward she traced a huge SOS in the sand and then hiked out to the rocky point to look for boats. At the tip, she took off her neon jacket and draped it over a stunted spruce clinging to the crevices in the rock. It wasn't much, but it was all she could do.

Satisfied, she returned to give Pim the last of their water. She was parched from her own exertions, but he needed the fluids more than her. Kneeling at his side, she massaged his limbs and chest to try to keep the circulation going. Finally, crossing her fingers and mouthing vague prayers to all the gods she could think of, she waited.

Dimly over the hiss of the surf, she heard the drone of a motor. She leaped to her feet and raced out to the end of the rocky point, twisting her ankle but barely feeling the pain. A small pinpoint appeared around the curve, coming from the top of the island. It grew louder and larger as it approached. She jumped, shouted, and waved her neon jacket. The boat veered toward her, a small ocean skiff with a single person at the helm. A moment later, it had navigated the narrow inlet, and the man stood up to pull the motor up.

Amidst her relief, Amanda stared. It was Tag.

"What are you doing here?"

"Looking for you," he replied as he jumped nimbly ashore.

CHAPTER SEVENTEEN

It was late in the evening before Amanda had a moment alone with Tag to ask him what he meant. Tag had used his marine radio to call for help, and before long the beach was swarming with RCMP officers and paramedics who attended to Pim quickly and efficiently before loading him onto a boat to take to Maaqtusiis. They wanted to medevac him directly to the trauma centre in Victoria, worried there was a possible fractured skull or subdural hematoma, but Pim roused himself long enough to insist on Tofino.

Tag stayed with Amanda on Flores Island while the police dealt with the follow-up. The Emergency Response Team had been called in to conduct the search for DeeDee, but until they arrived, Sergeant Saint-Laurent and his team took charge. Saint-Laurent fixed a solemn, skeptical eye on her the moment he stepped onto the beach.

"You get around, Ms. Doucette."

She couldn't rouse the energy to think of a retort, so she said nothing. He listened impassively as she described meeting DeeDee and her driver on the trail and deciding to follow them.

He scowled. "Why?"

"We heard her say she had a gun, and we were worried about Luke."

His eyes narrowed. "Do you know where Luke Lafferty is?"

"No. But Pim —" She broke off, not wanting to give away Luke's hiding place or arouse Saint-Laurent's curiosity. She told him instead about the driver absconding and Pim asking her to wait behind while he followed DeeDee, because he could move faster alone.

"So, you didn't actually witness the shooting?"

"Well, Pim was right behind her, and she had a gun, so ..."

Saint-Laurent continued to look skeptical. "You're sure it was Ms. Vali? Perhaps it was Luke?"

Amanda was shocked. "No! Pim is Luke's friend. Besides, he's not around."

"I thought you said you didn't know where he is." When Amanda didn't rise to the bait, he shifted his gaze out over the channel. "What was she doing on Flores Island?"

"I think she was trying to find Luke."

"Why?"

"How should I know? When you find her, you can ask her." Amanda reined in her impatience. "I assume it has something to do with her brother's death. She is very angry."

"I'm aware she thinks we aren't doing our job," he said dryly before closing his notebook. He gestured to the woods, now just a black smudge in the darkness. His search team was standing at the entrance, bristling with gear. "Walk me to the scene."

Tag had been sitting by his boat, excluded from the police interview but reluctant to leave her. He rose to intervene. "Can't this wait until tomorrow?"

Amanda could see Saint-Laurent sizing him up. The tattoos, the muscular biceps, and the steely challenge in his gaze. "A violent crime has been committed, sir," he said calmly. "And an armed and dangerous suspect is on the loose. It's also a crime scene, so if you'll just wait here ..."

"But she's exhausted."

Amanda looked at Tag curiously. It was not like him to show such concern. She tucked that observation at the back of her mind to figure out later as she picked up Kaylee's leash and obediently led Saint-Laurent and his team down the path.

Much later, Tag took her out to dinner at one of Tofino's small but exquisite restaurants. The moment they were seated on the waterfront patio surrounded by lights reflecting in the water, Kaylee fell fast asleep under the table. Because she was still feeling shaky, Amanda ordered only a light salmon salad and a glass of wine, but in the embrace of patio lights and soft jazz, with some food in her system, she began to revive.

"What were you really doing off Flores Island, Tag? I thought you were in Victoria."

He nodded. "I was. But I got concerned when Matthew said you were staying in Tofino because you were worried about this artist Luke. I thought ..." He shook his head, vacillating. "I thought that wasn't a good idea, not just because our trip is very close, but because that guy is trouble."

"How did you know I was on Flores Island?"

"The guys at the boat dock told me Pim had taken you there. So, I borrowed one of their boats and went looking for you."

She picked at her salad. "But you were coming down the channel from the north. From where Luke's place is."

"Yeah, well, that's where I thought you'd gone." He had ordered a glass of mineral water along with his fish tacos and was twirling the ice with his straw, avoiding her gaze. "When I didn't see Pim's boat there, I started looking farther down the channel."

Amanda tried to make sense of the story. It just didn't ring true. She didn't know Tag that well, and their relationship had been strictly businesslike, but he was a no-nonsense, straight-shooting, unsentimental guy. This sudden protective streak was out of character, as were his evasive eyes.

But after half a glass of wine, exhaustion was closing in. She couldn't marshal her doubts to question him further. Instead, she picked up another thread.

"You said Luke is trouble. What do you know about him?"

He shrugged. "Not much, except that he paints yellow trees, and everybody says he's crazy. But I know a man died on his island."

"There's no proof he was involved in that. Almost nobody knows him, Tag. Yet everyone judges him."

"One of the guys in my treatment program knew him years ago, when they were both on a psych ward. Said he used to lose it. Hallucinate and see things. It took a shitload of Haldol and three staff to hold him down."

"I don't doubt that. But that's not who he is."

He sat back with his arms folded and his gaze defiant. The Tag she knew was back. "Okay, then tell me about him. What you see in him."

"He's resourceful and inventive, in his own way. You should see his place. He grows his own food, raises his own chickens, built an amazing cabin out of the forest. A lot of guys would be down in the gutter or dead, but he's trying to live a life that keeps him safe and respects the land that he shares. He doesn't kill —"

Tag twitched.

"He doesn't pollute, he puts his feelings, his dreams, and his fears into his painting. It helps keep him sane."

"All of us want to be safe, but we don't hide away in the wilderness. Most of us find a way to participate in society, maybe even help."

"I know. There may be other mental illness or drug effects going on, but he was in Vietnam, and it still torments him. The atrocities that he witnessed, those he experienced, and also ..." She hesitated. "I suspect, those he committed."

Tag's eyes narrowed. "What did he commit?"

"He was a soldier, so I'm sure he had to kill." She pushed aside her salad and sipped her wine, picking her way through her impressions. "Up close, in the adrenalin and panic of battle, you do things that later you can't believe you did. And if you were a naive, eighteen-year-old boy from small-town America, straight out of high school, who'd never experienced terror before or seen friends blown apart in front of you, never experienced the powerful urge to retaliate, the trauma can be catastrophic. I think that's why now he can't kill anything. I think he made a vow to keep that violent Luke locked inside and never give him the chance to escape again."

Tag nodded slowly. "I've known a few guys like that," he said. "They don't let anyone close because of it."

"The thing about guerrilla warfare is that it destroys your trust." She thought back to the young guards they'd hired to protect their village in Nigeria. Guards who'd turned tail or joined the terrorists. Government officials who hadn't passed on the warnings. "When you're in the middle of it, you don't know if your best friend will help you or will stab you in the back. It's like standing on shifting sands. Terrifying and soul-destroying."

He was studying her closely, the defiance and skepticism fading from his eyes. "There are many ways to be traumatized, but being betrayed is the worst," he said finally. "The memories are always there, waiting to leap out of the dark at you. And that bottled-up anger does feel very scary indeed. You do build fences around it, to make sure it never escapes."

She looked at him, wondering. Who had betrayed him? She felt a new understanding. He was prickly and unsentimental, but he was not without pain. Fences indeed.

The next morning, Tag joined her in her favourite alcove in the breakfast room. He glanced at her plate piled high with eggs, bacon, and home fries, and he raised an eyebrow before ordering granola and fruit salad. She resisted the urge to defend her choice; after eating almost nothing the day before, she was famished and figured she could double up on calories. Besides, he was not her mother. Not that her mother would have even noticed.

She was stiff and sore all over. Her sore ankle was propped up on an ice pack, and her back and shoulder muscles screamed. She'd been woken too early by a frantic phone call from Chris, who'd seen the report of Pim's shooting on the RCMP feed and was already trying to wheedle a week off. In her exhausted state, the idea flooded her with relief, but she barely had the strength to discuss it. She had downed two Advil before bed and two more as they talked, but the pills had not yet kicked in. "Let me shower and have breakfast," she'd said, "and then find out the news this morning, and we'll talk later."

Even once she had showered and washed her hair, she still felt bedraggled and beaten up. Tag, on the other hand, looked scrubbed and fresh in a cornflower T-shirt that matched his eyes and showed off his muscles.

"Are you going back to Victoria today?" he asked as he sipped his tea. Some weird chai thing, she observed as she clung to her double-shot latte.

She'd thought about little else last night before she crashed into sleep. Luke was still out there, vulnerable and cornered, and now trigger-happy DeeDee was hunting him down with a gun. Why had she shot Pim? Had she thought he was Luke and feared for her life? Had she thought he was an animal stalking her? A bear or a cougar? Or had she fired blindly when she heard a noise behind her? She had hit him in the head, one shot in a million if it was a fluke.

DeeDee was military, from a proud warrior family. Chances were she was a good shot. Chances were she knew what she was shooting at too.

Why was she looking for Luke? Did she just want to ask him what he knew about her brother's death, since he was one of the few occupants on that part of the island? Or had she already tried and convicted him, based on rumours about his odd lifestyle? Was she going to make sure he paid because she thought the police wouldn't? Or was she so blinded by grief that she wanted her own revenge?

All these questions had haunted her restless sleep, and now she debated what to tell Tag. In her exhaustion and vulnerability of last night, she had shared more about Luke's private story than she should have, and she wasn't sure how to backtrack.

She picked up a slice of bacon and stalled as she chewed. Eventually she shook her head. "I'd like to stick around a couple of days to see how Pim is. I feel responsible for what happened to him, since he was helping me, after all. And I want to see how this plays out for both Luke and DeeDee." She paused. "Plus if they find Luke, if they arrest him, I want to be there for him."

"There's nothing you can do, Amanda."

"I can find him a lawyer, provide advice, maybe even act as a go-between. He trusts me."

"If they find him. This is a waste of precious time. We have work to do."

She glared at him and stabbed another bacon. "No, we don't. The trip is almost all planned. We're ready for the orientation session next week. I have a spare day or two, so I'm staying. Period. But you go back and get yourself organized."

"If you're staying, so am I."

She rolled her eyes. Again the protectiveness? Had Matthew put him up to it? Had he told Tag to keep an eye on her, to keep her from doing something stupid? Matthew had left half a dozen frantic messages last night, but she'd been too exhausted to reply with anything more than *call you tomorrow.*

"Fine." She laid down her fork. "Tag, I'm very grateful you showed up yesterday, but you don't have to stick to me like glue. I'm going to take a couple of hikes through the old forests and maybe try a surfing lesson, if the Advil works its magic."

"I might just explore. Check out a couple of kayak trips. I won't get in your hair."

Matthew woke up furious with Amanda. He'd lain awake half the night worrying about her latest brush with danger and had gone on to worry about whether this was the end for them. He was fighting the battle of his life with no guarantee that he would win it or how long he had left. He needed all his energy. His conversation with Owen Rhys had opened his eyes. Nothing was certain. He had a follow-up appointment with his doctor today to discuss next steps, and that might tell the tale. Worrying about it was pointless, but the apprehension hung like a pall over his spirits.

He'd loved working with Amanda; she made him feel alive, and their work together had given him purpose when he'd limped back from overseas, jaded and burned out. But the relationship had changed since Chris took priority in her life. Matthew needed to build his own life for whatever time he had left.

But that discussion with her would wait until this trip was over and the file wrapped up. Meanwhile, he had to find out how she was. He was about to phone her for the sixth time when his call display lit up with an incoming video call.

"About time!" he exclaimed.

"I'm sorry, Matthew," she said wearily. "It's been a hellish twenty-four hours."

His anger evaporated at the sight of her drooping shoulders and the dark circles under her eyes. "I know, love. How is your friend Pim?"

"I checked first thing this morning. He's stable, but he refused to go to Victoria, and treatment is limited at the local hospital. The doctor says the next forty-eight hours will be crucial."

"Doctors always say that."

"I know. And I know he's strong. He should be fine, no thanks to me. Why does this keep happening to me?"

It was almost a wail. Perhaps it wasn't the time to remind her why. "Are you coming back now?"

"I'd prefer to stay here until I know they've caught the woman who shot him, and Luke is safe."

His anger flared again. "What can you do, Amanda? Except get into more trouble."

"It's not that I'll do anything. It's that I'll be close if I'm needed. Luke asked for me, Matthew. That's why Pim and I were going in the first place." When he said nothing, she ploughed on. "I don't think I actually need to come back until orientation next week. Everything is in place. Plus, Tag's here. We —"

"Tag is there? Why?"

"He said he was looking for me. He was concerned I was still trying to find Luke."

Matthew digested this peculiar twist. "That's bull. He was distracted at our last meeting, and Bonnie said some woman was asking about him."

"Who?"

"American, Bonnie thought. Tough customer."

Amanda sucked in her breath. "I bet that was Richie's sister. What would she want with Tag?"

"It's certainly a new twist. But speaking of new twists, there's someone digging around in the past." He told her about his phone call to Patricia's cousin. "Unfortunately, his very elderly father couldn't remember any details, including who called. But the cousin did remember one thing: Patricia's partner was Bertie Keen."

Her eyes widened in surprise. "Keen? Or Keenan?" Her mind raced. Could it be Keener's brother or cousin? "Bertie could be short for Albert. AK, the painter of the blond girl on the beach! It makes sense! It explains why Keener kept it all these years."

He could see the excitement on her face. That quest for answers. "Could be. He died about a month after Patricia died in the fire Luke was implicated in."

"Implicated in, but cleared," she interjected sharply. "You said it was deemed an accident."

"Hard to prove otherwise," he said, determined to remind her of Luke's dangerous side.

She was too excited to be deterred. "Still, it gives us yet another strange thread that ties in somehow. Richie Vali from the US and Keener right here in BC."

After signing off, Amanda went on the hunt for Tag. The man had some explaining to do. But he was not in his room or on the grounds. In the process, she found Keener wiping down the breakfast tables. Keener had seen Tag heading off toward downtown at top speed right after breakfast.

"While I have you," Amanda said chattily, reaching for a cloth to help him, "I'm trying to figure out how everyone is connected and where the artist Luke fits in. There has been one murder and one attempted murder, and I'm right smack in the middle of both. I'm wondering if it has anything to do with Luke's past."

Keener had stopped cleaning and was looking at her warily. "What's your question?" he snapped.

"That artist, AK, is his name Albert Keenan?"

Keener stiffened. "Where'd you hear that?"

"Was he your brother?"

He went back to cleaning, slowly and deliberately. "I don't see why it's your business."

"Again, I'm in the middle of this, and both Luke and this woman DeeDee Vali, who shot Pim, are on the loose out there. I don't want to be flying blind."

"It's ancient history."

"This whole thing seems to be about ancient history. Someone phoned Patricia Decker's family just a few weeks ago, inquiring about Bertie."

Keener looked up, his eyes widening. "Who?"

Rather than answering, Amanda let the silence dangle. He became engrossed in another table, but eventually he tightened his lips and nodded. "He was my big brother. It's no secret. Just a chapter in my life I don't like to think about."

She laid down her cloth, and her voice softened. "I'm sorry, Keener. But I think it's connected to what's going on now. Was he Patricia's partner? The woman in that painting?"

"His last painting."

"What happened to him?"

"He's dead. Years ago."

"A month after Patricia's death, I know. How was Luke involved?"

"How do you think he was involved?"

Amanda pieced together the bits of information she'd learned. Luke had been badly burned in a fire, and now he was frightened by fire. Fire featured prominently in his paintings. She had thought it went back to napalm in Vietnam, but perhaps it was the fatal beach house fire. Or both. Carefully, she phrased the question she didn't want to ask. "Did he set the fire?"

Keener set his jaw and wiped the table viciously. "If he'd left Patsy alone, none of this would have happened."

"Was the baby Luke's?"

"Bertie thought so. She didn't even put his name on the birth certificate," he shot back. "She didn't put any father's name on it. How does a man handle news like that? Bertie was a kind soul, not tough like me, and he was trying to help Luke. They gave him a roof over his head when he stumbled into the camp, all broken and on the run. It wasn't much, just a lean-to attached to their shack, but back then, nobody had much. Nobody needed much." He broke off, his jaw working.

"I can tell by the painting that Bertie loved her very much." *And so did Luke*, she thought. She remembered the simple memorial plaque she and Tag had seen in the old cemetery. *My Nootka Rose, September 19, 1971*. The Nootka rose was a pink flower, like the ones in the painting.

"Did he put the plaque in the cemetery for her?" she asked gently.

For a moment, she thought he'd feign ignorance, but then he flushed. "Bertie was looking for a deeper meaning to life. He went to Tofino hoping to find it in the peace, love, and communal lifestyle there. But all he found was sex, drugs, and the same old human failings. He was devastated by Patsy's death. It ate away at him, and in the end he couldn't live with himself."

Amanda held her breath. He hadn't answered her question, but he'd hinted at something far more important. She was reluctant to probe the wound further, but old grudges were bubbling up into new deaths. "Are you saying Bertie set the fire?"

"The fire marshal was inconclusive, but said it was most likely an accident. A candle got knocked over. There was no electricity in those shacks, and they were always burning incense. Lighting up."

"But people heard shouting."

Keener gazed out the window toward the ocean. He looked resigned, his defences spent. "They were all stoned, celebrating Bertie's birthday. Some of those drugs can make you paranoid as hell. Maybe, in a fit of rage …" He shrugged. "I always wondered if that's why he killed himself. Stupid fool. Left a baby son with no one."

Amanda looked at him. "Why not you?"

Keener jerked as if stung. "Nothing to do with me. I was eighteen years old. What was I gonna do with a kid? No, the authorities swooped in and snatched him up. Better that way, I'm sure."

When the second call came in, Matthew was sitting on a bench overlooking the harbour, trying to absorb what he'd learned from the first. Not good news, not bad. His oncologist was never one to jump for joy, but he declared himself pleased with the latest tests. "Not nearly the spread I was expecting" was how he put it. "Does that mean the chemo is working," Matthew had asked. "Somewhat" had been the enigmatic reply. *I'll take it*, Matthew thought.

The second call was a WhatsApp video call. Owen Rhys's cancer-ravaged face filled his screen, reminding him of what might lie ahead.

Rhys was holding a large drink, which he slurped noisily through a straw. For a man clinging to life by a thread, he looked surprisingly cheerful. "I've been digging around some more. Man, I love this stuff. It's like teasing apart a Chinese puzzle, isn't it?"

Matthew found those frustrating rather than challenging. "Any luck with that?"

"Some," Rhys said. "Not sure what use it is. The Vali family is pretty tight, and General Damon Vali is a decorated hero, so the military records are squeaky clean. Sanitized, I'm guessing, because

Vietnam was an unpopular war. The government and the military suppressed a lot of the ugly stuff, especially after the My Lai massacre came to light. The antiwar protest movement was huge, not just in the US but across the world, and politicians and military brass were trying to keep the shit from blowing back on them. There were lots of lies and spin even as they threw the returning vets under a bus."

Matthew waited impatiently for the point of the call but knew better than to rush a good storyteller. He made encouraging noises.

"It was a dirty war on both sides," Rhys said. "The VC were no choirboys. But we incinerated whole forests and villages in their own country, and we poisoned others. We dropped about four hundred thousand tons of napalm on Vietnam, trying to burn the crops and jungle, and twelve million gallons of the lethal herbicide Agent Orange, killing half a million Vietnamese along with the trees. Damon Vali was a helicopter pilot, so odds are good he was part of all that. He would have seen the villagers fleeing from the flames, the farm animals torched, even as he pressed the button. But he was also part of rescue missions, going behind enemy lines to extract trapped and wounded GIs. He went above and beyond. 'Let no man be left behind,' because they had heard what the Viet Cong were doing to captured soldiers. That's what he got most of his early medals and commendations for."

"But no investigations? No cover-ups?"

"Not that I could find. But I did find that there was a brother — Damon's younger brother — who died in the war. His recon mission was ambushed, and he was caught behind enemy lines. Maybe that's what made Damon so determined to get them out. There was no big military fanfare for the kid, but the family gave him a private family funeral, and he was awarded a Purple Heart for trying to save a South Vietnamese village from the Viet Cong. There's a plaque somewhere in Texas."

Ancient history, Matthew thought. But wasn't that what this was all about? "You got the brother's name?"

"Yep. Lucas Jefferson Vali."

CHAPTER EIGHTEEN

Amanda listened with growing astonishment as Matthew filled her in. Her thoughts were whirling. Was this the key to the whole mystery? Luke, Richie, and DeeDee were family! Yet as the connection clicked into place, it only raised more questions. What was the true story of Luke's desertion? She tried to piece together the disjointed story he had told her. About napalm, hiding in the field, and a young boy with a gun.

"You're sure it's the same guy?" she asked.

"No, but Lucas is not that common a name. And the Vietnam connection fits."

"Is it possible he escaped from behind enemy lines? Could the army make that mistake?"

"Crazier things have happened. Napalm incinerated whatever it touched, so there would have been no trace of him left. But I think those guys would be listed as MIA unless there was an eyewitness." Matthew looked thoughtful. "The psychiatrist I talked to said many soldiers deserted when they returned home on leave. There were organized networks on the army bases to help them fake the documents and make the trip to Canada. The fact he showed up where lots of resisters were going suggests that."

"But surely there would be records of his desertion. The military keep scrupulous track of these things. His father, and even his brother, were big names in the military. They would have had access to his postings and his desertion."

Matthew was silent a moment. "Yeah, and my source suspects they could have buried the truth. Better a dead war hero than a deserter, especially when his brother was just building a name for himself."

"Good God," Amanda said. "Would they have the power to do that? To falsify documents and create an alternate narrative?"

Matthew shrugged. "If nobody dug too deeply, and they let it lie low for a while. Remember, it was back in the days of illegible triplicate carbon copies buried in boxes, not instant digital searches. It may be why they gave him a private family funeral instead of a big military fanfare. Hoping to avoid close scrutiny."

"But the family! Luke's mother! Other siblings."

"Damon Vali was the only other sibling, and he was overseas in Vietnam at the time. It's possible their father was the only one who knew the truth. After all, he had powerful connections in the high command and even in the political sphere. He was making millions handling military contracts. It would be a terrible stain on his reputation if people knew his son was a deserter. He might take it as a blow to his military honour. And I bet he did have the power to make military records disappear."

"Leaving his wife, his other son, and later his grandchildren completely in the dark."

Matthew sighed. "All we know for sure, Amanda, is that contrary to the official story and the heroic narrative the family promotes, it looks like Lucas Vali is alive and living in Canada. And that's a secret they've kept for over fifty years."

"Until now." She grasped at straws to figure out how it fit together. "But why would it even matter now? Why would it be worth killing someone over now? You said yourself the old man died last year. I bet there was a funeral with full military honours.

And didn't President Jimmy Carter grant amnesty to Vietnam war resisters years ago?"

"If there was a cover-up, that complicates matters."

"But even so, fifty years later, it's a pretty dead issue."

Matthew gave a wry smile. "Well, there's always the old adage my source mentioned. Follow the money."

She turned that idea over in her head. "The inheritance? All those arms millions? Luke has no use for any of that. He was selling his paintings for ten bucks on street corners before Nancy stepped in. Unless ..." She broke off as a thought occurred to her. "Unless the next generation down — the old man's grandchildren Richie and DeeDee — suddenly got concerned about their share. But how would they find out about Luke? If it was a well-buried secret and the official documents declared Luke dead, how did they find out he wasn't? No one up here knows his real name, so how would Richie trace Luke to Tofino? Because now, goddamn it, Matthew, I'm sure that's why he came here!"

"Maybe Luke contacted them?"

"Not in a million years. He doesn't even know how to use a phone."

Matthew's eyes suddenly widened. "Speaking of phones, I wonder if this is connected to that mystery phone call to Patricia Decker's family. Somebody has been poking around in ancient family history."

"Richie? But why? That's the key."

His brow furrowed in worry. "Amanda. Honey, you're exhausted."

Disconnected fragments of the mystery tumbled through her mind. She'd been bouncing from crisis to crisis so fast that she hadn't had time to make sense of them. Some crucial piece of the puzzle was missing. Who could help her find it? Who could she talk to?

She reached out to touch her fingertips to the computer screen. "I'll be fine, Matthew. Just give me time to think."

After a hasty goodbye, she hung up and headed into the kitchen, but neither Helen nor Keener was there. Piling Kaylee into the car, she drove to the Java Bean, where she found Jesse working alone.

"Nana's taken the morning off," Jesse said. "She's been working flat out for ages."

Amanda tamped down her frustration. "Where would she go on her time off? Beach? Or would she just stay home?"

Jesse shrugged. "Anywhere. But …" she wavered, "when she really needs to recharge, she sometimes goes to the rainforest trail off the highway. Trees are her happy place."

Amanda had hiked the nearby rainforest trail herself and knew there were a couple of peaceful lookout spots. Waving Jesse a quick thank-you, she jumped back in the car. There were few people on the forest hike, and within seconds she was swallowed up by massive old-growth cedars and hemlocks. Splashes of sunlight danced through the canopy and dappled the trail.

She found Nancy on the second loop, sitting in a red Muskoka chair overlooking a ravine. She seemed very far away and blinked in bewilderment at the sight of Amanda.

"Remembering my glory days," she said with a sheepish smile. "Imagine cutting down these magnificent giants."

Amanda took a deep breath and sank into the adjacent chair. For a moment she let the silence linger. "I'm sorry to disturb your peace. I know you're exhausted."

Nancy shut her eyes and turned her face toward a sunbeam. "Nothing compared to you. How are you holding up?"

"I need to pick your brains."

Nancy chuckled. "Good luck finding them."

"About Luke. The old days."

Nancy said nothing, but her dreamy smile vanished.

"Did you know he was a US Army deserter? And that Richie was his nephew?"

Nancy's eyes flew open. She blinked several times, her tongue poking her broken tooth. "Wow," she breathed.

"Wow to what part?"

"The nephew bit."

"So, you knew he was a deserter?"

"We guessed. He never talked about it."

"Do you have any idea how he and Richie might have connected? Do you think Luke finally reached out?"

Nancy shook her head. "After fifty years? I doubt it. He hates to venture outside his comfort zone. Maybe Richie found out from his own family?"

"They may not have even known. Luke was believed to have died in the Vietnam War."

"Then from someone else?"

"Who?" Amanda demanded. "Who might have known about his past?" The mystery call to the Decker family came to mind. "Maybe someone connected to Patricia Decker? Someone — a man — called her family last month to ask about her. About what happened to her and her baby, who'd be a grown man by now."

Alarm flashed across Nancy's face before she shut her eyes.

"What are you thinking?" Amanda asked. "About the man who called?"

Nancy shook her head. "Nothing. Just an old woman's exhaustion. Look, I have to recharge my batteries, Amanda. I promised Jesse I'd be back."

Amanda hesitated. She could see the weariness etched into the woman's face, but there was something else. Silence. She had retreated behind the veil of secrecy that shrouded those days.

Amanda quelled her impatience as she stood up, thanking her and urging her to rest. As she walked back along the trail, she mulled over Nancy's reaction. The fleeting alarm. The look of surprise. At what? The phone call?

Amanda's breath caught. No, not surprise, recognition. And what if it wasn't the phone call, but the baby!

Abruptly the puzzle shifted, and another piece tumbled into place. Nancy's reaction to Tag and her warning against taking him to Luke's place, Tag's previous visit to the Silver Surf B&B and his interest in the painting of the young woman. DeeDee's search for him.

And all his mysterious behaviour over the past week.

Was it possible?

Amanda raced back to the B&B and pulled up the trip data on her laptop. Her fingers flew as she flipped through the medical records, then froze when she opened the file.

Michael McTaggart, Date of Birth March 10, 1971.

Her heart pounding, she reached for her phone to call Matthew. She hated to even think it, but what did they really know about Tag?

Bonnie accepted the lunch invitation with alacrity, giving Matthew a quiver of desire mixed with shame. He loved the sound of her voice, low and faintly throaty. Her soft laughter reminded him of a cat purring.

He hoped she would not feel used when he pumped her for information on Tag. He really did want to see her, and this time he was determined to build on the tenuous affection that was slowly developing between them. If it were anyone else but Amanda and the fact she was in potential harm's way, he would have refused her request.

At first, they chatted about last-minute plans while they sipped their drinks and waited for their appetizers. It was a blustery day with a chilly, salt-laden wind blowing in from the ocean, so they had chosen to sit inside the restaurant and enjoy the waterfront view through the panoramic window.

It was Bonnie herself who opened the door to more serious conversation. She cocked her head and smiled. "What will you and Amanda do for your next tour, if that's not a state secret?"

"I don't know." He tinkled the ice around in his Coke. "I'm not sure there will be a next tour. There's only so long you can keep the momentum going, only so many donors ready to pony up, and only so long I want to live out of a suitcase. Amanda has a partner now, back in Newfoundland, and I expect she'll be wanting to settle down and make a home. Neither of us has had a real home in years. These tours have taken us across the country, living in short-term sublets and never really making friends. Before that, we were both overseas on assignments. Nomadic life can be exciting and adventurous, but it's also rootless and lonely. There comes a time when you take stock and wonder what's ahead and where you'll be in five years."

He broke off, ducking his head to hide his flush of embarrassment. He'd said way too much and revealed far more than he'd ever really considered before. But she was a good listener, smiling gently and nodding as if she understood.

"Where is your home?"

"If you mean, where did I grow up? First in New Brunswick and then Toronto. But I wouldn't want to live in either place. Toronto is a big, clamouring, crowded place, and I've had my fill of those. I want someplace simpler. Someplace with culture but a sense of community." He looked out over the harbour with its bobbing boats, its boardwalk buskers, and the majestic buildings in the background. Taking a deep breath, he ventured further. "I like Victoria, actually."

She sipped her drink and eyed him over the rim of her glass. "It's a pretty place, for sure. Laid-back, but maybe a bit boring for you."

"Beats dodging rocket fire in the streets. Boring is what you make of it."

"True. I was born in a little Inuit village near Inuvik. Nothing much happens there, but I know what you mean about a sense of community. It will always be home for me."

He felt a twinge of dismay. He'd never survive in a little Inuit village near Inuvik. Inuvik was twelve hundred wilderness kilometres north of Whitehorse on the Mackenzie River delta near the Arctic Ocean, where the cold freezes your piss and winter darkness lasts three months. "Will you move back there?"

She shook her head. "For visits, yes, to reconnect with my family and replenish myself, but no, not to live. I have a life, friends, and purpose here in Victoria."

He hesitated, his heart racing. While he debated how to phrase his next question, their fish and chips arrived amid a flurry of cutlery and condiments. After dousing his fries in vinegar, he tucked in, trying to sound casual. "Is there anyone special?"

She chuckled, that catlike rumble that he loved. "If you mean *special* special, no. There was, but it didn't work out. So, I know what you mean about looking to the future and wondering what lies ahead."

"But you're not old."

She laughed again. "Neither are you."

He met her eyes. There was a clear message in that. He wanted desperately to reach out and touch her. To make a move. But he felt paralyzed. Paralyzed that he had nothing to offer her but possibly pain and grief. Paralyzed that he was using her.

While he wrestled with his indecision, she made the move. She reached across the table to touch two fingers to his. "I think you're pretty exciting."

As if she'd read his mind. He curled his fingers around hers. Felt her electric warmth. Words stuck in his throat as panic rushed in.

He thought of Amanda, who at this moment was waiting for news and counting on him. He tightened his grip as if to hang on to her.

"I have to ask you something."

She grinned. "Anything."

"No. I mean ... about Tag."

She withdrew her hand, her smile fading. "Tag?" she said in bewilderment.

He nodded. "Something has happened in Tofino. Tag has turned up there out of the blue. Remember he was distracted at our last meeting and asked for personal time? And a woman was nosing around asking about him? That woman was the sister of the man who was murdered, and she herself shot the guide Amanda was with."

Bonnie's eyes widened and her jaw dropped. "Someone shot at Amanda?"

"She's fine," he said quickly. "But it was that woman asking for Tag. And right afterward, Tag shows up to the rescue. It looked like he was following Amanda."

Bonnie looked confused. "Omigod, what's ... what did he say?"

"That he was worried about her. But Bonnie, what if he's mixed up in this?"

"I don't see how he could be. I've known him for years, here in Victoria."

"What do you really know about him? About his past?"

They had both forgotten their lunch, but now she picked up a french fry. "He's very private, and I don't pry. Of course, I know he's a recovering addict, about ten years clean, and he did disclose that he'd been in prison for robbery and assault. It was in prison that he got clean and started his training as an addictions counsellor. He's been getting steadily better, building a life and friendships, showing more trust in people."

She picked up another fry and stopped with it halfway to her mouth. "Come to think of it, recently he's been talking about wanting to know more about his past. It used to be a closed door to him, too painful to open. But he became curious about his family of origin, and I know he was looking into genealogy. That's part of the healing process for kids like him who've spent their whole childhood in the system. They want to know where they came from, they imagine what their family was like. They even wonder if their parents are still alive, what they're like, if they have any brothers and sisters. They're not just in survival mode anymore. They're beginning to want answers about where they came from and why they were given up. He said he was a troubled kid and a handful from the get-go. Kids like that begin to think they're not worthy, they're bad. He was getting past that." She looked sad. "He's a nice guy. Rough around the edges, but considering what he's been through — multiple foster homes and group homes, we can only imagine a tenth of it — he's still got a lot of heart. I can't imagine him being mixed up in murder."

Matthew thought about the phone call the Decker family had received. "Has he found out who his parents were?"

"I think he found his mother. He had his original birth certificate, after all, but as far as he told me last month, he was having no luck with the father."

"Is McTaggart his mother's name?"

"No, that was the family that adopted him when he was three. They gave him their name, but it didn't work out, and they surrendered him a couple of years later. But he said they were nice, so he kept that name. It probably made him feel like he was part of a family, however briefly."

Heartbreaking, Matthew thought. "Do you know how he was searching? Public records?"

"Genealogy records, I suppose. Like Ancestry.ca."

By the time Matthew phoned Amanda back, it was late afternoon and he sounded both frazzled and elated. When he told her he'd had lunch with Bonnie, he sounded more alive than he had in months. She could hear the thrill in his voice as he told her what Bonnie had said. But more questions clamoured for answers. What could Tag possibly have learned on Ancestry.ca? No one even knew Luke's real name, and Lucas Vali was listed as dead before Tag was even conceived. How could there be anything to connect Luke to Richie? More chilling still, what did it have to do with Richie's death?

She glanced anxiously out her window. She could see the sun slowly sinking toward the ocean. Another night was settling in, with Luke and DeeDee on Flores Island, playing cat and mouse, and Tag nowhere to be found.

CHAPTER NINETEEN

Chris paced his small office at the Deer Lake detachment, fighting his rising anxiety. Amanda was in Tofino, safe and sound. Tag was with her. He never thought he'd be putting his trust in a recovering addict and ex-con, but at least the man had probably learned a few street-fighting tricks over the years. Before Chris put in his request for emergency personal leave, he should probably get an up-to-date report on how much danger she was actually in.

As soon as he heard Chris's voice, Travis Nihls chuckled. "I was wondering how long it would take you to call. I had bets with myself. You're twelve hours late."

"Time difference," Chris shot back, feigning humour. "She's okay, she's safe. I just talked to her. But I want to know if I should be packing my bags."

"Officially? We've got half the Mounties in BC on this case, so no. But if you're wanting a break from your beautiful island corner of the country to come to this one, absolutely."

"How close are you to wrapping this up?"

"You do know it's not my command, don't you? I'm just here to lend an extra hand."

"But you hear things."

"Yeah. All the rural detachments are pitching in. We've got surveillance on the whole of Clayoquot Sound, and everything is calm.

I can tell you this, as long as you keep it under your hat. We're nowhere near knowing what's going on, let alone wrapping it up. We have two potential suspects on the loose, at least one of them armed, and a possible third."

"Third? Who?"

"The group of surfers our victim was with have finally turned up. At least, Dovid Lantos, the main guy in the BOLO, showed up. Walked into the Tofino detachment this morning, all apologies, saying they'd spent the last few days hiking the Cape Scott trail up north, out of cellphone and internet range, and they only just picked up their messages yesterday when they got back to Campbell River. They wanted to be completely unplugged, they said, and that trail would do it. Anyway, he made a statement that, lucky for you, I just heard about."

Travis seemed settled in for a long chat to draw out the suspense. The only reassuring thing was that his chatty tone suggested nothing critical had been revealed. Things moved as slowly on the west coast as they did on the east. Nonetheless, Chris had to bite back his impatience.

"So, he added to the complications, did he?"

"Maybe. He said he didn't know Richard Vali well. None of them did. They met him one day on Chesterman Beach when the weather was really wild and the waves rough. They were not experienced surfers — Ontario boys with a couple of lessons under their belt. One of them got into trouble, and Vali went out to help bring the guy in. Guided him out of a riptide, apparently. They invited him to join them for a beer to thank him, but turns out he was way richer than they were and staying in this fancy resort nearby, so they went there instead, and he picked up the tab. From there, they hit a patio bar on the inlet waterfront to listen to a live band. Vali was quite a bit older than them — forty-seven, Dovid Lantos is twenty-nine — and I think the kids thought they'd hit on a lucky mark. A rich American dude from California willing to buy rounds and foot the bill for some luxuries, maybe even a boat rental."

"Did he tell them what he was doing there?"

"Yeah, he said he had some business."

"Business? That's it?"

"That's it. He did say he was in financials, so they figured he was working some sort of deal. There's some big investment potential in Tofino. Anyhooo …" Travis cleared his throat. "They hung out together a couple of times, trying out different beaches, and then Richie suggested they check out some of the less travelled islands up in the sound. Fewer tourists, empty beaches. He rented them a boat from some local guy, told Lantos he'd found it online, but the next morning when they were loading their gear in the harbour, he didn't show up. Sent a text saying he had his own boat and he'd meet them. They were going to Flores Island, and he said he'd find them."

"That's weird."

"Yeah, they thought so, since it was his idea to try Flores, said he was keen to explore it. But they said he often disappeared for a bit, so anyhooo …" Travis stopped for breath. "Whew, this is getting to be quite a story! Just trying to tell it exactly like I heard it, not to forget details. Apparently, Lantos was really nervous and talked a mile a minute because he was scared they were going to be suspects, because Vali was rich and the rest of them were all crammed into one campervan. So he wanted to spill everything he knew. So … where was I?"

"Finally getting to the point of this tale," Chris said dryly. "Vali was going to meet them on Flores Island."

"Right. And he did. Showed up in a little powerboat pretending everything was cool but acting really wired. Kept checking his phone. He drank quite a bit at lunch, and then suddenly he wanted to leave to check out some beaches on the other side. The others were having fun, so they said they'd be along in a bit."

Chris drew in his breath as he played the scenario in his head. Amanda had told him about their encounters, but none of the dynamics behind them.

"They headed up the coast — this is the inside channel — keeping an eye out but not caring too much because Richie was acting too intense for their chill mood anyway. They came to a beautiful beach on the outer side of the island and decided to stop for lunch, figuring Richie had gone on. But then he roars up, coming from up the island, so they figure they must have missed him in one of the coves, but when they asked where he'd gone, he just shrugged. Took the wrong channel, he said, man, it's easy to get lost in all those islands and inlets. Anyway, they fooled around, surfed some, smoked some, and then your girlfriend shows up with that Indigenous dude and gives them hell for being disruptive and reckless. Apparently, that really pissed Richie off."

Despite his impatience, Chris chuckled. "Amanda doesn't pull her punches."

"Yeah. Anyway, then he got a phone call — the kids said he was arguing —"

"Wait a minute," Chris said. "There was cell reception?"

"The kids thought it was a sat phone. Yeah, so after that call, he said he had to get back to town. The weather was beginning to look tricky, and they were worried about his boat, and wanted to go with him. But he told them to fuck off, he'd do fine on his own, and he took off toward town."

Chris felt a wave of disappointment. All that buildup for nothing? "That's it? They think it was an accident?"

"No, no!" Travis exclaimed. In the background, Chris could hear the murmur of voices and the occasional phone ringing. "I'm just coming to the best part! They got to worrying about the weather and were just packing up when this boat comes up the shore. Lantos noticed it because it was heading up toward Hot Springs, and by now all the boats were coming back in — whale watchers and fishing charters — because the weather was turning. There were two guys on deck, arguing. Richie was one."

"Could they hear what it was about?"

"Too much wind and waves. But they figured it was an argument judging from the arm waving and stomping. Then the older guy —"

"Older guy?"

"That's what Lantos called him. Said he was a tall guy with white hair. Anyway, then the older guy sees them on the beach, guns it, and the boat continues up the bay."

Chris's mind raced to keep track. "What time was this?"

"Well, the kids were busy getting their gear packed and didn't check the time, but it would have been about four p.m."

"And sometime in the next twenty hours, Richie is dead."

"Yep."

"What's the working theory? That the older guy was Luke?"

"Yes. Nothing conclusive yet until the kids can ID him and his boat, but things point to Luke. Because here's the extra little kicker. Richie must have left his own boat on a beach farther south, which means it probably floated away on its own at high tide, and however his body got to those rocks the next day, it wasn't in his own boat."

Before heading out the next day, Amanda banged on Tag's door one last time. No answer again. What the hell was he up to? Her thoughts were still reeling from her latest discoveries. Had this been Tag's secret agenda all along? Not to come on a wilderness healing journey with fathers and sons, but to find his own father? And do what? Confront him? Exact revenge for being abandoned by him? Had he known when he volunteered for the tour that his father was Luke, or had he pieced that together from Ancestry.ca or from inquiries he'd made here in Tofino? What if he'd discovered his father might have been implicated in his mother's death? Had that curiosity and yearning then turned more deadly?

She thought back over the past two weeks. Tag had shown no interest or knowledge of Luke when he first arrived. He'd dismissed the paintings in Nancy's gallery as weird. In fact, his only interest in paintings had been in the one by AK of the young woman who had presumably been his mother. Something about it had aroused his curiosity, as had the plaque in the cemetery dedicated to "My Nootka Rose."

Only later, after Richie was murdered and Luke was on the run, had he shown any interest in Luke, and even then it had been contempt and dismissal until Amanda had shared some of his background.

Only then had there been a glimmer of compassion.

What was he up to now? And why did that question fill her with unease? She hurried through the B&B to the breakfast room, which was empty, but Keener was in the kitchen, cleaning fish.

"Keener, have you seen Tag?"

His red, weathered face puckered with concern as he shook his head. "Nope. Never came to breakfast. Helen saw him real early, making a cup of coffee, and she gave him a muffin. She said he seemed like a man on a mission."

Helen had been working quietly nearby, peeling apples, and Amanda turned to her. "Did he say where he was going?"

She hesitated before shaking her head. "He was dressed for weather, but then you should always dress for the weather in Tofino."

Amanda sensed she was worried. "What?"

"It's just ..." she waved her paring knife in the air, "we've always been very discreet about our customers' privacy. You have to be in this business and in this fishbowl town, especially when you've been part of the community for decades. Everyone has their secrets, and they deserve to stay that way."

Amanda felt a twinge of anxiety. What was she talking about? "Where was he going?"

Helen glanced across at her husband and raised her eyebrows. He shrugged and said, "He came in here late one night, sometime last week. I was making bread, and he started asking all sorts of questions about Luke. He said it was because he was worried about you. You were going on these visits to him, and he was worried how crazy Luke was. He said he'd heard we knew him years ago on the commune, and he wanted to know what he was like back then. Always a recluse, unstable? I told him Luke was basically a harmless soul unless he was triggered, and then most of the time he'd run away and hide. He especially hated the huge bonfires the weekend beach campers lit, and the fireworks. He'd go into the forest behind Wreck Bay, and nobody could find him until he came back. He'd survive on berries, roots, and plant shoots that he'd learned about from the First Nations in the area. I told Tag I didn't think you were in danger."

"Did he want to know anything about Luke's life back then?" Amanda gestured to the painting of the woman. "About Patsy, for example?"

Keener's eyes widened in surprise. "He did. He wanted to know how she died, about the fire, who was inside the hut."

"Didn't he ask if Luke started it?" Helen interrupted.

"I think he was trying to find out what Luke was capable of. I told him no one knows who set it, but that was everyone's theory at the time." Keener laid down his fish knife, avoiding her eyes. "Look, I didn't like Luke. I've made no secret of that. He came into my brother and Patsy's life, and he turned it upside down. He got between them. My brother was never a very confident man. He struggled with a lot of self-doubts. Luke was bigger and stronger than him, he was a better painter than him, and when Bertie realized Luke had got between him and Patsy, he was crushed. That's something I'll never forgive Luke for."

"He asked about the baby too," Helen said. "He asked if it was Luke's."

Amanda's excitement grew. "What did you tell him?"

"I told him it was none of his business," Keener said. "I wanted my brother's memory to retain some dignity. To be honest, I never thought Patsy was right for him. Any one of several men could have been the father. But my brother ... well, he took that love to the grave."

"Actually, it *may* have been his business," Amanda said slowly. Her heart was pounding. Tag had been digging, and it looked as if he'd uncovered the truth. "I believe Tag is that baby."

They both stared at her. Helen's jaw dropped, and Keener blinked rapidly several times before recognition dawned in his eyes. He wagged his finger at Helen. "I should have seen that. There was always something about Tag that niggled at me. The eyes. The set of the mouth. Didn't I say he reminds me of someone?" He paused, his eyes narrowing. "But I haven't seen Luke in years, and he and Tag are so different. Luke always looked like he was trying to dissolve into his own shadow. Tag is a confident, seasoned man who looks like he's been through hell and come out the other side." He shook his head in wonder. "Wow, Luke and Patsy's baby. Patsy always had a soft spot for Luke, protected him, stood up for him. For all her wildness, she had a maternal streak. So that cute, little, bald butterball that Patsy never let out of her sight is Tag!"

Amanda nodded. "I think so. Tag has been trying to find out his origin story. That's a lovely memory that you can share with him sometime."

Helen set aside her paring knife and came to stand by Keener, hands on her hips. "I think you should tell her the rest."

He whipped his head back and forth. "No. It's bad enough I hinted Luke might have started the fire."

"You let him believe that?" Helen's lips tightened. "Not only did Luke not set the fire, but he saved the baby when Bertie —"

"Please, Helen! No one knows for sure what happened."

"*I* know!" She flushed, breathing hard. "Luke could only save one of them, so he wrapped the baby in his clothes and ran."

Keener stared at her, agape. "What?"

She bowed her head. "I've never told anyone that. Everybody was so sure it was Luke, and you ..." She cast Keener a fleeting glance. "You were so upset for Bertie. I was just a kid ... but I remember it, clear as day."

Keener was still staring at her, half a century of unspoken secrets quivering between them. Amanda didn't press them further. Keener had already told her he suspected his brother might have caused the fire in a fit of jealous rage. An action of a second that could never be called back. But if Tag believed that his father was responsible for his mother's death and for his own placement in the foster system, that could break the fence he himself had described that corralled his anger safely out of reach.

He needed to know that his father had, in fact, saved his life.

CHAPTER TWENTY

Amanda spent the afternoon driving around town, checking with water taxi drivers down at the docks and asking Nancy whether she'd seen Tag. To no avail. However, Nancy didn't look shocked when Amanda said Tag might be Luke's son. They were sitting on Nancy's patio, sipping tea and enjoying a rare lull in customer traffic. Nancy's shoulders relaxed, as if a burden had been lifted.

Amanda cocked her head thoughtfully. "You knew that already, didn't you? You recognized the resemblance that first day at the café. Were you ever going to tell me?"

"It wasn't my story to tell." Nancy studied her teacup as if weighing her words. "It wasn't easy for Luke. Bertie was the man who took him in and helped him through some very rough times. Whatever Luke's problems, he always had a strong sense of right and wrong."

"But maybe in a weak moment? Lots of things can happen under the influence of drugs. Weed and alcohol both lower inhibitions, not to mention what LSD and magic mushrooms might do. Would they even know what they were doing?"

Nancy looked skeptical. "Luke was a shy kid, straitlaced in a naive way. Not what you'd call worldly."

It was Amanda's turn to be dubious. "I think Vietnam opened his eyes pretty quickly. The drugs flowed freely there too, and sex was standard currency with the locals." *As it still is in many parts of the world*, she thought wryly.

Nancy shrugged. "It was almost certainly Patsy's doing, not his, because unlike Luke, she was worldly way beyond her years. She liked to … sample widely."

Amanda remembered what Keener had said about Bertie's self-doubts. "And Bertie didn't mind?"

"Well, it was the way it was." She chuckled. "Still is, in some circles. Free love was part of the religion. Besides, Bertie didn't know the half of it. He was off in Tofino or Ucluelet much of the time, peddling his paintings to make a buck or two." She cocked her head as if rifling through her memories. "They were an odd pair, really. I think Bertie believed he'd hit the jackpot when Patsy agreed to marry him. Out of all the guys she could have had, she chose him. It gave his ego a huge boost."

"Why *did* she choose him?"

Nancy looked at her with a grim smile. "Oldest reason in the world. It might have been the dawning of the Age of Aquarius, but bottom line, she was pregnant, and she needed a decent breadwinner. Bertie was one of the few guys in the commune who was seriously trying to earn money. He was a hell of a better bargain than Luke, that's for sure, with his voices and his panic attacks."

Amanda gazed into the distance, barely seeing the other patrons or the birds flitting in the nearby bushes. A picture was emerging of the complex web surrounding Tag's birth. Had Luke suspected the baby might be his, and if so, how had he felt when Patsy instead chose a reliable money source over a sensitive but damaged artist?

She skirted that uncomfortable question. "But I understand it was Luke who rescued the baby from the fire."

"Is that so?"

"Yet three days later he's found wandering the street alone in a psychotic state. Did he bring the baby back to Bertie? Or just leave him on someone's doorstep?"

Nancy began collecting up their plates and teacups. "I'm not comfortable discussing this further behind his back. Luke is a private man who's been through a lot, and he should be the one to tell you these things. But I will say, even at his most strung out, Luke was always an honourable man."

Nancy moved briskly and methodically, but the slight tremor in her hands betrayed her. There was a bond between her and Luke, one that had been forged at least fifty years ago in the commune. It was no accident that she was the only one he trusted with his paintings. Had she also been the one he'd entrusted the baby to during his headlong, panicked flight from the fire?

Amanda thought back to the paintings in Luke's studio. The ones of children were tucked into remote corners or stacked against the walls. "He painted a lot of children. Children running through the field, children crying —"

"Yes, and those rarely sold." Nancy turned toward the restaurant, dishes in hand. "He did paint happier children, and when those became popular, he stopped doing them. Perverse bugger. Almost like he didn't want to be a success. But the children were all dark-haired and brown-eyed. Not blue-eyed and blond like Patsy or ginger like him."

Dark-eyed and brown-haired like the children in Vietnam, Amanda thought. Poor man, so tormented by his guilt and failure that he wouldn't even profit from their memory. She sighed. The sun was sinking behind the trees toward the ocean, lighting the sky with a soft luminescence. Perhaps Tag had returned from his mystery trip by now. She thanked Nancy, asked her to tell Tag she was looking for him, and headed back toward the Silver Surf B&B.

On her way back up Campbell Street, she passed the handsome new glass-and-timber building that housed the RCMP. On a whim, she turned in. The police needed to know all the information she had uncovered. The place felt virtually empty, but Mr. Sensitive was manning the front desk, and he grinned at her cheerfully. Her enthusiasm faded.

"Another body, Ms. Doucette?"

"Working on it," she shot back. Probably not a wise retort when talking to a cop, not all of whom had Chris's sense of humour. "Is the sergeant around?"

"Nope. Out catching our man." His grin widened. "Can I help you?"

She hoped that was a generic reference rather than one about Luke. "I'd like to talk to him about some information I've learned that might be relevant."

He raised one lazy eyebrow. "What information?"

Reluctantly she plunged ahead. "About the connection between Luke Lafferty and Richard and DeeDee Vali, and about —" She broke off. Mr. Sensitive's second eyebrow had joined his first, and she could almost see the glee emanating from him. A juicy piece of intel, and he'd be the one to deliver it. Not only would he probably skip the nuances, but he'd also make Luke look even guiltier than before.

"Actually," she said, "it's complicated. I'll write it down and try to catch Sergeant Saint-Laurent in the morning."

"He'll be back out at dawn," Mr. Sensitive said, leaning forward as if to reach through the Plexiglas and grab her. "Assisting —"

She was already breezing out the door. "That's okay, I'm an early riser."

Before she headed back to the Silver Surf, she detoured to pick up fish and chips from the Wildside Grill and returned to her room just as the sun was dipping into the ocean, casting a trail of orange sparks across the rolling surf. She knocked on Tag's door, but there was no answer. After feeding Kaylee and letting her out to romp in the bush, she settled at the table on her terrace to enjoy her dinner.

Somewhere in the bushes, Kaylee barked. Amanda looked up but saw no sign of her. The bushes were in deep shadow, but she heard the rustling of leaves and a cascade of stones. Fear shot through her. There were frequent signs warning of cougars and bears in the area. Rationally, she knew the dangers were minimal, because both species were shy and avoided humans, but there were exceptions. And an innocent dog might be a tempting dinner.

She had to call Kaylee several times before the dog came trotting back, looking alert and wary.

"We can't have you encountering critters, princess," Amanda said, snapping on her leash and tying her to the chair while she continued her dinner. Kaylee kept staring into the bushes, and the occasional growl bubbled in her throat, but when Amanda strained her eyes, she could see nothing. Finally, too unnerved to sit out in the deepening dusk, she picked up her plate and retreated inside to settle on her bed with her laptop. Almost immediately, a video call came in.

All her fears evaporated as Chris's smiling face filled her screen. "Hey you," she said.

They exchanged affectionate greetings before his expression sobered. "I'm worried about you, honey. I don't want you to keep trying to see Luke."

"Chris, I'm safely here in Tofino! Not going anywhere. But why the sudden hard line?"

"I'm ... just worried, darling."

"Why?"

"The police have uncovered some things."

"What things?"

"I can't tell you. I'm sorry. It's part of the investigation. But will you trust me if I say he's a person of interest, and the police have evidence that puts him in the frame?"

Anxiety mixed with her annoyance. "Is it about his relationship to Richard and DeeDee Vali?"

His eyes widened. "What do you know?"

"What do *you* know?"

"Amanda, stop playing games. This guy may be a killer. What do you know about his relationship to the Valis?"

She gave herself a shake. Chris was right. She knew she was in over her head, and she'd been on the brink of turning all her information and suspicions over to Sergeant Saint-Laurent anyway. Who better to tell than Chris, whose judgment and sensitivity she trusted as much as her own?

So she told him. He listened without interruption while she told him about the commune, Patsy, Bertie, the baby and its unknown father, the fire that killed Patsy, and the subsequent death of Bertie. She described Bertie's connection to Keener, and Helen's admission that Bertie, not Luke, set the fire that killed Patsy. She told him about the mystery man who had called Patsy's family inquiring about the identity of the father and the fate of the baby.

And finally, hesitantly and reluctantly, she told him about Tag.

Only then did Chris erupt. "Jesus fucking Christ! Don't tell me he's right smack in the middle of this?"

"Yes, and I can't check any of it out, because he has disappeared."

"You have to report this, Amanda."

"I'm going to, but till now it's been all conjecture. The birthdates, people's recollections and suspicions ..."

"Tag's disappearance is real."

"I don't even know he's disappeared. I haven't seen him since yesterday, but he isn't tethered to me. He's free to go off and make his own plans."

Chris's forehead crinkled. She could see him trying to tease apart the solid evidence from the background details that, although crucial to the whole picture, were mostly third-hand speculation.

"I still think the detectives have to know. Speculation or not, those are leads they can follow up on."

"I know." As Amanda wrestled with her reluctance, she glanced out her patio door at the last streaks of coral and mauve glowing through the trees. Against that backdrop, a shadow moved. She sat up with a gasp. Blinked. The shadow was gone, flitting by so quickly that she wasn't even sure it was real.

"Amanda, what is it?" Chris's voice was urgent with alarm.

"I don't know. Maybe nothing." She glanced at Kaylee, who was staring fixedly out the window. "I thought I saw something outside."

"Something? Like what?"

Fear made her short. "I don't know, Chris! A shape, maybe watching me. Earlier too. Probably a bear curious about my fish and chips. I'm just spooked from finding that body and then Pim getting shot."

"Darling, listen to me. Please take this seriously. Tomorrow morning, I want you to get in your car and drive straight back to Victoria and stay there."

"My tour starts —"

"Until your tour starts. And find yourself another counsellor, for God's sake. I'm getting on a plane tomorrow. This is serious. Please, please, darling."

To her shock, his voice quavered, and his eyes glistened. She reached out her fingertips to touch him. "Honey, I'll be fine. And I promise I'll go back to Victoria as soon as I can."

CHAPTER TWENTY-ONE

Amanda tossed and turned half the night, listening to the rhythmic swish of the ocean surf on the rocks below and attuned for any sound that didn't belong. A footstep, a dislodged rock, a snapped twig.

There was nothing. She rose at first dawn, hoping to catch Sergeant Saint-Laurent, and after feeding Kaylee and grabbing a coffee from the cart, she headed out toward her car. The Silver Surf B&B was just beyond the town, perched on a point and surrounded by hardy Sitka spruce that clung to outcrops of black rock. In a shallow dip beside the gravel parking lot, ferns and salal bushes bright with little pink and white flowers had gained a foothold.

The flowers on one of the branches quivered. Amanda froze. Kaylee was alert, staring.

"Hello?" Amanda called. The bush swayed gently, but she could see nothing. It could be a cougar or bear or just a squirrel foraging for food. She could ignore it, or she could try to find out whether someone was spying on her.

She headed back into the B&B, cut through her room and out her patio door. "If you can keep quiet, you can come with me," she whispered to Kaylee, who cocked her head as if trying to understand. Together they crept out into the bush and circled back to approach the salal bushes from the other side. Halfway along, she came upon a flattened, mossy patch. Kaylee snuffled around the edge to uncover a rolled-up sleeping bag and a large backpack tucked beneath salmonberry bushes. Amanda stared at it, frowning. She knew expensive, scarce accommodation had forced many to sleep rough when they couldn't find a room, and illegal camps had become a problem. Was that what she was looking at? Or was it something more sinister?

She picked up the backpack, which was stuffed with clothes and weighted down with a couple of solid items. One felt like a laptop, the other like a … She sucked in her breath and dropped the bag. A gun.

Signalling Kaylee to stay at heel, she crept forward, praying the rustle of leaves would not alert her watcher. The Silver Surf's parking lot was in sight now, as was the back of the salal bush. There was nobody there. She turned slowly in place, her eyes sifting the changing shapes of green and brown.

Kaylee barked, and Amanda whirled around just as a figure stepped out from behind a tree trunk not five feet away.

Amanda's heart rate spiked. "You!"

DeeDee held up her hand. "I'm not here to cause trouble."

"You've been spying on me!"

DeeDee glanced around nervously. The B&B was quiet. "I have to talk to you."

Amanda's heart rate gradually slowed. The woman looked rough. Her clothing was dishevelled and muddy, her face and hands caked with dirt. But she had no weapon in her hand, and her blue eyes were pleading.

"What do you want?" Amanda demanded.

"I want you to tell me where Luke is."

"I don't know where he is."

A car rumbled by on the nearby road, and DeeDee shrank back. "Let's go down on the beach. Too many eyes around here."

Amanda pictured the beach at the bottom of the bluff. Beautiful, peaceful, and deserted. Too deserted. "No, we can talk right over there in your hideout."

"Don't fuck with me. You know where he is."

Amanda had started to walk to the hideout. "I don't."

"Then your Indian friend does. He was taking you to him."

They stood in the small, mossy clearing, glaring at each other, neither giving way. Amanda felt anger settling in. "I have no idea. You shot him before we could go anywhere."

"I didn't mean to do that. I thought he was a bear."

"He's a good, kind man, and he's fighting for his life now."

DeeDee's gaze flickered, and she raised her hands. "I've never been in a forest like that. I was spooked. I saw a brown shape and ... I just fired."

"It was a perfect shot to the head."

"That's how I was trained."

Amanda stared her down in silence, weighing the explanation. She knew from Chris that police were trained to aim for the chest to maximize their chances of disabling the adversary. Soldiers were probably taught the same, but she decided not to challenge her.

"Then you have to turn yourself in and tell that to the police. They are looking for you."

DeeDee whipped her head back and forth.

"Why not?"

"What chance would I have? I'm in a foreign country, I don't know your laws."

Amanda bit back a sarcastic retort about Canada recently getting rid of the guillotine. "They're perfectly reasonable laws. Innocent until proven guilty and all that."

"But ..." DeeDee faltered and looked at her hands. "I smuggled a gun into the country, and I shot a local man — an Indian — on his own land. I'll be railroaded."

"That's nonsense. You can't escape the consequences, but I can help you."

DeeDee shook her head. "No. I need to find Luke, and then I need to get the hell out of here."

"Why are you looking for Luke?"

DeeDee squared her shoulders, her equilibrium returning. "Because he killed my brother."

"What makes you think that?"

"Because he's running a scam. Richie went to see him, and I bet he figured it out."

Amanda frowned. "What are you talking about?"

DeeDee's expression grew shuttered. "Doesn't matter."

"It does if you're going to accuse Luke of murder. Is this about Vietnam?"

DeeDee stiffened. "Vietnam? What the hell does that have to do with it?"

"Because Luke was in Vietnam, and he went AWOL. He's your uncle, isn't he?"

"That's absolute bull. Our uncle is dead. I told Richie so. Dad's furious. Dad was in Vietnam too, and he knows his brother died. Our uncle was a war hero. This guy is an imposter trying to muscle in."

The notion of Luke contriving such an elaborate scheme was so ludicrous that Amanda almost laughed. She forced herself to be patient. "Luke has lived a reclusive lifestyle for fifty years. Why would he want to muscle in now?"

"That's none of your damn business."

Amanda abandoned patience. "It became my business the minute you shot at us."

DeeDee stared at the ground and then raised her eyes to gaze out toward the ocean. Anywhere but straight ahead. "Our grandfather died last year, and the will is still working its way through the process. There's a hell of a lot of money. The family vultures are out."

Amanda considered the implications. The idea that Luke even knew about the money, let alone wanted it, was outrageous, but there was no way DeeDee and Richie could know that. She felt a chill. People had killed for far less. "DeeDee, why was Richie really looking for Luke?"

DeeDee threw her hands up in the air in exasperation. "Because the fool really wanted to know. He wanted to see for himself."

Footsteps crunched on the gravel nearby, and Kaylee barked. DeeDee broke off, growing rigid in alarm, and snatched up her belongings. "Gotta go."

"Wait! Where are you going? How can I reach you?"

"Nowhere." DeeDee's face hardened. "If I have something to say to you, I'll find you."

Amanda climbed in her car, locked the doors, and sat for a few minutes, stroking Kaylee's fur and breathing deeply. Sensing her distress, the dog nuzzled her hand gently.

The woman's intensity had unnerved her. What did she really want, and why had she brought a gun with her? She seemed determined to find Luke. Was it just to find out the truth about her brother's death or to avenge it?

As she thought back over the conversation, a sudden shiver raced through her. Pim! DeeDee thought Pim knew where Luke was. Pim was a tough, savvy guy, but right now he was lying in a hospital bed, exposed and vulnerable.

She revved her car, groping for Sergeant Saint-Laurent's card with her free hand as she peeled out of the parking lot. He would be out on the search by now, but surely someone would answer the main number.

Mr. Sensitive. Her heart sank when she heard his voice, but this was no time to be picky. She filled him in on DeeDee's visit and her fear that she might go after Pim to find out where Luke was.

"Pim doesn't know where Luke is," the officer said. "Or if he does, he's closed up tighter than a clam. Believe me, we've tried."

"You're limited to legal means. She's not. And she has a gun."

"There's a security guard at the hospital."

"Are they armed?"

Mr. Sensitive was silent a moment. "I'll run it by the sarge," he finally muttered. "And we'll send a unit out to the B&B. You learn anything else, you let us know."

She thanked him, tossed the phone on the seat, and careened around the corner. The hospital was only a few blocks away, a boxy, one-storey structure that looked more like a temporary storage facility than a modern medical facility. Only the helipad on the lawn beside it and the sign outside provided clues.

She was dismayed to see no one manning the nursing station and no security guard in sight. She went down the hall peering into rooms and was halfway along before she was accosted by a nurse with a friendly but no-nonsense expression. She asked about Pim and explained her connection. The nurse's face lit up with a smile, and she pointed to a closed door back up the hall.

"We put him in the room right beside the nursing station so we could keep an eye on him. He really should have been transferred to Victoria, but luckily he's been doing really well. He may go home in a couple of days."

"Has he had any visitors?"

"Lots."

Amanda's concern spiked. "Anyone unusual?"

"Just villagers. He's a popular guy."

"Anyone inquiring by phone how he's doing?"

The nurse looked at her oddly. "Well, you've been calling."

Amanda pasted on a genial smile. "Besides me."

"There was one strange thing. A woman called wanting to know if he was conscious and able to talk."

"What did you tell her?"

"Nothing. Patient confidentiality. The strange thing is she said she was you, but I knew you'd called not long before."

"Thank you. I'm worried about that woman, so keep a close eye. I've alerted the police."

A bell sounded, and the nurse looked up the hall. "I've got to go, but you go ahead in to see Pim. He's awake and bored. We don't want him walking out of here before his discharge."

Pim was sitting up in bed, propped up by pillows in a darkened room. His laptop was open on the bed table in front of him, along with the remains of breakfast. Other than the bandage around his head and purple circles around his eyes, he looked his usual self. His craggy face crinkled in a rare smile at the sight of her, and he pushed his laptop aside.

"I'm not supposed to look at this thing for too long, but I'm not a guy to lie around." They chatted briefly about how he was doing before he sobered. "Thank you. I owe you."

"Do you remember what happened?"

"Some is coming back to me. Not the rescue or the first night in hospital."

Amanda hesitated. Pim was recovering and needed to avoid stress, but he held answers no one else did. She ventured carefully ahead. "You remember being shot?"

He nodded, trying to conceal a grimace of pain from the movement. "I remember the blow. Lucky it cracked the skull. The doctor said that saved me from a worse injury."

"Do you think she shot you on purpose?"

He squinted toward the darkened window. "I didn't see her till it was too late. I was behind a bush, and when I came around, bam. It could have been an accident."

"She says she thought you were a bear."

He grinned. "That's a new one for me."

"But it's possible she shot too fast?"

"Yeah, that's what I told the police."

Amanda pictured the scenario. It was possible, especially for a soldier trained to shoot at the first hint of danger because the enemy didn't give second chances. "Pim, she's still looking for Luke, and she's on a mission. She thinks he killed Richie."

Pim grunted his objection.

"You saw Luke after Richie's death. You talked to him, maybe the only person who has. Did he tell you what happened?"

"He hardly spoke."

"Did he know Richie was dead?"

Pim nodded slowly. "He was very upset. Panicked. When he gets that way, he goes silent, like he doesn't know you're there. He goes into himself."

"Did he come to the village to see you?"

"No, he sent me a message."

"How?"

"He has his ways."

She let that slide. "Okay. But before this happened, he wanted to see me. Do you know why?"

"No. Said you would understand."

She felt a chill. Understand what? What had he done that she alone would understand? "Do you think ... he might have ..." She broke off, not wanting to put the thought into words. "Do you know what he meant?"

"He just said something bad happened. Bad, bad, he said many times. He said he had to hide."

"Bad, bad." Dear God. Amanda tried to keep her voice calm, barely daring to pose the next question. "The police are looking for him. Worse, DeeDee is looking for him. He has a shotgun. Do you think he's dangerous?"

"Everyone is dangerous, pushed too far. A bear will avoid you, but if he's trapped ..." He paused, and his expression shuttered as if at a dark thought.

"What?"

"Sometimes he goes someplace else in his head. His visions are not spiritual; they don't show him the path. They're like a nightmare pulling him back in the past. To the jungle in Vietnam. He knows how to disappear and pop up somewhere else. Not like a spirit, but like a guerrilla. He will set booby traps."

Her resolve strengthened. "Search and detection techniques have changed a lot since Vietnam. For everyone's safety, especially his, he needs to come in."

"What for? To be put in a cage?"

"We don't know that he's done anything wrong yet. I want to stop things from getting worse." She reached out to touch his arm. "Pim, tell me how to send him a message. At least give him the choice to talk to me."

Pim leaned his head back on his pillow with a sigh. He suddenly looked very weary, and she felt a stab of guilt. It was a heavy burden for a man still recovering. She gathered her things, preparing to leave.

"The police are mostly on the inner side of the island," he said unexpectedly. "He'll use the other side. There is a creek that runs down from Mount Flores to the beach not far from where Richie's body was found. Not at Cow Bay but a smaller beach farther up. A path leads up beside the creek, and maybe a kilometre up, there's a culturally modified tree. An old red cedar, maybe eight hundred years old, with a plank cut from its side. If you go ..."

He paused and shut his eyes as if trying to picture it. "I'll draw you a map."

She fished her notebook from her knapsack and tore off a sheet. His hand was shaky and uncertain, but eventually he drew her a rough sketch.

"Call Gil to take you. He should be in the village today, and he can use my brother's boat."

"Does Gilligan know where this hiding place is?"

"Nobody knows but me."

Amanda was full of apprehension as she thanked him and headed out of the hospital. As she was walking to her car, Nash came up on his bike and braked in front of her. She stopped, startled to see him out of context.

"What are you doing here?" she blurted, then flushed. "Sorry, none of my business."

He grinned. "Visiting my uncle. Thank you for taking care of him."

"Pim's your uncle?" It hadn't occurred to her to wonder where Nash was from or what his background was. He was just her kayak guide.

"Everyone in Maaqtusiis is related." He was reaching for the hospital door when he turned. "Have you heard from Tag at all?"

"Tag? Not in a couple of days. Why? Is there a problem?"

Nash's brows knitted. "Not exactly. It's just he's supposed to check in once a day so we know he's okay, but he missed last night."

Kaylee, watching them from the car, began to bark in outrage. Amanda moved toward her car. "Wait a minute. What are you talking about? What's he doing?"

"He's out on a solo paddle. He didn't know how long he'd be, because he wanted to test out a particular route through Clayoquot Sound. We weren't thrilled he was going alone. He's an experienced paddler, but the tides and currents in the sound are like nowhere else. He said you were too busy, and anyway he wanted to do it solo. So we outfitted him for four nights and provided him with some safety gear."

Amanda tried to make sense of this latest twist. What the hell was Tag up to? They'd already decided on the Broken Islands kayak route. "He hasn't answered any of my texts or phone calls," she said. "Where in Clayoquot Sound was he planning to go?"

"He was going to go up to Hot Springs and try to circumnavigate Flores Island. Climb Mount Flores if he had time. The outer shore can be damn tricky in any small craft, as you know. And there's another storm in the forecast."

"I'm headed up that way now, so I'll keep an eye out for him. What colour is his kayak?"

"Neon green." Nash flashed his cheerful, ready grin. "He wasn't thrilled with that, but we insisted. We wanted him to be visible."

CHAPTER TWENTY-TWO

Amanda had just finished her call to Gilligan and was on her way down to meet him at the wharf when she spotted activity around the Tofino police station. RCMP officers in full ERT uniform were coming and going, heading out in vehicles and on foot down toward the wharf. They moved with an intensity and speed that suggested urgency. As she approached the door, Mr. Sensitive burst out, forcing her to dive out of the way. Without even noticing her, he headed for the parking lot.

Amanda's heart accelerated with a mixture of apprehension and excitement. Inside, she found Janine on the phone at the front desk. Amanda shouted through the Plexiglas divider. "What's going on? Have they found him?"

Janine held up her finger, finished her call, and let Amanda inside. "No."

"But something has happened."

"There's been a development, yes."

"Is it about Luke? Have they had a tip?"

"Luke is still at large, as is Ms. Vali, so the risk to the public remains. That's all I can say."

Amanda stifled her frustration. After all her time with Chris, she knew the rules. Janine could not comment, even if she wanted to. Even saying as much as she had could be grounds for disciplinary action. She took a deep breath and steeled herself. It was time.

"I have learned some information I think the police should have."

"I can't leave the desk," said Janine, pulling out a piece of paper. "Can you give me the highlights and write the details in a witness statement?"

"Luke has a shotgun. It's the same one he's always had."

Janine grew rigid. "What kind?"

"I don't know guns. Old. Double-barrelled, break action, I know that much."

"How long have you known this?"

"Since ... since the day after he disappeared."

Swearing, Janine reached for her police radio.

"Wait, there's more. There may be another man on the island looking for Luke."

"Yes, we know about him."

Amanda was startled. "You know about Tag?"

It was Janine's turn for surprise. "Who's Tag?"

"His name is Michael McTaggart. He's a counsellor from Victoria who's working with me on the tour. But he took off on his own in a kayak a couple of days ago, and I'm pretty sure he's looking for Luke."

Janine had recovered and was staring at Amanda suspiciously. "What are his intentions?"

"I don't know. But what I suspect is that he's just learned Luke is his father."

"Luke?" Janine's mouth gaped in disbelief. "Luke! That crazy old man?"

"It happened a long time ago, obviously, when Luke lived down here in the Wreck Bay commune. McTaggart is the right age. But I don't think Luke knows about him."

Janine was muttering as she typed into her computer. "McTaggart, Michael, date of birth 10-3-1971. He's done time. Assault. Fucking hell. Does he have a firearm too?"

"I have no idea."

"Do you have any other surprises for me?"

"Well, I already told the officer here that DeeDee Vali waylaid me early this morning. She's been on the lam, living rough, but she's still determined to find Luke. And she does have a gun."

Janine grabbed her radio again. "I've got to call this in ASAP to alert the team. Luke's firearm makes it a whole other alert level." Amanda moved to leave. "Wait! The witness statement!"

"I'll come by and fill it out later," Amanda said. "I've got something I need to do first."

"What?" Janine shouted, but Amanda was already out the door. Her heart was pounding. She'd had to tell the police about the shotgun and about Tag, but although she had no regrets, the implications terrified her. Now there were three people running around the island with unknown motives. At least two of them had guns and knew how to use them. After the life Tag had lived, she didn't put it past him to have a gun stashed away somewhere too. Probably illegal.

As she drove down to meet Gilligan, she replayed the conversation with Janine, worrying that she'd set the wrong tone and sent the police into high alert. Something Janine said stopped her short. *Yes, we know who he is.* In her rush, Amanda had assumed she meant Tag, but Janine's surprised reaction belied that. *Who's Tag?*

Was she expecting someone else?

After standing in line for twenty minutes at the Tim Hortons in Toronto's Pearson Airport, Chris managed to buy a breakfast sandwich and large dark roast coffee before racing to the departure gate. The waiting area was packed and all the seats taken up with people or their bags, so he propped himself against a column and tried to eat. He wolfed the sandwich down as fast as he could while the line filed slowly toward the counter.

He had a long, tedious travel day ahead of him. He had sent Amanda his arrival information, but he hadn't heard back from her. There was no time to call her now. Once he had stored his bags in the overhead bin and settled into his seat, he took out his phone for one last check if she'd responded. Instead, a text from Nihls popped up. *Are you free to call? Got some news!*

Too late, he thought with dismay as the announcements came on and the plane taxied from the gate. It would have to wait until he landed in Vancouver, a frustratingly long five hours from now.

Clouds were lurking along the western horizon, and the wind was already picking up as Amanda waited on the dock for Gilligan to arrive. She wasn't sure her idea would work, but she could think of no other solution. Pim had said no one else in the village knew its location, so if Luke knew Pim had been shot, he might not even check their secret message drop. She'd asked Gilligan whether anyone else in the village had heard from Luke, but no one had.

She felt frustratingly out of touch. There had still been no word from Tag, and his cellphone went directly to voice mail, probably because he was out of range. While waiting for Gilligan to arrive, she sat on the edge of the dock and watched a couple of seals frolicking about while she phoned Chris. She wanted to update him on her meeting with the RCMP, but he didn't answer his phone either. She left a brief, cheery message that she had told the police all she knew, and it was now in their hands. She knew she would be out of range once she got to Flores Island, and she didn't want him fretting about her safety. She would see him soon enough.

Her last call was to Matthew. She wanted to ask him to find out more about Tag's background, specifically his conviction for assault and any other evidence of violence. But he, too, didn't answer his phone. After leaving him a long, rambling message and telling him Tag was still missing, she hung up in frustration.

"Where is everyone?" she asked Kaylee. The dog, fascinated by the seals, barely gave Amanda a glance. "Oh, that's great," Amanda muttered. "Ignore me too."

A small, steel-hulled ocean skiff came down the harbour, dodging a seaplane and a fleet of kayaks as it steered toward to dock. The small, skinny driver stood at the console, barely able to see over the instruments, but his smile was a welcoming sight. Suddenly she didn't feel so alone.

Soon they were bouncing over the swells, threading through the inlet and north past Vargas and Bartlett Islands on their way to Flores. Gilligan stood tall at the wheel, scanning the water with a practised eye and glancing uneasily to the west. Even Kaylee, perched in the bow, had flattened her ears. "A storm's on its way," he said, "so we better not stay long." The tide was coming in, increasing the risk of dangerous seas, and he was watching for submerged shoals as well as for the mouth of the creek that would guide their landing. As they passed beautiful swaths of white sand beaches, Amanda recognized the rocky headland where Richie's body had lain. She suppressed a shiver.

"I'll get as close to shore as possible," Gilligan shouted over the sound of the engine. "With the tide coming in, we won't get stuck."

He eased off the throttle and pointed ahead to a creek at the far end of a small, curved beach. The boat slowed to a low growl and rocked in the swell as he steered it toward the far end of the beach.

"I'll beach it way over in the protection of the curve, and we'll walk from there. My uncle would kill me if I wrecked his boat. Hang on!"

He ran to the stern to raise the motor, and the boat ground up on the sand with a jolt. While he secured the anchors, Amanda climbed down the ladder and jumped into the ankle-deep surf. Kaylee whined and peered anxiously over the edge.

"I'll make a seadog out of you yet," Amanda said as she reached up to lift her down.

Once they were safely on the beach, Gilligan eyed the high-tide mark doubtfully. "I hope I can trust those new anchors, or this boat is going to float away."

Amanda was already walking up the beach toward the tree line. Pim had said the path was beside the creek, but as she scanned the impenetrable bush, she could see no sign of a path. Pushing aside the shrubs and overhanging spruce boughs didn't help.

Gilligan came up behind her, casting frequent glances over his shoulder at the boat and the brooding sky. His anxiety was palpable. "Anything?"

"It will be here somewhere," she muttered as she guided Kaylee over, hoping the dog would pick up the trail. To her relief, Kaylee immediately poked her head through the underbrush and pulled ahead. Amanda turned to Gilligan. "I want you to stay with the boat and make sure it's okay."

He shook his head. "Uncle Pim would kill me if I let you go alone."

"It's only a kilometre hike. It shouldn't take long."

"This isn't a stroll through town, Amanda. Hiking a kilometre through that bush could take hours."

I don't spend a lot of time strolling through town, she wanted to protest but thought better of it. "That's why you need to stay with the boat. I'll be fine. I have my compass, my whistle, and my bear spray. This way, if you have to, you can move the boat. I'll feel better knowing our way out of here is secure." She didn't feel nearly as confident as she pretended, but Pim had been nervous about others knowing about the secret drop, and she was afraid that if by chance Luke was watching, he would freak out at the sight of another person.

Kaylee was snuffling the ground and tugging on her leash. Amanda checked her watch. "If I'm not back in three hours, you can start up the trail."

Gilligan looked from her to the boat, his brow creased in distress. It took some persuading, but he ultimately capitulated after making her promise to blast her whistle the instant she sensed trouble.

"And don't get lost! Everything looks the same in the forest. Mark your path and make sure you don't take a wrong turn. At the worst, follow the creek back downhill, and it will bring you here."

Taking a deep breath, Amanda plunged forward and was immediately enveloped by the forest. Kaylee kept her nose to the ground, zigzagging a track, and Amanda let her lead, keeping a close eye on her for signs of alarm.

They made slow progress, crawling over giant, moss-covered logs, ducking under prickly spruce branches, and squelching through soggy ferns. Nearby, the creek swished by, invisible beneath the lush grasses and ferns. "This hardly qualifies as a path," Amanda muttered to herself, but Kaylee pulled ahead, her tail high and wagging.

In the canopy high overhead, the birds followed her progress, and crows flapped from tree to tree. Ravens heckled and treetops swayed in the wind. Sunlight and blue sky still peeked through the branches, but Amanda knew darker clouds were gathering offshore.

She panted and cursed as she clambered up steep slopes over slippery rocks and clung to branches to keep from falling. She glanced at her phone. Forty-five minutes. How far had she come? How far could this culturally modified tree be?

Twenty minutes later, stopping on a mossy log to peer at Pim's shaky map, she noticed a massive red cedar soaring up out of the forest just up the slope. Over eight hundred years old, Pim had said, the largest one around. Surely that was it. With renewed heart, she resumed her climb and soon reached the base of the huge tree. Circling it, she found the long strip carefully carved out of one side, the way the Ahousaht harvested planks for building without killing the tree. Bingo.

She studied the map again. From here she was to turn a sharp left and walk two hundred paces to a small stream that flowed beneath an old stump. On that stump was a hemlock, and in its trunk was a small cache.

Kaylee was sniffing the air. Her excitement had given way to wariness. Amanda peered through the trees and lichen-draped branches but could see nothing. Like her, the forest seemed to be holding its breath. Reaching down to reassure the dog, she set off to count the paces.

Up ahead, a shadow flitted through the trees. Kaylee barked. Amanda gripped her bear spray and began to talk quietly as she moved forward. It seemed a long two hundred paces before she came to the stream trickling over the rocks and followed it up toward the cedar stump. She could see the hemlock now, draped like a ghoulish bride in lichen. "Please let there be a message," she murmured as she slogged through the damp to the tree.

Kaylee barked again, her gaze fixed on the forest on the other side of the stream. But her body conveyed not so much alarm as puzzlement, and her tail wagged tentatively.

Amanda could see nothing moving. She circled the hemlock and groped through the moss and lichen to feel the small hole hidden behind. Her relief turned to dismay when she stuck her hand in. The cache was empty. Luke had left no message.

Plan B. She opened her knapsack and pulled out the note she had written. She had wrapped it in a compostable doggie bag to keep it dry. *Luke, Pim sent me. He is in hospital but recovering. Can we meet? Leave me a note where and when.*

She shoved the bag into the hole and straightened the moss and small plants over it again. Kaylee was still staring expectantly at the forest. As Amanda turned to leave, she felt as if eyes were watching her. She shook herself. *Calm down, Amanda.* Kaylee isn't worried, and whatever it is, it's keeping its distance. More curious than hostile.

Nonetheless, she picked up the pace as she slipped and stumbled back over to the ancient cedar and started down the creek path. Her heart was hammering. Kaylee was sniffing cheerfully through the underbrush now, delighted with the outing. Fear slowly loosened its grip, and Amanda's stomach unknotted. She glanced at her phone. Nearly two and a half hours. Overhead, clouds were thickening, and the wind was rattling the branches. She strained to hear the hiss of surf. Finally, the forest thinned up ahead, and the pale ocean light peeked through. Relief washed over her. She was almost at the beach when a scrap of bright green in the distance caught her eye. She peered at it, then pawed her way through the bushes toward it, knowing what it was before she reached it.

A neon-green kayak, tucked in off the beach behind a screen of salal bushes.

CHAPTER TWENTY-THREE

The minute the plane touched down at Vancouver International Airport, Chris activated his phone. To his delight, a message from Amanda popped up. *I've told the Tofino RCMP everything I know,* it said, *and now it's out of my hands. See you tonight, love you.* Her phone went to voice mail, but even so, he breathed a sigh of relief. That was one worry out of the way.

He had some time to kill in the airport before his flight to Victoria. It had been a long, draining trip, and he still had one more leg and then a four-hour drive before he reached Tofino. By then he would have been awake almost twenty-four hours. He decided to treat himself to a proper sit-down lunch, maybe even a beer provided it didn't put him to sleep.

Inside the restaurant, he sat on a high stool at the bar and ordered fish tacos and a bottle of Corona. As he waited, he pulled out his phone to call Nihls.

"About time!" Travis exclaimed. "You guys run off your feet out there on the Rock?"

"Busier than you'd be up in Campbell River, I bet. What's this news? Have you caught Luke?"

"Nope. But his boat was found moored in a hidden inlet on the mainland across from Flores Island. There's nothing up there but rugged backcountry, and we'd never have spotted it if it hadn't been for a local fisherman."

"Luke will be right at home, then."

"Yeah, he will be. ERT has moved the search over there, but he's going to be a bitch to find. The forest is so thick, you can hardly see twenty feet in front of you, and the place is full of caves."

The server brought his Corona, and Chris took a deep, satisfying swig. "Have they at least found DeeDee Vali?"

"No, but we know she's been sleeping rough on the edge of town. But we found the boat she stole docked back at the small craft harbour. None of the water taxi or kayak companies have seen her, so we don't know what she's up to."

"Is she even still in the region? She might be trying to flee the country."

"Yep. RCMP and CBSA have been monitoring the borders in case she does try to slip back across into the US. So far, she hasn't, but the search did turn up another Vali who came across the border last week."

"Richie? Or was he already dead?"

"Nope." Travis chuckled. He was trying to drag out the suspense, but Chris could hear the excitement in his voice. "Three days before Richie died and five days before DeeDee herself crossed over, their old man came across the land border driving a fully loaded, heavy-duty Ram pickup with Texas plates. He came across not at the obvious Peace Arch crossing, but at Nighthawk, an obscure outpost in the middle of the mountains. He must think we don't have computers up here."

Chris tried to make sense of the twist. "Their father? *Before* Richie died?"

"Yep." Travis sounded triumphant. "The sequence is, Richie comes up, then five days later Pops comes across, three days later Richie dies, and two days after that, DeeDee shows up. She'd been notified of his death as his next of kin because no one could get hold of the father. In all probability because he was already up in Tofino."

"But he … I mean, surely he's not a suspect. He wouldn't kill his own son."

"How long you been a cop? He sneaks across an obscure crossing, and he's not responding to attempts to reach him. He has a cellphone, but it's still in Texas. If he has a new one for use in Canada, it's a burner. So we don't know where he fits in."

"Where's he staying?"

"Can't track that down either. Maybe in the cab of his truck, for all we know. It's a big wilderness if you want to hide."

His plate of tacos arrived. Chris picked out a juicy shrimp absent-mindedly as he mulled over possible scenarios. "Well, we know why DeeDee came up. Maybe the father wanted to meet Luke too. He was his brother, after all."

"To stop Richie from seeing him may be more likely," Travis said. "Since I sent you that message early this morning, some other things have come to light, courtesy of your girlfriend. The family doesn't believe Luke is the long-lost brother who disappeared in Vietnam. They insist that guy is dead. The father, Damon Vali, as much as witnessed it from his helicopter according to DeeDee. They think Luke is running a scam, out for their money."

Chris thought back over the details Amanda had shared about Luke. Fragile, sensitive, artistic, off the grid. "That doesn't sound like a man who has hidden out in the wilderness for half a century."

Travis grunted. "Like I said, how long you been a cop? But there *is* one other guy in the mix, and that's an ex-con from Victoria named Michael McTaggart. Seems he may be Luke's son, in which case he'd be in line for some money too. And nobody can find him either."

When Amanda emerged from the creek path onto the beach, Gilligan was standing on the bow of his boat, listening to a weather update. Gloomy clouds now pressed in, and the ocean was steely grey and angry. The tide was peaking, and Gilligan had moved the boat out to safety. He greeted her with a wave of relief.

"Just in time!" he shouted as he manoeuvred the boat closer to shore, trying to avoid the waves. "It may take slightly longer, but I want to take the inner channel to get back to town. It's more protected."

The boat pitched in the surf as Amanda waded out to grab the ladder and hoist Kaylee aboard. "That's good. I want to check out Luke's cove and the other side of the island anyway. I'm worried. It looks as if Tag is here somewhere."

Gilligan fought the wheel and throttle to keep the boat steady. "I'd prefer not to stop."

"Let's see if there's any sign of trouble at least," she said as she clambered up the ladder and pulled it up. "If we see anything, we can report it to the police search team. They're still on the inner side, right?"

Gilligan shook his head as he wheeled in the bow anchor. "They all took off up Millar Channel in a big hurry earlier."

Had they found Luke? "Do you know what happened?"

He shrugged as he reversed the boat away from the dangers of the shore. Within minutes, he had pointed it northward and gunned the engine, giving the rocky, unpredictable shoreline a wide berth.

Spray shot up as the bow slammed through the waves. She took out her binoculars to scan the land, but the boat pitched so much in the swells that she couldn't focus. Frustrated, she dug out her rain gear and went up to the bow to see more clearly. Out to the west, the ocean was swallowed in a billow of charcoal grey. The wind had turned icy, and the spray stung. As they rounded the tip of the island, the land across the channel vanished from view in a curtain of mist and rain. Gilligan had to cut his speed and ordered her to keep a sharp eye out for rocks and shoals.

Icy needles stung her cheeks. Was that sleet or slashing rain? Squinting against it, she strained to see ahead. "Slow down," she shouted. "I think Luke's cove is around here somewhere."

Gilligan was pale and grim, but he maintained a steady speed. Amanda peered into each inlet and cove as they drove by, and when they rounded the rocky point beside Luke's cove, she gasped. Inside the cove, banging against his dock, was a sleek yacht with a red-and-white cabin and powerful twin outboards.

Bigger and newer than Luke's boat by far.

"What the hell?" she shouted over the engine. "Do you know whose that is?"

Gilligan kept his eyes glued to the ocean.

"It could be trouble. We should check it out," she said.

"I don't think … in this weather …"

"We'll be safer on shore. Maybe we should wait out the worst on land. Besides, maybe it's DeeDee. Luke could be in danger."

"He knows how to take care of himself."

The boat bucked violently, throwing them off balance. Gilligan cursed. "I think we hit something."

She glanced anxiously around at the boat hull. It was an old boat, full of dents and patches, and there was already an inch of water in the bottom, but it could be the rain and spray. "I think we should get off the ocean. If we're taking on water …"

He looked drawn and frightened as he guided the boat toward the dock. Behind the protection of the point, the wind was quieter, and the rain pelted straight down. There was barely room in front of the larger boat, and Gilligan studied the shoreline nervously as he manoeuvred into place. "We're above the low-tide mark. If we stay long, we'll be stuck here until the tide comes in again."

Amanda jumped onto the dock to secure the boat, and Kaylee leaped off too, thrilled to be on firm ground. She snuffled about, reacquainting herself.

While Gilligan inspected his boat, Amanda peered inside the cabin of the other one. Besides the requisite safety equipment and a collection of diving gear piled in a deck box, she saw a khaki duffel bag and a sleeping roll. It didn't look like DeeDee's gear. Just a random stranger taking refuge from the storm? Or something more sinister.

Clambering aboard, she did a quick search inside the cabin, turning up the boat registration papers from a marina in Port Alberni, but no wallet or personal papers. She threw propriety to the winds and unzipped the duffel bag. A pile of men's clothing spilled out: a few sweaters, thermal pants, a thick jacket, and men's sports sandals. Judging by the labels, all of it top quality. She held up the jacket. A big man, by the looks of it.

She laid the jacket down and looked around, puzzled. Tag was wandering around here somewhere. What was he up to? He'd last been seen heading off in a kayak, which he'd stashed farther down the island. Had he somehow obtained this boat instead, and if so, from whom?

The questions left her uneasy. Too many secrets and too many people looking for Luke.

Gilligan appeared in the open doorway, looking more relaxed. "It doesn't look like the boat was damaged, but I radioed the Coast Guard, and they advised me to sit tight here and wait out the storm. It's supposed to be fast and fierce, but you never know. We may be here all night."

Her heart sank. Chris was on his way across the Island to Tofino, and he would be frantic if she was missing after nightfall in the middle of a storm. "Do you know that Coast Guard guy well? Could you ask him to take a message from me?"

He nodded. "Yeah, he's married to my cousin."

"Are you related to everyone?"

He grinned. "Pretty much. Who do you want to send a message to?"

She settled on alerting Keener, who would tell Chris when he arrived. "Make sure he says we're safe and sound and off the water."

When he returned from his boat, he was carrying a large bag. "Now we have to plan how we're going to wait out the storm. Around here, we're used to unexpected delays due to weather, so I brought food, dry clothes, and there are warm blankets and a tent stored in the bench on my uncle's boat. We can hunker down here."

"I think we should go up to Luke's cabin."

"In this weather?"

"We're wearing rain gear, and the forest will shelter us from the worst. I know the way. We'll be much warmer and more comfortable at his place, with its wood stove."

"The Coast Guard may come looking for us."

"Then tell your cousin-in-law where we're going."

He gave her a long look. "You just want to check out the cabin."

"Well, that's a bonus."

An icy blast of rain hammered the window, and the thin walls were no match for the wind. She cocked her eyebrow.

"Fine," he muttered, picking up the bag again. They stuffed the blankets, food, and warm clothes in dry sacks inside their backpacks, and once they had secured his boat, they set off. Amanda let Kaylee lead. The dog's eager presence was reassuring. The rain was cascading down through the canopy, drenching them and turning the path into an unfamiliar torrent. Rain-swollen mist obscured their view, and Amanda was grateful for Kaylee's unerring nose as they slipped and stumbled their way up the mountain. It seemed an eternity before they reached the lookout near the summit. Gazing out over the vista, she could see nothing but swirls of grey and white. Somewhere down there was the channel and the mainland opposite, but she could barely see the trees fifty feet away.

Gilligan raised his head, his nostrils flaring. "I smell something."

She sniffed. Sniffed again. Just whiffs, carried on a gust of wind. "Fire."

Kaylee had turned to look up the path, her nose twitching too. Amanda frowned in confusion. "But surely there wouldn't be forest fires in a rainstorm like this!"

Gilligan shook his head. "It's not a forest fire. Someone has lit a fire up at the cabin."

CHAPTER TWENTY-FOUR

By midafternoon, Chris found his eyelids repeatedly drifting shut despite blasting music at full volume and singing along at the top of his lungs. Afraid he'd fall asleep while navigating the twisty, mountainous road to the western coast of the Island, he stopped in the City of Port Alberni for a coffee and an energy snack. The sky was leaden, and the wind cut through his thin jacket. He glanced anxiously at his phone.

He'd had no signal for much of the drive through the mountains, but his relief at seeing three bars was quickly overtaken by disappointment. No call from Amanda. When he checked the weather forecast in Tofino, he saw that the storm was already at full force, with strong winds and rain mixed with sleet. Where the hell was she?

He phoned Nihls. "Sorry to bug you, but is there any news? I haven't heard from Amanda."

"No news, but we're battling a major storm out here, so cell-phone reception may be iffy. If Amanda was out on the water, she's probably taken shelter somewhere."

"What do you mean 'out on the water'? Has she gone somewhere?"

"I don't babysit your girlfriend, Tymko. There's a lot of water out here. I'm just saying she may not be able to call."

"Sorry," Chris muttered, rubbing his eyes. "I'm just on edge. No sleep."

"Yeah, we're all on edge. It's a massive search area, and this weather isn't making it any easier. We can't put officers at risk. Ask the Coast Guard if they've had any word."

"Thanks, Travis. Seriously. I know you're sticking your neck out for me."

"I'm just glad I lured you out here. By the time you get here, I may have even more interesting news. The search team found several trail cams with video up around Luke's place. They're bringing them down here now. Maybe they'll tell us where Luke is. Who knows, they may even have caught Richard Vali's killing on camera. Or at least give us some clues."

Luke's compound was drenched. The chicken coop was a mud puddle, and water poured off the roof to form rivulets across the yard. A dim light glowed through the windows of the main cabin, and the smell of woodsmoke was strong. Amanda put her finger to her lips and signalled Gilligan to circle around the back.

"We don't know who's in there," she whispered. "It could be DeeDee."

After he'd slipped out of sight, she started forward, gripping Kaylee tight to her side. Water dripped from her hood, and her boots squelched over the ground as she crept up, trembling all over with apprehension. Could this be Luke? Would he risk coming home with half the Mounties on Vancouver Island looking for him? His boat was not in the cove. Someone else's was.

Unless he had switched boats to throw off the searchers.

She reached the window and peeked cautiously over the sill. A fire blazed brightly in the wood stove, but the room was empty. She waited. Watched. Nothing. She turned to look around the compound. The animals were all gone, and the place looked forlorn and abandoned. Then she noticed the door to Luke's studio was slightly ajar, and a pinpoint of light danced through the windows.

She crouched down, tiptoed over to the studio, and edged along the wall to the door. Holding her breath, she peeked through the crack.

A man was standing in the middle of the room, his back to the door and a flashlight in his hand. He was wearing a raincoat draped over his shoulders, obscuring his shape. The weak light pierced the late afternoon gloom as it played over the walls.

The man lifted his gaze to the ceiling, agape, and his breath quickened. He turned slowly in place until he saw her. He froze. She sucked in her breath and stared back.

His astonishment hardened to anger. "Who the hell are you?"

In an instant, she took in the marked Southern drawl, the tall, commanding presence, the bristle of white hair, and the familiar blue eyes deep set in the weather-beaten face. Her mind was whirling. Sensing her anxiety, Kaylee gave a low growl, which snapped Amanda out of her paralysis.

"I'm Amanda Doucette, a friend of Luke's," she said in as calm and steady a voice as she could muster. "I could ask the same of you, although maybe I know."

His eyes narrowed in suspicion. "I doubt that. I'm not from around here. A tourist who stumbled upon this place and took refuge when the storm hit."

She scrambled to take stock of her options. She was alone in the room with a man far bigger and stronger than her, despite his age. Kaylee would do her best to protect her and might inflict a bite or two, but a vicious kick would silence her. Gilligan was out there somewhere and might come to help, but she couldn't count on his intervening in time.

Over the years, she had faced many angry men, some desperate to escape or to rescue their families, others furious at her for thwarting their will. She had learned to hide her fear. She had two choices: challenge him or play along.

She forced a smile. "His paintings are quite extraordinary, aren't they?"

"That's not how I'd describe them. More like crazy."

"They're tormented, yes, but they all mean something."

He stood stock-still but flicked a contemptuous gaze around the room. She'd been debating what to do. She'd wanted to get him back outside, where Gilligan would see them, but she also wanted to show him what the paintings meant. To make him understand.

But that contemptuous dismissal made up her mind. She stepped forward toward the painting of the exploding heart. "This is a portrait of a dying man. I don't know everything that it symbolizes, and maybe even he doesn't, but it could be a broken heart or it could be a soldier blown apart by a bomb."

His stony stare flickered. She pointed to the gun held to the temple. "This one is self-evident."

The contempt returned. "Suicide. Proves my point. Crazy."

"But he hasn't pulled the trigger." She took a calculated risk. "Haven't you ever been at the brink?"

He turned away abruptly. "This is pure exhibitionism. Putting all this ... this horror on public display for the world."

"But it's not on public display. This is his own private universe, where he pours all his horror, as you call it, out of his mind."

He was silent. She looked up at the ceiling at the shooting shards of black and yellow and orange and for the first time saw what they depicted. She sucked in her breath, almost wanting to run for cover from the attack.

"Were you ever in Vietnam?"

He was leaning against the wall by the door, feigning disinterest, but his body went rigid. "What makes you ask that?"

"You're the right age, so I wondered. Luke was in Vietnam, in a village that was firebombed with napalm."

"Did he tell you that? Did he remember that, or did he make it up?"

She nodded at the ceiling. "No one can make that up. He told me fragments. He remembers crouching in the field, hanging on to his gun, he remembers helicopters. And here ..." She pointed to the tiny figures, human and animal, racing away from the boiling black. "The villagers are trying to outrun the flames. But this ..." She gestured back up to the sky, raw and terrifying. "This fire is the heart of his terror."

He barely glanced at the ceiling. "That crap could be anything. One of the West Coast's famous forest fires, or even an image of what's inside his crazy mind."

She had to fight back her anger. "It's overwhelming his whole being. It's what happened to him. It's why he's up here, hiding as far away as possible."

"If you say so." He started to open the door. "It's getting cold, so how about we go into the cabin by the fire."

"Luke was your brother, wasn't he?"

"Bullshit," he snapped before reining himself in. "Why the hell would you say that?"

"Because you look alike, and I'm told he had a brother in Vietnam. That's why this painting affects you."

"I can see the man told you his ridiculous lie. I had a brother, yes, and he died in Vietnam. This man's claim is an outrage to his memory. And that ..." he pointed a shaking finger at the ceiling, "is all too close to the bone."

Amanda glanced up at the painting again. She was wondering whether it was too personal to probe deeper when she noticed

247

for the first time a tiny, luminescent shape amid the boiling black smoke. She squinted at it. A helicopter? Matthew had said Luke's brother was a helicopter pilot. Was the painting just a general depiction of the horrors of napalm, or was it more personal? The flashes of yellow and orange seemed to come straight down from the ceiling, as if Luke was right underneath.

She thought of the burn scars on his body. Her heart hammered. Was it possible? She found her voice through the dryness in her mouth. "How do you know he died? Did they retrieve his body?"

"I've had enough of this bull. The man decides, fifty years after the fact, to announce he's back from the dead, just when my father dies and a whole pile of inheritance is up for grabs. I don't think so."

He yanked open the door and came face to face with Gilligan, who was standing outside.

"Who the fuck are you?"

Amanda felt a wash of relief at the sight of Gilligan. He'd obviously heard enough through the door that he recognized the tension. He was six inches shorter than the older man, and not a fighter by nature, but he drew himself up the best he could.

"I'm Gilligan George from the Ahousaht First Nation. This island is our territory, and when I saw an unauthorized boat moored in the cove, I came to investigate."

"Well, fine. Since we're all here, let's get out of this hellhole and go to the main cabin."

Gilligan didn't move. "And may I have your name, sir?"

The man glowered at him. "Damon Vali." He shot a glance at Amanda. "General Damon Vali."

"I see. Was Richard Vali your son?"

"It seems y'all know my whole damn family history!" Damon snapped, pushing past them to head toward the cabin.

"My sympathies on your loss, General Vali," Gilligan said as he followed him across the yard.

Damon whirled and stabbed his finger at the studio. "And that crazy man killed him!"

"Why?" Amanda asked mildly.

"My son came up here to check out his claim. Defying my orders. As soon as I found out where he was going, I came up too, hoping to intercept him." He slammed into the cabin and stalked over to the slab of cedar that served as a counter. He rummaged through the shelves. "But I was too late. Doesn't the man even have a decent drink in this place?"

"Did you see your son?" Amanda asked.

Damon hesitated, maybe trying to decide how closely he should adhere to the truth. Remembering, perhaps, that he may have been spotted by Richie's surfing buddies on the beach. "I did, briefly. But he was determined to follow up. He said there was some kind of proof, and he had to see it for himself. He had the nerve to say wouldn't it be wonderful if Uncle Luke was alive?"

"Well, wouldn't it be?"

"It's a scam. My brother is dead. I saw it with —" Damon broke off. "A friend of mine saw it during a search-and-destroy mission of the enemy village that had attacked Luke's platoon. He called in the hun bomber, said too late he saw two soldiers running across the field. I ... I flew in later, nothing but charred and smoking ruins. He would have been incinerated. Dead within seconds."

"Dead by friendly fire," Amanda said quietly.

He nodded. The memory had transported him back, and he looked bleak.

"He made a painting of those charred and smoking ruins."

Damon shrugged. "Maybe this guy saw photos. Maybe he was even in Vietnam. But he's not Luke."

"He told me he ran into the jungle. Maybe he kept running until he reached the South China Sea."

Damon snorted. "An impossible feat."

Amanda thought of her own escape to freedom across four hundred kilometres of hostile countryside. *The unthinkable becomes possible if you're desperate enough.* "I looked it up. It's about sixty miles."

"Sixty miles of VC-infested jungle." Damon leaned back against the counter, trying to look dismissive. His jacket slid back to reveal the butt of a pistol in a holster on his hip. Alarm shot through her. Was that gesture deliberate?

"I know Luke," she said quietly. "He's not interested in your money. And I can think of no reason why he'd kill Richie."

Damon waved an impatient hand in the direction of the studio. "Does a man like that need a reason?"

"How did Richie even connect with him? Why would he think a hermit living out in a remote corner of Canada might be his uncle?"

"Bullshit science." He shoved away from the counter and strode to the door. "Now, I've wasted enough time. Has it stopped raining enough that I can get the hell out of here?"

Near blackness greeted him and rain lashed in. "Fuck," he muttered and was about to slam the door shut when he stopped short and peered into the shadows. "There's someone out there."

CHAPTER TWENTY-FIVE

Chris parked his rental car and dashed through the rain to the front door of the Silver Surf B&B. Inside, he was relieved to be greeted by warmth, light, and a matronly woman with a cloud of white hair piled on top of her head, who peeked around the corner at the back of the lobby.

"Mrs. Keenan?" Chris introduced himself and said he was staying with Amanda.

The woman's cheery smile vanished, and her brow furrowed in bewilderment. "She said nothing about that to me. My husband may know, but he's out."

"It was only just arranged. Is she here?"

The furrow deepened. "No, I haven't seen her since early this morning."

"What about Tag? Michael McTaggart."

"We haven't seen him in a couple of days. The rooms are paid for, of course."

"Do you know where they went?"

She shook her head, the cloud of hair flopping in her eyes. "It's not a night to be out, that's for sure."

Chris handed her his card. "If they show up, Mrs. Keenan, or you learn anything, please call me."

At the sight of the official card, her expression cleared with relief. "For sure. And call me Helen."

He smiled. "Now how do I get to the police station?"

He followed the woman's directions through the dark, sodden streets and found the station easily. Tofino was less than half the size of Deer Lake and had only two main streets. On this night, almost no one was out, and businesses were closed. Miraculously, the power was still on, but he suspected it might go out at any moment.

The inside of the station was quiet too. The low buzz of conversation drifted from the interior, punctuated by occasional laughter. The smell of coffee and reheated food seeped through the walls. A lone female officer manned the front desk behind the partition, and she smiled brightly at the sight of his ID.

"Newfoundland! You're a long way from home, b'y!"

Chris grinned. "Are you from the Rock?"

"Cape Breton, so we're almost neighbours! What can I do for you?"

"I'm here to see an old work mate, Sergeant Nihls. Is he here?"

"Along with half of Vancouver Island. Can't get rid of him. I'll call him."

Within seconds, Chris heard hurried footsteps, and Travis Nihls flung open the inner door. "You made it!" To Chris's surprise, Travis enveloped him in a back-thumping hug. Since when had Poker-Ass Nihls gone all touchy-feely? Island life obviously agreed with him, for he was pot-bellied and double-chinned now, and his once military buzz cut was a soft silver swoop.

"Dude, you're soaked! How do you like our West Coast weather?"

"This little sprinkle? It's got nothing on a nor'easter."

"Still gets you wet, though. Come on in, and I'll get you a cup of coffee."

Travis led the way down a corridor to the break room at the back, where a handful of officers were slumped around tables. There was no sense of urgency or triumph, merely defeat. They barely mustered the enthusiasm to say hello. Chris held his impatience in check until he was cradling a cup of hot coffee. Its warmth radiated through him, and he realized how much he craved it.

"So, any updates?"

"Still no sighting of the principal suspects, and with this weather, we had to pull everyone in, at least until morning." Travis looked uncomfortable, as if debating whether to say more.

"What?"

"Nothing. Except the noose around Luke's neck may be tightening."

"What the hell does that mean?"

"The trail cam footage I told you about. We've started going through it, and Luke had a visitor last week. According to the time-stamp on the video, Richie was up at Luke's cabin the day before he died. The camera picked him up outside the cabin. No sign of Luke in the footage, so we can't definitively say the two of them met, but it's not looking good. There was another man with him that we're working to identify."

"Richie visited Luke," Chris said.

Travis nodded. "Him and another man."

Chris ignored that. "And the next day, he's dead."

"Yeah, like I said, the noose —"

Chris's gut tightened. "Where the hell is Amanda? She hasn't been back to the B&B, and no one has seen her."

"That I do have good news on. The Coast Guard heard from them, and they're safe. She and her guide, Gilligan George, a kid from Maaqtusiis, they were out in his uncle's boat, and they moored up in what is known as Luke's Cove."

Chris nearly leaped out of his chair. "She's with Luke?"

"Don't worry, Luke's not there. His boat was found up on the main peninsula. But he has a dock and a path to his place from there."

"Do you think they'd go up to the cabin for shelter?"

Travis shrugged. "They might stay on the boat. I'm told it's a long hike up the mountain, and in this weather ..."

"But they'd have no heat on the boat."

"There would be emergency blankets and probably a portable heater."

Chris thrust aside his half-finished coffee and jumped up. "We have to go up there."

"Dude, there's absolutely no way anyone is going out on the water in this. In the dark."

"But if Luke finds them —"

"I told you, Luke is nowhere near there. He knows that's the first place we'd look."

"I can't just sit on my ass all night while two, maybe three possible killers are roaming about. Can I take a Zodiac?"

"It would bounce around like a cork out there."

"A bigger boat, then. What do you have?"

"Saint-Laurent would never authorize it." Travis shook his head firmly. "Chris, you're not going out there tonight. Let's see what the weather is like in the morning."

Chris took a deep breath in a futile bid to control his rising anxiety. He had to get out of the station. He had to move. He'd seen the weather, and he knew Travis was right. To go out in those conditions would be suicidal and would put other first responders at risk trying to rescue him. But that rational knowledge did not stop him from driving down to the small-craft harbour and jogging down the wharf past the crowded slips to stare out at the sea. Mist swallowed up the deserted harbour, but blurry halos of light shimmered in the distance, presumably from small islands in the inlet. Boats rocked and clanged in the water, and even in this protected inlet, ocean swell broke against the pylons, sending up spray.

His heart ached as he pictured Amanda huddled under an emergency blanket, wet and hungry, while a possible killer, a man she'd befriended, lurked in the shadows. *Fuck!* Feeling the despair of helplessness, he turned, wrapped his rain jacket tightly around him, and headed back to the station. At least there he'd be on the front lines of information coming in, and in the morning, as soon as the first boat could safely get out of the harbour, he'd be on it.

He was just greeting Janine when the door swung open behind him, bringing in a blast of cold, damp air, and a woman strode in, her face grim and a laptop tucked under her arm.

"I'm DeeDee Vali. Y'all have a warrant out for my arrest. I'm here of my own volition." She laid the laptop down on the counter. "I believe my father is trying to kill his brother."

Damon rushed out the cabin door, groping under his jacket and pulling out a black, deadly-looking pistol.

"Wait!" Amanda cried, but he had vanished into the darkness. "Fuck! Gilligan, did you see anything? Could it have been a bear?"

Gilligan shook his head. "I didn't smell it."

A shot rang out. Amanda dived for the door and slammed it shut. Another shot and a scream. Then a single blast, louder and deeper. Kaylee set up a volley of frantic barking, and by the time Amanda had quieted her, she heard cursing and scuffling outside. Coming closer. Kaylee growled.

Galvanized, Amanda dragged Kaylee with her and ran to crouch behind the bed. Gilligan stood in the centre of the room as if rooted to the floor. There was only one door to the cabin, and he was staring at it, mesmerized.

Someone was outside the door, breathing heavily and fumbling with the latch. Amanda grabbed the hatchet from the woodbox and clutched Kaylee to her. Then the door burst open, and Damon stumbled in, his face a mask of pain.

"He shot me! The sonofabitch shot me!"

His pistol was gone, and bright red blood pumped down his shredded right sleeve and splattered on the floor. Amanda rushed to close the door and then took Damon's good arm to guide him to a chair.

"That's arterial blood. We need to stop the bleeding fast. Gilligan, get my knapsack for me and grab that piece of rope from the hook."

Damon fell into the chair, pale and tremulous. Was he already going into shock? She checked his pulse, which was racing but strong. She worked quickly, fashioning a tourniquet from the rope before cutting away his jacket sleeve to examine the wound. Wounds. As if he'd been peppered with half a dozen pellets.

From a shotgun.

Corralling her wild thoughts, she forced herself to concentrate on the task, removing the pellets, disinfecting and packing the wounds, wrapping the area, and applying pressure. As she instructed Gilligan to keep up the pressure, she and he exchanged glances. Luke had a shotgun, but so did almost everyone who lived in the country.

Damon sat quietly, not uttering a word despite all her probing. She pressed a cup of water to his lips. "You need to drink. You need the fluid."

Damon studied her efforts with a critical eye and finally nodded. "Good job, little lady."

"Keep drinking. Did you see who shot you?"

"Too dark, but pretty sure it was Luke."

"You know what Luke looks like?"

Damon blinked rapidly. "Well, no. I mean the guy who lives here."

"Did you hit him?"

"I think so. I heard a cry, then a thud."

Fresh alarm shot through her. She had not heard a sound from outside since Damon came in. "I have to go look for him. He might be injured."

"He deserves to rot in hell as far as I'm concerned."

"Damon, that's not how I operate."

"All right, but consider this, young lady. He'll probably kill you."

Anger chased out her alarm, and she stood up. "No, he won't. Gilligan, give him more water and keep that pressure up."

She pulled her rain gear tight, took out her flashlight, and signalled Kaylee to follow her as she stepped out into the dark. She stood on the doorstep for a moment, processing the sounds and allowing her eyes to adjust to the dark. Kaylee was whining and pulling her in the direction of the forest. She heard faint rustling ahead, and Kaylee barked. Amanda crept forward, letting Kaylee lead, her heart pounding. Luke would not hurt her or Kaylee, she told herself, no matter how freaked out he was.

Her mind ran over the sequence of the earlier fight. Two gunshots about a second apart. Loud, distinctive pops. Followed by a thud and then a louder blast, deeper than the other two. The shotgun?

Her horror spiked. If so, Damon had shot first, twice, like a professional, and only then had the shotgun fired in response.

A moan stopped her short. She played the flashlight beam over the sodden ferns and grasses ahead. Kaylee tugged her forward impatiently, and soon her flashlight found a dark shape sprawled on the ground. She rushed over, pushed the ferns away from the face contorted in pain, and sat back in shock.

Tag.

What the hell?

He was shaking all over, and as she probed his neck for a pulse, he moaned, opened his eyes, and blinked at her blearily. "Amanda?"

"You're okay," she said, not knowing if it was true. "Where are you shot?"

"I ... I hurt all over. My thigh burns, and my shoulder. Jesus, it's a bitch!"

She shined the flashlight over the ground nearby. "What happened to your shotgun?"

"My what?" His voice faded and his eyes closed.

"I have to get you to shelter. I have to look at your wounds."

He opened his eyes again with an effort. "He did it deliberately, Amanda."

"Maybe he was frightened. It was dark."

"It was almost point-blank. He was looking right at me. Shined the light in my face."

"Do you know who he is?"

Tag turned his face away. His chin trembled. "I think ... I think it was my father."

Every ounce of her shouted in silent protest. It wasn't possible. "Did you actually see him?"

Tag nodded. "Just for ... for a second." His eyes rolled, and he slipped into unconsciousness before she could reply. Damon was the one with the gun. Even if Luke was afraid and had no idea who Tag was, he wouldn't shoot. She shined the light around the compound wildly. The closest shelter was the woodshed, near the edge of the forest and far from the cabin. She tapped his cheeks sharply, and his eyes drifted open. "Tag, I have to hide you. I'm going to get you into the woodshed. Can you help at all?"

His head moved weakly.

Tag was about six feet and probably at least one eighty. An impossible weight for her. "If you stay here, you'll die. Try!" She seized his good arm and tugged. "Push with your good leg."

Bit by bit, they inched over to the woodshed. She rolled him inside and stacked some logs in front of him. He was shivering and barely conscious now, exhausted by the effort and the pain. Blood pooled around his leg. Desperately, she yanked off her scarf and wrapped it tightly around the area. Not enough! She called Kaylee to lie beside him.

"I'm going to get a blanket and some supplies from the cabin to treat your wounds. I'll do what I can, but I have to get you out of here."

When he didn't respond, she left him and raced back to the cabin. Her thoughts were in turmoil. She was not a doctor, not even a nurse. She was running out of first-aid supplies, and she was stuck with two injured men on top of a mountain in the dark in the middle of a storm.

Jesus fucking Christ!

She fought the flash of hysteria bubbling up. Tag had said the shooting was deliberate. It had to have been Damon, not Luke. Surely. But had Tag fired back, thinking it was Luke? And how the hell did he get here in the first place? If she couldn't save both, who should she save?

CHAPTER TWENTY-SIX

When Amanda returned to the cabin, she found Damon peering out the window into the rain-slicked darkness. He looked fired up for action.

"Did you find him?" he demanded.

Amanda shook her head. "Maybe you missed." She busied herself checking the packing on his wound. Blood was still seeping, but at least it wasn't pouring. "You should get some rest. I think it's safe to stay here until morning."

Damon paced back to the window. "We're sitting ducks here. We should establish some plan of defence."

"We can cover the windows and turn the table on its side for a shield," Gilligan said.

"Good idea." Damon grabbed the blanket off the pallet on the floor and struggled to drape it over a window with one arm before collapsing back into the chair. Amanda covered the other window with a large painting from the wall.

"The oil lamps," Gilligan said, and he blew them out. Lit only by the eerie orange glow of the wood stove, the cabin plunged into gloom, and blurry shadows flickered on the walls. The light was ghostly as it played over Gilligan's anxious face. Tag urgently needed medical attention, and she felt guilty for dragging poor Gilligan into danger. Like Pim, he had no part in the drama and yet here he was, caught in the centre.

"I think we should put a guard outside," she said. "Gilligan, can you take the first watch while Damon rests?"

Gilligan looked alarmed. She knew he was in no danger, but he didn't know that. Damon immediately stood up. He wavered but fought for balance.

"No, I'll do it. I feel fine, and I've got the training. This young man is not a soldier."

He grabbed the hatchet and headed out the door. *Damn*, Amanda thought, racing to peek around the blanket to see whether he would search the grounds for Tag. She prayed Kaylee didn't bark or run out of the shed to check him out. All she could see through the blackness of the storm was a faint smudge of his silhouette pressed against the studio wall. Far from the woodshed, and far from the path back down to the shore.

She seized Gilligan's arm. "There's no danger," she said, "but he shot my friend Tag. I've hidden Tag in the woodshed with Kaylee for now, but he's badly wounded, and we need to get him to help. He's a big man. I don't think you can carry him, so I want you to sneak around the side of the cabin and go down to the boat to radio for help. Tell them what's happened and get ERT and the paramedics up here."

He looked ghostly pale. "In this weather?"

"Maybe it will blow over by the time you get down there."

"But you! I can't leave you by yourself with a gunman on the loose."

She shook her head. "The shotgun came after the pistol shots. Tag only shot in self-defence. Damon shot first."

"But then … I can't leave you alone with him!"

"I'll figure it out," she said with a confidence she didn't feel. She could only focus on the goal. "Damon is weak, and his shooting arm is injured. I don't know where his pistol is, but maybe the shot-gun hit it. I can stall him until you can get help."

"But he'll see I'm gone!"

"I'll think of something. I'll do what I can to play along." She pressed her flashlight into his hand. "Gilligan, our only way out is to get help. I think Damon tried to kill Tag deliberately, thinking he was Luke. Now, get out of here before he comes back in! Please?"

Gilligan nodded and slipped silently out into the darkness. She peered out after him, but the night had swallowed him up. No tell-tale light, and the rain drumming on the leaves deadened all other sounds. Damon had not moved from his post.

She pressed her shaking fingers to her lips and breathed a deep sigh. One problem solved. Now she had to solve the next one: caring for Tag.

She collected up the remains of the first-aid supplies and packed them under her raincoat, along with an extra blanket. But before she could figure out how to get to Tag, something thumped hard against the cabin door, and it flew open. Damon stumbled in, his pallor a death mask in the firelight. He was dripping wet, and the stench of gunpowder wafted around him. Dread chilled her as she saw, dangling from his left hand, a black pistol. He had found his weapon.

"Any whisky in here? Take the edge off?"

She drew him toward the wood stove. When she reached to extract the gun from his trembling fingers, he tightened his grip. "I need that."

"Okay, but let's get your wet clothes off and warm you up by the fire."

With a grunt, he fell into the chair and glanced around the room. "Where's the Indian?"

"He ran away. He said this isn't his fight."

Damon sneered. "Figures. Coward."

Amanda ignored the slur. "I'll check to see if there is anything to help with the pain." She had seen some small bottles of dried herbs on Luke's shelf, probably native plant remedies, but there was nothing except incomprehensible initials scrawled on the bottles. She knew that willow bark helped to reduce pain and fever, but there was nothing marked *W*. There was a bottle of honey, a natural antibiotic that might come in handy.

A small bottle of dried roots marked *Val* caught her eye. She took it down and opened it. The sharp, pungent smell made her recoil. Could it be valerian? She knew little about the plant, except that the oil was a strong natural sedative. For a few moments, she waged a quiet war with herself. The mystery root might be a sedative, but it might also make him stoned. Or kill him. Pim had said Luke used magic mushrooms and natural hallucinogens.

Damon was shivering. In the end, she put the bottle back on the shelf before returning to his side. She wrapped a blanket around his shoulders, and as she glanced at the fire, a stroke of brilliance came to her.

"We need more wood. I'll get some from the woodshed. That will help you."

He was already fading, his body listing in the chair. Quickly, she dragged the pallet over in front of the fire. "You lie down. Sleep if you can."

Wincing, he eased himself down on the pallet, still clutching his gun. His eyes were already closing by the time she reached the door. *Maybe he'll be asleep when I get back*, she thought, *and I can get the gun later.*

She eased the door shut softly and raced across the compound toward the woodshed. Halfway there, Kaylee emerged from the shadows, whining and wagging her tail.

"Kaylee, I told you to stay," she whispered, burying her face in the dog's wet fur. It had been a difficult demand for the dog, but

Amanda had hoped she'd stay close to the injured man. Dogs have empathy for the sick.

She opened the door to the woodshed. Silence. Fear shot through her. Was he dead? She peered behind the pile of wood.

No. He was gone.

She searched all the corners of the shed and then the grounds around it. As she widened her search circle, bafflement replaced panic. Where the hell was he? How could he have gone so far? He'd been unconscious, and with his injured leg, he could barely move.

"Kaylee, where's Tag? Find him."

It was a game they played, usually for treats or toys hidden in the house. But Kaylee had become quite skilled at tracking down toys. Amanda prayed she would understand this version of the game.

The dog cocked her head and glanced at the entrance of the path to the shore.

"Tag's gone down there?" she whispered as Kaylee looked from her to the path. "How did he manage that?" Amanda stood at the top of the path, listening. Rain dropped steadily from the trees and wind rattled the boughs, but she could hear no human sounds.

He can't have gone far, she thought as she started down the path. That trip would probably kill him. A hundred feet down the sodden path, she stopped again to listen. Still no sound of movement or groaning. But Kaylee had wandered off the path into the bush and had stopped to sniff at something. With trepidation, Amanda followed and found a shotgun leaning against a tree.

She touched the barrel. It was cold, but when she leaned over to sniff it, the acrid stench of burnt gunpowder made her recoil. She studied the shotgun warily. She had a visceral aversion to guns, having seen all sorts of ragtag firearms in the developing world. She remembered the single-barrelled shotgun her aunt Joan kept at her cottage in Quebec's Laurentian Mountains. Aunt Joan claimed she kept it to chase off groundhogs and muskrats, but Amanda had never seen her actually fire it. This one was a double-barrelled, break-action antique just like Luke's.

Luke! It *was* Luke's, abandoned just off the path. Suddenly it all made sense. Luke had found Tag and was now carrying him to safety. A near-impossible feat for a man in his seventies, no matter how strong he was from years in the bush. Maybe he had left the shotgun so he could carry Tag more easily. Or maybe he'd left it for her to find.

She picked it up and poked at it nervously until it broke at the barrel. Could she shoot the thing? Could she go back to the cabin and use it to disarm Damon? Or ... Her heart beat faster, for the first time with hope. She could follow Luke down the path! Now that both Tag and Gilligan were out of harm's way, there was no need to stay with Damon. She could leave the man in the cabin, hopefully getting some much-needed sleep, and let the Emergency Response Team deal with him in the morning.

The choice was an easy one. They all had a much better chance of escaping if there were two of them to carry Tag. Without another moment's hesitation, she set off down the path, letting Kaylee lead the way through the dark.

Once she was seated in the station's interview room, DeeDee clutched the laptop to her chest and looked defiantly at the circle of officers surrounding her. Saint-Laurent had been roused from his bed, Travis had joined them, and Chris, having followed her upstairs unnoticed in the flurry of excitement, had slipped unobtrusively into the back.

Saint-Laurent extended his hand to take the laptop, but DeeDee didn't move. "Now that I've turned myself in voluntarily and am prepared to hand over key information, I'd like some guarantee from y'all first."

Saint-Laurent drew his lips in a thin, disapproving line. "Like what?"

"Like dropping all potential charges. Doesn't it work like that up here?"

"You almost killed a man."

"That was an accident. He had a brown hat, and I thought he was a bear. Look, I'm not familiar with these woods, I didn't know about the dangers, and there are *Bears in the area* signs all over the place. I was spooked."

Saint-Laurent seemed to consider that. Chris suspected he would capitulate. It was a strong defence argument and would likely result in an acquittal on reasonable doubt if it went to trial. Meanwhile, there was tantalizing evidence right here in the laptop.

"I'll discuss it with the Crown."

A small smirk crossed her face. "What's the crown? Some kind of oracle?"

"The Crown attorney."

Her smirk faded. "Discuss won't do it."

"I think it will. Take it or leave it."

DeeDee held his stare for a few seconds before silently opening up the laptop. "My brother's laptop. It's all in here. Once I got possession of his things, it took me a while to crack the password. Our grandfather's birthdate."

Saint-Laurent nodded to the laptop. "We were looking for that, and his phone."

"Yeah, well, I got there first."

Chris could tell that Saint-Laurent was displeased. The detectives investigating the case had screwed up, and now crucial evidence was contaminated. But all he said was "Fine. What have you got?"

"An interesting trail of websites and emails. First clue ..." She typed in a few words and opened a display. "A 23andme DNA chart. Richie had sent his DNA to a few sites a little while ago. On a lark after our grandfather died, he said, to see what skeletons there might be in our closet. Granddaddy had served overseas in North Africa and Italy during the Second World War. Lots of hanky-panky went on with the local girls. And Daddy was posted to all sorts of nasty places over his career, starting in Saigon." She gave a twisted smile. "Richie didn't like the way everyone made them out to be big heroes. He was not a fan of military culture."

She hesitated, stroking the keys gently as if touching her brother himself. "On the home front, neither man was very honourable. Sons of bitches, mostly, especially to the women in the family. It wasn't hard to imagine they treated the women overseas the same way."

Chris was finding this background fascinating, but Saint-Laurent shifted impatiently. He waved at the laptop. "So did he find some long-lost half sibling?"

"He found something he wasn't expecting. To match with a relative, of course, that relative's DNA must be in the database too. And bingo, someone's was."

"Who?"

"Your very own Michael McTaggart of Victoria, BC. A 14.7% match."

The other officers frowned in bewilderment, but for Chris, a number of pieces began to fall into place. This was how Tag fit into the picture!

"Richie talked to me about it, maybe a couple of months ago. Fourteen percent means he's either a first cousin or half sibling, but who the hell could he be? One of Daddy's or Mummy's little accidents? This McTaggart dude was born on March 10, 1971, so he was conceived in the summer of 1970. Our mother couldn't possibly have gotten pregnant then because Daddy was overseas and she was home with a three-month-old. Me. Believe me, you can't keep a secret like that from the other wives on the base, and sex was never her thing anyway. I heard them arguing about it often enough. Daddy, on the other hand ... he was in Vietnam, so a child from him was possible, but Michael McTaggart's ethnic heritage is solidly northern European. That made the half-sibling connection unlikely. But first cousin ..."

She clicked on a link that displayed the Vali family tree and pointed at various entries. "Richie started filling this out so we could figure out what the connection might be. Our mother had one sibling, a sister, and at that time she was unhappily married to our uncle in Dallas and pregnant with her first son. Our father had one brother who died in Vietnam in 1969. So a first cousin connection didn't make sense either."

"There are some other explanations," Saint-Laurent said.

"Yeah, and Richie thought of them. He had his DNA retested with another company. Same result. He talked to our father about our uncle who died in Vietnam two years before this dude was even born. His body was incinerated by napalm but never actually recovered. We asked if he could have survived. Daddy was outraged. Furious. He said he had an irrefutable eyewitness who saw Uncle Luke just before the napalm hit. He said this was all a scam because McTaggart was after our money. Richie and he had a big fight about it, and Richie was supposed to drop it. But then a few weeks ago, this Michael McTaggart messaged him. He said he was trying to locate his father, and 23andme said Richie and he might be first cousins. He wanted to know which of our relatives might be his father."

DeeDee flipped to another site. An email program, Chris thought, straining to see from his distant vantage point. "Next, an email correspondence started between them. McTaggart told him there was no father listed on his birth certificate, but he'd learned his mother was living on a commune on Vancouver Island where there were a lot of American draft dodgers and deserters. Maybe his father was one of those, he said? Richie was intrigued. This shot a big hole in our family's military history, but again, Daddy went ballistic. Nothing riles him more than pacifists and shirkers. The DNA doesn't lie, Richie said. Of course it does, Daddy shot back. That fourteen percent just tells the amount of shared DNA, not where it came from. It could be from our grandparents. Maybe one of them had an illegitimate child during World War II, and they would be a half-sib to Daddy. Any kid of theirs would be our first cousin. That DNA stuff is a hornet's nest, Daddy said, stirs up nothing but trouble."

Chris was trying to untangle the chains of lineage as DeeDee talked. Would an illegitimate grandchild of the grandfather have the same percentage of DNA in common? But DeeDee carried on. "Richie put that theory to McTaggart, who said he'd learned that an American deserter had actually been living with his mother and her partner at the time. The dude had been an artist and maybe still lived in the area. McTaggart wanted to track him down."

At this point all the officers were on the edge of their seats. "And?" Saint-Laurent snapped. "Did he?"

DeeDee opened up another long email chain. "Yep. McTaggart told Richie he was going up to Tofino on business and planned to ask around and find the artist, hear his story for himself, and get his DNA. In the next email, he says he's pretty sure it's a crazy hermit living off-grid on a remote island, and he's going up to visit him. Richie says he wanted to come with him. By this time, our father had found out McTaggart was a drug addict and an ex-con, and he was even more convinced it was a scam. 'I'm not giving him my millions,' Richie replied, 'I want to know if the Vietnam war-hero story is a load of crap.'" She smiled wryly. "Richie had a way of turning Daddy's crank."

"So, they met up and went together to Flores Island," Saint-Laurent said.

"I guess. Their last email is them setting up a meet at Tofino Harbour, two days before Richie was found dead." She grew sad. "I should've come with him. Richie can be a huge pain in the ass, and he and I didn't see eye to eye most times, but he was my baby brother. My only sibling. Maybe if I had ..." Her voice grew ragged.

Saint-Laurent had been jotting some notes on his paper. Chris could see the paper was filled with boxes and arrows between them. Now the sergeant exchanged looks with the other officers and signalled them to confer in the corner. Chris edged over to hear.

"Here's the timeline," Saint-Laurent murmured. "Richie and McTaggart go up to Flores on Tuesday — McTaggart is probably the other guy caught on the trail cam — and on Wednesday Pim and Ms. Doucette spot him on a beach with Dovid Lantos and his friends. Thursday, his body shows up. Time of death is between Wednesday afternoon and Thursday noon, but the last time he was seen alive was late Wednesday afternoon, when Lantos saw him in a boat going up toward Luke's cove. We need to confirm the ID of that boat and of the older man with him. Let's get a photo of McTaggart, and get Lantos back in here to —" He broke off mid-sentence and turned back to DeeDee. "Wait a minute. Didn't you tell the desk officer downstairs that you thought your father was trying to kill his brother?"

DeeDee had used the time to regain her composure and was sitting rigidly still. She nodded.

"Why?"

"To shut the guy up, whoever he is. Daddy was furious. There's a lot of money at stake, but more important, the family's reputation. We don't need a deserter and an ex-con bastard in the family. Daddy refused to admit Luke might have escaped that firebombing. He refused to give a DNA sample, said he wouldn't pander to bullshit theories. But now ..." She rocked forward, once again looking shaky. "No one knows where he is. He's gone to ground. The military couldn't find him when they came to inform him of Richie's death. Our mother told them he was at some top-secret military conference, and maybe that's what he told her, but she'd lie to the president to cover for him, so that's worth crap-all. She asked me to come up here to ID Richie's body and handle things. But Daddy hasn't responded to one damn message from me, and Mom finally admitted he's up in Canada!"

Saint-Laurent was deadpan. "Did she say how long he'd been here?"

"A few days. But like I said, Mom is a wizard at covering his ass. At first, I thought he came up to avenge Richie's death. That's the kind of shoot-between-the-eyes guy he is. But now, with him still not showing up ... what if it was more? What if he'd do anything to keep the truth hidden? What if it's not Richie being dead that's the problem, but Luke being alive?"

At that moment, footsteps pounded down the hallway, and someone hammered on the interview room door. The desk officer burst in without waiting for an answer. "Sir, news. I've got Coast Guard on the radio. They need a full ERT and paramedic response at Luke's cove, ASAP!"

CHAPTER TWENTY-SEVEN

The rain had eased to a drizzle and the wind had died down, but black clouds still hung in the treetops, enveloping Amanda in a smothering darkness that her eyes couldn't penetrate. She didn't dare turn on her flashlight in case Damon was coming in pursuit. Instead, she groped blindly down the path, letting Kaylee lead. The heavy shotgun drooped in her arm. Praying she wouldn't shoot off her foot, she waved it like a stick to feel ahead as she tried to dodge the roots, deadfall, and low-hanging boughs blocking her path. Rain dripped through the canopy, turning the moss and leaves slick. Water ran in rivulets down the path, and within minutes, despite her rain gear, she was soaked.

On and on she slogged, trying to recognize landmarks along the trail. The large cedar log, the sharp bend around an old stump, the rushing stream now swollen to a torrent, overlaid with a hand-hewn boardwalk that was now below water.

Kaylee stopped so abruptly that Amanda ran into her. The dog was staring straight ahead, her body rigid. Amanda reached to soothe her. She could see nothing in the darkness, but through the drumming of rain and the gurgle of the stream, she heard a new sound. A thud. A grunt.

She froze, trying to stifle her breathing and quiet the hammering of her heart as she sifted the forest sounds. Where had the sound come from? Behind her on the trail? She glanced back the way she had come, but there was no light, no hint of footsteps. Up ahead? All was quiet there too, as if they were also listening.

She thought about cocking the shotgun to prepare for an attack. But she wasn't even sure it was loaded, and if she tripped and the gun went off, one of them might get hurt. Instead, she gripped it in readiness and began to edge carefully down the trail, alert for an ambush. It could be Luke. It could be a cougar, crouched to spring. She held Kaylee on a tight leash and watched her behaviour. Her head was high and her ears forward. She moved with confident excitement, not fear.

Nonetheless, all Amanda's senses were hyperalert as she slithered down the path. She could see nothing ahead. No moving shadows, no dark shapes in the rainy gloom. Whoever it was, where had they gone? Had they left the path? She was just beginning to doubt the sounds she'd heard when Kaylee veered off the path and plunged into the mossy undergrowth. Moss-draped tree branches slapped her in the face, and roots tangled her feet. Amanda stumbled on blindly, eyes on the ground.

"Kaylee! What the …?"

Kaylee had stopped, her tail wagging. Amanda risked turning on her light. Standing in the shelter of a massive cedar was Luke. In the dim light, their eyes met.

"Thank God!" she exclaimed. She was so relieved, she wanted to hug him. "Where's Tag?"

"Where's Damon?" Luke countered.

"I left him in the cabin, hopefully asleep."

Luke scowled. "I know my brother. He'll come looking for us. Tag is here." He stepped behind the tree. "We need to get him to safety."

"Rescue should be on its way to your cove," she said as she followed him around the tree. "I sent Gilligan to radio for help."

Tag lay on the ground, his leg splinted and his wounds bound up with vines and strips of bark. Willow, Amanda realized, well known among Indigenous people for its healing powers. His colour was slightly better, and as she leaned over him, he opened his eyes. "Amanda."

"We need to keep moving," she said. "Soon Damon will realize I'm gone."

"I'll take care of Damon," Luke said. "You take him to the boat."

"No. I can't carry him by myself. It's too far."

"This is my fault," Tag murmured. "Leave me here and get down to the boat. You can send the paramedics up here."

"Out of the question," Amanda replied. "We go together."

Tag shook his head. "He's after me."

"No, he's not," Luke replied quietly. "He's after me."

With an effort, Tag shifted his gaze to Luke. "Why?"

Amanda glanced nervously back toward the path. "Can we save this discussion for a later time? Luke, you carry his upper body, and I'll carry his legs."

Tag cringed. "Too much pain. Broken leg."

Luke nodded to Amanda. "You keep watch. You've got the gun." He squatted down and handed Tag a piece of wood. "Bite on this so you don't scream."

"I won't." No sooner had Tag taken the wood than Luke bent to seize his good arm and hoisted him up across his back in one fluid movement. In spite of himself, Tag cried aloud.

Luke's face contorted with the effort as he staggered back to the path. He obviously knew the way by heart, because he moved without hesitation through the dark. Amanda switched off her light and followed, clutching the gun over one arm and Kaylee's leash in the other hand. The cold, heavy weapon felt deadly, and she prayed she wouldn't have to use it.

"Is this thing loaded?" she whispered.

"Yes," Luke said between grunts. "When you lock the barrel up, it's ready to go. Did Damon have his pistol?"

"Yes."

"Did it look broken?"

"I don't know. It looked okay to me."

Luke gasped as he shifted Tag's weight. "I guess I missed."

"But his shooting arm is injured."

"Damon can shoot with either arm."

Tag had lapsed into unconsciousness and lay limply over Luke's back. Amanda tried not to think of the strain on the older man or the precious moments slipping away as they made slow progress toward the dock. Amanda tuned her ears for the roar of boats, but there was nothing.

Luke paused to catch his breath and shift the burden on his back again.

"How far are we?" she asked.

"About a quarter mile. How does he look?"

Amanda checked Tag's pulse. "Hanging in." She paused. "Do you know who he is?"

For a moment, Luke didn't answer, and she was worried she'd probed too far. When he spoke, he was barely audible. "He's Leo Decker, and I've known him all his life."

Amanda was glad the darkness hid her astonishment. "You remember him?"

"Like in a dream. Through a haze of madness that rose and fell."

"Did you ever meet him? Before now, I mean?"

He shook his head. "But Nancy kept me —"

A gunshot cracked the night. Kaylee burst out barking, and Amanda dived forward to clamp her muzzle. Luke stumbled and nearly dropped Tag as he veered off the path. Amanda crouched low as she scrambled to follow him. Luke careened through the choking underbrush, fighting the ferns, fallen logs, and thick roots until he reached a massive, uprooted cedar. He laid Tag down behind the root ball, pressed his finger to his lips, and reached for the shotgun in her arms.

As they waited, Amanda's eyes gradually adjusted to the darkness. Through it, she saw the first faint hints of lightening. She could distinguish Luke and Tag, and farther away, the shapes of trees against the sky. She had lost track of time, but dawn was coming and, with it, the risk of being seen.

The silence was eerie. There were no more shots, no boots tramping through the mud, no heavy breathing. What was the man up to? She peeked cautiously over the top of the root ball but could see no movement or flash of light through the darkness. To her dismay, she saw fog was rolling in off the sea, hanging in pallid shreds in the dark trees. *Fog could also be our friend*, she thought. Maybe Damon would pass on by, oblivious to their hiding place, until he reached the dock. A twinge of fear ran through her. Gilligan was a sitting duck there, and he knew too much for Damon to leave him alive.

Luke was curled in a ball, the whites of his eyes glistening in the darkness. His every muscle seemed to quiver. At his side, deathly pale against the dark ground, Tag didn't move. Luke leaned over to check his pulse, and his breath quickened. He hugged his shotgun and began to rock gently. A blank, lost look stole across his face. "I carried a man like this once, running from the VC. I don't know how long. When I was too tired to keep going, I put him down to rest and he was dead." He rocked.

"Luke, Tag — Leo — is still very much alive. We will save him."

He shifted his gaze to her, as if calling himself back from a faraway place. And nodded. He rose to a crouch.

"I'm going to take the fight to him. Draw his fire to me."

A protest died on her lips at the sight of him. Grim anger had replaced the haunted look. This had been a long time coming.

Suddenly, Kaylee sprang up to face the woods behind them and barked. Luke and Amanda spun around to see Damon silhouetted against the trees, barely fifteen feet away, pale and breathing hard, with his deadly pistol wavering in his left hand. He turned on his headlamp and tilted his head back to shine it on the scene. The blinding light settled on Luke's face.

"Holy sonofabitch," Damon whispered. "It *is* you."

Luke shielded his eyes. "Put the gun down, Damon."

"But you were dead."

"You thought so. Hoped so."

Amanda held her breath. Damon's gun was still trained on Luke, and although she couldn't see his face in the darkness, she could see his white-knuckled grip.

The challenge of Luke's words hung in the air for a long moment. "Those were crazy times," Damon said. "Split-second life-and-death decisions. By the time I —" He stopped. Shook his head. "There was no time to call off the bomber."

"And wiping out an enemy village was worth a dead GI or two, even if one was your brother."

Luke, this is not deescalating, Amanda thought, and she was just searching for words to intervene when Damon erupted.

"Jesus! How could I know? Smoke, explosions all around, villagers running. I knew your unit had been evacuated. I did the goddamn evacuation!"

"But you knew two of us were left behind. Or did you even bother to check?"

Damon's body had been swaying with fatigue, but now he stiffened. "Is that what all this is about? Payback for what happened fifty years ago?"

Amanda rose and stepped forward. "Can we do this later? No one is dead yet, so whatever happened up there at the cabin, it's reversible if we get this man to safety. But we have to act now."

It was as if she hadn't spoken. The men glared at each other, one in a beam of light and the other in shadows. "Is that how you did it?" Damon said. "By getting your son to manipulate my son? Why should I care about your son, now that mine is dead?"

"And whose fault is that?" Luke muttered, so quietly that Amanda wasn't sure Damon had heard. But the man stumbled a half-step backward. Shock or exhaustion? In the silence, Tag moaned, and pain spasmed across this face. Amanda took a calculated risk and stepped between the two brothers.

"Damon, you need medical help, and so does Tag. Without it, both of you will probably die. You can't walk away from this. You'd have to kill all three of us and hope you can escape on your boat, injured and all alone on the open ocean. In the fog. Is that what you want your legacy to be? Not a decorated general and war hero but a fugitive and three-time murderer? The Coast Guard and RCMP will be here any minute. You can bet they will hunt you to the end of the earth." Outrage powered her voice. "Or … you can put this aside for now and help us get Tag down to safety. At least then you won't have a murder charge hanging over your head, whatever else you might face."

Damon stood rigid, his headlamp beam quivering in the darkness.

"Shoot us or help us. Time is running out."

His gun drooped ever so slightly. It was a small sign, but Amanda softened her tone. "Your brother has been paying for fifty years for your split-second decision. You two are old. It might be time to reset the scales."

Behind her, Amanda could hear Luke's ragged breath. She risked a glance and saw that he had bowed his head and was looking at Tag. She wanted to reach out but didn't dare. Not with emotions teetering on the brink. "Can you pick him up again?" she whispered.

Luke crouched down, looking infinitely weary. Damon lowered his headlamp beam to look at the injured man. Amanda flinched as he shifted his gun. In the next moment, however, he slipped it into its holster and stepped forward.

"We need to improvise a stretcher," he said.

It felt like an eternity before Amanda heard the muffled growl of engines and the first murmur of voices. Up ahead, the fog took on a pale, eerie glow from the searchlights. Tears of relief rose to her eyes. Her arms were spasming with pain; one carried the shotgun and the other one pole of the stretcher. Beside her, Damon was barely able to support his pole, and at the other end Luke staggered beneath the weight of the rear poles.

As they drew closer, the pale outlines of vessels emerged from the fog, three bobbing in the cove and two smaller ones pulled up on the beach. They seemed to float in nothingness, their lights catching the dense, shifting tendrils of fog. The invisible ocean lapped against the dock, and overhead the paling sky heralded the coming dawn.

Nothing moved. They were waiting.

Suddenly, a shout cracked the silence. "Police! Stop!"

She stumbled onto the beach, and with her last bit of strength, she set her pole down on the sand. "We're fine! We're safe."

A powerful spotlight caught them in its beam. "Drop your weapons!" the disembodied voice ordered. Not a voice she recognized.

She let the shotgun slip from her hand and glanced at Damon. Sweat beaded his pallid face, and he blinked in the light as if he didn't know where he was. He had set Tag down, but now he backed up and reached across for his gun.

"Damon!" she whispered. "This is the police! Undo your holster and put your gun down."

He stood wavering in the light, and behind the searchlight Amanda knew at least half a dozen firearms were trained directly on him. Luke had been caught in the light, as if frozen, but in that standoff, he stepped around Tag's stretcher and approached his brother. Amanda imagined half a dozen firearms shifting their aim. Without saying a word, he unsnapped his brother's pistol belt and tossed the whole apparatus far down the beach, where it landed with an invisible splash.

Damon turned to him, and Amanda could see a look of blank incomprehension cross his face. "This man shot at me," he said before he sagged forward and collapsed in the sand.

The minute the pistol hit the water, figures materialized from the fog, shouting orders and thudding along the dock as they descended on the foursome. Engines coughed to life. In the swirl of shapes, she saw paramedics down in the sand, tending to Tag.

"How is he?" she asked. One of the paramedics glanced up and gestured with his hand. Touch and go. She headed toward them, anxious to see for herself, but managed only two steps before she was swept into a powerful hug. Chris whirled her around and around, covering her in kisses. Every inch of him shook.

"I was never so fucking scared in all my life!" he gasped.

"To tell you the truth, neither was I."

Officers clustered around her, peppering her with questions. They were trying to be professional, but their excitement and relief bubbled over. Even Sergeant Saint-Laurent looked a little less grim and disapproving.

He gave her a ghost of a smile. "How much longer will you be staying on our beautiful island, Ms. Doucette?"

"Time to find you more trouble, I promise. But right now, I want to sleep for a week."

"We're relieved this was resolved without further violence," the sergeant said.

"You should know, Luke only shot in —"

"We'll be taking everyone's statements later. Our first priority is to get you all back to town. The injured men will be airlifted directly from Tofino to Victoria General Hospital. The helicopters are already standing by. As for you and Mr. Lafferty, EMS will want to assess you both, but you seem ..." Saint-Laurent glanced around as he spoke. "Where is he?"

"He was right ..." The other officers peered through the fog.

Saint-Laurent's grim face returned. "*Merde*! Find him!"

The officers fanned out, leaving Amanda huddled in Chris's arms. She could hear them shouting and talking with increased frustration.

But Luke had vanished into the fog.

CHAPTER TWENTY-EIGHT

"If you know where he is, you have to tell us, Amanda," Chris said. He had waited until they were back at the Silver Surf and she was curled up in bed with a cup of tea and a plate of strawberry pancakes before he broached the topic.

She cast him a reproachful look. She was doped up on painkillers and so tired that her body quivered all over. After the long, cold wait and the constant questions from the police, she just wanted to sleep.

Seeing her look, he squeezed her hand. "I'm sorry, honey. I know you're exhausted. If this could wait, it would. But we need to find Luke. His brother claims he shot him."

She shook her head slowly, wincing at the movement. "He was defending Tag. His son. Damon had already shot him twice."

"Did you witness that?"

She hesitated. How easy it would be to say she'd looked out the window and seen the whole altercation? "No. But Gilligan and I both heard it. Two pops from the service pistol, followed by the shotgun blast. And Luke didn't shoot to kill. He just disabled the arm holding the gun."

"In the dark, in the pressure of the moment, that would be a near-impossible shot."

"Luke is apparently a crack marksman."

"I thought you told me he hated killing. Hated guns."

She could see the skepticism on his face. How could he not believe her? What kind of trust was that? She shrugged. "Maybe that's the paradox of a war survivor." She leaned forward. "What did Gilligan say?"

"The same as you. I don't doubt that's what you heard, and you're probably right about the sequence of shots. We'll know more when we can question Tag, but meanwhile, we need to find Luke. We have to follow up on Damon's accusation and hear what Luke has to say. But he's not in his cabin, and his boat is still moored across the channel."

She sighed as she pushed her half-finished plate away and laid her head back on the pillow. "I don't know where he is. Honestly."

"But you know where some of his hideouts are."

She didn't open her eyes, afraid he would see the evasion in them. "He has several hideouts, and the paths that criss-cross the island are impossible to follow. No one is going to find Luke until he decides to come out." Her eyes opened as a thought struck her. "But he might, because of Tag. He'll want to know how Tag is doing."

"You're saying he'd travel all the way to Victoria to visit him? How?"

"No, that would be too overwhelming for him. He'd contact somebody —" She stopped short as her weary mind made the next connection.

"Somebody like you."

"More likely someone from Ahousaht."

"We have an officer in the village."

Sadness washed over her. They were going to cut him off from his friends and hunt him down, keep him from the one thing he cared about the most: Tag. The little, bald baby he had carried to safety from the flames of his makeshift shack.

"He's not going to hurt anyone, Chris. As long as it takes to find him, be patient. Don't corner him, don't hurt him."

Chris gave her a long, hard look. In his eyes, she saw the struggle between his police instincts and his tenderness for her. He leaned over to stroke her cheek. "You have such a loving soul."

"I just know, in this instance, he's innocent."

Chris withdrew his hand. "Maybe. But there's still the unsolved question of Richie Vali's death. Someone smashed his head in and dumped him in the sea. We know from his emails that he was going to meet Luke. We know from the trail cam video that he did go to Luke's place with Tag. We know he was spotted in a boat with an older man not long before his probable death. Both Damon and the sister, DeeDee, believe Luke killed him. Possibly even on that boat ride."

She said nothing, remembering Luke's cryptic comment of the night before. "When my own son is dead," Damon had said. "And whose fault is that?" Luke had replied. Damon had reacted as if slapped. That had touched a nerve.

"I think it's more complicated than that," she said.

"Maybe. But we won't know until we can question Luke. You do see that, Amanda."

Profoundly weary, she just wanted him to stop. She sighed, nodded, and shut her eyes. "Trail cam?" she murmured.

"Yeah, the crime scene guys found a couple of trail cams around Luke's property. They're still reviewing them."

"Tell them to look ..." Her voice faded. With a supreme effort, she opened her eyes again. "Tell them to look for one down at the dock."

Once again, the police spent three days scouring Flores Island. ERT and K9 continued their search, while helicopters combed the shoreline and even Chris was put to work in the grid air search. The Ident

Unit went over every inch of Luke's compound and the trail down to the cove. The rain had washed away much of the physical evidence, but enough traces remained to tell part of the tale. Two shell casings of the right calibre for Damon's pistol had been recovered about twenty feet in front of the cabin, and patches of blood were detected in the soggy soil. A large spill was also found about fifteen feet from the pistol casings. Although the rain had ruined all hope of accurate blood spatter analysis, the pattern did suggest the presence of both splattered blood and pooled blood from two wounds about two to three feet apart. DNA results would take weeks, but the blood type matched Tag's. It looked as if Damon had shot Tag twice from fifteen feet away, bringing him down instantly.

A second patch of blood, along with scattered buckshot and fabric, was found near the site of the bullet casings. The pattern suggested splatter as well as dripping, but very little pooling. That blood type matched Damon's, and the buckshot matched that found in the remaining live shell in the shotgun recovered at the beach.

The Ident team had been able to tell who shot who, and to some extent from where, but on the evidence, not who shot first, as Sergeant Saint-Laurent pointed out in the incident briefing two days later.

"Well, not from the evidence, no," the lead Ident officer said. "But Damon Vali could not have made those two shots with that mangled arm. So, logically, he shot first."

Saint-Laurent flushed and retreated behind his notes. Chris smiled. Score one for Amanda's theory.

The Ident officer wasn't finished. With a drawing of the layout of the compound, he traced the movement of Tag's body from the point of injury to the woodshed, where a blood-soaked scarf and leaves confirmed Amanda's story of how she'd helped him. Amanda's clothing itself was covered in blood from both Tag and Damon, and inside the cabin there were drips and pools of blood, as well as bloody first-aid materials.

"Your girlfriend was quite the hero of the hour," the lead detective said to Chris. "We'll be putting her in for a civilian commendation."

Watching the story unfold, Chris was suddenly overwhelmed by the bravery and resourcefulness of the woman he loved. To see her actions so dispassionately and meticulously laid bare through the forensic reports brought a lump to his throat.

And yet, the night of the rescue, all he'd done was grill her on her refusal to think ill of Luke. It had taken a complete stranger to see the extraordinary heroism she had displayed.

He knew she'd flown to Victoria for the day, courtesy of the Tofino Air pilots who'd been impressed by her bravery. After several surgeries, Tag's condition had been upgraded from critical to stable, and he was awake, clamouring to see her. The police had cleared the visit, but only once the Victoria police had interviewed him first, and the Tofino police wanted her back in Tofino as soon as possible for further assistance in the days ahead.

As soon as she returned, hopefully later that day, he was going to treat her to the most extravagant and elegant dinner Tofino had to offer. But first he had some shopping to do.

The moment Amanda stepped off the seaplane onto the dock in the inner harbour, Matthew enveloped her in a long, fierce hug. "God, you have nine lives, girl!"

It was a warm midmorning in Victoria, and the sun beat down on the water, yet Matthew was wearing a light leather jacket. Even through the fabric, she could feel his bones. His smile was wide with relief and excitement, but alarm niggled at her gut.

"I'll drive you to see Tag, and then Bonnie wants to meet us for lunch to discuss next steps. Are you up for that? She doesn't want to overwhelm Tag with visitors so soon."

Amanda nodded and hooked her arm through his as they headed up the stairs to the street. His pace slowed, and by the time he reached the top, he was breathless.

"How is Bonnie?" she asked, pretending not to notice.

"She's great. She's been really busy reorganizing the tour and finding a new counsellor —"

Amanda stopped abruptly. "Wait a minute, Matthew. She's thinking of continuing the tour?"

"We both are. It was all set to go, everything booked, food ordered, and the men are so excited. This is a highlight for them. You can't imagine what it means to them. Both fathers and sons."

She thought of Tag's determined search to reconnect with his own father. Yet she was exhausted. Spent. She wasn't sure she had anything left to give.

He glanced at her with alarm. "You think you're not up to it?"

"I don't know, Matthew. I'm not sure I can."

He headed to the parking lot. "Well, we postponed it a week and rebooked a few things, which is quite a feat in Tofino in June. And we lined up a new counsellor who's already reviewed all the files and is meeting with each man over the next day or two." He paused by his orange Kia. "Bonnie says this is what Tag wants. He wouldn't want to disappoint the men."

"Tag would want to participate. If we postpone it to the fall, maybe he can."

He climbed into the car. "We don't have the time to set up a brand-new tour this summer. Bonnie is a busy woman. If you want a charity tour this summer, this is it."

There was a frenetic edge to his insistence. When he moved to start the car, she reached over to catch his hand. "What's really going on, Matthew?"

He pulled his hand away and let it fall. Bowed his head.

"You're more than rundown, aren't you? You're sick."

"A little."

"With what?"

"Lung cancer."

She felt the words like a physical blow to the chest. Tears sprang to her eyes, and she swung around to clutch his arms. "Fuck, Matthew, that's more than a little sick!"

He extricated himself. "I'm not dead yet."

"I didn't mean ... How long have you known? What do the doctors say? What are they doing?"

"It's a work in progress. Right now, I'm getting some cocktail of things that is supposed to slow things down, and then maybe they can operate. It's not the fast-moving type. We won't know for a while, but unfortunately the cocktail makes me feel like shit sometimes."

"None of the trip — none of the rest of this — matters next to you taking care of yourself." She saw now just how wan and thin he was. She wanted to wail, but she wouldn't do that to him. Matthew had always been her rock, always there to catch her when she fell and boost her up when she flagged. She'd never considered that one day he wouldn't be there.

She reached gently for his hand again, and this time he didn't pull back. "This is your time. You have to put yourself first to fight this thing. Let us pick up the slack this time. It doesn't matter what Tag wants, or Bonnie, or even the men. It matters what you want."

"I want the tour to go ahead. But after that ..." He struggled for calm. "This is not a death sentence, Amanda. The doctors have a few tricks up their sleeve, and nowadays lots of people live a long time with cancer in their lives. I hope to. There's still lots of juice in the old bugger yet."

He raised his head and looked out over the harbour, bobbing with boats. At the elegant legislative building across the water and the commanding old Empress Hotel on the left. "But I like

Victoria. It isn't Paris or Bangkok, but I like the feel of the place. It's got a good cancer hospital, and for the first time in a long time, I really like my apartment overlooking the ocean. I think I'd like to stop off here for a while." He gave a chuckle. "A bit late in life, but there it is."

She relinquished his hand and instead leaned over to wrap her arms around him awkwardly. She knew what he was saying, but this wasn't about her. He was telling her what he needed, to be set free, and she was so happy it was something she could give.

She herself had been wondering what lay ahead. What her future was, and where. She had loved these past two years with Chris, but Deer Lake, Newfoundland, was a very small world compared to what she was used to. He might soon be posted someplace else, possibly even more remote. Someplace even farther from the complex, teeming challenges and needs that were her life's work.

Did she love him enough to leave all that behind? Or could they find a path through?

"I'm sorry I haven't been much of a friend these past couple of weeks" was all she trusted herself to say.

He cleared his throat. "Jesus, Amanda, can we get on with it? We're meeting Bonnie at one o'clock."

Amanda took a few minutes to centre herself and shake off the mantle of sadness. Today was truly not a day for self-indulgence. She had to be strong for Tag now.

Tag was a shadow of his former self. He was propped up on pillows, and even though it had only been three days, he looked as if he'd aged ten years and shrivelled half a foot. Nonetheless, he looked infinitely better than he had on the floor of the woodshed, so pale from pain and blood loss that he'd been almost translucent.

His shoulder and arm were immobilized in a cast and his leg in another, trussed to a pulley to ease the pressure on it. He was lying back on the pillow with his eyes shut and his jaw slack, looking worn out. She wondered if the police had pushed him too hard, and she debated simply leaving the book she had bought him and tiptoeing out.

But as she laid down the book, his eyes flickered open, and he managed a smile. "Florence Nightingale."

"Not my preferred occupation," she said. "They've got you tied up like a turkey here."

"Yeah, and there might be more surgeries if the leg doesn't co-operate. I told them I want to be able to bike again."

"You will. Meanwhile you can learn something about art. I brought you a book for while you're waiting. It's Emily Carr's paintings. Sorry, I couldn't find a book of your father's."

She had meant it as a joke, but a shadow flitted across his face. "I suppose you're angry at me. For not telling you what I was up to."

Now wasn't the time to quiz him on that. In any case, what he did on his own time was his own business. "I just wish you'd told me. I could have helped."

"At first, I was just nosing around. I didn't know who I was looking for. My DNA had matched to Richie Vali, who didn't have a clue why. But I figured my father must be American, so I asked around about Americans who knew my mother in 1969. There were tons of American draft dodgers in the area. Then I learned about the fire and about Luke. He fit the bill. Richie and I decided to check him out. To be honest, I was nervous how he'd react. Some weird, crazy artist hanging out on top of a mountain, and I walk in and say, 'Hiya, are you my father?'"

She smiled. "He already knew. Nancy at the Java Bean is his art dealer, and she's been keeping him up to date on you all along."

He grimaced. "Oh, there's a story."

"It was him who carried you on his back almost the whole way down the mountain."

"I hope I get a chance to meet him. Properly, I mean."

She was startled. "Didn't you and Richie go to visit him? I heard a water taxi took you over there."

"Yeah, but we never found him. We found his cabin, but he wasn't there. The place wasn't locked, and all his animals were there, but he wasn't. We waited around as long as we could, until we figured he didn't want to see us." The long speech had left him breathless, and he leaned back to gather his strength. "Richie was really disappointed. In fact, he was angry. He wanted to see Luke for himself. I figured he might be the uncle who everyone thought had died in Vietnam, but Richie said his father thought it was a trick."

"What about you? Did you think he was really your father?"

"I needed to get his DNA. DNA doesn't lie. I was just concerned that I'd tracked down the wrong American war resister, and I'd be back to square one."

Tag coughed and gripped his side to stop the pain. The spasm left him gasping for breath. Amanda rose to go. "Tag, we don't have to talk about all this today. I just wanted to check how you're doing. Can I get you anything before I go?"

"What about Luke? How's he doing?"

"I don't have any news. He's gone to ground again."

Tag fought back another cough. "I followed all kinds of trails trying to find him after they found Richie's body, spent two days wandering around in the bush."

"Why?"

"I had to know what happened. Did Richie go back? I was scared they'd had a fight —" He stopped to breathe and shook his head. "Never mind. He's never going to let the cops find him. I told them everything I know about that night, that Luke only shot to protect me, but I'm afraid he won't trust the process."

She suspected he was right. The coughing had subsided, and he lay back, spent. "I'll let you rest, and I'll come back in a day or two."

He spoke with his eyes shut. "Richie and I saw his paintings. We stood in that hut, the one with *There but for fortune* over the door. It was ... terrifying. I've seen some crazy shit street art, but this was ... wow. His whole life, his guts, poured out on those walls."

"And the ceiling."

He nodded. "The ceiling was what really got to Richie. He kept staring up and turning around, saying 'holy fuck' over and over. Finally, he said, 'It's true. This is real. This is the war.' And then he said he had to get his dad up there, because his dad had to see this."

CHAPTER TWENTY-NINE

"Honey, do you think Luke is in that cave you and Pim went to?"

Chris's tone was casual, almost conversational, as they shared a bottle of wine on the terrace outside their room. Shorebirds wheeled overhead, the ocean whispered below, and golden evening light glowed through the trees. In a curious move, Chris had brought his daypack out and, without saying a word, had propped it on the ground by his chair. When she had questioned him, he merely smiled and raised his glass to her in a toast.

He had wanted to take her to the Wild Point Inn to get the best view and the best meal in all of Tofino, but Keener insisted he could prepare just as good a feast without subjecting Amanda to the crowds and din of Tofino's night scene.

Amanda had been grateful. While they nibbled prawns ceviche, she had filled Chris in on Matthew's news, and he had told her about his day with the police search. She'd begun to feel mellow, almost at peace.

Now, as he slipped the casual question in, she tensed. "As it happens, I don't know, but I'm not happy you think I'd withhold that."

"I'm sorry. It's just ..." His gaze lingered on the backpack, and he lifted his shoulders in weak surrender. "He needs to come in. We need to talk to him. Damon is in custody at Victoria General, charged for now with the attempted murder of Tag, but Luke's evidence is crucial." He paused, toying with the last prawn on the plate before leaving it for her. "Tag's statement confirms yours and Gilligan's about that night. Luke needs to know he's not facing any charges, but Richard Vali's death still has multiple questions. We've made inroads. Today, Dovid Lantos identified the boat they saw carrying Richie and the older man up the coast of Flores Island that afternoon. He couldn't identify Damon, so it's not airtight, but it was Damon's boat, not Luke's. So Richie was last seen alive with his father. The boat has been impounded, and forensics has found trace amounts of blood on the decking. The rain washed a lot away, but there is still some caught in the cracks and crevices."

"Richie's blood?"

"Too degraded to tell, but it's not fish blood." He hesitated. "We also found the trail cam hidden by the dock, as you suggested. It was late afternoon, so the cove was in shadow, and it just caught a side glimpse, but it showed Richie walking up toward the trail, followed by Damon. Time was last Wednesday."

The day Richie probably died, Amanda thought with alarm. Had Luke been involved after all? "What about the other cams?"

"No sign of either man on the two other cams, but maybe the angle was wrong. But about thirty minutes later, a bulky shape passed by the dock cam again. It's too dark to tell what it was, even with our enhancement techniques, but it might have been a person carrying a bulky object on his back."

Her mind raced ahead in horror. "They're thinking Damon killed his own son?"

Chris shrugged. "There are a lot of dots to connect. Luke probably doesn't figure in the scenario, since thirty minutes isn't enough time to get up to his cabin and back, but we need his evidence to nail this down."

Amanda left the prawn untouched, but she picked up her wine. Her hand shook as she replayed the scene in the forest that night:

Damon brandishing his gun and screaming about his son being dead. Luke's quiet response. *And whose fault is that?*

Good God, why would the man kill his own son? "I have to talk to Luke."

He drew back, frowning. "Then you do know where he is."

"No, I don't, Chris. But I have some ideas." She held up her hand to forestall his objections. "I know him, Chris. You and the search team can't find him."

He gave her a long, searching look. "But you can."

"I don't know. But except for Pim, I'm the only one who might."

"I'm coming with you."

She shook her head. He reddened and thrust his plate away. "You're not going by yourself. Out of the question. For one thing, this is an official police search. And for another, after all you've been through, after your narrow escapes, I'm not letting you go alone."

She glared at him. Keener ventured by to remove the plate and eyed them uneasily. "Do you want to wait a bit before the black cod?"

"We'll wait," Chris said.

In his sharp tone, she recognized the cop in control but also the lover in a panic, and gradually her anger faded. "Compromise. Come with me to the island but wait on the shore. If he sees you, he'll run, and we'll lose him." When he opened his mouth to object, she held up her hand. "I can leave him alone, and he will melt into the forest forever, taking all his answers with him. Or I can try to find him. If I'm lucky, he'll talk to me."

"Amanda, I can't authorize —"

"You're not authorizing a fucking thing!" she snapped. "Don't make it official, don't tell your colleagues. Just you and me. I'll try to persuade him to come talk. But only to Saint-Laurent. You bring some officious heavyweight in from Victoria, and Luke's gone."

"And if you can't persuade him?"

"Then I'll show you where he is." She could see the skepticism in his face, and she locked her gaze on his. "That's the deal, Chris. Can I trust you on this?"

He peered back at her. In the fading light, she could see the hurt and anger in his face. The rebuke. He leaned over and picked up his backpack. "If you don't trust me, what have we got?"

The next morning, after leaving Chris in the small cove, Amanda considered that question as she worked her way inland along the narrow trail that led to Luke's secret cave. At the shore, the path had been trampled by dozens of officers searching the area for Luke and for forensic evidence related to Pim's shooting. But as Kaylee led the way deeper into the dense forest, past the many decoy side paths and the spot where Pim was shot, the trail became almost invisible. Amanda was grateful for Kaylee's unerring nose.

She hadn't told Chris about Luke's battered old canoe, which she'd spotted tucked into the brush at the start of the trail. Secrecy was an ingrained habit.

Chris was a wonderful man, as caring and committed to fairness and justice as she was, but he had chosen a different path to find it. Even he knew sometimes that path wandered far from the goal, but in his view, the rule of law was still the best route. Without law came chaos.

Even more than where they would live, this question troubled her. If she didn't trust him, what *did* they have? He had a sworn loyalty to his profession and to the law. It was unfair to ask him to break it. But she stood on the other side of that line, free to choose when and if she would ignore it for the greater good. She'd been in too many parts of the world where people were betrayed for the cost of a loaf of bread and where the law did not lead to justice but to control, or worse. Trust was a fragile thread; once broken or doubted, it would fray to nothing. Would trust always be fragile between them, too often questioned to endure?

Her heart was heavy as she approached the cliffside that hid the entrance to Luke's cave. She put the sadness aside with an effort and stopped to scan her surroundings. If Luke was here, he was probably aware of her presence and watching her from a safe distance.

"Luke?" she called softly.

No answer. Kaylee pulled her eagerly toward the entrance. Giving in, Amanda let go of her leash, and the dog disappeared through the hole in a flash. Amanda crouched down and felt her way through the darkness on her hands and knees. A gentle breeze wafted through, bringing with it the fresh smell of smoky loam, wool, leather, and oil. A light glowed up ahead, and within a minute she emerged into the dimly lit cave.

Luke sat in the corner on his makeshift bed of spruce boughs. He was ruffling Kaylee's fur and looked up, as if he'd been expecting her. The cave was filled with objects she recognized from the cabin. An oil lamp, his dishes, blankets, and fur parka. And leaning against the walls, stacks of paintings.

He had moved himself in.

"Leo? Tag?" were the first words he uttered.

"He's recovering well in Victoria General. I saw him yesterday."

"And my brother?"

"He'll be fine too. He needs surgery on his arm. The shot pretty much shredded it." She paused. "He's in custody at the hospital, charged for now with the attempted murder of Tag."

He peered at the ground. "I think he thought it was me."

"Maybe he was just afraid."

He shook his head. "In my family, we lived by a very narrow code. If it's in the way, kill it."

She hesitated. It sounded too monstrous. She'd seen Damon's shock when he shined his headlamp on Luke's face. Up to that moment, he might not have believed his brother was alive. He might have thought there was a bad man out to swindle him, and he might have shot at Tag not out of ruthless premeditation but out of panic. He was a man alone in a dark, alien landscape, reacting as his training had taught him to.

"Luke, the police don't suspect you of any wrongdoing. They know Damon shot first and you were only protecting Tag. They just want to talk to you, to get your statement about what happened."

"But they have your story, Gilligan's, and Tag's."

"They want to know about Richard Vali's death."

Luke recoiled, as if he'd had an electric shock. He whipped his head back and forth. "They'll blame me."

"Is that why you ran away?"

He shifted farther into the corner.

She softened her voice. "The police don't suspect you anymore, Luke. They found blood on Damon's boat and saw the trail cam footage of the two of them. But you were watching them, weren't you? You saw something."

"I should have saved him."

"Why did you say it was Damon's fault?"

Luke sighed. He looked up at the ceiling as if imagining another scene. "Richie saw my paintings. The ceiling. He saw the helicopter." He paused, his jaw working. "Coming up the trail, they argued. My brother thought I was a fake, that I was in on it with Tag. Richie said, 'That war was real. That helicopter was real. You knew, didn't you?'" Luke's breath quickened. "'You knew Uncle Luke was there, and you ordered the bomb.'"

Amanda's eyes widened. "Was that true?"

"Until the other night, I wasn't sure. My brother was a soldier. He saw black and white and the glory of serving our country. I saw miracles in the desert flowers after the rain, in the butterflies landing on my jacket. Growing up, I used to steal moments to draw and paint. My father and Damon never understood." He shrugged ruefully. "I think they were ashamed of me."

She waited until he pulled himself back from the sadness. "After the napalm bombing, I wondered — did he do that on purpose? Or did he just not see the little things? Like me and my friend crouching in the hayfield. The children running. Did he only see the glory?"

He paused again, struggling to articulate what he thought. "Richie wanted him to face that. He wanted the truth. A truth Damon wouldn't face. They were yelling. Richie asked was a medal more important than your own brother's life? Damon hammered him. Two, three times, shouting he was as bad as me and he wouldn't have the family dragged through the mud. It would be an insult to all the brave men who fought and died in that war."

Amanda pictured the scene playing out on the narrow, precarious path up the mountain.

"Richie tried to duck. He slipped and fell. You know that steep drop?" Luke gave a soft whimper, wrestling back the images. "I should have helped him, but I ran away. That's something I live with every day. I ran away. Again. I should have helped."

The oil lamp flickered, and Amanda wondered fleetingly whether Chris had run out of patience. Whether even now, the police were on their way up the trail. "Luke, please tell all this to the police. I'll go with you. Help you."

He didn't seem to hear. "I knew Damon would blame it on the crazy hermit. That night when Gilligan and you came to the cabin, I was watching. Afraid for you. I knew Damon had come back looking for me. Then Tag showed up, and Damon saw him. In the dark, maybe he thought Tag was me. Do we look alike? I mean, without my scars? He looked at Tag, said, 'Time to put an end to this,' and shot him. Point-blank, before Tag could even ask why."

Jesus! It had not been a moment of panic, but a ruthless choice. "Luke, you have to tell the police. Your brother is a dangerous man. He can't get away with this."

Luke shook his head and cradled himself as if for comfort.

"My boyfriend is waiting down at the shore. He's RCMP, but he's a good man, I promise you. You don't have to go to the big city and talk to some stranger. He will take you to see Sergeant Saint-Laurent right here in Tofino, and we'll stay with you. We'll make sure he understands."

Luke said nothing, but she could picture his mind racing over the terrors. Sensing his distress, Kaylee nestled against him. Amanda let her plea hang in the air, unsure what she would do if he refused. Damon Vali had to be stopped.

Eventually, she broke the silence. "It's time to stop being afraid. Time to stop running away."

He kneaded Kaylee's fur. "Okay. I will come. But not yet. Let me find my way."

She gave him a long, searching look. "You promise you will come?"

He nodded.

She left him then, and as she walked back down the path, her thoughts turned over the horrors she had learned. How would she explain this to Chris, and how would he react?

She found him where she'd left him, sitting on the rocky headland by the little cove, watching the boats go by. Her heart swelled as she ran into his arms. He had not followed her. He hadn't called his colleagues. He had trusted her.

Now she needed him to trust her one more time.

CHAPTER THIRTY

The Pacific Ocean was afire with colour as the sun dipped into it. Golds, corals, and on the tips of the dancing waves, silvery white. Along the vast stretch of Long Beach, silhouettes of walkers and surfers cast long shadows up the sand. People strolled hand in hand, children chased each other, and dogs raced down the sand, ears flying.

"My God, this is beautiful," Chris murmured.

He had looped his backpack over his shoulder, saying he thought he might try a swim. They had taken off their sandals and were walking barefoot in the surf, which tickled their toes every time it rushed in. Kaylee had found a small piece of driftwood to play with in the waves.

A lingering tension hung between them. A question unanswered. She slipped her hand into his and squeezed it, trying to reassure him that all would turn out well, all the while fighting her own nagging doubts. She knew he had told Saint-Laurent nothing about her visit to Luke, and she knew what it was costing him.

She heard a shout and turned to see a young man jogging along the beach toward them, carrying a large, bulky package. As he drew near, she recognized Gilligan. Her momentary alarm disappeared at the sight of his big grin.

"I'm glad I found you," he gasped once he reached their side. "Mr. Keenan told me you might be here. This afternoon, Luke paddled his canoe into Maaqtusiis and turned himself in to our tribal police. Sergeant Saint-Laurent is on his way over there to talk to him."

Amanda felt as if she was floating, so great was the weight that lifted off her shoulders. She could hardly catch her breath as she turned to Chris. He, too, was smiling. The cloud between them had lifted.

Gilligan handed her the package. "He wanted you to have this. He said I should make sure you still want it and give it to Nancy if you don't."

She took the package and walked over to a nearby driftwood log to unwrap it. She already knew what it was. She looked at the sunlit field, the boiling charcoal sky, and the vivid oranges of fire licking at the edge. At the glint of honey gold in the woman's hair and the child running toward her out of the fire.

"Good God," Chris breathed.

"Do you still want it?" Gilligan asked.

She looked around at the beach. At the sunset now gilding the sand and the people walking hand in hand. At the outstretched arms in the painting. Running away from fire, yes, but running toward safety.

"Yes, I do," she said. "It's scary, it's my journey, but ultimately it's about hope."

After Gilligan left, Amanda rewrapped the painting with reverence. Chris took it, leaned it against the log, and put his arm around her. "It's going to transform our living room."

"Are you okay with that?" He didn't know it, but it was the most important question she'd ever asked him.

He looked down at her, and his expression grew intense. Maybe he did know after all. He nodded. "I have my own present for you, in my backpack. But there's a caveat. Only open it if you trust me."

She unzipped his knapsack and rummaged past the shoes, bathing suit, and towel to pull out a cardboard box. Opening it, she found a mini bottle of champagne and two champagne flutes. She grinned at him.

"Champagne on a sunset beach. Perfect."

"There's more. Inside the glass."

When she extracted one of the glasses, a small, silver-wrapped package fell out into the sand. She unwrapped it. Seconds ticked by. She took a deep breath.

"Yes," she said, slipping the ring on her finger.

ACKNOWLEDGEMENTS

The Amanda Doucette series has taken this Montreal-born Ottawa resident all across this vast country, from the Great Northern Peninsula of Newfoundland to the Pacific Rim of Vancouver Island. *Wreck Bay* found me far from my familiar turf and trying to acquire a lifetime's experience in the eighteen months it took to write the book. I read multiple books, combed the internet for information, photos, videos, and podcasts, and picked the brains of my West Coast friends, both old and new. I am grateful to all the people who shared their insights about everything from the Wild Side Trail on Flores Island to the history of the logging protests and the Vietnam War.

Since I came of age in the sixties, I have many memories of the counterculture and the utopian dreams of the communes, as well as the horrors of the Vietnam War. Researching this book was also a fascinating trip into my past.

But a book does not feel complete until I have visited the locations and walked in the steps of my characters. During my West Coast stay, I took two kayaking trips, a bear-watching tour, a whale-watching boat tour, and a seaplane excursion, as well as numerous rainforest hikes and beach strolls. Along the way I talked to everyone from tour guides, wait staff, B&B hosts, and park officials to the people at adjacent tables in restaurants. Thanks for all the fascinating tidbits. As well, a special thanks to my Vancouver Island friends who welcomed me and provided an insider's perspective, especially Veronica Shelford, Louise Crossgrove, and Kathie Janzen Wagner.

Many people help to bring a book from its rough beginnings to the polished product that hits the bookstores. As usual, my very dear friends and long-time critiquing group, the Ladies Killing Circle, got first crack at it, so a huge thank-you to Mary Jane Maffini, Linda Wiken, and Sue Pike for your incisive eye. A huge thanks also to my friend and gentle editor, Allister Thompson, whose understated but astute comments always make the book better, and to Laura Boyle and her design team at Dundurn for the perfect cover. I am forever grateful to Dundurn Press for championing Canadian writers and stories and for continuing to believe in me. Thanks especially to Kirk Howard for his vision, and to Kwame Scott Fraser, Kathryn Lane, Jenny McWha, Erin Pinksen, Heather Wood, Alyssa Boyden, Kendra Martin, and Maria Zuppardi, as well as all those working behind the scenes.

And lastly, thank you, readers, for making this crazy journey worthwhile.

ABOUT THE AUTHOR

Barbara Fradkin was born in Montreal and worked for more than twenty-five years as a child psychologist before retiring in order to devote more time to her first passion, writing. Her Inspector Green series has garnered an impressive four Best Novel nominations and two wins from the Crime Writers of Canada. She is also the author of the critically acclaimed Amanda Doucette Mysteries and the Cedric O'Toole series, and her short stories have appeared in mystery magazines and anthologies such as the New Canadian Noir series and the Ladies Killing Circle series. She is a two-time winner in *Storyteller Magazine*'s annual Great Canadian Short Story Contest, as well as a four-time nominee for the Crime Writers of Canada Award for Best Short Story. She has three children, two grandchildren, and a dog, and in whatever spare time she can find, she loves outdoor activities like travelling, skiing, and kayaking, as well as reading, of course.

Check out more

AMANDA DOUCETTE MYSTERIES

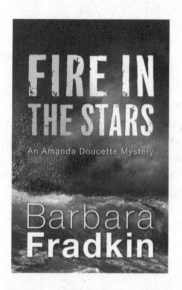

A former aid worker returns home haunted by her time in Africa and channels her pain into a murder investigation that's all too personal.

A winter camping trip turns deadly as two missing teenagers, a twisted love triangle, and the spectre of radicalism create turmoil in the remote Laurentian wilderness.

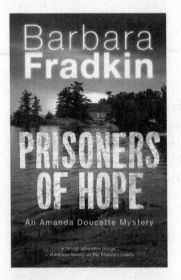
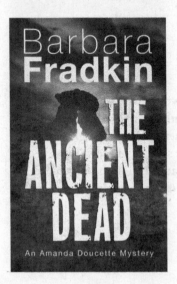

Discover more mysteries from Barbara Fradkin with the award-winning Inspector Green Series

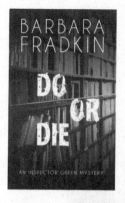

BARBARA FRADKIN

DO OR DIE

AN INSPECTOR GREEN MYSTERY

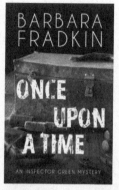

BARBARA FRADKIN

ONCE UPON A TIME

AN INSPECTOR GREEN MYSTERY

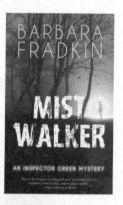

BARBARA FRADKIN

MIST WALKER

AN INSPECTOR GREEN MYSTERY

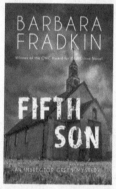

BARBARA FRADKIN

FIFTH SON

AN INSPECTOR GREEN MYSTERY

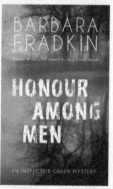

BARBARA FRADKIN

HONOUR AMONG MEN

AN INSPECTOR GREEN MYSTERY

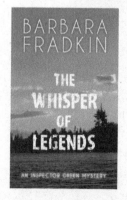

BARBARA FRADKIN

THE WHISPER OF LEGENDS

AN INSPECTOR GREEN MYSTERY

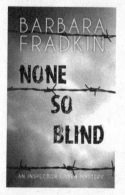

BARBARA FRADKIN

NONE SO BLIND

AN INSPECTOR GREEN MYSTERY

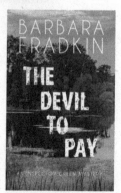

BARBARA FRADKIN

THE DEVIL TO PAY

AN INSPECTOR GREEN MYSTERY

Available at your favourite bookseller or at Dundurn.com